BY OLIVIA ROSE DARLING

Fear the Flames

Wrath of the Dragons

WRATH OF THE DRAGONS

WRATH
OF THE
DRAGONS

A Novel

OLIVIA ROSE DARLING

DELACORTE PRESS
New York

Delacorte Press
An imprint of Random House
A division of Penguin Random House LLC
1745 Broadway, New York, NY 10019
randomhousebooks.com
penguinrandomhouse.com

Library of Congress Cataloging-in-Publication Data
Names: Darling, Olivia Rose author
Title: Wrath of the dragons: a novel / Olivia Rose Darling.
Description: First edition. | New York: Delacorte Press, 2025.
Identifiers: LCCN 2025013034 (print) | LCCN 2025013035 (ebook) |
ISBN 9780593873922 hardcover acid-free paper | ISBN 9780593873939 ebook
Subjects: LCGFT: Fantasy fiction | Romance fiction | Novels
Classification: LCC PS3604.A7465 W73 2025 (print) | LCC PS3604.A7465 (ebook) |
DDC 813/.6—dc23/eng/20250331
LC record available at https://lccn.loc.gov/2025013034
LC ebook record available at https://lccn.loc.gov/2025013035
International ISBN 978-0-593-98490-1

Printed in the United States of America on acid-free paper

2 4 6 8 9 7 5 3 1

First Edition

BOOK TEAM: Production editor: Robert Siek • Managing editor: Saige Francis •
Production manager: Angela McNally • Proofreaders: Alissa Fitzgerald, Bridget
Sweet, and Pam Rehm

Book design by Caroline Cunningham
Front endpapers map, front matter map, and part openers art by Andrés Aguirre
Back endpapers illustration by Lucy Walls

The authorized representative in the EU for product safety and compliance is
Penguin Random House Ireland, Morrison Chambers, 32 Nassau Street,
Dublin D02 YH68, Ireland. https://eu-contact.penguin.ie

To those who would walk through hell for the people they love.

*And to my dear friend Grace. A woman who lit up
every room she entered.*

I miss you every day.

THE WO

ELDHELM GODLY LAND DREGOR
GODLY LAND THIRWEN

DOLENT
SEA

ZRAKA
GALAKIN
GODLY LAND ZARIO

AUTHOR'S NOTE

Wrath of the Dragons is the second book in the Fear the Flames series. *Fear the Flames* was originally independently published in 2022 and republished by Delacorte Press in 2024. Changes were made in *Fear the Flames* upon rerelease, and I highly recommend reading the new version before *Wrath of the Dragons!*

TEN SLEEPING GODS

Goddess of Flames, Life, and Stars

God of Water, Death, and the Moon

Goddess of Souls, Mercy, and Destiny

God of Illusion, the Mind, and Memory

Goddess of Air and Storms

God of the Sun and Light

God of Earth and Harvest

Goddess of Grief and Sorrow

Goddess of Love, Marriage, and Fertility

God of War and Strategy

RULING HOUSES AND SIGILS

HOUSE VELES

Rulers of Vareveth

Sigil: Five black dragons with eyes of varying colors behind a pair of crossed golden swords on a dark blue banner

HOUSE ATARAH

Rulers of Imirath

Sigil: A golden trident spearing a crown on a dark purple banner

HOUSE DUSKBANE

Rulers of Feynadra

Sigil: A snarling silver wolf on a dark gray banner

HOUSE ILARIA

Rulers of Galakin

Sigil: A red sea serpent coiled around a yellow sun on an orange banner

HOUSE LILURIA

Rulers of Thirwen

*Sigil: A black kraken wrapped around a ship
on a dark red banner*

HOUSE WARTHORNE

Rulers of Urasos

*Sigil: Brown stag antlers framing a mountain
on a dark green banner*

DECEASED HOUSES

HOUSE DASTERIAN

Former Rulers of Vareveth

*Sigil: A golden oak tree with sprawling roots
set on an emerald-green banner*

Conquered by House Veles

HOUSE VELLGRAVE

Former Rulers of the Southern Isles

Sigil: A white crescent moon on a purple banner

Conquered by House Atarah

PRONUNCIATION GUIDE

PLACES

Aestilian: uh-still-e-an

Avaloria: a-va-lor-ia

Caleum River: cai-leum

Dolent Sea: doe-lent

Emer River: ee-mer

Erebos: ere-bos

Etril Forest: et-rill

Feynadra: faye-na-dra

Fintan River: fin-tan

Galakin: gal-ah-kin

Imirath: im-ir-ath

Kallistar Prison: cal-i-star

Ladislava: la-dis-lava

Lake Neera: nee-ra

Port Celestria: ce-les-tri-ah

Ravaryn: ra-var-in

Seren Mountains: se-ren

Sweven Forest: swe-ven

Syssa Falls: si-sa

Terrwyn Forest: ter-win

Thirwen: thir-wen

Urasos: u-ra-sos

Vareveth: var-eh-veth

Verendus: ve-ren-dus

Zario: za-ri-oh

Zinambra: zi-nam-bra

Zraka: zuh-ra-ka

PEOPLE

Ailliard: Ail-liard

Alexus: uh-lek-suhs

Asena: uh-sen-uh

Asterin: as-ter-in

Aveline Lilura, queen of Thirwen: ave-line lil-ur-a

Braxton: brax-ton

Caspian: caspi-an

Cayden Veles, king of Vareveth: kay-den vuh-lez

Cordelia Ilaria, queen of Galakin: cor-delia ih-lar-e-uh

Cyra: see-ra

Cyrus: cy-rus

Drystan: dris-tan

Eagor Dasterian, former king of Vareveth:
ee-ah-gor das-ter-e-in

Elowen Atarah: el-o-win uh-tar-uh

Erix Ilaria, king of Galakin: eh-rix ih-lar-e-uh

Esmeralla: es-mer-alla

Evrin: ev-rin

Fallon Lilura, king of Thirwen: fal-uhn lil-ur-a

Finnian Eira: fin-e-in ey-ra

Garrick Atarah: ga-rick uh-tar-uh

Gryffin: gryf-fin

Hale Warthorne, prince of Urasos: hail war-thorne

Hyacinth: hy-acinth

Isira, queen of Imirath: isir-a

Jarek: jar-ek

Killian: kil-lian

Koa: koh-uh

Lethia Warthorne, princess of Urasos: lee-thia war-thorne

Lycidias Duskbane, king of Feynadra:
ly-cid-ias dusk-bane

Lycus: ly-cus

Nasha Duskbane, queen of Feynadra: nah-sha dusk-bane

Nessa: nes-sa

Nykeem: ny-keem

Nyrinn: ny-rinn

Ophir: oh-fer

Rhys Froydin: reese froy-din

Ruella Liluria, former queen of Thirwen: ru-ella lil-ur-a

Ryder Neredras: ry-der ne-re-dras

Saskia Neredras: sas-kia ne-re-dras

Sillas, lord of House Baelyn: sil-las bae-lyn

*Valia Dasterian, former queen of Vareveth: va-lia
das-ter-e-in*

Xantheus, lord of House Baelyn: xan-theus bae-lyn

Zale Ilaria, prince of Galakin: zale ih-lar-e-uh

Zander: zan-der

DRAGONS

In order from largest to smallest:

Basilius: ba-sil-ius
- thunder-wraith, male, lavender with lavender eyes

Delmira: del-mira
- sky-striker, female, sky-blue with yellow markings,
blue eyes

Sorin: sor-in
- deathclaw, male, emerald green with black-tipped
wings and horns, green eyes

Venatrix: ven-a-trix
* bloodfury, female, crimson with pink and gold markings, red eyes

Calithea: cal-ithea
* star-eater, female, silver with silver eyes and white-tipped wings

RAVARIAN

Addi: addi

Amito evidani: am-ito evi-dani

Ardama: ard-ama

Essa: eh-ssa

Nunti: nun-ti

Ravarian: ra-var-ian

Sirantia: sir-an-tia

Sirse: sir-se

Sosta: sos-ta

Tasuri: ta-suri

Tesis: te-sis

Ulessi: ul-essi

Veantia: vean-tia

DRAGON COMMANDS

Veta: vè-ta

◆ Definition: attack

Solka: sol-ka

◆ Definition: fly

Zayèra: zay-e-ra

◆ Definition: dragonfire

Lotas: lo-tas

◆ Definition: obey

Andula: an-dula

◆ Definition: faster

Part I

THE
WEIGHT OF THE
CROWN

CHAPTER
ONE

CAYDEN

THE NIGHT IS NEARLY SURRENDERING TO DAWN BY THE time I make it back to the castle and dismount from my horse. The cold cloaking the cobblestones seeps through the soles of my boots, and the wind nips at the cracked, split skin on my knuckles. I fist Koa's reins in one hand and bring the other to my mouth to pull a splinter out with my teeth.

Two stable hands begin rushing toward me, but I wave them off. Their quick dismissal of the man they were assisting seems to vex him further if the stiffening of his shoulders is anything to go by. It's best that I have more tasks to complete; if I sit idly by, I know I'll end up where I'm not supposed to be.

I unlatch the door and lead Koa into his stall that smells of fresh hay before unhooking his saddle and grabbing a brush to glide down his shiny coat. He huffs impatiently while stomping his front hooves.

"You're no better than a spoiled child," I say while stepping out of the stall to haul a barrel of fresh oats inside. He nudges my shoulder with his muzzle before diving into his early breakfast. I continue brushing him while half-listening to the aggravated orders echoing outside. The man is most likely a lord that was loyal to Eagor, but he's certainly a prick. They began vacating the castle the night I overthrew Eagor, but another wave followed after Elowen rode her dragons.

House Dasterian ruled over Vareveth for centuries, but Eagor never sired an heir to challenge my claim.

Once Koa is taken care of, I leave him to rest, nodding to the guards at the mouth of the stables. I manage to keep the sneer off my face while bypassing a large, gaudy carriage surrounded by several trunks. There is so much gold embellishment on it that if I were still living on the streets, it would serve as a beacon to my thieving hands.

His voice continues booming off the stone walls that surround the square, all hugged by frost-tipped vines. Banners bearing the House Veles sigil hang on either side of the entrance, matching the one embellishing the gate, and all that Elowen has done in such a small amount of time makes her appear like an eager bride. Bitterness surges within me knowing that she keeps to her tasks for the sake of maintaining our appearances.

The one thing Elowen asked of me after I carried her out of that banquet hall was space, and I couldn't stay in our gods-damned chambers knowing she was farther away from me than she had ever been when I was searching for her. Silence cloaked the room like a plague, and yet that's exactly where my instincts urge me to go, no matter how painful it is to watch her withdraw.

My jaw clenches when I glance up at the tallest tower that Venatrix and Sorin loop around, fading moonlight painting their scales.

"Murderer!" the man shouts at my back, and it seems as if every guard holds their breath while they wait for my reaction.

I slowly glance over my shoulder, taking in the short, portly man in an embroidered coat more obnoxious than his mode of transportation. "If you wish to discuss one of my kills, specify which. Corpses get added to my list by the day." When these men speak, I often wonder if they think themselves intelligent for stating common knowledge loudly, or brave for insulting me in public. One must step into the darkness eventually, and what awaits them is entirely determined by their actions and what I have to gain.

Two guards step forward, but I hold up a hand to halt their approach. A lord that can hold his wine better than he can hold a sword is no threat to me, and he's more useful to me alive . . . for now.

"Eagor Dasterian was the rightful king of Vareveth. You're nothing but a usurper."

"You're welcome to challenge me."

"You never should have challenged *him!*" he seethes, his cheeks reddening. "A bitch sired by our enemy spread her legs for you and you—"

He swallows his vitriol, eyes widening when I spin on my heels as the world fades away, and I zone in on my target. I wrap my fingers around the clammy flesh of his throat and slam his back into the carriage hard enough to gag him and jostle the monstrosity. A woman screams within but doesn't come out to investigate. The vein in his forehead protrudes as I tighten my grip, and I cock my head like a predator, inhaling his fear.

"I am one of the eight lords of Vareveth!" he chokes out, clawing at my hand. "You cannot kill me!"

"Don't overestimate your worth. There was one king and that didn't stop me." I lean down to emphasize our vast height difference. "Insult my woman again and I'll rip out your tongue. I won't kill you right away because I can't torture a corpse, but I will make you beg for death before I bestow the mercy upon you."

"You are playing a dangerous game, Your Highness."

The honorific is wasted on me.

"I'm not playing your game. You're playing mine."

I release my grip and slide my hand into my pocket as he hunches over, gulping in air as if he's run for miles. "Scurry back to your estate. If you're still organizing your trunks come midday, my patience will be gone, and how will you pass along my warning to the other lords?"

His polished boots slip on the step as he scrambles into the carriage while still gulping in air, and I turn away as he slams the door behind him. I get his name from one of the guards at the entrance before stepping through.

Lord Xantheus of House Baelyn.

The support of the nobility is important to the prosperity of the kingdom, considering their lands supply most of our food and create jobs for the people, but they will not forget to fear me as they never feared Eagor. The previous king of Vareveth let the nobles sink their claws into him and guide him wherever they wanted. They didn't support him out of loyalty, but for the same reason I did—he was malleable. They were all perched on his shoulders, whispering into his ears, and they hate me because I was above them all, controlling puppet strings they didn't know were attached.

The castle is bathed in shades of twilight rather than the emerald green and gold of House Dasterian with their sprawling oak tree sigil. High, vaulted ceilings have been painted to resemble the night sky, and dragons are carved into the stone archways lining the halls. Dark blue and gold drapery adorn windows and alcoves, sitting rooms have been reupholstered, and even the smallest details cater to our reign. Despite the early hour, glaziers climb ladders to create stained-glass mosaics reflecting the Veles colors of dark blue, gold, and black.

The Dasterians were a long line of warrior kings, some of whom wielded earth magic, thus earning their sigil. Eagor was the first to outlaw magic in these lands that were once rampant with earth-wielders and accepting of mages that delved into soul magic and dark magic. Now earth mages seek refuge within the earth cult that travels through godly land, or in Urasos, though most of the population despises them. The longer the gods slumber, the more volatile people become, and the more crimes they commit against mages.

I round the corner and slow my steps while passing the entrance to the throne room. On either side of the door stands a massive statue of a dragon with a wing flared out and a sword clutched in its talons that cross above the walkway. I stride forward and pinch the velvety midnight-blue fabric that ripples beside the dragons, and pride swells within my chest. Five black dragons, all facing the same direction with one wing tipped up, are stitched into a circle, almost like a wheel, set behind a pair of crossed golden swords. The colors of the dragons' eyes are an homage to Elowen's dragons: red, blue, green, silver, and lavender. No matter who comes after us, they will know the founders of House Veles. The queen who brought dragons back into the world, and the king who conquered a kingdom to have her.

I continue my path up several flights of curved stairs and tug the hood of my cloak down as I tap my knuckles against Ryder's door before shoving it open since I can hear him and Saskia arguing through the wood. Sure enough, Saskia is ready for the day, as she always is when dawn comes, and helping Ryder redress the wound on his stomach he obtained while helping me overthrow the crown. He groans a curse into his mug as Saskia tightens the wrappings, only opening his half-shut eyes when he notes my presence.

"I take it you weren't warming the betrothal bed last night," he says, glancing over my muddy boots, weapons, and black leather chest guard over my matching tunic.

"I take it you'll never be warming a betrothal bed."

He mutters something unintelligible into his cup again before Saskia's healing abilities cause him to flinch. "I'm assuming you rode to the border to check on the security of the kingdom. Any issues?"

"None. Eagor never cared for militaristic involvement, so his death doesn't affect the soldiers." I walk toward the window and feel the tension in my shoulders loosen when I note the remaining three dragons by the lake. Calithea rests on the shore beside Basilius, who is so massive he makes her look like a hatchling, but Delmira spreads her wings and glides her claws through the water. "You never protect your left."

"I'll learn one day," Ryder replies with a chuckle in his voice. "You shouldn't be riding to the border without me. The kingdom is volatile. Nobles have been fleeing the castle since Elowen rode her dragons yesterday."

"Yes, you're in such good condition to fight should someone attack Cayden on the road," Saskia mutters.

"I would be if your healing skills were better. I'd have asked Elowen if she wasn't getting ready for the day." Ryder grins when Saskia's glare intensifies.

I clear my throat and claim a chair on the other side of the coffee table. "Have you seen her?"

Saskia's glare slides to me, but quickly becomes more contemplative, making me feel like one of the coded letters she looks forward to deciphering. I think it's always irked her that she's never been able to read me as well as she can other people. She finishes bandaging Ryder, making him wince again. "Only briefly. She came to my chambers an hour ago and asked if I'd accompany her into Verendus today."

"How did she look?"

Saskia grabs a small bowl of fruit off the tray before leaning back on the couch. "She looked fine."

She didn't sleep. She's not fine. Her uncle betrayed her, and even if she wants to pretend his death doesn't faze her, I know it does. She wanted his approval and love, and he never granted her either. She was constantly reaching out her hand and left it there with blood pooling in her palm as the man that should've cherished her, loathed her. When I carried her out of that banquet hall covered in his blood, she looked shattered.

"I'm hoping to get some wedding planning done while we're out. You need to solidify your claim to the throne as quickly as possible."

"Give her some time," I state. "Just get her out of this castle."

Saskia's eyes soften a fraction, but she remains silent. I'd have taken her away from the castle after she said good night to her dragons, but her eyes filled with pain as soon as she landed in the grass and saw me waiting for her. She took to the skies after the dragon ceremony and didn't come down until she was so cold she could hardly walk. She wants time away from me, and though it goes against my instincts, I'm trying to respect it. But I can't sit by and watch her torture herself within the confines of her mind. She internalizes all the pain around her, trying to take it away from everyone while brushing her own aside as the knife twists in her heart. She wants to protect everyone else, and all I want to protect is her.

Ryder fills a cup of coffee halfway before pulling a whiskey bottle from the shelf under the table and topping it off. "You look like you could use this."

I note the label painted with black flames. "Did you take that out of my reserve?"

He shrugs. "You import the good stuff."

I take the cup from him, making a mental note to replace the lock. Saskia's eyes still burn into my face, so I gesture for her to voice whatever thought is brewing. "Let's get this over with."

"You're in love with her . . ." she softly states. "And it's killing you."

"All hells, Sas," Ryder mutters. "At least let the man finish his drink before you begin analyzing him."

Love.

Love latches on to a person and drains them until they have nothing left to give. It reinvents someone and makes them unrecognizable. One of the many flaws in human nature is regarding a heart as anything more than an organ that pumps blood. I've lived a life of endless battles, always needing to have my weapons raised against threats in front of my face and behind my back. There is no room for love. It's a weakness I could never afford and never wanted.

And yet, when I think of Elowen, the fire that's raged within me for as long as I can remember is tamed. Her presence is a moment of peace in a lifetime of pain. What I feel for her defies the logic I've lived by. I don't like calling it love; it seems too mundane a word and too hypocritical. Men say they love their wives but slide their hand adorned with a wedding band across the skin of another. Elowen is tethered to my soul in an unbreakable way. I would do anything for her, but she's never felt like a weakness. It's true that if someone wants to hurt me, they'd target her, but Elowen's existence makes me more ruthless than I've ever been, to ensure she's never taken from me.

She's the poison I'd willingly lift to my lips without an antidote in sight, and force myself to survive, knowing death would offer me no relief if it cleaves me from her.

I ignore Saskia's observation. I don't know what love is, but whatever I feel for Elowen Atarah is something unknown to this world. "I'll serve as her guard today."

"We'll have Finnian and Braxton and five dragons that are never too far from her." Saskia sighs. "Let me try to talk to her. She won't be able to think as clearly if you're there. People can't process their pain when surrounded by it."

Not good enough is on the tip of my tongue, but I douse the words in whiskey. "If anything happens to her . . ."

"We'll all be on our guard."

I crack the tension in my neck. "You have the day, but she's mine tonight. Make sure Finnian knows that, too."

CHAPTER
TWO

ELOWEN

S NOW BLOWS IN THE WINTER WIND AND FLUTTERS TO THE ground, making the cobblestone streets resemble the sugar-dusted pastries behind the counter. Their aroma hangs heavy in Lemon Drop Bakery as the fireplace makes me forget about the chill beyond the window. Just as it was last time we were here, honeybuns, fruit tarts, and cakes with more layers than I thought possible are beautifully displayed. I've added a few jam jars into my basket, and will also be requesting a fresh loaf of bread to take with me as soon as it's ready.

"Do you have a color palette in mind?" Saskia asks, drawing my eyes away from the mountain range in the distance.

"For . . . ?"

"The wedding."

"We'll use the house colors." I force a laugh. "I suppose that's the benefit of choosing them yourself. Nobody would select colors that don't complement them."

After the dragon ceremony, I spent several hours deciding on the design of the House Veles sigil, along with our house colors and re-decorating of the castle. Everyone kept looking at me like I needed to rest, but I couldn't. Tasks keep my mind distracted from all the things I don't want to think about. Every time I tried to fall asleep, I kept seeing Ailliard's charred flesh and could swear I smelled it.

A petty part of me debated selecting a flower as our sigil and making the house colors pink and purple, but sigils are a way to show the world who we are. Vareveth is the kingdom of the dragon queen and demon king, and our banners must reflect that.

I'm spared from speaking on the wedding any further when the baker's apprentice approaches, carrying a three-tiered tray in each hand. "Your Highness." She curtsies after placing them on our table and offers me a shy smile. "All of our flavors are there as you requested, but please let us know if you require anything else."

I try to ease her nerves by returning her smile. "Thank you. I'm sure this will be more than enough."

She nods enthusiastically, looking over her shoulder as she rushes back to the kitchen. It draws my attention to the counter and my heart pinches in my chest. The memory of Cayden tucking a flower behind my ear flares so brightly in my mind, I bring the lavender cake to my nose to quell a forming headache.

"What was that about?" Finnian asks. "I didn't realize your presence could cause such giddiness."

"Elowen ordered a cake tasting. They probably think she's here to sample the flavors for her wedding," Saskia answers for me as she sips her tea. "Is that not why we're here?"

"No." I reach for a small rectangle of dark chocolate cake with raspberry filling, bringing a finger to my mouth to lick off some of the dark pink icing. "We're here to fulfill my wishes. Birthday cakes for the dragons."

My two companions exchange a perplexed look before Finnian turns to me and rests his hand on my shoulder. He speaks to me slowly. "Darling, they eat live animals. They don't need birthday cakes."

"They all have a sweet tooth."

"Fang," Saskia mutters.

"And besides," Finnian continues. "Don't you share a birthday? That's not for another few weeks."

"I'm making up for lost time." I polish off the chocolate cake and gesture for Saskia to write that flavor down in her notebook before placing two cakes on Finnian's plate and taking the blueberry for my-self. "Tell me if you like the lemon or orange better."

Finnian's puzzlement is replaced by excitement. He's used to going along with my absurd ideas; we've had practically a lifetime of them. He stuffs the lemon cake into his mouth and groans while nodding. I give Saskia a thumbs up to add it to the approved flavors list while I hand Finnian some tea so he doesn't choke to death. She rolls her eyes, but the way her lips tilt up on one side gives away her true emotions.

"The lemon for sure, but not the orange." Finnian looks down at his half-eaten cake with a frown.

"Interesting. I thought you'd prefer the orange considering the color of your hair."

He furrows his brows. "That has no effect on one's palate."

"My hair is nearly black, and my favorite was the dark chocolate."

He snaps his fingers. "You have a point."

"No, she doesn't," Saskia interjects, hesitating a moment before reaching across the table to take my hand in hers. "You don't have to hide your pain from us. You can tell us what's going on in your head."

Two sets of eyes burn into me, and it feels as if I'm standing aboard a ship, on trial for madness, with weights tied around my ankles. I force another smile, ensuring this one is better than all the others I've given today, and though my body rebels, I turn my hand over to squeeze Saskia's. "I've been reunited with my dragons, which is more than I could've hoped for in a lifetime, and I'm betrothed to my fa-ther's enemy. I'm fine, Sas. I promise. Besides, I've never had a bad day that couldn't be improved by a sweet treat."

She regards me for several more seconds in silence. "You're sure?"

I slip my other hand under the table and dig my nails into my palm, not letting my eyes flick to the cut on Finnian's throat, caused by an Imirath soldier who plotted with Ailliard. Ailliard had known Finnian since he was an orphaned child and watched him grow up beside me, and still he handed him over to my enemy. He knew me well enough to know I'll always trade my life for Finnian's. Even if he hadn't plotted to return me to Garrick, I would've killed him for harming Finnian.

I could've lost him. Guilt slithers through me like serpents wrapping around my lungs and strangling me from within. Finnian wouldn't be here if it weren't for me. He needs a morning void of strife and filled with ease, and though the mask I've cast over my emotions grows heavier by the second, I'll hide my pain to see him happy.

There will be a time to get my revenge, but not today. Beyond taking care of Finnian, I wanted to come out today to show the world that Eagor, Ailliard, and Garrick failed. I will not cower in the dark when I can be wreathed in light created by dragonfire. The people need to see their rulers unruffled and unbothered to quell any anxiety regarding our rise in power. I've had a lifetime to learn how to live without revealing my true emotions. The key to hiding pain and anger is never living a day without it.

"I'm positive." I remove my hand from hers as a blur of movement in the corner of the bay window catches my eye. I pull back the parted pink curtain and find a royal messenger handing off a letter to Braxton. Lemon Drop Bakery has one entrance and aside from us and the staff, nobody is allowed inside.

Finnian moves through the sea of lace-covered tables to retrieve the letter, keeping one hand on the hilt of his sword as he cracks open the door, letting in a gust of winter air that cuts through the narrow street like a blade. He drops the parchment in front of me and I dryly swallow when I note my name scrawled in Cayden's hand. Despite the urge to toss it into the fire, I eagerly tear open the seal and unfold the letter like the blushing bride-to-be the kingdom must believe I am. Manipulation is just as useful as battles when it comes to war. Battles help you gain territory and lessen your enemies, but manipulation lets you sink your claws into someone's mind and control an outsider's perspective, and *that* is a powerful thing. Only show people what you want them to think, never how you truly feel.

"It's an address somewhere in Ladislava." It says nothing else, and I choose to ignore the disappointment that prods at me. I asked for space. He's giving it to me. This is what I need. I don't want to see him.

But even as I repeat the words in my head they sound like a lie.

"May I?" Saskia asks, and I hand the letter over to her. She blinks slowly before clarity washes over her and she licks her lips to hide her growing grin. "Braxton can easily take you there. I unfortunately must get back to the castle."

"Give me a hint."

"No."

"Is it a shop?"

"If it was a shop I'd go with you."

I roll my eyes and stand while threading my arms through my coat, curiosity propelling me forward. The silhouette reminds me of a snow angel with its full skirts and bell sleeves; thankfully the sash around my waist gives it some definition and the fur lining the interior keeps me warm. Delicate golden dragons are embroidered on the front and circle the hem and cuffs.

I pay for the cakes and offer a bit more to cover the cost of closing their shop for me before leaving. My dragons screech when they spot me in the street, and I wave up at Basilius, who's closest to me, before handing my letter to the carriage driver since he'll be taking me where I need to go. I'd ride my dragons, but I don't want to leave Saskia and Finnian, considering I planned our outing, and the bruises on my ribs have been bothering me today.

We travel through winding streets bordered by quaint shops, cafés, and several icy rivers that cut through the kingdom. Lantern posts that were once fashioned to look like twisting tree limbs now depict dragons spitting fire on either side of the golden pole. Finnian rests his head on my shoulder and closes his eyes as the steady trot of the horses and his full stomach lull him to sleep. I pretend not to notice Saskia analyzing me across the carriage as we cross over an arched bridge that takes us to the circle in front of the castle, and the sound of picks slamming into stone stirs Finnian. I peek out of the window to see what the artists are working on, but it's too early in their process to tell. It must be something Cayden commissioned.

"I'll keep Braxton with me, but you should rest," I tell him.

"Are you sure?" Finnian asks through a yawn.

"Cayden requested her presence tonight, so I imagine he'll find her soon," Saskia says.

My heart lurches in my chest, and I tighten my grip on the bench beneath me. "Go," I urge him with an ease I don't feel.

He nods while wrapping an arm around my shoulders before stepping out of the carriage and offering Saskia his hand. She pauses to look at me. "I'm here if you need anything."

"Thank you, Sas." I keep the smile on my face until the door shuts, letting it melt once I'm alone and the carriage begins moving again. If only it were as easy to fool myself. I keep the curtains drawn so I'm able to admire the forest that stretches between Verendus and Ladislava, watching a herd of deer drink from a half-frozen stream before my dragons' shadows overtake them and they run for shelter.

We cross into Ladislava, and I sink back from the window until the carriage turns onto a street with a sign that reads HEALER'S ROW. Several stone cottages with warm light pouring from them capture my attention and make me think of Nyrinn. I wonder if she's heard the news of Ailliard's treachery by now. I listen as Braxton's horse stops behind the carriage, and his boots slosh through the snow as he approaches.

"My Queen," he says while opening the door and offering me a hand down.

"Thank you, general." The short iron gate squeaks as he unlatches it and follows me up the path leading to the cottage that matches the address Cayden gave me. "Would you like to come inside?"

"No, thank you, Your Majesty. I'll stand guard on your porch." He gestures to the cast-iron chimney nestled into the corner. "I'll make a fire and be more content here than I'd be at the border watching over soldiers as if they're children."

"I'll leave it unlocked should you change your mind."

He nods as I twist the handle and let myself in, pressing my back to the door and letting out a sigh of relief at the silence. Quickly unfastening the sash around my waist, I slide the coat off my shoulders and caress the throbbing bruises on my ribs. My eyes squeeze shut, and I press my lips together to keep all sounds of pain trapped within.

Cayden must've just been here because a fire with fresh logs burns in the hearth. Aside from that, I can feel his presence like a soul with unfinished business lingering in a graveyard. I can't help but cross the room and crack open the first door, which leads to a small storage closet, and the second, which leads to a washroom.

This is what I asked for.

Space is what I need to sort out my mind.

It's what has always helped me in the past.

I jump and cover my mouth with my hands when a loud bang on the roof makes several jars lining the shelves rattle, and I'd bet all my money that it's Sorin perched up there. Sometimes I think he believes himself to be as small as he was when he perched on my shoulder.

Dark wood beams line the ceiling and walls, with pale yellow wall-paper between them. There's a long desk with empty vials for tonics, a blank book and quill, and a mortar and pestle set in front of the herb-filled jars Sorin almost sent to their doom. A small couch and chair that look as soft as clouds rest close to the stone fireplace, with a table topped with a few books and a set of tea that I realize is still warm when I press my hand against the porcelain.

My heart is in my throat as I sink onto the couch and pluck the letter off the tea tray. The ink on it is still wet and I smudge Cayden's name with my finger.

Angel,

Despite the cottage being located on Healer's Row, you don't need to open your doors to anyone until you're ready. You can use this place as an escape if you don't wish to go to the castle or Veles Manor. I've compiled some books on dragons I believe you'll find interesting and brought your current read from the castle.

Enjoy the quiet. I'll be seeing you later.

Always yours,

Cayden

I lie down and curl my legs on the couch as I clutch the letter to my chest and stare into the flames. The scent of lavender, pine, and rosemary calms me, and with only myself as company, I drop the façade. Sometimes I pretend to be something I'm not for so long I think I'll be able to become that version of myself, but no matter how much I've tried, I can't simply force myself to be fine. I don't want to hurt, but I do, and I hate that I do.

Sometimes I feel like I'm drowning but I don't know where the water is coming from, and I don't know how to make it stop.

CHAPTER
THREE

CAYDEN

I PULL MY FIST BACK AND SLAM IT INTO MY OPPONENT'S FACE, watching as he drops to the floor. The familiar ache in my knuckles does nothing to subdue the frustration burning inside me, and even as the bell goes off and the crowd roars, I'm numb. The useless lump of flesh stays down on the sweat-and-blood-splattered ground as people shout for him to get up.

"The Viper wins!" the announcer declares, and I raise my wrapped fist in the air before he has the chance to touch me.

"Give me another."

From the corner of my eye, I watch as Ryder heckles the crowd to manipulate their bets, swaying some to go against me. It's been our routine for years and increases our earnings considerably. Nobody recognizes me. If they did our scheme would never work. The tonic I took will make me drowsy as hell in a few hours but hides the scars littering my skin and the tattoo on my ribs. Nobody cared about who I was when I was younger, just another scarred criminal trying to make some coin with his fists, but I had to take precautions when I became commander.

I'd have taken the tonic in Imirath but not having my wits about me on the heist wasn't a risk I could take. Like most of my time behind enemy lines, a black mask covers the lower part of my face, and a matching bandanna keeps my hair back aside from the few sweaty strands that stick to my forehead. Ryder takes the same precautions, using a hat to cover his curls and wearing a face mask, which isn't uncommon in the slums of Verendus. It's not as if many soldiers come this deep into Verendus, and the people that frequent establishments such as this spend their days avoiding someone like the Commander of Vareveth.

Beads of sweat slide down my chest and I roll my neck while moving around the sloped, misshapen ring as the next man ducks under the ropes. He's stockier than me, but not taller, and makes a show of amping up the crowd. I grab my bad shoulder and roll it a few times, knowing it'll help Ryder if the crowd thinks I'm injured.

"Fight!" the announcer shouts above the crowd as the bell goes off.

I tap my fists together and bounce on the balls of my feet as my opponent charges, sidestepping him at the last moment and jamming my elbow between his shoulder blades. He stumbles forward, catching himself on the ropes as a mixture of cheering and booing makes my ears ring. He finds his balance again and snarls, making his cheeks as red as his hair, and I smirk behind my mask. He charges again, but I let him back me into the corner and pound his meaty fists into my ribs. The bones ache from years of abuse but I hold firm. Honestly no beating I take in this ring will be worse than Ryder's whining if I don't play my part, and there's a strong force within me that craves the pain, knowing I've hurt the one person I never wanted to. I take another hit as I think of Elowen's tears as I tried to apologize, her doubt, her pain, her anger.

He switches tactics and swings at my face, but I shove my forearm out to block his hit and advance. My opponent stumbles back when I jab him in the stomach, but a glimpse of long dark curls pulls my attention away from the match. My head normally quiets whenever I step into the ring or engage in any fight, but I'm not here mentally, only physically. His fist slams into the left side of my face and splits my cheek open, causing blood to seep into my mask.

I chuckle despite my mounting irritation. "Very good."

I force the eerie calm that settles within me every fight to awaken. Though it's the rarest of cases, I'm thankful Elowen is not here. If she were in a place like this, I certainly wouldn't be anywhere but right next to her. Fighting is the one thing I'm good at; my father made sure of that. My knuckles throb with each hit I land, splitting open and soaking my wrappings, but I don't stop. I keep going until the man crashes to the ground like a felled tree, with blood trickling from his mouth, and pounds his fist to the ground to signal surrender.

The crowd erupts again but I don't wait for the announcer before ducking under the ropes and jumping down from the platform. Ryder's had enough time to play his game, and it's not as if we're strapped for funds like we were when we first started this charade. People practically jump out of my way to let me through the crowd as they rush to collect their winnings.

I bought this building when I was twenty, after spending enough years working both as an assassin and in a ring just like this. Though I continued both pursuits, I needed this place to widen my business endeavors. I was still a child when I escaped my father and crossed the border from Imirath into Vareveth. I stayed by the coast, and the dampness in the air made it one of the worst places to be without a roof over my head, but it felt like a haven compared to what I fled.

The buildings nestled closely together shielded me from the wind blustering off the sea, so there was that small mercy. My first job was unloading shipments on the docks in Verendus that were rife with crime. It was easy to learn the art of smuggling and to steal contacts from ledgers when nobody suspected the gangly orphan boy to have an ulterior motive. The pay was abysmal, but it was enough to get me off the streets and into a room, if the box above a tavern that reeked of fish could be considered that.

There were days when I felt like the hatred within me was a pit of tar that I was forced to trudge through, knowing one day I'd eventually give up the fight and let it overtake me, and it did. The boy I was drowned in that pit, and the demon the citizens of Ravaryn believe me to be stepped out of it. Strong emotions often make people irrational, but I wield mine like a blade, ensuring whoever stands against me is slain. This world took and took until I had nothing left to give, and darkness filled the shell of who I was.

The shadows that cling to the corner conceal me as I push open the hidden door and slip into the stairwell that leads to the office that once served as my bedroom. Shouting, music, and clinking glasses penetrate the thin walls as I pass the main level that leads to the tavern—the front for the illegal betting going on below. Very few trusted employees know I own the Demon's Den, but I take extra measures to ensure I remain anonymous to most.

Saskia wanted to invest in something more refined, but lips get loose when alcohol is involved, and not only did I need the business front, but I needed a way to collect whatever rumors I could. I bartended before my face became recognizable while listening for any murmurings about the lost dragon princess of the enemy kingdom, but aside from Elowen, there was also information to be gained regarding those in power. I knew Eagor's supplier who sold him the powder he loved to snort, and throwing it in his face at the ball was well worth any suspicions it may have created.

"Gods, I love the rush of a win." Ryder's voice rises like steam up the stairway when he enters, and I continue my path up to the second story. "The hit you took at the end was perfect, but you really could have embellished how much pain you were in."

I take off my mask and tuck it into my pocket. "If you think crying will help us then you're more than welcome to trade places with me. We both know you're better suited for wailing than I am."

"Hilarious," he drawls. "Firstly, I'm not ashamed of my emotions. Not all of us are perturbed by the notion of vulnerability. Secondly, you'd never be able to work the crowd like I do. They love me."

"Well, I'm glad someone does."

I shove open the door that leads to a short hallway and unlock my office, one of the two rooms up here. The other being the one that Saskia and Ryder shared, which was a nightmare that made me debate on more than one occasion if I should abandon them. The room is lit by a few lanterns and has no personal effects. All recordings of my dealings are kept in a safe at Veles Manor, but to keep up the front should anyone ever break in, records of the tavern organized by Saskia are kept in cabinets along the wall.

I grab the box of smokes off my desk before opening the shutters to the only window in here. The cold air caresses my skin as I place one smoke between my lips and another behind my ear before striking a match and lighting it. I wipe the blood off my cheek with a spare rag, take a deep drag, and tilt my head back to blow out the smoke. There's some sick irony surrounding the fact that I've spent my life avoiding people and preferring solitude, and the one person whose presence I crave like a drug currently wants me to stay away.

"Now *that* is something I haven't seen you do in quite some time," Ryder says, handing me a vial of the antidote to the tonic I took to disguise my features, with a smoke of his own pressed between his lips. "Elowen has done a number on you, brother."

He has no idea.

I smoked for several reasons when I was younger: to curb hunger, to mask the odor of the slums, or to give myself something to do with my hands. Some people develop an addiction to it, but I never have. I just feel like I'm going out of my damn mind. Thank the gods the sun has set. I need to see her, to talk to her, to find a way to remedy the rift between us.

A light knock vibrates the door, three short taps and then two separated by a brief pause. I step away from the window to let Alexus inside, locking it again once he enters. He's a fair-haired man with stubble along his jaw and the ability to move around and obtain the knowledge I employ him to seek. There are too many people at the castle and the border to meet with my spies, and though Alexus knows how to get into my house unnoticed, meeting here is the ideal place.

He nods my way before taking a seat in front of the desk. "Sir."

"I assume you have news regarding the nobles," I say while taking a seat. "Are they gathering?"

"Not yet, but with the last of them vacating the castle, I imagine they soon will. They'll most likely be working to try to find something to use against you or Queen Elowen to manipulate you as they did Eagor and Valia." He holds up a piece of folded parchment. "I've compiled a list of the eight noble houses from most to least loyal based off of how close they were to Eagor."

Alexus is one of my best spies and has been since I first became commander. We first met when we were both assassins in Verendus. We weren't friends—the only people I grudgingly granted that title were Ryder and Saskia—but if we had any insight on jobs, we'd share it, as long as it didn't cut into our individual profits or reputations.

"Seek employment in House Baelyn." As I glance through the list, I note that Lord Xantheus is second to last. "He's already proven himself to be vocal. I'll increase your fee by forty thousand syndrils."

"I'll take the job but you earned my loyalty long ago. I don't require more pay."

I ignore his protest and continue my orders, "The first whisper you hear of a meeting or a possible revolt, I want it reported to me immediately."

"I'll go there first thing in the morning. If he's just vacated the castle, there will be positions open on the estate." He pulls a flask out of his cloak and takes a swig. He never drinks while on assignment so he's probably getting the last of his whiskey while he can. "What's your plan if they never publicly state their treason?"

"Elowen and I will do something to enrage them enough to reveal themselves, or we'll play the long game, depending on how quickly this war pans out." I put out my smoke and take a mint leaf out of the tin beside the pack, chewing on it as I throw on a fresh shirt and my black cloak that absorbs the darkness around me. With my hood up, my features are obscured just enough to not be identified, but I don a fresh face mask to be safe. "The nobles are sheep—they'll fall in line when herded in the right direction, and if not, they'll be sent to slaughter. With proof, nobody will be able to contest their executions."

"I have the forged reference letter Ryder transcribed the last time I

sought employment, so I don't foresee an issue with acquiring a position." Alexus rises from his seat, closing his eyes and tilting his head
up to the ceiling. "Gods, I hate nobles."

"You're our bravest soldier for dealing with them," Ryder says. "I
couldn't do it, and I was born to."

Alexus chuckles and slips from the office without a sound as I unlock the corner cabinet, pulling out a bouquet of purple starsnaps and
blue irises I bought for Elowen earlier.

Ryder snickers as we step into the hall. "This is an endearing image.
Maybe I'll paint it one day to show children that even death has a soft
spot."

"Do you never get tired of hearing your own voice?" I lock up behind us and take the staircase to the back entrance. "Only a fool shows
up empty-handed when their woman is upset. If you took notes, perhaps you wouldn't be in a long-term courtship with your hand."

"Yeah, well, let's see if you make it to the ceremony." Ryder's laugh
bounces off the narrow walls. "Before you get too close, make sure she
doesn't have her knives on her."

I smile to myself. "I hope she does. It keeps things interesting."

His laughter increases. "Deranged bastard."

CHAPTER
FOUR

CAYDEN

I PULL ON THE REINS AS I TURN ONTO HEALER'S ROW AND note three male figures lurking across the road from Elowen's cottage. Soldiers often congregate here, as well as citizens seeking medical attention, either for themselves or someone in need of their escorting, but judging by the way they sway in place, I'd reckon they're drunk.

Koa's hooves clack on the cobblestones as I slow his pace and pull down my hood and mask, riding between them and her. Their laughter soon fades, as does the color in their cheeks when they realize who I am. Braxton stands at the top of the stairs leading to the porch with a hand on the hilt of his blade, his shoulders relaxed as if he welcomes the threat should they approach.

I stare without emotion and jut my chin toward the mouth of the road.

"Go," one of them commands, setting them off, disappearing in a sloppy sprint.

My protectiveness of Elowen doesn't stem only from selfish reasons, it's also because I've seen how cruel this world is, especially to women. The sharpest memory I have of my mother is her screams the night she died. Not her laughter. Not her smile. Pain shapes us like a blacksmith honing a blade that we point at anyone who threatens to take what little joy we find in this corrupt world.

"How long were those men here?"

"They arrived only a few minutes before you," Braxton answers. "I'd have confronted them myself if you hadn't come."

"Seize them if they return," I order as I dismount and tie the reins on a post. "I don't care if they're bleeding out and Elowen is the last healer in Ravaryn. They will never cross this threshold. Am I clear?"

"Yes, sir." Like Alexus, Braxton has known me for years, and I'm thankful they didn't conform to the rules of society and call me *Your Highness*. I've never cared much for propriety.

Aside from Ryder, Braxton is the only general I trust to guard Elowen. I've seen him take on several enemies at once and come out without a scratch. He swore to die for her before he even knew her, and Braxton is not a man that takes an oath lightly. He lost his wife and child on the birthing bed over twenty years ago yet still wears his wedding band.

"I have her from here. Have a good night, Braxton."

He dips his head before gliding down the path that leads to the road. I tighten my grip on the bouquet and shove the door open. My impatience is too strong to delay this a moment longer. Bundles of dried flowers tied with ribbons now hang from the rafters. She must've found them in the basket I left in the storage closet. I recalled her saying something about how Nyrinn's shop had bundles, so I figured she might want some here. Several books are open and facing downward on the table and couch to hold her place, and something loosens in my chest when my eyes land on her.

I wish I could hate her for having this control over me: to consume my thoughts and reinvent the man I am despite my not wanting to let the old version go. She's my only exception, the one crack within a heart made of stone. Braxton must've been in and out because she doesn't turn to face me. Spiraling curls spill down her back as she balances on a stool, desperately trying to reach a jar at the back of the top shelf. I see the very moment she knows it's me. Her shoulders stiffen as I close the distance between us and reach above her with ease. The dark strands of her hair that smell like a spring breeze smack me in the face as she spins, rattling several vials as her back slams into the wood.

I shove my irritation with how careless she is with herself aside as she stares up at me with wide eyes that make me want to drown in a pool of honey. I look for her in everything, everywhere. I see her eyes in the mundane details of my day that make me crave the moment I'll be with her again.

She takes the jar out of my hand, successfully ignoring the massive bouquet in the other. "Where did Braxton go?"

"Gone," I say as she hops down from the stool and strides to her desk while holding the glass up to the light to examine its contents. "No sense in keeping him here when I'm perfectly capable of guarding my wife."

The quill pressed between her fingers snaps in half, splattering her inventory log with ink. "I'm *not* your wife."

"I'm happy to remedy that mistake within the hour."

"Unless you have a ring worth my time on your person, you'll be waiting for quite some time." She scrunches her nose and narrows her eyes on the bouquet. "Though I've always believed it's best to get things over with, like yanking an arrow out of a limb."

I rip off one of the starsnaps and tuck it behind her ear as she continues to glare at me. "Have dinner with me."

She yanks the flowers out of my grip and tosses them to the floor without even looking. "No."

"I wasn't asking."

"How shocking," she mutters before gliding toward the mantel on the far side of the room to pluck off a random book and flip through the pages carelessly. I follow her like a damn dog on a leash and pull it from her grip, setting it aside as she spins on her heels, ready to busy herself with some other diversion. Normally, I'd love this, but not when I note the way she's limping. I bend down to wrap my arms around her waist and hoist her in the air, not caring if we're putting on a show for anyone outside and careful to avoid her injuries as she squeals.

"You are such a——" She cuts herself off with a growl when I gently set her down on the couch and take a seat on the coffee table, keeping my hands on her hips.

"Finish the sentence, love. I'm eager to know what you think of me."

She crosses her arms and sharpens her glare, and gods, if it doesn't make me want to kiss the spot on her neck that'll make her melt in my hands until she's begging me to keep them on her. "At the moment I'm thinking about how stupid you were to go on a midnight ride through the kingdom when we're supposed to be happily betrothed. There was gossip about a potential rift all throughout the castle—even Finnian knew about it before I saw him."

"I built you a library in our chambers before I left," I flatly state.

"Yes, and I'm sure you carrying wood and broken furniture up and down the tower was a sure sign of a satisfied man."

If Elowen wasn't upset with me, I'd keep her occupied well into the night, and I tried to sleep on the couch to give her some privacy before I nearly went mad. She can be angry for as long as she needs, but that doesn't mean I'll make it easy for her, and I refuse to accept living separate lives behind closed doors now that I know what it's like to truly be with her. "Couples argue."

"Not us. We don't have the privilege of making mistakes. We can't fail. There's too much—" Her breathing quickens, and she places a hand on her ribs as her face contorts in pain. "I will not lose this war because of our inability to put on a convincing front for the kingdom."

"Elowen," I say her name with a gentleness I didn't think myself capable of and slowly slide my hand beneath hers, knowing it's both warmer and larger. "I made you a promise. We will not lose this war." She lets out a shuddering breath, though I'm unsure if it's from my touch or my words.

"We cannot afford an internal rebellion. All our strength must be focused on Imirath, especially now that they're aligned with Thirwen. We'll be fighting two armies, and I don't know if Galakin will entertain us now that I'm betrothed to you and not their prince as they wished."

"I'll send my condolences if it helps sway them." She grants me a half smile before wiping it clean off her face. "Alexus took the job to spy on the nobles so the situation will be easier to monitor with a man on the inside. Internal conflict will be terminated swiftly and without mercy."

She nods as the tension in her body slowly loosens. Her face is mere inches from mine, and the warmth of her skin burns the tips of my fingers like hot iron. "No matter what you do, it won't change the blood in my veins. People will always care about that. You should—"

I quirk a brow. "I should care? You know I've never cared about your relation to Garrick."

Her cold fingers wrap around my wrists and remove my hands from her body. "Perhaps you don't right now, but . . ."

Talk to me.

I can practically see the walls she's trying to build between us again. This doesn't sound like her. *No.* It sounds like Ailliard. She never told me what he said to her the night she killed him, but I'd wager it had something to do with that.

"I'd never judge you for who your father is, nor where you come from."

"Why?"

Because mine was the worst man I've ever met.

"Because they never deserved you." I shake my head. She may be Elowen Atarah, princess of Imirath, but she's always been so much more than that. I've seen her soul, and the darkness within it just makes the light that much more beautiful.

She sucks in a sharp breath and tries to stand, but I rest a hand on her uninjured thigh to keep her down. She needs to rest, and to keep weight off her bad leg, but she tries again, and it will only hurt her more if she struggles against me.

"W-what happened to your eye?" She stiffly walks toward a cabinet in the corner, pulling out a tin and a rag.

"I lost focus and got hit while fighting."

"That seems unlike you. You're not one to get distracted."

"No, I'm not," I say, my eyes locked on her face. Denying her aid is on the tip of my tongue, and if she were anyone else I would without hesitation, but I swallow my discomfort as she dips the rag into a bowl of water and comes closer. "I own a tavern in the slums of Verendus. I bought it with the money I made as an assassin and increased my profits by smuggling goods and putting a fighting ring in the basement."

"Why?"

"Renting a room felt like throwing money away, and I needed a place to meet with spies." I shrug. "I was also tired of not having a way to make money unless I worked for someone else."

"And you fought in the fighting pit tonight."

"I take a tonic to disguise my features, so nobody knows it's me."

Her throat bobs as she swallows. "Is that why you're richer than other commanders?"

"And some kings."

"Then why bother working your way through the army? You could've bought one with the amount of money you must have."

"Money doesn't buy loyalty, blood does, and mine has spilled beside my soldiers'. I needed a steadfast army to stand between us and Garrick once I found you."

She tips her head to the ceiling before uncapping the tin of salve. "And you expect me to believe you did all of this strategizing and didn't factor the marriage clause into your plan?"

"I didn't. You—"

She holds up her hand, exhaustion evident on her features, and I grind my teeth. "Is this something you smuggled? It's infused with healing magic, and we've only just lifted the bans on it."

"Yes, it's from Galakin. They have healers that channel light magic into medicine."

Her fingertips brush my cheekbone, and her touch slows, becoming more of a caress. I remain still, afraid that any movement on my part will break whatever trance she's fallen into. It's like a knife is twisting in my gut, knowing I can't close the distance. Wanting her is the cruelest form of torture.

A horse whinnies outside, and Elowen's gaze clears as she turns away. The celestial and draconic beading on her light blue velvet gown shimmers as she glides away, and I close my hands into fists, trying to use the pain of my nails digging into my skin to curb the longing pulsing through me.

"I'm assuming you're still against separate chambers, considering you got rid of the furniture in your bedroom to add the library to our suite."

I clench my jaw. "Yes."

"It's entirely normal for—"

"I don't give a fuck about other royals or couples or what's normal for them." I risk her ire, standing from the table and tightening my hands in her thick curls until I can tilt her head up exactly where I want it. "Be angry at me all you wish, but you'll never be rid of me."

A flush creeps up her neck and cheeks. "Starting tonight you'll sleep in the bed with me and remain there until dawn. I don't care how painful it is for you to lay there; in fact, I hope it is. You're too tall for the couch and we can't risk a servant seeing you, but I will bind your hands if they reach for me."

"Quite the imagination you have."

She throws the rag at my face and rolls her eyes before darting them to the side, noting the few people lingering in the road to get a glimpse of us through the window. Just as easily as she adopted theatrics in Imirath, a smile slides onto her lips as she looks up at me, rises onto the tips of her toes, and kisses my unscarred cheek. She's never done that, and something like shame pumps into my blood.

She scoops the flowers she tossed on the floor into her arms and cradles them to her chest, gently smiling down. It's the first hint that I've done something right since the betrothal. I pluck her coat off the hook by the door and help her into it, flicking my eyes between her and the bouquet as I offer her my arm.

"The flowers are innocent," she insists.

CHAPTER
FIVE

ELOWEN

O NE DAY I'LL LEARN TO LIMIT MY SELF-DESTRUCTIVE
habits, but today is not that day. I stare out the window of
the carriage, hardly absorbing any of the sights, but also not
granting a glance to the man across from me. He takes up more than
half the damn carriage, but his presence alone makes me feel as if I'm
pressed against the wall and starved for air.

I cross one knee over the other as the horses trot on, pursing my
lips when Cayden *chuckles.* Oh, how the sound makes me want to
scream. "Has anyone ever told you it's rude to stare?"

"Has anyone ever told you that I'm rude?"

"Nobody had to. I caught on rather early."

He chuckles again. "Why am I going to look at snow and buildings
when I've been starving for the sight of you all day?"

Warmth floods my chest like someone spilled hot tea within me,
but I force ice into my tone. "Flattery and flowers will get you nowhere."

"I'm right where I want to be."

I scoff and finally face him, not letting the pain slicing through me
show on my features. "On my bad side?"

He pushes off the wall as if it were impossible to stay away, lazily
twirling one of my curls around his finger, but he doesn't answer the
question. We begin to slow and voices of citizens along the street filter

in through the gilded wood, excitedly chattering about spotting the royal carriage. I gasp as Cayden pulls me forward and catch my balance on his chest as he settles me on his lap.

His scent and warmth surround me, and I try to shove myself off though all I want to do is sink into it . . . into him. I want to rest my head on his shoulder like I've done so many times before and forget the world, but I can't let myself. I've been used by my father and then by Ailliard, and though I knew Cayden and I were using each other in the beginning, I didn't think we'd end up here. He's never hid his cunning nature from me, but I never thought I'd be a casualty of it. I don't even know if I am. I feel like I don't know anything, and my own mind traps me in the dark. How can you trust what anyone says when you can't even trust yourself?

"If you think I'm going to let you touch me after you deceived me—"

"We have been apart all day and when that door opens there will be several citizens trying to get a glimpse of us," he cuts me off, circling my hips with an arm and pressing me closer. "If you wish to push the narrative of a happy couple then you need to take into account what I'd be doing." His eyes darken as they flash to my lips, and I can't suppress my shiver when his fingers glide up the column of my neck before wrapping around the back.

I do my best to keep another tremble hidden. It's not as if my feelings for him have disappeared. I wouldn't be in as much pain if they had. Trying to cut him out of me would be like trying to rip my soul in half. "What would you be doing?"

His sigh caresses my skin, and he leans forward to graze his lips above the spot on my neck he knows I love. "I'd ensure space would be the last thing you wanted from me, and I'd take my sweet time proving that."

My thighs press together of their own volition, but I shove my desire aside, lacing my fingers through his hair to pull him away from my neck. His pupils dominate his eyes as I lower my lips to hover just above his, never granting him what he so desperately wants. Uneven breaths dance within the small space as my chest both tightens and fills with butterflies. "This is not real."

His hold tightens as the door is pulled open, looking ready to tell the driver to fuck off and lock us in here so he can savor the proximity for a few more seconds, but I whip my head toward the bashful man and slide farther up Cayden's lap to brush my hips over his bulge, making his shoulders stiffen.

"Oh, I'm so sorry!" I cover my mouth to suppress a laugh.

"I-I didn't mean to interrupt, Your Majesties," he stutters, flicking his eyes over his shoulder to take in the small crowd that's gathered by the entrance of the restaurant. "Would you like me to take you back to the castle?"

"Nonsense." I smile to ease his nerves. "We'll be just a moment."

"Of course, my queen." He bows and swiftly shuts the door, allowing me to climb off Cayden's lap. I'm thankful for the winter wind that filled the carriage and cools my flushed skin.

"Do you need me to leave so you can sort yourself out?" I ask in a sickeningly sweet voice.

He rests his elbows on his knees and drags his hands down his face, whispering my name a few times under his breath as he shakes his head. "If this is how you wish to play, then I'm happy to oblige."

I narrow my eyes and tilt my chin up as the rush of a challenge fills me. Cayden shoves the door open once enough time has passed, offering a hand to help me down then sliding mine through the crook of his arm as he tosses two coins to the driver.

"A drink while you wait," he says over his shoulder as he escorts me through a stone archway chiseled with swirling blue designs that glow as if a lantern were encased within.

I stay close to Cayden as he leads us through the small crowd, not entirely as a façade. I've never liked being surrounded by people. Ailliard told me I'd get over it as time passed, but I never have, and he never missed the opportunity to tell me how weak it makes me. The shame that used to accompany his words has faded from a twisting knife to the sting of a slap.

I rest my head on Cayden's bicep as the hostess rushes around the white marble podium to greet us, dropping into a low curtsy that makes her gown ripple around her like waves crashing on the shore. "Your Majesties, welcome to Starry Night. It's an honor to serve you this evening."

Cayden steps behind me to slide my coat down my arms and remove his cloak, handing it off to the servant awaiting them. I'm thankful the gown I chose this morning is fit for an establishment such as this. The sleeves widen below my elbows and drape dramatically, making the dark blue jewels and golden embroidery shimmer as I walk. The hostess leads us through a parted set of curtains, and a staff thumps against the floor, vibrating the soles of my shoes as a man with a deep voice announces us.

"King Cayden Veles and Queen Elowen Atarah. The conquerors of Vareveth."

Chairs scrape against the floor as all in attendance rise as we glide through the room. I don't let myself falter under their prodding gazes. Every move, every step, every breath is up for scrutiny, assessed for weakness. Those that remain loyal to Eagor are waiting for us to fail, but I'll claw my way to victory, no matter the odds. I will no longer be at the mercy of men, but they will beg for mine.

I grasp my skirts to keep from tripping as we're led up a set of immaculately polished steps to a singular table on a risen platform. Several ivy-covered columns circle the space to create the illusion of privacy, though we'll be visible to the entirety of those gathered. Golden candelabras cast a warm glow from where they stand in the gaps, making it feel incredibly intimate.

Cayden moves past a server to grip the back of a chair and slides it in behind me before filling the silent establishment with the sound of him *slowly* dragging the seat across the table closer to mine.

"I wonder, are you this obnoxious with everyone or do you reserve this charming attribute for me?" I whisper, despite the chatter resuming as people return to their meals.

"It serves no purpose with anyone else." He leans back in his chair, draping an arm over the back of mine. "I don't wish to be associated with them."

"Vos essa un nunti tasuri." *You are a stupid man.*

"Vet vos essa tesis mas ulessi ardama en Ravaryn." He smiles so wide his dimples deepen in his cheeks as I blush. *And you are the most beautiful woman in Ravaryn.* "I see you've been studying the Ravarian texts."

I've been devouring them for several hours. He left me books on both the ancient language and dragon lore, and each time I cracked one open I kept wanting more. They're all packed safely in the carriage, ready for me to continue once we get back to the castle.

Ravarian is a forgotten language used only by the cults who pass it down orally and a few select scholars who meticulously record it and lock it away. Mages often use it to cast spells even if they're not in a cult. It was the language spoken in Ravaryn centuries ago before we adopted the common tongue.

"You never told me you speak a second language." My brows crease. "How did you even acquire the book?" The pages are yellowed with age and show signs of water damage along with smudged ink. Some pages are falling out, but none are missing, thankfully.

He shrugs. "I have many skills I've yet to reveal. As for how I got it, I was a thief before I was anything else."

"Are you fluent?"

"Yes, sirantia." The way he rolls the R makes me wish he'd say it again. His voice is deep and raspy. I've always loved it. It reminds me of how he sounds in the morning, but I quickly shove that memory aside. Gods, when will someone bring me a drink?

I clear my throat. "What does that mean?"

"I seem to have forgotten." He continues grinning at me. "Tell me what you learned about the dragons."

I purse my lips and fight the urge to roll my eyes as a servant *finally* begins ascending the steps. "I seem to have forgotten."

I file the term into the back of my mind, prepared for a full night of hunting for the meaning of it. I turn my gaze to the approaching man in impeccable garb. "Good evening, Your Majesties. Can I get you started with some drinks?"

"Oh, yes. A meal is not complete without wine." I prop my chin on my clasped hands. "Bring me a bottle of your most expensive. Something that's collecting dust in the cellar. The king and I haven't toasted our betrothal yet and this seems like the perfect opportunity." I turn to him, though if he's bothered by my request, he doesn't let it show. "How does that sound, *lamb chop?*"

"If it's to celebrate our betrothal then bring me your most expensive whiskey as well." His mouth twitches. "Anything for you, *peaches.*"

I scrunch my nose and hum, smiling as if the term didn't curb my appetite. Though that doesn't matter, considering Cayden orders for me after the server lists off the chef's specials, annoying me further by choosing the correct options to my exact specifications. I pluck a piece of warm bread from the basket and dip it into a small dish of oil and red pepper flakes to avoid speaking to him as the waiter leaves. His gaze is glued to the side of my face, but I ignore it in hopes of vexing him.

It's not hard to find something to look at. The night sky is visible through the glass domed ceiling adorned with enchanted candles twinkling above to act as stars. My dragons fly above as if they can sense where my gaze rests, and the knot in my chest loosens as they calmly swirl through the clouds. The whole establishment looks like it belongs in the Vareveth castle now that the servants have worked tirelessly to transition the appearance. I glance over my shoulder, watching two manmade waterfalls flow on either side of our table and gather in a pool in front of us filled with silver fish.

The server returns to place the bottles and glasses on the table, but Cayden chooses to uncork them himself. I force myself to look anywhere other than at his fingers wrapped around them, but he slides the crystal glass in front of me, bringing attention to the exact thing I'm trying to avoid. The golden rings on a few of his fingers reflect the dim light around us, and the cuts on his knuckles send a wave of nostalgia rushing over me.

"What is your opinion on divorce?" I ask before taking a very needed and very large gulp of wine.

"I think it's a mutually beneficial agreement between two parties that wish to be free from the torments of a crumbling union." He swirls his whiskey. "However, I don't think much on things that have no relevance in my life."

I laugh softly, as if Cayden had said something amusing, as the server returns with our dinner. Taking a sip of wine, I lean into him. His eyes soften slightly when he looks at me, knowing this is fake but wishing it were real. It makes me take another sip and another until my glass is empty and he pours me a second glass.

I know there is no getting out of this union, and I suppose I consider myself lucky in a way. Most royal marriages are arranged when the heirs are infants and are notoriously unhappy, but there's a petty part of me that wants to twist the knife a bit. "Through our marriage I gain an army, and you gain a crown and the allegiance of the woman bonded to five dragons. This is a political union, so what's to happen when the war is over and none of the benefits apply any longer?" I cross one leg over the other, tilting my head. "Most would say divorce is the obvious course of action."

"Most people are idiots and disregarding their opinions has served me well so far." He scans my features like he's trying to figure out what's truly going on in my mind. "You speak as if this were a betrothal of convenience, yet you were anything but. How many men must conquer a kingdom to have the woman they want?" My shoulders stiffen, and he never stops assessing me. "I never said you weren't worth it. I'll spill whatever blood I must, Elowen."

I suck in a sharp breath and drink half my glass, letting the familiar light sensation flood through me as the alcohol takes effect. "I'm sure the crown embellishes the outcome."

He traces his fingers along the back of my neck, bringing his face so close to mine we're almost nose-to-nose. His eyes have flecks of gold despite the pupils nearly dominating them. "If we were merely a political agreement, I wouldn't have committed the details I adore about you to memory. I wouldn't have tasted you and realized I was starving. I wouldn't know where to touch you, how to touch you, or give a fuck about any of it and yet I do, and I can't stop."

Oh gods.

I can't do this.

Without thinking of the consequences or how it might look, I try to shove away from him, but his hands shoot out to clasp my wrists and tug me forward until I'm pressed against his chest. His lips graze my ear, making me want to arch into him like a cat in the sun. "Play nice, angel. People are watching."

"You said you don't care what they think."

"But you do." He slides his hands to my sides, making me shudder as he caresses my aching bruises. "And I wanted you closer."

I want to give him a biting remark, but it gets lodged in my throat. I turn toward the table to try to locate my wine. He's always had a way of making me forget everything else in the world exists. He tilts my chin back toward him and I'm trapped. Lost in him. Helplessly treading water in the middle of a stormy ocean.

"If the roles were reversed, how do you think I would've reacted to you bringing up marriage?"

I shake my head, the pain in my chest sharpening. "Don't do that."

"Answer the question, El," he states with unyielding resolve.

"You didn't bring up a betrothal when we were at the inn or any other better suited moment," I hiss. "You didn't speak of a future—"

"I didn't speak of a future with you because I've never planned my future beyond getting revenge, but that doesn't mean I didn't want you to be in it."

"You brought it up in a banquet hall drenched in blood moments after my uncle betrayed and attacked me and plotted with your king to send me back to my father."

He sneers when I bring up Eagor. "When we were at the inn did I not say I'd never let you go? For months, have I not said I'll do anything for you and to have you? What did you think that would entail for people in our position?" I bite the inside of my cheek to stop myself from succumbing to my emotions. "Nothing in this world will ever be more valuable than you in my eyes. I did what I had to do to keep you safe, and I will not apologize for something that I don't regret."

I don't bother holding myself up anymore, letting the exhaustion crush me into his chest and taking advantage of being able to hide from the world for a few moments. He continues stroking my side with one hand, and I swear I feel a slight tremor in the other when he rests it on the back of my head to keep me pressed against him. The darkness comforts me, as does his scent of teakwood, amber, and leather. I know he'll keep me safe; it's never been a question of that, but people get a taste of power and let it lead them like a hound chasing a scent. I've always allowed myself to love, but I've never believed it was meant for me. It's so much easier to give and expect nothing in return.

"You know me, El. Come back to me."

I'm right here, I want to say, but I'm not. I'm lost in the maze of my mind with staggeringly high walls crafted from doubt and betrayal. "Do I?"

"More than anyone."

CHAPTER
SIX

CAYDEN

I KNOW I'VE DONE TERRIBLE THINGS IN MY LIFE, TAKEN JOBS for the sake of deepening my pockets, fought without honor, and told more lies than I remember, but this woman—*this woman*—is my personal brand of torture.

"How long are you going to keep at this?"

Normally I relish silence and crave it when someone's voice fills a room, but Elowen's silence is grating on my every nerve like walking on nails without shoes. I lean against the doorframe that leads to our bedchamber, watching as she kicks off her boots and glides toward the vanity against the wall.

She sighs, a contented smile painting her lips as she pretends to be engrossed in the task of slowly removing every ring on her fingers before moving on to her earrings.

"Elowen." I genuinely don't think anyone in Ravaryn has her audacity, and it both intrigues and irritates me. She hasn't spoken since we began the journey to the castle, blatantly ignoring all my attempts at conversation. She uses a few cotton pads to wipe off her makeup and piles her curls on top of her head before striding toward the couch laid with several decorative pillows the maid must've removed when turning down the bed. "I'm thinking of cutting my hair, perhaps shaving it all off."

She throws me an icy glare over her shoulder and shakes her head.

"Ah, so you *can* hear me."

She presses her lips together, no doubt swallowing some sarcastic comment about how unfortunate a fate that is and hoists the mountain of pillows into her arms, throwing them down on the bed and arranging them into a line down the middle. I leave her to her... task... and pour myself another whiskey. Maybe I should just drink from the bottle. Gods know I need it.

She's packing them in with the amount of vigor one would exercise while building defenses against an enemy, and just to annoy her, I pinch one of the mounds between my fingers and lift it high. "Foolproof plan, love." She glares at me, a stubborn curl falling in her eye, and yanks the pillow from my grip to slam it back to where it was. "Isn't the whole point of sleeping in the same bed to appear normal? Do you often try to suffocate yourself with feathers while you sleep?"

"Death seems a merciful fate compared to—" She slaps a hand over her mouth and grabs a book off the nightstand, all but sprinting into the bathing chamber.

"All hells," I mutter while pinching the bridge of my nose and following her like a gods-damned dog *again*. I bite my tongue so hard that I taste the coppery tang of blood as she ignores me and prances around the room to light candles and pour some oils into the oversized tub. Her lips quirk up when she takes in the state of me and sets her book on the table beside the bath.

I drag a hand down my face as she slides her gown off her shoulders and shimmies it over her hips until she's wearing nothing but the moonstone necklace she never removes. Though it doesn't accomplish what I'm sure she sought out to do. My irritation from her attitude is nothing compared to the molten hot fury beating in my chest like a second heart. If she thought I'd turn into a mindless man fueled by lust at the sight of her, then she should've factored in the state of her injuries I'm now able to see. Dark bruises mar both sides of her torso and legs. They're all I can focus on. Knowing Ailliard beat her and shoved his nails into the cut on her thigh while I was only in the other room turns my stomach. When she came limping into the banquet hall with blood spilling down her leg, I was prepared to torture every single prick that had a hand in her pain and set the entire castle ablaze.

"I'm sorry."

Her lips part and eyes widen as she takes a step back before shaking her head and lowering herself into the bubbly water.

"How are you feeling, love?"

I try to wipe the anger from my features, but she's already seen it. She's known me long enough to know that the constant anger burning within me will never burn her. I'd sooner fall on my own sword before I ever raised a hand to her or made her feel unsafe with me. Her father tortured and imprisoned her, her uncle beat and betrayed her, her mother sat silently as she was abused, and I deceived her.

I know I deserve this silence from her, probably even worse. She can give me all the grief she wants, but I will not be another person to discard her. Nothing she does to me will ever compare to the hell my life would've become if Imirath had taken her.

She grabs her book on dragon lore and cracks it open. It rests against the side of the tub, but her eyes don't move over the words as she stares down at it. Tossing back the remaining whiskey in my glass, I turn away.

My eyes land on the desk nestled across from Elowen's in an alcove hewn into the stone. I moved it from my old bedchamber, now a library off the main sitting room in our suite. We could've moved into the king and queen's chambers, but they're separate from each other, and neither Elowen nor I were keen on the idea of living in the same chambers as Eagor and Valia once did. I walk through the parted midnight curtains held back by draconic hooks and unlock the top drawer. There's not much in here aside from a few reports, my reading glasses, and the small velvet pouch I grasp.

I step closer to one of the floor-to-ceiling windows in the rounded alcove while holding the ring up to the moonlight spilling through the frosty panes. Something pinches in my chest when I look at it, but it's sat in the dark long enough. I shove down my unease and return to Elowen. She peeks over the top of her book when I reenter and raises her brows when I sink to my knees beside her. I gently take hold of her wrist and slide the ring onto her index finger—a glittering star sapphire framed by diamonds set into a gold band.

She blinks slowly while looking down at it before shaking herself from the trance and tracing the oval stone with her eyes. I hadn't planned on giving this to her yet, but it was always going to be hers. A mixture of pride and possession twine together within me, and I don't miss the irony of it being our house colors.

"Keep it safe for me."

I don't offer her any information as she continues to stare, and I leave her to ponder her theories. Women don't wear rings to signify a betrothal, and if it were for that purpose I would've placed it on the opposite hand and ring finger, but it feels right to see it on her.

Returning to my desk, I grab the stack of sealed reports from the drawer and rest my glasses on the bridge of my nose. The dragons swirl around the spires, and I watch them from the corner of my eye as their wings cut through the clouds. Calithea looks like she was born from the night itself with her silver scales that resemble a shining star.

Imirath's front has been quiet, but I don't mistake the lull for peace. Garrick will never surrender, nor will I. He's too proud, and if he's figured out who I am by now then he knows I'll never let him live.

There is no ending to this war where we both survive.

I exit the alcove and toss the stack of reports into the fire across from the four-poster bed. There's nothing of value within the words, so there's no sense in keeping them. I rest my hands on the mantel and bow my head while listening to the crackling logs and Elowen getting dressed.

She steps back into the room but pauses in the doorway. I feel her eyes burning into my back like a brand and slowly look over my shoulder to take her in. Her cheeks are flushed from the bath and damp, dark curls hang down to her hips. A sage slip with golden embroidery brushes the tops of her thighs and a robe made of white lace drapes behind her and down her arms.

I swallow thickly and avert my gaze to the wall as she climbs into bed, still clutching the same book in a white-knuckled fist. My nails dig into the wood before I push off the mantel and retrieve some medical supplies from an ornate box on a small table. She holds the book against her chest like a shield as I approach and sit beside her.

"I can't watch you be in pain and do nothing about it," I state.

"Why?" She whispers the word, and it's weighed down by exhaustion, but something else lurks beneath the surface. There's a twinge of desperation, like she needs to hear the answer to quell the doubts in her mind cultivated by my actions.

I run my tongue over my teeth as I contemplate how to articulate my thoughts. "From the moment you stepped into my life I've had this incessant need to ensure your well-being, and I'm too much of a jealous prick to watch someone else tend to you."

She laughs quietly while propping herself on the pillows at her back and bending her knees so I'm able to work.

"Fuck," I mutter while breathing deeply, though that doesn't help considering all I'm inhaling is her intoxicating scent of lavender and vanilla. She laughs again because the temptress knows exactly what she's doing to me. I unroll the heated bandages I've used on her before while raking my eyes over her. A small scrap of lace covers the apex of her thighs that I could easily pull aside, and her nipples press against the silk covering her chest as it rises and falls unevenly.

She hums in relief when I get halfway up her thigh, and I pause my actions briefly. "Do you wake up every day and think of new ways to torture me?"

"Yes."

Her voice.

Her laugh.

It's like hearing a ballad after stepping off a battlefield.

She sits up once I finish her thigh, but I get no relief from our new position considering all it does is bring her face closer to mine. She shivers beneath my touch as I dip my hands under her slip and gently dust my fingers along her torso. Her eyes don't leave mine, and she doesn't back away, doesn't avoid looking at me as she did in the bath.

I press my hand into her back, selfishly bringing us closer and tilting my head down while I begin wrapping the bandages around her. She sucks in a sharp breath as her hands shoot forward and digs her nails into my shoulders.

"I'd raise him from the dead just to kill him again. You know that, right?" I murmur against the side of her head. She nods in the crook of my neck. "Just breathe for me. Once you're wrapped it'll feel better, but the injuries will take longer to heal if I don't do this." Her exhale fans against me as I continue my movements slowly, no matter how hard it is to be close to her knowing she'll withdraw in mere seconds. "What other words did you learn while studying Ravarian?"

"I mainly focused on the basics, and some dragon commands, also phrases to insult you successfully." She relaxes against me and my lips quirk up. "I'm going to continue after you finish. I took a break to read about dragon origins. I want to know if there's a reason I share a bond with them."

"What did you find out?"

"Asena, the high priestess, told me I'm blessed by the Goddess of Flames. During the dragon ceremony she said that my soul was forged in the fire of the gods." She leans back to look at me as she speaks. "Dragons came into the world centuries ago during the Age of Dragons. They first hatched from stars, but the goddess sensed something lurking within the earth's core. Every day for five years she would place her palms to the ground and let her magic seep from her. She was plagued by dreams that made others think she was mad, but the dragons began clawing their way out. It was said there were so many dragons you could never step outside without seeing one in the sky."

My brows crease. "Did it say what happened to them all?"

"It didn't say what caused their downfall, but I'd like to ask Asena about it when I have the chance." Her eyes come alive in a way I haven't seen since the night Ailliard died. "If she is correct, the soundest explanation for my bond is that the dragons sensed the fire within me when the eggs were placed around my cradle. My soul summoned them when it came into the world."

"And do you believe her?" I don't want to crush her hope, but Asena isn't the strongest resource. Blind faith is the absence of logic. It may work for some people, but not me.

Elowen's eyes drift to the window, tracking her dragons' movements as she contemplates. "I've never worshipped the gods, but I'm not opposed to hearing all theories as I continue my research to widen my perspective. There's always some truth to be found in legends if you read carefully." She brushes past the topic without giving me the chance to respond, and asks, "Will you tell me about the ring?"

"One day." The words taste bitter on my tongue. It's not the answer she wants, but it's the one she needs. It'll cause her to pull away, but she's not ready to hear about the origins. I wish I could be selfish enough to tell her, to be how I am with everyone else, but I can't. Even in her anger, her heart remains soft, and I want to win it back with my actions, not with a story from my past.

She huffs and flops back onto the pillows, cracking her book open to shield her gaze from mine. "You don't need to keep up the mysterious façade. You're nice to look at so I'm sure that'll keep me interested as the years tick by."

The ghost of the caress burns my flesh, and I flex my hands to rid them of the emptiness. "Are you implying that you think I'm handsome and would've married me had I asked properly?"

She drops the book to her chest. "I never said that."

I tap a finger against her lips. "You didn't need to, sirantia."

CHAPTER
SEVEN

ELOWEN

MY HEART POUNDS AS VENATRIX FLIES PARALLEL TO the sea below. Ocean spray dots my cheeks, stealing the breath from my lungs at the frigid temperature. I release my grip on the saddle horns, spreading my arms wide and letting the wind whoosh through my gloved fingers.

Sometimes my mind feels like I'm standing on the edge of a fathomless canyon, and other times I feel like I'm at the bottom of it, staring up through the darkness with no way to claw to the top. A week has quickly passed, and I've realized that most of my problems are drowned out by the sounds of dragon wings flapping on either side of me, so that's why I've spent more time in the air than on the ground.

"Andula, Venatrix," I command, using the Ravarian word for *faster*. When I'm not flying, I continue to study the language. Cayden has been occupied with war meetings, but we both agreed that training with the dragons as much as I possibly can will benefit both myself and the army more than poring over maps or discussing strategies.

Sorin shoots forward, attempting to overtake Venatrix, but I order him back in line. A displeased groan rumbles in his throat as he obeys, and I glance over my shoulder. "I rode you yesterday, you spoiled boy."

I switch between both the common tongue and Ravarian often and though they seem to understand both, I prefer the way the latter sounds. Sorin is the fastest and he doesn't let any of them forget it, especially Venatrix, whose growl vibrates my legs. I catch myself on her scales when Sorin bumps her from behind.

"Lotas." *Obey.*

Sorin groans again but doesn't challenge me, and I make sure to offer him my back before my smile breaks free. I don't think I'd be able to rein him in if he caught a hint of me enjoying his playful antics. I'd entertain him if we weren't about to begin a training drill, but the jagged maze of rocks looms into view. Mist coats the dark stones in an eerie blanket as the surf crashes against the staggering pillars.

I need to ensure they're ready for the battles to come. A dragon's life is not worth my father's, no matter what he's done to me. I will not forsake their love and loyalty to fulfill my vendetta. The cold has seeped into the steel saddle horns, but I tighten my grip despite it. Each dragon wears a black saddle with straps that attach to my belt and keep me from falling off when they twirl and twist. A dragon and rider must be one, and I don't want to restrict their movements. Their attention is split when I ride bareback, and I wouldn't be able to live with myself if my carelessness is the catalyst of them getting hurt.

I stroke a hand down Venatrix's crimson scales, and she hums softly. Something about the comfort laced within the small gesture makes me want to lie on her back and forget the world exists, but I grit my teeth knowing that's not an option. People often cast judgment on things they can't control and wear their animosity like armor to defend themselves against the unknown. Ailliard believed my dragons to be cursed beasts, but his treachery sealed his fate, not the fire that melted the flesh from his bones. Just because someone believes something to be monstrous doesn't make it so.

I was born into a world that doesn't accept my power, but I'll carve a place here for myself and my dragons with both blades and flames.

The wind whips at my cheeks like thousands of tiny needles as we cross into the shadow of the first cliff. The ruins of what was once a godly temple dedicated to the God of Death, Water, and the Moon stand as a labyrinth of obsidian stone. A haunting feeling pulses through the air, but we stay the course. I lean closer to Venatrix as she turns her body to enter the maze through a small gap.

There is nothing like flying.

She sharply ducks through a narrow passage created by two pillars that collided—the sea moss growing at the apex makes me believe it's been like this for centuries. She swirls around a column with grace, and rights herself just above the surface. Churning surf cuts through the sea-worn walls, and the waves smashing against it boom like thunder. Sharp rocks peek through the whitecaps as she zigzags through them.

My head jolts back when Venatrix takes a sharp upturn, tucking her claws close to her to keep them from scraping on the ruins. I press my chest into the saddle, staying as close to her as I possibly can. Her wings flare out on either side, pushing us back up and above a stone leaning horizontally in another pile of fallen rocks.

Venatrix is fierce in everything she does, and I wonder if it has something to do with her origins. The deep red of her scales hints toward her being a bloodfury. They hatched within volcanoes where their mothers laid their eggs in pools of boiling blood. Human or animal, it mattered little. It's believed the incubation process was how they gained their crimson coloring, and their lust for blood is stronger than that of other dragons. The mother would dive into a killing frenzy just before laying her clutch so her hatchlings could come into this world with a feast.

My throat tightens when I note the sliver leading to a long shaft, just wide enough for her to squeeze through as long as she gets enough momentum before entering. Her back is too large for me to fit my legs around—I even must kneel on Calithea—so I unhook my saddle straps and lie flat on my stomach. Her heart pounds beneath my cheek, and I use the sound to ground me as she enters. Darkness envelops me. The stone is so close that the dampness caresses my skin. If I were to move an inch, I'd shred my cheek. Venatrix continues at a steady, even glide, and my heart beats in time with hers.

For the first time in my life, I do not fear confinement, though I think the credit for that is owed to the dragon beneath me. The sea fades away, and for a moment, all that exists in the world is shadow and fire.

Sunlight sears my eyes when she makes it through, and my braid whips behind me as I sit up, leaving the temple ruins in our wake. Sorin and Calithea follow Venatrix's path, but Basilius and Delmira swoop over the top of the final pillar. Basilius never would've fit through the gap, and I doubt Delmira could either. Pride swells in my chest as I watch their scales shimmering in the sun as they tumble and play with each other.

Sometimes I get emotional just looking at them, and the magnitude of what I feel for them overtakes me. No matter the pain the bond has caused me, I could never run from it. I think it's brave to open your heart knowing love can become loss in a matter of seconds. I'd consider myself a coward if I didn't cherish my dragons as they deserve.

My smallest dragon is Calithea, though she's by no means little. She's considered a star-eater with her silver scales and white-tipped wings that remind me of snowflakes, hailing from the first dragons that existed. Her egg would've been kept on the bank of a hot spring within a mountain, and she would have glowed upon hatching. Star-eater hatchlings were said to look like shooting stars when they had a burst of energy. They only learned to dim their glow after their first three months and were kept in the cavern until they did to protect them from predators. The dragons never left my side as a baby, so she was safe within my chambers.

My next largest is Venatrix, then Sorin. The emerald-green menace with black markings on his wings and horns. He's always been the most reckless of them all—he was just a baby when he bit off Garrick's pinkie for raising a hand to me. He's undoubtedly a deathclaw. His mother would have flown to the densest forest in the wilderness of Urasos or farther north in godly land to lay her clutch at the base of an elder tree. She would have picked off anyone who entered the forest seeking to steal her unborn hatchlings and fed their blood into the roots that locked around the eggs as if they truly were claws.

After that is Delmira; her light blue coloring with yellow markings is that of a sky-striker. Delmira is soft like a summer day but can also bring forth the might of a storm. She not only has the ability to turn her scales black to blend with the night, but she can also blend with the day. To protect her eggs, a female sky-striker would fly for months, keeping her unborn babies warm with her flames as she waited for them to hatch.

Basilius is both the most timid and the largest. I've had the hardest time finding information on him, but apparently there is a series of volcanoes in the Galakin desert called the Ring of Fire and he is likely from the center of it. The toxic gasses that rise into the air turn the sky purple. He's considered a thunder-wraith. Thunder-wraiths have the deepest roars, often compared to thunder itself, and the adults would roar so loudly upon the hatching of their clutches that the ground would rumble as if a volcano erupted.

Venatrix turns in the direction of the castle, and I slip my eyes shut again. This is the only place where I feel light and free. It's as if my exhaustion rises with the sun and stays shackled to me throughout the day. I'm too anxious to sleep, and every time I close my eyes, I see Ailliard's face just before I burned him. I hear the sickening sound of the knife sinking into him after I threw it, and the words he's burdened me with over the years.

His voice didn't die with him; it grates on me every day.

The things he said about me.

The things he said about Cayden.

I spent so many years trying to please him and everyone else to the point that I sometimes don't know who I am outside of who I thought I was supposed to be. He knew how to get in my head and manipulate me better than anyone. He knew where to strike, and I'm the one who has to live with it.

Sorin roars, and I crack my eyes open to look back at him. He flies close enough to nudge me in the shoulder, and I laugh at the mischief lining his emerald gaze. "Hello, my sweetling."

He spins quickly before righting himself and coming close again.

"Ah, you want to play."

He screeches in response.

I remove my thick waist belt and winter coat, strapping it onto Venatrix's saddle to keep it from becoming a casualty of Sorin's chaos craving. I suppose I should've bundled up beneath my coat, but I left the castle in a hurry when I sensed Delmira having a nightmare. Sheer lavender sleeves dotted with dark blue jewels drape down my arms and billow in the wind, but at least my dragon scale pants are lined with fleece, and my ribs are nearly healed so the corset doesn't sit uncomfortably on me anymore. I place my hands beneath me and slowly get to my feet as Venatrix flaps evenly. Sorin keeps his eyes on me as I spread my arms wide and quiet my mind again. Anticipation whirls through me like a storm, and I wink at him before jumping off Venatrix.

A series of different emotions are fired down the bond. Fear from Calithea and Basilius, anger from Venatrix and Delmira for my recklessness, but Sorin is pure joy. A scream rips free from my throat as I free-fall toward the sea as Sorin sharply dives. I laugh and tumble, knowing he'll never let me fall. The wind howls in my ears like a banshee, and blood pounds through my body. Every day with my dragons is a privilege, and I don't intend on wasting a single second. I manage to right myself and tilt my chin as he closes the distance between us and nudges his nose into the bottom of my boot, making me laugh again.

He flaps his wings and drops his mighty body beside mine until our eyes are level and we plummet together. He hums a sound of contentment low in his throat as the other dragons chase us but are too far back to catch up. I reach forward and press my hand against his snout, and he leans into my touch. The ocean grows louder, but I don't move, and Sorin lives for it. This is more than just a moment of recklessness; it's a show of trust.

Venatrix roars, causing Sorin to huff, and he turns to bring me level with the saddle. I wrap my hands around the horns, and he slowly rights us until my chest presses into his back, and the surf is so close he's forced to veer right to avoid a wave crashing over us.

Sorin slows his pace once we're over the forest, letting the other dragons catch up as he gloats. I have a feeling Delmira and Venatrix would ram into him if I weren't on his back given the way their eyes are narrowed. I catch my breath, and I don't realize how much my cheeks hurt from smiling until I relax, letting Sorin carry me back to Verendus after snagging my coat off Venatrix.

A riding party carrying my house sigil is heading away from the castle, and I shoot up in the saddle, immediately alert. There are too many soldiers for this to be a routine patrol. It's still early in the day and I wasn't informed of anyone traveling north. Finnian is easy to spot, his ginger hair standing out against the frosty forest, and it's not hard to identify Cayden and Ryder after that. Sorin follows their path, casting them in a wing's shadow.

The same mist that coated the rocks hangs heavy over the forest, making the torchlight in the distance easy to spot amid the gray. The battalion comes to a stop beside a crystal-blue lake, and Sorin begins slowly swirling around it as he descends. Venatrix follows, but the other three remain in the air. Never out of sight, though.

The ice along the edge cracks as Sorin lands and dips his shoulder so I'm able to hop off . . . but Finnian's pinched brows when he looks back at me make me pause. Venatrix must sense the tension mounting inside me because she slides her head over my shoulder and growls at the four Aestilian soldiers kneeling in the mud.

CHAPTER
EIGHT

ELOWEN

SNOW CRUNCHES UNDERFOOT WHEN I DISMOUNT, BUT I don't move from between Sorin and Venatrix as I stare down four familiar faces across the bank. Their wings flare out behind my back and their front claws sink into the ground as they growl low in their throats. Jarek flinches and quickly moves his bound hands to where I'm sure his blade was before Vareveth soldiers confiscated it.

I click my tongue as Venatrix's growl sharpens. "Don't move too quickly. You'll startle the dragons, and they're quite protective of me. If they wish to kill you, I won't be able to stop them."

Cayden strides toward me, cutting out my old guards and Jarek from view. He doesn't have to tell me something is wrong; I know it is. Border patrols were ordered to grant any Aestilian citizen access into the kingdom and provide them with a safe escort to the castle. I run my thumb over the ring he gifted me despite it being covered by my glove. I've surmised it's important to him given how many times his gaze catches it, but I force myself not to ask of the origins again since I know he'll deny me. I don't want to grant him the satisfaction of knowing how much I think of it.

"Why are they here?" Nessa, Esme, and Zander were three of the four guards that escaped Imirath with Ailliard and me. The only one missing is Lycus. They moved as a pack, and I'll find him within the hour if he's lurking somewhere in my kingdom. They all bear the evidence of a struggle, with split lips and bloody cuts seeping into their clothes.

"The soldiers on patrol found pardons for all but Jarek on their persons. In each, Ailliard claims he blackmailed them into leaving Imirath and implores Garrick to show mercy and grant them positions in the infantry to prove their loyalty," he answers without emotion, which is what I need right now. This pales in comparison to Ailliard's betrayal, and if Cayden were to look at me with pity my anger would only worsen.

A discarded princess, Ailliard's voice slams into my mind before I have the chance to shut it out. But I need to be more than a title. I need to be more than the other rulers of Ravaryn. The weight of the crown crushes most, but where they falter, I will fly.

"We can take them back to the castle for questioning if you prefer," he offers while handing me the stack of pardons. "I was notified of their movements shortly after you left for flight training and alerted the dungeon guards to keep them separate, but it's your decision how we proceed."

I roll my lips together, contemplating his proposal. "We'd have to escort them through the streets of Verendus, alerting everyone to the treachery within my kingdom. I refuse to let spineless traitors make me look weak. Why didn't they travel by sea to avoid our kingdom?"

"The emerald storms are traveling up the Dolent Sea. They probably thought their odds were better if they could face an opponent that they could kill rather than a sea storm." An emerald storm warning is not something to regard lightly and not easy to predict. The storms earned their name because it's said once the sea turns green, your death is near. You could be fishing on the calmest waters one moment and be pummeled by waves the size of mountains in the next.

I would've taken the same risk with traveling on foot, but I sure as hell wouldn't be dumb enough to get caught. Even if they made it to Imirath, they would have been thrown in the dungeon and tortured if they weren't killed on the spot. Stealing a princess from a castle isn't a crime that's forgiven or forgotten over time. Garrick would have made an example of them the moment he had them in his grasp. Part of me wants to let them cross the border to prove that, but I don't have the patience.

I rip the pardons in half and drop them into the mud. "And Jarek? What's his purpose?"

"He refused to speak to the soldiers, but it's nothing I can't handle if you require my skills."

I smirk up at him. "I'm sure I'll manage."

"I hope you do."

He rests a hand on the hilt of his blade as he turns away and escorts me closer to the prisoners. Sorin and Venatrix shake the ground as they follow, and the other three circle the skies above like they're searching for prey. The captives at least have the good sense to tremble, so it appears they're not entirely dense.

"They're beautiful, aren't they?" I gesture to the dragons at my back.

"Y-yes, my queen," Jarek stammers.

"Did you know dragons are also highly intelligent? Far more intelligent than most people, though that's not really a compliment." I latch my fingers around Jarek's chin and jerk his head up. "Where is Lycus? Tell me now and I'll grant him the mercy of a quick death. Fail to inform me and I'll make him beg for it once I find him."

"He's not here," Jarek states. "He did not betray you, nor did I."

"Quiet," Zander growls, but Jarek continues despite the order.

"He refused his pardon, apparently told Ailliard to burn it several years ago and to never speak of the matter again. They were kept under a loose floorboard in Ailliard's room at your house. Lycus drew his sword against us as we left Aestilian but was wounded. I don't know how he fares."

I tighten my grip, bitterness and fear for Lycus swelling within me. I can only hope he made it to Nyrinn. She's never needed magic to perform miracles with a needle and herbs. "And I suppose it's a mere coincidence you're traveling with traitors?"

I roughly release him, letting his head hang in shame as I glare at the other three. I wonder how many times they spoke of returning to Imirath over tables filled with food provided by me.

"In a time of war, allegiances are swayed," Nessa begins. "Once we learned of your betrothal, we knew you would return to Aestilian to seek soldiers to fight for your cause, but we could never fight against King Garrick."

"So you try to scurry through the kingdom like rats to get back to a king that doesn't want you," Finnian snarls, his face contorting in disgust as he steps up beside me with a hand on the hilt of his blade.

"You murdered Ailliard!" Zander cries out, voice shaking for his fallen friend.

"You'll soon realize that's how I solve many of my problems."

He spits, but it lands short of my boot. Cayden is the first to unsheathe his sword, followed by the soldiers around me. "He was your family. Your flesh and blood. You murdered him!"

"What I did was necessary." I place my hand on Cayden's to keep him from ending the interrogation, and he moves the blade in front of me to form a steel barrier. "And there is no need to repeat yourself. I believe we all heard you the first time."

I turn to Nessa and Esme next. It was only a few weeks ago that I spoke to Nessa about Aestilian and her and Esme's daughter while we drank tea. "Did you abandon Moriko?"

Nessa sucks in a sharp breath. "She died of a fever. Nyrinn couldn't save her."

"My condolences." Something in my chest twists painfully. Moriko was an innocent just starting out in life and was taken away unfairly soon.

Cayden takes over for me and addresses Jarek. "You never stated your purpose."

"Ailliard entrusted me with Queen Elowen's safety on several occasions and blatantly stated his disapproval of this union," Jarek states with more confidence than one should possess on their knees.

A beat of confused silence passes before Cayden speaks. "And?"

"A queen deserves better than a demon," he spits.

Esme chuckles under her breath. "We took him with us because he's a good soldier, but we didn't think his request would be granted. Ailliard promised Elowen to Jarek if she didn't find a suitable match after coming to court."

"Esme," Jarek growls.

"He wanted to prove his worth in the war and negotiate her survival to marry her. Garrick has no other heirs and Jarek would agree to whatever Garrick's terms were, even if it meant keeping Elowen confined to their chambers. He wouldn't shut up about it the entire time we rode here. We would've taken a boat if it weren't for the storms, and I'd have thrown him over the edge."

"Bitch," Jarek snarls.

"We're already dead," she answers calmly. "We may be on different sides of a war, but she's still Elowen. I'll give her answers where I can."

She's still Elowen.

A sentence that should bring me comfort only turns my stomach. I've spent years beside these people, bled for them, fed them, fought for them, and even that wasn't enough.

I wonder what it would feel like to be enough exactly as you are. Sometimes it feels like I could fight until I'm an inch away from death and still fall short even then.

Cayden tilts his head in my direction, and I nod. His blade shimmers in the rising sun as it strikes, cutting off Jarek's plea as Cayden beheads him in one swift swipe. Blood splatters Zander's face and the head thumps on the ground. I nudge it away when it comes close to my boot.

"I find you guilty of treason against the crown. I, Elowen Atarah, queen of Vareveth, queen of Aestilian, princess of Imirath, dragon queen, sentence you to die." I've spent years of my life beside them. Though I suppose it's true that love and hatred walk a fine line, and the latter can slowly bleed into the former, poisoning it without someone realizing.

I step forward after ordering the soldiers standing behind the prisoners to move away and lower my voice so only they're able to hear.

"You knew what Garrick was doing to my dragons when you left them behind. You watched me walk through life with five missing limbs and never once did you offer any information of the Imirath castle no matter how much I begged."

"We thought it a fool's errand." Nessa's voice shakes as Sorin's head looms above mine.

"It appears the only fools are you."

With nothing left to say, I turn my back on them, but Zander speaks before I get far, keeping his voice low as I did. "Do you truly think you can build a future with a man who hates the blood that runs through your veins? Your father will always be his enemy, and when you have heirs, those children might look just like him. Go back to your father and do your duty, Princess."

The plea isn't coated with condescension, it's genuine. His last gift to the Atarah line before he leaves this world. I clasp my hands together to keep him from seeing the tremor that travels through me. "The future shouldn't concern you; you have no place in it."

"Elowen, wait!" Esme cries.

But I don't.

Neither do Sorin or Venatrix as their jaws unhinge and flames spill on either side of me.

CHAPTER
NINE

CAYDEN

MY HEAD POUNDS IN THE AFTERMATH OF SPENDING the day surrounded by people. War meetings are currently pointless considering we haven't heard anything of Imirath's or Thirwen's movements, and yet my generals insist on meeting. If they weren't good soldiers, I wouldn't bother attending, but unfortunately for me, they are. Though I brought forth the matter of Aestilian after what transpired, and included Finnian in the discussion since he's Elowen's most trusted advisor. My generals needed to be warned that she and I will be leaving the kingdom when war is breathing down our necks.

I don't want to lose more soldiers in another fruitless skirmish on the border, and I don't want to advance the army before Thirwen arrives. If they dock in Vareveth while we're in Imirath, we risk fighting a war on two fronts. I've walked the path to war since I was a child, and I will not be outwitted by a king who orders his army from behind castle walls while my sword is raised on the field.

I shove open the door to the suite and relish in the silence. Elowen only just got back an hour ago after flying all day, and I forced myself to listen to my generals ponder strategies to grant her some peace and privacy. I've made it clear that she's welcome to join the meetings, but her time is best spent learning her dragons and testing commands. Knowing how gruesome battles can become, I'm relieved she won't be fighting on the ground, though picturing her hundreds of feet in the air doesn't exactly ease my nerves.

A fire crackles in the living room hearth, casting a warm glow over the dark blue and golden upholstery. I stride past the couch, but rather than turning left, I veer right, bringing me to the rooms that were once my chamber in this shared suite. Tucking my hands into my pockets, I lean against the doorframe. Dark wood shelves line the walls wherever windows and sconces don't interrupt. I kept the seating area by the fireplace and added stained-glass lanterns on the end tables to provide more light.

If Elowen knows I'm here, she doesn't make it known and continues gazing through the balcony doors. The dragons fly above the icy lake as snow falls, casting a thicker blanket over the forest that stretches between here and Ladislava.

"Elowen," I murmur while stepping forward, not wanting to startle her if she's lost in her mind. "El." My fingertips glide along the soft fabric of her lavender gown, and she sharply inhales when I slide my hand beneath her hair and rub the column of her neck.

"Aestilian." She takes a choppy breath. "It must be evacuated." I remain quiet to give her time to finish her thought. "We both know Garrick will try to hurt me however he can, even if it means killing an entire kingdom. Aestilian doesn't have the power to face Imirath."

"They can come here." During the meeting, I compiled a list of houses in Verendus vacated by those loyal to Eagor or who have fled to the countryside to escape potential conflict as a result of the coup.

"If anyone chooses not to follow, I need you to promise me you'll let them go. Don't threaten them. They've been through enough."

You've been through enough, I want to say. *Too much.* She's been treated so poorly that she's confused by kindness. Ailliard's belittling treatment of Elowen was apparent from the moment I met the bastard. I'd have killed him that very day if I'd been sure it wouldn't have turned Elowen against me.

"I won't undermine you," I state as she turns into my hand. "But I will act if they show signs of treachery or aggression toward you."

I don't know how to deal with those who stood idly by while Ailliard hurt her. Even if someone only watches a murder, they're still an accomplice. Aestilian is practically defenseless, and we can't afford to send soldiers to defend the north while we're at war. Now that Imirath has united with Thirwen, we'll need to start pressuring Galakin to take our side. Feynadra and Urasos are notoriously neutral and given Garrick's conquering nature, as shown by the raids in the southern isles, they will likely remain so. Our best chance is Galakin. Not only do they have a terrible relationship with Imirath, they despise Thirwen.

Thirty-five years ago, the Crimson Tide War broke out between Thirwen and Galakin. Queen Cordelia, a princess at the time, had two sisters, not only one as she does now. The king didn't have a son and named Cordelia his heir with the stipulation that she retain the Ilaria name instead of taking her husband's. He promised his second daughter, Nasha, to the crown prince of Feynadra who currently rules the kingdom. But it's unknown what truly happened to his third daughter, Cyra.

Galakin claims the second-born prince of Thirwen, King Fallon's younger brother, stole her away after falling in love with her at a banquet, but Thirwen claims the late king of Galakin killed them both for their rebellion. Some people believe the pair of them escaped entirely and made a life for themselves. One of the bloodiest wars in the history of Ravaryn was fought over a misunderstanding that still isn't solved. It's called the Crimson Tide because for leagues, the sea ran red. Neither side was declared a winner considering the immense casualties.

Though the war ended, their hatred has only grown.

Imirath is a peninsula, and with the added force of the conquered isles, their navy is formidable. Thirwen is an island kingdom, as is Galakin, and both draw their power from the sea. Vareveth is landlocked in every direction but west, and though I've spent the last several years building my navy, the other kingdoms dominate in that sphere.

My first instinct is to keep Elowen here where the army surrounds her. The well-being of the people of Aestilian doesn't keep me awake at night—but Elowen will find a way to help them with or without me, and I need to be with her for the sake of my sanity.

She tries to drop my gaze, but I tilt her chin up. "What's wrong?"

I saw the way she shifted when Zander spoke his final words, but I couldn't hear him over the wind. If she weren't still icing me out, I'd have found a way to keep her from flying away. I don't know how to navigate this. I've never cared about someone's reaction to my actions, but I'd rather Elowen scream at me than disappear into her thoughts, slipping through my fingers like grains of sand.

A knot forms between her brows, and she pushes away from me to face the window again. "I'll command two dragons to guard the border between here and Imirath and two to guard the castle in our absence. Asena remains in the kingdom, and I sought her out before I returned to the castle. Ophir, the leader of the water cult, also entered the kingdom after we lifted the bans on magic. They combined their camp within the woods near Ladislava and said they can open a portal for us with their combined strength."

If I clench my jaw any tighter my teeth will break, but I force my tone to be even. "We'll be gone for two days at most. You won't be parted from the dragons long, and you'll be able to test the bond over a great distance."

She nods, twisting her fingers around her curls. Words I don't know how to form burn in my throat as I watch her. I feel as if I've broken the one thing in my life that I held above everything else, and all I think about every waking moment is how to put the pieces back together to make us whole again. I open my mouth to say something . . . anything, but three—*aggravating*—voices enter the suite when the door slams open.

"Hello?" Ryder calls out, and I don't bother answering. Elowen blankly stares across the room before lifting her shoulders and plastering on a smile none of them will see through as they appear in the doorway. "Well isn't this a cozy addition to your love nest."

Ryder sinks into the chair closest to the fire, propping his boots up on the table. If I believed in the gods, I'd pray for patience.

"Cayden would probably agree, considering he was more than happy to make a show of destroying all of his furniture that used to be in here."

"Don't put words in my mouth." I narrow my eyes at Elowen. I'd never refer to something as a *love nest*.

She smirks. "How can I when they never seem to stop coming out?"

I roll my eyes and locate the whiskey bottle before taking a decent swig. Prayers don't work but alcohol hasn't failed me yet.

"Are we all set to leave tomorrow?" Finnian asks as Elowen takes the spot beside him on the couch.

Elowen's shoulders stiffen as she looks around at our group. "Have you already met to discuss the evacuation?" She rests her arms against the back of the couch and settles her eyes on me. "I only just told you of my plans."

"Evacuation is the only option. We don't know what Ailliard revealed to Imirath while negotiating your capture, and as you said, Garrick will slaughter your kingdom simply because it will hurt you. If Lycus truly was injured while defending you and sought medical attention, your people will know of further treachery by prominent figures within Aestilian and will be on edge."

Not only that, but there is too much land between here and Aestilian. She cannot rule both while Urasos and Feynadra stand between the kingdoms.

"We'll leave at first light?" she asks, and I nod as she faces forward. I place my whiskey on the mantel and sink my hands into the cushions on either side of Elowen's head. "Are you excited to be back on your lumpy mattress?"

Finnian groans in response, as Ryder's voice fills the space. "Why is it always first light? I think we should start appreciating afternoon travel."

"Because there are people who could die," Saskia flatly states before handing Elowen a piece of parchment. "Cayden and I compiled a list of available housing in Verendus. He advised against Ladislava because many of your people are refugees. They'll be farther away from the border in the inner city."

"Thank you." She quickly buries her nose in the paper. "This is perfect." There's a smile in her voice that's mirrored on Saskia's face. Sas has needed someone like Elowen since I met her, and the same goes for Elowen. "Are any buildings large enough to serve as an orphanage? I'd like to keep the children together."

I lean down and rest my forearm on the couch. The pulse in Elowen's neck jumps and the list slips from her fingers. I ghost my finger down her thigh. "These two." She doesn't spare me a glance as I point them out, and accepts a pen from Saskia to underline the addresses, though they look more like lightning bolts.

"Stop," she grumbles.

"I didn't say anything."

"I can practically feel the arrogance radiating off you." I snicker, and Elowen quickly changes the subject. "I don't want anyone in Vareveth knowing my guards betrayed me. We won't be able to hide it from Aestilian, but the nobles here hate me, and I don't want their malice extending to my people through rumors they orchestrate to cause chaos within the kingdom. There are still a handful of citizens and soldiers that are wary of me, but perhaps they'll warm over time since many are loyal to Cayden."

"Anyone loyal to me will never harm you. I've made sure they know the consequences."

"I'm the daughter of your enemy—their enemy—sitting on the throne of this kingdom."

"And they will die a thousand deaths when their hatred reaches my ears." My lip curls. "A thousand more if they contemplate harming you."

Saskia sighs, but I don't remove my eyes from Elowen as Saskia speaks. "You can't use that remedy for every issue."

"It's effective."

"He's got a point there," Ryder tacks on.

Saskia continues over us, "As king and queen you need to consider your public image. Something I'm aware you've never cared about."

Elowen stands from the couch, cocking a hip and propping her hand on it. "When you invoked the marriage clause you erased the divide between king and commander. You cannot simply kill your way through Eagor's role because it vexes you."

"The nobles will never love us, but they will fear us. I'll have their compliance, or I'll have their heads. If a king can be replaced, anyone can." I step around the couch, closing the distance between us, forcing her to look up at me. "I didn't rise in rank by making friends with the right people, I did so by killing the right ones when necessary." Her lips part as she looks up at me, eyes flicking between mine. "And anyone who wishes you harm is the perfect one."

"There it is!" Saskia exclaims, rising from the chair so suddenly it startles Elowen as she turns, making her fall back into my chest. I wrap an arm around her waist to keep her here. "That's what's been missing this week!"

Ryder nods. "I agree."

"They're due for another public appearance. They haven't gone out together since the dinner in Ladislava. There are magical vendors at the night market since they've lifted the bans, so it would also be a show of support to the citizens," Finnian says, and Saskia glances at him curiously. "Yes, I am quite a good advisor, thank you."

"What's happening?" Elowen whispers.

"Do you want to leave?" Gods know I do.

"They're in our chambers."

I give her a flat look. "We have other rooms to lock them out of."

Saskia latches her hands on Elowen's shoulders, but I still keep my hold on her. "Everyone spoke of how enraptured you were with each other at Starry Night, but rumors of unrest will begin if you're not consistent with your appearances."

Elowen coughs. "Well, I wouldn't say *enraptured*."

"For months," Saskia begins, dismissing her words with a wave of a hand. "The people have watched the two of you fall for each other. We've been standing outside the world you escape into in each other's presence."

Elowen stiffens, and I rub her ribs through the dress. I know how her mind works, and she's probably fighting the guilt over not volunteering for another public appearance before it was brought up. I spin her toward me to give her something else to focus on, a different emotion—anger.

"Come on now, angel." I tilt her chin up with my free hand. "Was it not you who fooled the guard at the bridge crossing by pretending to be my doting wife?"

She purses her lips. "I'll never forgive myself for manifesting this miserable fate."

"That mouth," I mutter, dragging my thumb across her lower lip. "We could go out again tonight, but I understand if you're no longer up to it."

She pushes away from my chest. "What are you insinuating?"

I sigh. "Do your performance skills stem from the pressure of a moment? If there's no pressure, maybe there's no talent."

She glares up at me like she can't believe I'd ever say such a thing. *That's it*, I want to say. *Fight with me, challenge me, be the version of you I adore. No more of those damn empty smiles and stay here with me.*

"I know what you're doing." I hold up my hands in mock innocence "Need I remind you the guard at the gate wasn't the only man I fooled? What about the attentive soldier from the tavern?" My smirk drops. "What was his name? Do you know it, Cayden? Your memory is better than mine and you couldn't take your eyes off us. It's too bad you snapped his neck; he was quite charming."

Of course I remember him. Watching her flutter her lashes at an Imirath soldier was one of the worst sights I've ever witnessed. It made me want to throw her over my shoulder and burn the tavern to the ground, mission be damned.

She taps a finger against her chin. *Don't fucking say it.* "Evrin!"

Ryder, Finnian, and Saskia must note the way the room chills ten degrees and quickly exit the library, muttering something about meeting us downstairs after they get ready for the market. I slowly lower my hands while we glare at each other. The tension between us is palpable, and so alive it's practically bouncing off the walls.

"I'm going to remember this, Elowen."

"Is that supposed to be a threat?"

I chuckle humorlessly, remembering how close she sat to him, the way I had to sit there while he put his hands on my woman. I take a step closer, and her breasts heave against the fabric of her gown as her breathing quickens. I don't respond right away, opting to trail my fingers across her collarbone and up her neck, making her tremble as I cradle her head. "I'm going to treat you so well that every man you ever encounter will become a faceless blur in the back of your mind because there's no room for anyone but me. I'm going to remember this, and remember him, because one day you won't."

She steps forward until she's pressed against me, staring up with more fire in her eyes than I've seen in days, and I tighten my hold in her hair. "You sound quite sure of yourself for a man who practically locked me into a betrothal."

"You can despise our betrothal all you want, but if you're going to state your hatred for it at least be honest."

"Between the two of us, honesty is not *my* weakness."

I shake my head while leaning down to bring our faces closer together. "You hate our betrothal because it's exactly what you crave in the depths of your soul. You want to be mine, and I'm no stranger to waiting for you, so you take as much time as you need to accept it because I'm not going anywhere."

She scoffs. "Your arrogance truly is astounding."

"I don't speak out of arrogance."

"Then what's making you say this?"

Obsession. Addiction. Need. "I'm sure you'll figure it out one of these days."

CHAPTER
TEN

ELOWEN

S ASKIA AND I LOOP OUR ARMS TOGETHER TO FEND OFF THE
cold. I'm tempted to pull the hood of my coat up for extra
warmth, but Hyacinth took extra care in crafting my appearance. The top half of my hair is pulled back, and tiny braids twist
together to form a wreath at the back of my head. The dark blue
jewels laced throughout the strands match my coat. It's a similar silhouette to my white one, and a black sash embroidered with golden
dragon scales cinches my waist.

Sweet and savory scents spill from the booths that line the circle at
the base of the castle steps, hardly giving me enough time to distin-
guish one before entering a cloud of the next. Basilius is perched at the
top of the waterfall beside the castle, and I feel his lavender eyes tracking my every step as the other four circle above. "Do you think not
having Cayden beside me will hinder the image we're trying to por-
tray?"

Saskia's painted red lips part in a small smile. "His eyes have been
drilling into your back since we stepped away. I'd say he's playing his
part flawlessly."

We pause briefly by one of the stone firepits that reside at the center of the lane and soak in the warmth. As if I'm pulled by some force
unknown to me, I glance over my shoulder, and my gaze immediately
collides with Cayden's. An intriguing, dark aura pumps off him as he

rests one boot on the wall at his back and balances a smoke between his lips. A black coat, made of a mixture of rich night-spun fabric and leather, hugs his broad shoulders, and I force myself to face forward and pull Saskia toward the closest distraction.

"My queen." A man with round goggles that magnify his blue eyes stands within a red booth. His wispy white hair sticks out haphazardly and matches the apron he wears over his coat. "What a pleasure it is to see you in the market."

Many of these people were forced to sell their wares in private under the reign of Eagor and Valia. The magic infused in the trinkets is hardly harmful, mainly things to enhance daily life—gloves and muffs enchanted by fire magic to keep you warm, books with a simple spell cast upon them to keep your place, dresses and cloaks with hems that never get dirty, to name a few.

There are those who can wield the elements and those who have the lesser ability of enchanting objects. Vareveth was once accepting of earth magic—which doesn't surprise me considering the Dasterian sigil was an oak tree. It was said the first Dasterian king could rival the God of Earth in his abilities. Many have fled to Craigon, the capital of Urasos, and a few surrounding cities. However, outlying villages have taken it upon themselves to persecute those with the ability to wield the earth. They believe that possessing this magic is mocking the god himself, and most elemental mages keep their abilities hidden.

I set my basket on the counter and unlatch myself from Saskia, grasping one of the small vials with perfume that seems to flicker inside. "What's this made of?"

"It's a light floral scent infused with starfire to give it a hint of smokiness."

I trail my finger down the bottle, unable to pull my gaze away. I didn't realize how sheltered I was in Aestilian, not only from the world but from knowledge. I've been making up for lost time, because I realize now that Ailliard purposely kept me ignorant. I trusted him to inform me of the world, and without access to a proper education or a library, I never doubted him.

True freedom comes from education, which is why so many rulers lock up books, ban or burn them. Keeping them in the hands of the privileged and away from the masses. The key to tyranny and control is to keep someone ignorant. If they don't know anything different, they'll find comfort in what they know rather than fighting for something they could have.

"Can you wield starfire?" I ask.

"No, Your Highness, only the goddess herself can wield such an element. I have a very diluted supply considering she's also the only one able to conjure it and has been asleep for centuries. It's very hard to come by. Mine is just strong enough to add some shimmer to my scents."

"And it won't burn me?"

"Not at all." He gestures for me to try it out. "It'll feel warm, but no stronger than a summer breeze."

I uncork the bottle, dotting my neck and wrists before lifting it to my nose. It smells like a bottled garden at the peak of spring, but I do note the smoky undertone. It's subtle, but beautiful. "How much does it cost?"

"Consider it a gift for the queen." He fists his apron as he turns to the only full-size glowing bottle on a platform. He has a plethora of other perfumes, but it's clear this one is both rare and expensive. There's a knot between his brows when he places it in my hand, and before he pulls away, I place my coin pouch in his palm. Color rises in his cheeks as he stares down at it. "Oh, no, Your Majesty."

"I trust that covers this?"

"It's far too much. The king will call it theft."

"The king will not say anything as long as I'm happy." I add the perfume to my basket and slide it onto my arm. "Have a good night, sir."

He continues staring down in disbelief, but even at a distance I note the tears welling in his eyes when he finally manages a response. "A-and you as well, Your Majesty."

It wasn't long ago when I was merely scraping by, desperate for money and not knowing if I'd have enough to feed myself or those in

Aestilian. The gold band on his finger and heart locket around his neck hinted toward him being married; maybe he even has a family. I know I can't help everyone, but if more people realized how far one act of kindness can go, we'd live in a much better world.

Saskia smiles at me again as she stops us at a booth filled with candles. "What?"

She shakes her head, holding a water lily scent to her nose. "You are a sweetheart, Elowen Atarah."

I scoff, not offering a response as I stop her from reaching into her coin pouch and sign Cayden's name on the bill instead, along with his Ladislava address. Saskia laughs as she drops her items into her basket and adds two to mine.

"Do you think I can make the vein in his neck pop if I spend enough money?" Cayden challenged me to come here, and he's about to realize how much his smugness will cost him. After all, what's more romantic than doting on your betrothed?

"I don't know." She purses her lips. "But I'm never against testing a theory."

"I appreciate your support in my endeavors."

My basket continues to fill—pastries, a new book, a golden ring shaped like a dragon curling around my finger, hair chains and jewels, spices I'd like to use while baking . . . and oils. The snow isn't what makes me shiver when I think of the red, raised skin on Cayden's back. He mentioned that his shoulder didn't heal correctly, and I wonder if the lash marks also ache. No matter how much he hurt me, if there is something I can do to alleviate his pain, I'll do it.

We pass through a series of booths each selling specific crystals, candles, and carvings to decorate limbs or altars dedicated to the ten sleeping gods. Many ladies huddle together while deciding on which pink amethyst necklace or bracelet dedicated to the Goddess of Love, Marriage, and Fertility complements them. A more antsy crowd gathers around the table dedicated to the Goddess of Souls, who I've learned also presided over mercy and destiny, and I can practically feel their anxiety and desperation as they grasp lapis lazuli tokens. Swords with pommels encrusted in bloodstone are swung as people gather around the God of War and Strategy's booth, but the Goddess of Grief and Sorrow's is overlooked, the tourmaline towers remaining untouched within the gray drapes.

"What'd you buy, love?" Cayden asks as I approach, pulling the smoke from his lips and grinding it into the cobblestones before withdrawing a tin of mint leaves from his pocket.

"You didn't need to do that."

"It's not healthy for you to breathe it in."

"Then why were you smoking?"

"You told me I have to be nicer." He juts his chin to where Ryder and Finnian are giggling beside him, lost in their own conversation. "I needed something to do with my mouth so I didn't insult them."

I hide my smile behind my hand and respond to his earlier inquiry, "I bought copious amounts of alcohol to get me through this betrothal."

"Cheers to that." He transfers the heavy basket to his hand. "Do you need more money?"

"I thought of a rather simple solution once I ran out." I glide closer and stare up at him like a besotted betrothed. "I signed your name to all my bills."

"You could've signed yours," he says, unfazed by what I've just revealed.

"I don't have any accounts here." I don't have any accounts at all. Ailliard controlled my money. I kept a small tin under my bed in case of emergencies after he didn't loan me anything when Finnian needed medicine, but whatever I earned went into his pocket. He told me it was used for the people of Aestilian, but I don't know what to believe anymore. I wouldn't be surprised if he spent it on himself.

"*We* do." He pushes off the wall, dropping his face closer to mine. "I added you to all of mine." My mind feels as if it's trudging through thick syrup as I process his words. "I'm not changing it so don't bother arguing. When we ride to war, I need to make sure you're taken care of if something happens to me."

I dryly swallow. Images of Cayden being captured or killed dance along to a morbid ballad within my thoughts. "That's not— You don't have—"

"I'm very hard to kill, El. Put it out of your mind for now." He begins leading me through the market again. "But if you keep looking at me like that then I'll be silent while you spend whatever you wish."

I bite my lip, wrapping my hand around his arm and resting my head on his bicep. "All I have to do is smile and you'll let me drain your accounts?"

"Breathing works just fine."

I don't bother hiding my laughter since so many eyes are on us. Pushing ahead of him, I step toward a blue booth and accept a dish filled with sweet buns stuffed with savory pork before leading him over to the fountain at the center of the circle that the stone carvers have finished crafting. Both staggering in height and intricately designed, it looks like five dragons taking flight around a set of crossed swords with a crescent moon at the top.

The fountain in the castle's entrance hall that resembled the Dasterian oak was also replaced with a similar design. Dark blue flags atop the sharp spires billow in the wind as my dragons fly around them, and Cayden dusts some snow off the stone before guiding me to take a seat. He pulls me close, and I soak in his warmth while handing him the dish.

He chuckles. "Have you changed your mind already?"

"They're for you."

His brow is furrowed like my gesture perplexes him. "What?"

"You were in meetings all day." I fold my hands in my lap after he accepts the food. "You forget to eat sometimes." His fingers cease running along my arm, and he's silent for so long that I force myself to look up at him. "I can get you something else if you don't like it."

"No." He clears his throat, and his eyes soften as he drops them to the food. "This is perfect. Thank you."

I relax against him, throwing my legs over his lap and resting my head on his shoulder. The lack of sleep must be catching up to me because the steady beat of his heart makes my eyelids grow heavy. We may sleep in the same bed, but it's torturous. We stay on opposite sides, and I don't let myself succumb to exhaustion, not trusting myself to keep my hands off him in my unconscious state. I've even taken to napping on Basilius's back while flying.

"We'll return to the castle after this," he says.

I nod, trailing my fingers along the golden dragons circling the cuff of his sleeve. He's never cared for fanciful garb, dressing more like an assassin than a king, but it helps that one of our house colors is black. He always looks well put together but will never be the type of man to wear obnoxious fabrics and tight pants after the favored fashion of the wealthy. I prefer him this way, though. I don't want him to change his appearance. I love his scars, and the intensity of his eyes, and the messy waves that brush his forehead and the tops of his ears. He looks like a dark dream took on a human form.

My eyes drift around the colorful tents and the people dressed in decadent coats as they browse. Children smile at the enchanted objects, women walk arm in arm with their friends, and men trail behind their sweethearts with arms filled with purchases. Snow continues falling, collecting on my lashes and the ice that surrounds the perimeter of the fountain. I'm about to ask Cayden if we can stop for some mulled wine on our way back to the castle, but the hair rises on the back of my neck as my spine stiffens. *No.* The food I ate earlier threatens to make a reappearance as I squeeze my eyes shut, but a blue pair I'd know anywhere burn behind my lids. Ailliard is looking right at me with a hatred I never noticed until he betrayed me.

"It's not him," I whisper. "He's dead. *He's dead.*"

"El?" Cayden frames my face. "What's wrong?"

He rubs his thumbs along my cheeks and curses when I don't answer. Ice shatters after he removes one hand, and moments later, freezing fingers clutch the back of my neck. "Open your eyes," he demands, and I do, forcing myself to focus on the water dripping down my back instead of my panic. "Breathe."

"Ailliard." He rubs his thumb into my hair as I search the area again to spot the man. My palms moisten, but all it makes me think of is Ailliard's blood coating them as I tried to pull my knife free. The man that set me off bears a remarkable resemblance to Ailliard, but it's clearly not him. I haven't mourned him, haven't wanted to, and I wish I could crush the small sliver within me that felt relief at the thought of him being alive. Death makes idealists of us all.

"I thought—"

I shake my head, realizing how ridiculous I sound. I killed him myself. I threw the knife that took him down and commanded Calithea to engulf him in flames. I knelt in the blood of the man who was the closest thing I had to a father. He's gone.

I force hollow laughter to crawl up my throat. "Don't mind me. The mind plays tricks on us when we're sleep-deprived."

Cayden's green eyes sear my profile until I force myself to look at him. "You don't have to play this game with me."

I innocently shrug. "What game?"

"El." The way he says my name . . . the softness . . . the understanding. . . . It sends another tremor through my hands.

"Please don't," I whisper.

A muscle flutters in his jaw and a dark look crosses his features when he realizes he won't be able to breach my defenses tonight. I don't want to talk about Ailliard. I don't want to think of him. I don't want him to have any power over me anymore, but sometimes it feels as if even death can't retract the claws he dug into my mind. Cayden remains silent, locking himself in yet another battle of wills in our ongoing war of stubbornness, but he doesn't push me for now. It's neither the time nor the place, but the tension between us is like a kettle just about to start screaming over a fire.

CHAPTER
ELEVEN

ELOWEN

I T'S STILL DARK OUTSIDE AS I BOUND DOWN THE SIDE STEPS
of the castle, leading to the lake littered with frost-tipped rocks. I
am unable to be confined a moment longer. My dragons softly
snore along the shore, and the dampness within the earth seeps
through my pants as I kneel at the center of their circle. Calithea's
silver eyes blink open and she moves her head closer to me, allowing
me to trail my fingers along her snout as I hum a soothing tune. They
must've fallen asleep out of pure exhaustion and my heart twists in my
chest when I think of them sleeping huddled together in the dragon
chamber.

How old were they when they grew too large to fly within the confined space?

How many days did they wish to die while staring out at the skies
they now fly through?

There isn't a single thing I wouldn't do to save them from suffering.
Delmira curls her tail around me as the others inch closer, drawn to
my presence even in sleep. All I've ever wanted were my dragons, not a
crown or a kingdom. I've always known I'd kill Garrick for what he did
to them, to me, and now to Cayden. But when I think of what my
future looks like, it's as if I'm staring at a horizon I'll never reach. All
I've done with my life is wake up and try to survive to the point that
I've forgotten how to live.

Footsteps thump in the grass as the sun bleeds over the mountains, and pebbles dance along the lake's icy shore as Sorin's growl vibrates the ground. I soothe him down the bond and smile at Finnian over my shoulder.

"Are you ready?"

"Are you?" I ask. The green cloak and brown tunic he wears complement his features nicely; a pin with the Veles sigil sits proudly on his chest. In true Finnian fashion, a bow and quiver are thrown over his shoulder and a sword is at his waist.

His throat bobs, his voice coming out as a hoarse whisper, "No."

I release Calithea and rise to meet him. "You don't have to come if it's too much for you."

"I won't remain here while you're forced to lose our home."

"I'm losing land." My hand wraps around his. "I'm not losing my home."

He blinks away the water in his eyes, yanking me forward by our joined hands. "Wherever you go, I go."

The tension in my body loosens. Finnian has always been more than a friend to me from the moment he first made me laugh. Our bond has never been reliant on what I could give him, and most of the time I think he wished I wasn't the lost princess of Imirath. "Maybe one day that statement will take us somewhere warm." He laughs but it's strained, and I pull back to look up at him. "What is it?"

"I know we haven't spoken about it, but I need to say this." He bites the inside of his cheek as his chest rises on a deep inhale. "I've been doing a lot of thinking since the night Ailliard betrayed us . . . recalling memories of our childhood, the way he treated you, the way my life was easier because you shielded me."

"Finnian, stop."

"I remember how he screamed at you when you stayed by my side when I was sick with fever. I was delirious, but I remember you begging him for money to buy medicine when nothing was working, but he told you it was too selfish to spend that much on a remedy for one person." He swallows hard. "You left, and a few hours later came back with medicine I knew you couldn't afford, shaking and covered in blood with a bruise on your cheek. You never told me how you got it."

"Finnian." I latch my hands on to his biceps, forcing memories I keep locked away to remain there and ignoring my churning stomach. Some thoughts are best left untouched. "You will not bear the burden for whatever decisions I have made over the years. Do not lose sleep over choices I'd make again if given the opportunity. I didn't survive exile because of the anger that lived within me, I survived because of you."

He lets out a choppy breath and kisses my forehead, pulling me close again for several moments of silence before asking, "Have you decided which dragon you'll take?"

I sigh, rubbing at the relentless ache in my chest. "I can trust Venatrix to keep all the others in line aside from Sorin. He's unpredictable, and I don't know for certain he won't follow me against my orders."

A familiar smile slides over his features. "Good quality to have."

I nudge him on his shoulder, offering no reply as Saskia exits the castle in her warmest coat and a scarf spooled up to her chin. She wears the same pin as Finnian over her breast, and I tug at the chain that rests across my chest, a small replica of my sigil glinting in the sun. It matches the golden dragons swirling around the cuffs of my white winter coat.

"Asena and the water mage came to the front steps of the castle and are being escorted here by Braxton," Saskia says.

Finnian shudders. "Their presence is unsettling."

"I doubt they wear robes that cover their faces and chant in the woods to seem inviting," I mutter, and Finnian glares.

Cayden converses with Ryder as they stride to meet us, the pair of them clad in weapons and black winter garb that make their already muscular frames appear even larger. My dragons begin waking up now that they sense a forming crowd, and Basilius is the first to take to the skies.

Cayden sighs as he stops beside me. "I'm afraid we'll never be able to make the people of Aestilian believe you're choosing to marry me."

I narrow my eyes. "Why?"

"You're far too beautiful. People will inevitably talk."

"It helps that most people know you're wealthy."

His dimples deepen when he chuckles, the sound making me feel like I'm soaking in the sun. He escorted me to our chambers after the night market and only came in from standing on the balcony after I doused the lanterns and climbed into bed, informing me he had business to take care of at his tavern before disappearing for several hours. He didn't tell me what his tasks consisted of, but the fresh cuts on his knuckles lead me to believe he was fighting again.

Asena descends the steps with Ophir, both cloaked in heavy robes that hint toward their loyalties: red for Asena and blue for Ophir. I didn't have the chance to inquire about the origins of dragons when I saw her yesterday. My main focus was on Aestilian, and what she could do to help me. Only the gods can conjure elements, but she can wield flames within her vicinity. Ophir possesses a similar gift but with water. However, after training their entire lives, both are skilled in other magical abilities that enable them to open portals. The magic in their blood has been passed down for generations, more potent than those in the market who infuse objects with charms.

Asena's curls spill around her like a halo when she removes her hood and bows. "Your Majesties, may I present Ophir, renowned mage and the leader of the water cult."

Straight onyx hair frames his pale face and falls to the black sash tied around his waist. Reverence floods his dark gaze as he looks at Cayden and drops to one knee. "My king."

We exchange a confused glance.

"Why has the water cult come to Vareveth?" Cayden asks. "Speak plainly. We don't have time to waste."

Manners to envy, truly. Though at least he saves us time by being himself.

Mages and cults mainly keep to the Terrwyn and Sweven forests to avoid being targeted. The only kingdoms where magic is ingrained within the culture are Galakin and Thirwen. Galakin is accepting of fire magic, and many people in Thirwen study mind control and are bonded to animal familiars. Perhaps if my mother had been from Thirwen it would have explained my bond to the dragons, but she was a noble woman of Imirath. Imirath accepts water magic, Urasos accepts air and now earth, but magic is outlawed in Feynadra.

Kingdoms stick to one element to establish a balance of power between one another. Centuries ago, when magic in Ravaryn was stronger, more mages practiced their abilities without fear. Although Galakin claimed the element of fire, nobody can challenge my claim considering my bond to the dragons, but to anger Imirath, Cayden and I also lifted the bans on water magic.

"I am here for you in the same way Asena is here for Queen Elowen. The wind carries messages off the tide and has whispered your name." I share another glance with Cayden; it's close to what Asena said when she gifted me the amulet. "My people and I have traveled from the Terrwyn to pledge our fealty to you, the king blessed by the God of Water, Death, and the Moon. On your order, we will follow you to war and ruin."

"Just as the fire cult wishes to pledge ourselves to the queen blessed by the Goddess of Flames, Life, and Stars," Asena adds. "This union was destined by the gods and brings balance to our elements. It is divine and blessed in blood. The gods honor a sacrifice, the end of the Dasterian line for the birth of a power unknown to this world."

"Flames flood Queen Elowen's veins, and the salt of the sea runs through yours," Ophir says to Cayden. "I saw you kill Eagor Dasterian when I looked into the waves, and felt a shift in the air as you claimed the throne." It feels just as invasive as it did when Asena told me that she watched me steal the amulet in the flames.

"How are you co-existing so peacefully?" Cayden asks. "The cults are notorious for their rivalries, and I will not have your war on my land."

"Our allegiances reflect alliances the gods formed with one another. The Goddess of Souls cult resides deep within the Etril Forest, but we share a relationship with them, too. They don't inhabit any kingdoms; they're a bit strange."

"Yes, I'm sure." How peculiar must they be for *Asena* to call them so? I clear my throat. "You're welcome in our kingdom, but do not expect pious rulers. We'll be fair, but we do not worship the gods as you do."

"And if you wish to serve us then slice open your palms and take a blood oath," Cayden adds. A gruesome agreement. If someone breaks a blood oath, their blood will slowly boil them alive for several torturous hours. "I will not have you betraying us on that battlefield or running to a different ruler because *the wind* influences you."

"Yes, Your Majesty," Ophir and Asena each say in unison before unsheathing a blade from the ropes around their waists and slicing into their palms. Blood pools on their skin before they let it drop to the earth and state their vows to us. Their act is not something to take lightly, and it's not something that can be easily broken.

My head spins from all this new information so I choose to inquire about the Goddess of Flames and her relation to the dragons on another day. There's only so much knowledge I can absorb before noon. "How will you know when I need you to open the portal back to Vareveth?"

"Will you be able to command your dragons across a great distance?" Asena asks.

"Yes."

She nods. "We will build a pyre beside the lake. When the time comes to evacuate, command one of your dragons to light it, and we will make haste." Her eyes soften, making me wonder again how much she knows about dragons and their riders. "I'll leave you to your goodbyes."

"Thank you." I manage a smile, only letting it drop once they're gone.

I don't call my dragons down, wanting to watch them fly instead. They're magnificent . . . extraordinary . . . I'll never know how someone could look upon them and choose to chain them. I give Venatrix and Delmira the command to fly to the border, tracking them as they become smaller and smaller as the distance grows, and for a moment I pretend they're hatchlings again, small enough to perch on my shoulders. Calithea begins swirling around the spires, and Basilius dips over the waterfall and spreads his wings over Verendus.

I rub at the ache in my chest, forcing myself to stay calm.

"Do you want to know what Ryder was telling me earlier?" Cayden asks, and I wonder if he knows how badly I need a distraction.

"Hmm?"

"Apparently, in the eyes of the gods you'd already be my wife because I killed for you," he says. "If that's all it takes to be a husband, I'd say I'm a damn good one so far."

I roll my eyes. "You don't believe in the gods."

"Marriage has reformed me."

"Atonement isn't in your skill set, and Elowen Veles is not my name, so don't start drawing hearts around it on pieces of parchment."

His eyes darken as he watches my lips form the words, like he's trying to memorize the shape of them. Something bordering on obsession crosses his features, all traces of humor disappearing. His hand twitches at his side like he wants to reach forward and trace my mouth. He's always looked like this, even before we were betrothed, like I belong right here with him, and he'll kill anyone who tries to take me away. "Fuck that sounds good."

"It doesn't make it true."

His eyes flash to my pounding pulse. "Betrothed is an unnecessarily long word, too many syllables."

"My name has more, and you have no issue saying that."

"That's because I love the way your name tastes on my tongue, Elowen."

Heat and need course through me the longer he stares. If only the urge to have him had died down after our time at the inn, it would be so much easier to distance myself.

"Don't give me those eyes," he murmurs, stepping closer but still not touching me. "I'll carry you back upstairs and keep you there for days."

"I—" I shake my head. "I'm still upset with you."

"I'll get on my knees again if you want an apology. You'll be loving me by the time I'm finished."

Oh, sweet gods.

Sorin saves me from myself when he screeches, but the pulse pounding between my legs doesn't cease even when I turn away from Cayden. *Good boy*, I shoot across the bond, but then I see why he cried out. Asena and Ophir have their hands clasped, their heads bowed, as the air splits in two and a rift of purple and black wisps appears. I've never seen anything like it; it's like encapsulated colored fog.

Calithea and Basilius cry out as I get closer to the portal, and I stop in my tracks, but Cayden is there, pressing a hand into my back to keep me moving. Their screeches don't stop, no matter how much I caress the bond, and Venatrix's and Delmira's follow from the distance.

My eyes mist over but I don't let the tears fall. *I'll be back soon, sweetlings.*

They screech and screech and there's nothing I can do to soothe them right now. I'm helpless, powerless, shackled to a duty Ailliard placed on my shoulders since I was a child.

"Just keep walking, love," Cayden murmurs, wrapping an arm around my waist. I nod, unable to form words past the suffocating guilt. He's looking at me like he wishes he could take every ounce of my pain and live with it, knowing I'd be free of this agony.

Sorin dives through the portal, and we all follow suit. The sensation of thousands of tiny feathers dusts over my skin and disappears just as quickly as it came. My boots crunch in the snow and the crisp mountain air slams into me. Frost-covered trees and untouched snow stretch on for miles, and the frozen rivers and waterfalls make it look like an enchanted winter kingdom.

Sorin lands beside us and cries out like he's in pain. I draw two daggers from the sheaths on my thighs, and rush toward him . . . but there's no threat. His claws leave gashes in the snow as he paces, and his head thrashes side to side before tipping back to roar.

"Sorin." I sheathe the blades and run my hand along his leg. "You're all right. You'll be back with the others soon."

"I don't think it's that," Saskia says as Sorin sinks his claws into the earth on either side of me. "We're in godly land. Creatures sense things we can't."

"But they've been in godly land before," I say. "They were fine after Cayden and I released them."

"They were coming out of confinement." Cayden sheaths his sword. "Anything feels better than a cage."

I nod, knowing how true that statement is. "We'll make our visit as swift as possible, but I should go to Nyrinn first. That's where Lycus will be."

I slide my hand down Sorin's scales one last time before he takes flight, and I lead our battalion away from the misty wall in the distance that keeps the kingdom hidden and turn toward Aestilian one final time.

CHAPTER
TWELVE

CAYDEN

BEYOND THE FOREST STANDS A VILLAGE MADE OF SEVERAL cottages built around icy rivers and winding dirt roads. Smoke rises from chimneys and candlelight shines through several windows bordered by colorful shutters. Mountains reach high into the sky all around us, and a waterfall tumbles down one of the staggering cliffs in the distance.

"Gods," Saskia breathes, her boots crunching in the snow beside mine. "This place is beautiful."

I say nothing, not denying or confirming her statement as I keep my eyes on the back of Elowen's head, pulling away only to scan the surroundings. Sure, I suppose it's charming, but I'll never be able to overlook the way Elowen has spoken of the burden on her shoulders. My goal with moving these people is to make *her life* easier, not theirs.

She is the only reason I'm here, not because it's the right thing to do. Morals would've gotten me killed if I held them in high regard.

Reminiscing is pointless aside from using it to feed my anger, but as I watch a mother and son sip from mugs, buried in blankets while watching the sunrise, I can't help but think of my own mother. What would her life have been if she had left my father? If we'd found a place like this? I can still hear her screams, the way she choked on her own blood. Bitterness so potent it would sour the sweetest fruit curdles my stomach.

I've been forced to mourn her longer than I knew her. My father didn't even bury her after she died; for all I know she was burned, buried in an unmarked grave by the villagers, or left for an animal to feast upon.

I'd never belong in a place like this. Since the moment that Imirath soldier carved my face open, I've burned with an anger that grows by the day. Sometimes I feel as if I'm in this world, but I'm not of it. I was forged by hatred and sharpened in violence. I've survived everyone who has tried to kill me, and though I killed parts of myself to achieve such victories, I'd walk through this world as a corpse before I let an enemy escape me.

Being blessed by the God of Death is a laughable notion. The gods have no place in my life. They never have.

"Cayden." Saskia lowers her tone, slowing her steps slightly to keep our conversation private. "With Aestilian off Elowen's mind, we'll need to discuss Imirath's succession."

I grind my teeth, recalling when Elowen told me she has never wanted a permanent place in Imirath. Falling for her was never supposed to happen. I was supposed to take my revenge—kill Garrick, sign a treaty, and dust my hands of it, but that's impossible now. "I'll talk to her when we're home."

"Garrick has no other children? Not even bastards?" she rushes out, and if her concern wasn't so clear, I'd walk away.

"A bastard will never have a stronger claim than a legitimate daughter," I say. "And no, he does not."

From the corner of my eye, I watch as Saskia shoves her hands into her coat pockets. "I'll try to find out what's being discussed in Imirath. At least Elowen will have more information when it comes to making a decision."

Ryder gestures for Saskia to catch up as Finnian leads her and my soldiers to what I assume is the guard house. My strides quickly eat up the distance between me and Elowen, and I lace her arm through mine to keep her from slipping on any ice patches. I ignore the way people peek out of their windows to get a look at us, some even throwing their doors open and rejoicing for their returned queen.

Elowen tightens her hand on my arm, looking up at me with the kind of smile one might wear when bringing their lover home. "Smile, demon. You got us into this mess, so play your part."

"I hardly smiled before we were betrothed, and it didn't stop people from believing I'm in love with you." I look down at her when she flinches, but her expression hasn't wavered.

"My people will not be so easily fooled."

I grasp her chin with my free hand. "If you want me to kiss you, all you have to do is ask."

A flush creeps up her neck as she glances at my lips. "Don't flatter yourself."

"I'm just offering a way to strengthen our image." She glares at me before turning to knock on the door we've stopped in front of. "You know how much it enlivens my day to see your vexation written so plainly on your pretty features."

She ignores me as it's ripped open and the scent of rosemary, yarrow, and freshly brewed tea wafts down the steps. A woman with warm brown skin and shoulder-length raven hair cries out, pulling Elowen into her arms. Elowen stiffens at first, but soon melts into the quick embrace as she's ushered inside. I take another quick glance around before shutting the door behind me.

"My girl," Nyrinn says, her tone almost motherly. "I knew you'd be back."

Elowen brushes her fingers down one of the posts jutting from floor to ceiling. "You're our first stop."

Nyrinn whips her head toward the door with the realization that someone else is present, and she keeps her chin raised as she drops to a curtsy. "Apologies, Your Highness. I had assumed you were a guard."

"No formalities necessary, and I do serve as Elowen's guard." I stick my hand out, despite never doing this when meeting new people. "Cayden."

She clasps a calloused, much smaller hand around mine. "Nyrinn. If you haven't heard of me, I'll be gravely offended."

I manage a half smile. "What you taught Elowen has aided me on several occasions, and she's always spoken highly of you."

Nyrinn seems pleased by the response and turns to Elowen again. "Do commanders and kings often serve as guards over their women or are you still hell-bent on death finding you before it's ready?"

"I am not hell-bent on death." Elowen rolls her eyes, staring at the woman with a warmth I desperately miss. The memories sink claws into my mind, making me long for the past in a way I never have. I lament over the loss of her laughter, the softening of her eyes when she looks at me, the way she melts into my body because she feels safe in my arms. "Cayden is hell-bent on keeping me alive. There's a difference."

"Smart man," she huffs, her dark gaze pinging between the two of us. "However, it appears you left out quite a few details in your letter a few weeks ago."

"Can't seem to recall anything noteworthy." Elowen claps her hands. "Where is Lycus? I assume he'll be in one of the spare rooms?"

Nyrinn pulls out a chair at her table, her expression becoming remorseful while gesturing for Elowen to take the one beside her. She hesitates for only a moment, but does as Nyrinn wishes. Her fingers tug her moonstone pendant along the gold chain, and she whispers the words I already know. "He's dead, isn't he?"

"The guards cut him deep. There was too much damage, and too much blood loss. All I could do was make him comfortable." Nyrinn shakes her head. "However, he wanted me to pass on his last words to you. He said, 'It is an honor to die for the dragon queen.'"

Elowen releases her necklace, planting her elbows on the table and dropping her head into her hands. I push off the wall and kneel beside her, pulling the chair out enough to make her face me. "His blood is not on your hands. He did his duty as a loyal soldier and stood against those who betrayed you. You've already executed the guilty."

Elowen rubs at her arms like she's trying to clean some invisible filth from her skin. "He should've let them go."

"Loyalty and betrayal are old friends. One can't exist without the other, and we wouldn't know the value of the former without the presence of the latter," I say. "Death during wartime is unavoidable, but we will honor his sacrifice by winning."

She sinks her teeth into her bottom lip, tormented eyes latching on to mine. I know she has a hard time accepting comfort, but it doesn't stop me from trying. Sometimes I think she takes on the pain around her and internalizes it so that when she looks for someone to blame, it'll always be herself. "When is the funeral?" Elowen asks.

"Today," Nyrinn answers. "After news of Ailliard reached us, and the mutiny of the guards, we knew you'd return. It didn't feel right to burn him without you present. We also suspect you have a plan for how to handle the situation."

"I do." Elowen breathes deeply, turning to face Nyrinn as I get to my feet and slide my hand along her shoulders. "Aestilian must be evacuated for the safety of the people. As queen of Vareveth, I offer refuge to anyone willing to make the journey. Housing will be provided as well as funds for those who need it to help them get on their feet in a new kingdom."

Nyrinn looks around her shop, standing from the chair and trailing her fingers along the glass vials on the shelves, the bundled flowers hanging from the ceiling, taking her time as Elowen's knuckles become white while she grips the chair. "Please don't stay here, Nyrinn. It isn't safe. Cayden gifted me a healing shop and you're more than welcome to use it."

"Has he?" The woman turns toward us, curiosity lighting her eyes as she notes the hands I rest on Elowen's shoulders. "That sounds far more generous than the rumors report him to be."

"The rumors are correct," I state.

Nyrinn snorts as she opens the lid of an empty trunk pressed against the wall. Her hands grip the sides as she bows her head and takes a deep breath. "Inform me of the shop's inventory and start grabbing jars of whatever you lack."

✝ ✝ ✝

More people than I thought possible fill the place Elowen referred to as Mourning Meadow. Lycus rests on a grand pyre, his sword clasped between his sickly gray hands. The brown leathers he wears match the hair neatly braided down his skull.

"I don't know much about the afterlife," Elowen murmurs. "Ailliard usually spoke during the funerals."

"I know a bit."

"Do you know anything I can say to him as a final blessing?"

The memory slams into me: dirt-and-blood-caked hands clutching a token of the past as metal bars pressed into my back. I haven't said the words since, never had a reason. "May your soul cross the river and find peace."

It's said there are many layers to hell, and the closer to the top you are, the better you were in life, but there are rivers throughout. A soul can't find rest until they accept death and cross. Some are reincarnated if the God of Death thinks they deserve another chance to prove themselves, but he's known to be ruthless. I'll have to find a way to climb the mountains of the underworld after I die because Elowen will definitely be at the top, and my wretched soul will find a way to hers no matter the distance.

Elowen swipes a stray tear off her cheek and squeezes Lycus's hands. "May your soul cross the river and find peace, Lycus."

She tightens her hold on my arm as we return to Finnian, Saskia, and Ryder. Sorin lands beside the pyre, causing several parents to pull their children closer. Elowen's eyes glow gold for a moment, and the heat of Sorin's flames slams into my face as the pyre is set ablaze.

"Did you learn that from your books?" Elowen asks.

"No." I clear my throat. "My mother used to tell me tales while she knitted blankets in the winter."

Elowen steps closer to me. "What was her name?"

I swallow. "Asterin."

"That's beautiful," Elowen whispers.

"The blankets weren't," I murmur, wanting to give her a distraction as she's given me on numerous occasions. "She was never taught how to properly knit. Ladies at court practiced needlepoint. The blankets she made always came out misshapen and riddled with holes, but they were the warmest damn things I ever owned. If I could've saved one thing from the fire it would've been one of those."

"It makes me happy to know how deeply she loved you." Elowen's gloved hand slides into mine, the first sign of affection since the betrothal that I know to be true. "We will avenge her, Cayden."

I rub my thumb over her knuckles but cut myself off when Finnian steps forward. His slender shoulders are rigid when he turns to face the crowd, and the blazing flames at his back are reflected in his determined gaze.

"What's he doing?" Ryder asks.

"I don't know," Elowen answers. "He's never spoken at a funeral."

"I first came to Aestilian when I was a child—orphaned and alone," Finnian begins, his voice echoing throughout the valley. "My family lived on godly land, and I never thought much of kings and queens, never understood why so many people in great tales would give their lives for them. That was before I met a queen not much older than me: Elowen Atarah."

Her hand tightens on mine as Finnian continues.

"Lycus stood against those who betrayed her, and for that his soul will know peace in the afterlife. He was a brave and loyal soldier, and one who we should all strive to emulate. Do not let his sacrifice go in vain. Elowen is the only queen I will ever know. She is the ruler I choose to follow until the day the gods claim my soul. She has fought for us since she was a child, and now it is our time to return the favor. She rides to war against her father, and we must ride with her. If Lycus can raise his sword in her name against friends, then we should all be able to raise ours against foes. How many rulers have made a kingdom while exiled? How many people not only brought dragons into the world but ride them?"

Swords are unsheathed and hoisted in the air as the crowd grows louder. Finnian speaks in a tone I've never heard him use before. It demands attention, and commands respect. Sorin exposes his teeth and roars as Elowen strides toward Finnian. I don't hear what they say above the cheering, but the love shared between them is evident in their eyes. She's not wearing a crown, and yet anyone looking at her would know she's a queen by the way she carries herself.

"We fight for our queen!" Finnian unsheathes the sword at his waist, raising it high above his head. "The dragon queen!"

"The dragon queen!" the crowd echoes once, twice, until it becomes a chant and a sea of raised blades, glinting in the sun as all those in attendance drop to their knees.

The dragon queen.

Not the queen of Aestilian. Not the queen of Vareveth. A queen her people will follow to any land, to any end, to war and beyond.

Chapter
THIRTEEN

ELOWEN

THE MOON HAS OVERTHROWN THE SUN BY THE TIME WE make it back to my old home. The day was spent preparing everyone for the evacuation with Saskia and I taking charge of sorting the housing assignments, as Cayden, Ryder, Finnian, and the soldiers who accompanied us began loading trunks and crates onto wagons.

The housekeeper who's looked after the property lit the lanterns and fires once she heard I was back. I thought I'd feel comfort in coming back here, but it's strange to look at a site I once called home and realize it no longer is. My fingers glide against rough wood as I lift the latch, but the creaking gate doesn't make my shoulders loosen when the sound rises to my ears. I don't find solace while walking up the path that leads to the chipped green door I painted several summers ago.

Aestilian has remained frozen in time. It's me who's changed. I breathe deeply while twisting the handle, but the unease within me grows as I walk toward the fire blazing in the hearth, knowing that somewhere in the past, I walked here as a different person. A queen with no army, a rider with no dragons, a woman trying to hold a crumbling kingdom together. I toss my coat on top of the pile of others thrown over the couch and claim my seat beside Saskia at the table, the combined presence of my companions banishing the loneliness that once cloaked the space.

"Please tell me you have something other than ale," Saskia miserably mumbles.

"It's sad you felt the need to ask me that." I grin, reaching into the cabinet behind me to pull out a bottle of wine.

"You need to continue to expose yourself to ale to develop a taste for it," Ryder says after taking a large bite of the pot pie, somehow making meat, potatoes, peas, and gravy seem wholly unappetizing.

Cayden rolls his eyes toward the ceiling. "Can you refrain from exposing the food in your mouth?"

"Drink every time they bicker," I whisper to Saskia and Finnian.

Finnian shakes my hand beneath the table but Saskia blanches. "Do you want to die?"

I laugh into my chalice as Ryder casts Cayden a black stare. "You've seen innards fall out of a man's stomach but food disgusts you?"

Finnian smacks his fist onto the wood, rattling the plates and silverware. "No speaking of innards at the table."

"When did I become the enemy?" Ryder shouts incredulously.

"Change of plans." I stand from the table, drinking game forgotten, clasping my plate and chalice in each hand and biting down on the neck of the wine bottle so Saskia and I don't have to walk for refills. We sink onto the couch and get comfortable, clinking our glasses and filling them again.

The kitchen, sitting room, and dining area are all connected, so despite us moving away from the men, we didn't get far, and we certainly don't get silence. Ryder's chair screeches as he abruptly stands and carries his dinner the short distance, plopping down on the floor across from us. "Keep pouring, sunshine."

I look right at him while drinking straight from the bottle. Finnian squeezes into the spot beside me, and Cayden takes the chair closest to the fireplace.

"I set some goats loose in the field for Sorin," Cayden says.

"They're so adorable, though." Finnian groans, and I pat him on the shoulder.

"You can try to corral them while a dragon chases you for interfering with the hunt." Cayden doesn't bother looking up from his food while gesturing to the window. "We can watch."

"And you'll be out there saving his ass as soon as Elowen starts screaming," Ryder jests, and Cayden smacks him on the back of the head, causing them both to delve into laughter that the rest of us join in on.

Life is made up of a series of moments and can change in a minute. I've never known what tomorrow or even the next hour will bring—death, tragedy, or something else entirely. But on my worst days, sometimes it's the people I'm with who make it better.

"I'll show you to your rooms," I say once the ale and wine are gone and fatigue weighs on us all, leading them down the long hall that branches off into several rooms. The threadbare carpet that was once bright red is now a washed-out pink, most likely bleached from the sun and worn down by boots. "There are more blankets in the cupboard and extra wood beside every fireplace."

Ryder rubs his stomach while stumbling into his room, and Saskia claims the one beside his. The accommodations are plain, nothing more than a bed and dresser, but it'll do. Finnian opens his door and sighs. "I haven't missed that lumpy thing."

"You sleep like the dead and I'm sure your snores will be vibrating the floorboards soon enough."

"I don't snore that loud." He chuckles, but it soon dies out when I don't respond, and my smirk grows in the silence. "Ellie." My childhood nickname is drenched in betrayal. "How could you never tell me?"

"It's comforting." I innocently shrug. "It's like sleeping close to a big bear."

He looks at me like I've lost all capacity to form an intelligent thought, and I pull Cayden into my room, giggling to myself as I shut the door. "The bed is much smaller than you're used to, and your feet will hang off the edge, but—"

"It's fine." He unhooks the sword from his waist and sits down as he glances around my room, taking in the book stacks, chair, and small paintings in the corners of the walls that I did when I was bored. Sparse jewelry is piled into a bowl on my nightstand splattered with candlewax from nights I spent reading. "The first place I could afford was a glorified closet in a rat-infested building."

I grimace. "Was there at least a window?"

"Yes, though it wasn't much of a luxury unless you wanted to smell the filth of the streets or listen to the shouting drunks."

"How old were you?"

His brow furrows as he does the math in his head, and I glue my hands to my sides to keep from reaching forward to smooth it out. "Around fifteen." My stomach drops. "Don't give me that look."

"I'm not giving you any look." I avert my eyes and step over to the book stacks, running my fingers along the spines like greeting old friends.

"You wish to share a bed?"

I glance over my shoulder while undoing the braid Hyacinth did this morning and massaging my roots. "Why wouldn't we?"

"You don't have servants here," he says. "Isn't that why you wanted to share a bed in Vareveth? To avoid gossip if a servant entered our chambers and saw me sleeping on the floor?"

"Oh, right." I rise to my feet, tossing my hair behind my shoulders and clasping my hands. My bed here is also much smaller, so there's no way we'd be able to sleep beside each other and not touch. "I'll show you to a different room."

"You misunderstand me." He cuts into my path and grabs my wrist before I can twist the brass knob. "I'm staying in this room. The house isn't warded, we're in foreign territory, and although our enemies are miles away, we're still at war. I'm not taking any chances with your safety. I'll sleep on the floor if it makes you more comfortable."

He's so close, looking at me with eyes that make me feel like I've just stepped in front of a fire after trekking through a storm.

"I-I'm not going to make you sleep on the floor."

He draws me in like a weary traveler desperate for comfort, but I'm still stuck in the snow. Ailliard's voice echoes on a loop in my mind, making me want to press my palms to my ears and scream. I've faced terrifying things in life and yet the idea that someone could love me for all the years I have left in my life, and the fear that accompanies it, is the one thing I don't know how to conquer.

I drop my eyes and pull my wrist from his hold.

"El—"

"Can I have a moment? I'd like to be alone." The lie tastes bitter on my tongue. He's standing right in front of me, but *I miss him.* I miss tracing his scars with my fingers and lips. I miss the feeling of being at ease in his arms. Nothing happened in the way I wanted and yet I still want him.

Cayden has a power over me like nobody else, and I hate feeling like I'm building a barrier against my own happiness, but I mindlessly keep piling stones on top of each other, telling myself that what hurts me right now won't be able to hurt me again.

Nobody can love a vile creature.

He stares down at me for several prolonged beats as the silence between us suffocates me. It wraps around my throat like a ribbon, cowardice and pain twining together to form a bow. He reaches for his sword and exits the room, his boots thumping against the creaking wood. The front door to the house shuts, and I press my forehead into the wall while rubbing at the ache in my chest.

I can't just stand here, I'll go mad. Ailliard's heart thumps through the walls, beckoning me to seek out the source of what's been plaguing my mind since Jarek told me where the pardons were hidden. I dig my nails into my palms and step into the hall. Part of me didn't want to come back to the house, knowing this would be unavoidable.

The moon bathes the room with just enough light for me to see, and it smells of the dust that floats within the silvery rays. I tug my pendant along the chain as I step farther inside, scanning the surroundings of a room so familiar yet foreign. I didn't truly know the man that stayed here, despite sharing a roof.

My knees hit the floor hard when I sink to them in a daze, lifting the wooden trunk at the base of the bed. Several folded tunics are perfectly stacked in two piles, and it's like I'm watching myself outside of my body as I pick one up and hold it to my chest. I sink my teeth into my lip until I taste blood, throwing the tunic back into the trunk and slamming the lid shut.

The cut on my thigh is healed, but the fresh scar throbs when I recall Ailliard shoving his nails into the wound. He harbored such malice, such hatred, and here I am hugging his fucking tunic.

My blood chills when I get to my feet and round the dresser that juts awkwardly into the room. I press my hands into the floorboards until one pops up. I take a deep breath before lifting it and gracelessly let it slip from my limp fingers.

My stomach rolls and I force myself to look away from the contents within, squeezing my eyes shut as if it'll erase the image burned into my mind. *Why?* Why did he betray me? What day did he decide he regretted fleeing with me? What day did he look at me and realize he'd never care more for me than he cared for a king who wanted him dead?

Tears patter against the wood around me like the beginning of a storm, and I don't bother wiping them from my face as I trail my fingers over the ribbons I used to wear in my hair as a child. I'd never go anywhere without something colorful woven into my braids. Ailliard knew this, and each time he went on a raid he'd bring a new color back for me.

A sob rattles my frame when I flip through the old pages of a gardening manual he used to teach me how to read. Every inch of my body is shaking so badly I can't even read the words, so I set it aside and pull out the first gown he gifted me, made of lavender and white fabric. I practically lived in it before I outgrew it. I throw everything on the floor, pressing the heels of my palms into my eyes as if that'll stop the tears, but more keep pouring from me in violent waves.

My breathing quickens and my vision gets spotty. I try to calm myself down, to not succumb to my emotions, but they overpower me and drag me down into the shadowy depths. I feel like there's no escaping when they have me in their thrall. I claw at my throat, trying to remove an invisible noose but it's pointless. Frustrated with myself, I pile all my belongings onto the dress and fold them up.

I can't be in here anymore.

My boots pound as I make my way to the back of the house and shove the door open, tossing my childhood into the yard before spinning on my heels. I grab whatever reminds me of Ailliard: clothing, blankets, boots, the mug he always used, the daggers I bought him after saving for months, his seat at the dining table.

I don't stop until my chest is heaving from exertion instead of anxiety. "Sorin!" My voice is nothing more than a rasp, but the familiar sight of his emerald-green scales brings me comfort. "Burn it all!"

Flames engulf the pile, but it's not the fire that destroys the tokens of the past; it's the present.

CHAPTER
FOURTEEN

CAYDEN

I GUIDE THE WHETSTONE ALONG MY SWORD AS THE SNOW swirls around me, not bothering to look up when several people in the road stop to stare before quickening their steps to get back to whatever last-minute tasks they need to complete before departure. I'm counting down the seconds until we're able to leave. My patience is holding on by a frayed piece of string, and my temper winds through me like a storm.

I couldn't manage to go farther than the front porch. Despite wanting a distraction, protecting Elowen is my duty. I swore an oath to her when we struck our deal, and I won't falter. Violence has shaped my life and even in the quiet moments, I'm prepared for it to appear. The people of Vareveth coined the term *demon of Ravaryn*, but sometimes I think that one really did possess me as a boy and slowly eats away at my soul. My name is whispered in fear, shrouded in shadow, and drenched in blood.

Someone rounds the side of the house, boots crunching in the snow as the Vareveth soldier on patrol quickens their pace. I drop the whetstone beside me to give them my full attention. "Sir, it's the queen. She's—"

I grip the hilt of my blade and rush to the back of the house, immediately spotting the evidence of her pain. Ashes drift along the winter-kissed ground and sparks rise high above the flames. "No soldier is to come back here until I get the queen inside," I shout over my shoulder.

Footsteps lead toward a lake coated in ice and bordered by jagged mountains. The only flaw in the otherwise perfect surface is the gap beneath the gushing waterfall spilling over black rocks.

Elowen paces along the shore, wrapping her arms around herself like she's desperate for comfort. I wonder how many times she's broken down in silence and hugged herself, wishing she could have someone there to hold her. Fucking hells, she's not even wearing a coat, and her trembling is evident the closer I get. The golden dragons embroidered on the bell sleeves of her long blue tunic glimmer as she moves. It remains open in the front to reveal knife-clad legs with more delicate embroidery in a line down her thighs. Sorin isn't far from her, rustling his wings and stomping his feet as he watches his rider.

My coat is already off by the time I reach her, and her head shoots up when I wrap it around her. "What happened? Why are you crying?"

A feral growl tears free of her lips as she rips the coat off and shoves it at my chest. "I don't want you here."

She's not sleeping. She's barely eating. She's lost in her mind most of the time and I need to pull her out of it. I clutch the coat, not letting it fall in the snow because I'm getting this damn thing on her. She covers her mouth, eyes widening in fear as they flash back to the house. "Nobody can hear you but me. I've given you space when you asked for it in the past, but I'm done with that because clearly it's not working."

"You don't get to hurt me and be privy to my every thought." She angrily swats some of her tears away.

"I can't fix anything if you don't talk to me."

"Talk to you?" She laughs shrilly. "Communication was the one thing I asked of you and emphasized the importance of, and you blindsided me in a room filled with enemies, so you don't get to stand there and speak to me as if I'm the one who faltered." Her breath clouds in front of her lips, coming out in short gasps. "Has it ever occurred to you that maybe I request space because it pains me to look at you?" Lightning shoots through my chest, making it hard to breathe, but I don't let it show on my face. "You have always wanted power, and I will not be your pawn as you grasp for it."

"Which is why I made you my queen." I step forward, forcing her arms through the coat as she struggles against me. "Keep it on," I state in a low growl before releasing her. She can fight with me until the sun rises but not unless she's warm. If this were any other moment, I'd laugh at how large it is on her, but I have a feeling she'd castrate me if I smiled. "The voice in your head telling you that I utilized the marriage clause because I wanted to be king more than I wanted you isn't mine."

She flinches, tightening her arms around her middle again. "Don't talk about Ailliard."

"I didn't say his name, love." She shakes her head again, and I wonder if Ailliard is in there right now. I'll never understand how someone I completely adore could see herself so terribly. "I have been in much worse positions in life, so yes, I have taken to the role of king and will do whatever is necessary. I was born with nearly nothing and even that was taken from me before I rebuilt myself brick by brick. If I fail at being king, if I even falter and give our enemies an opening to exploit, I will lose you. I will lose everything I'm not willing to let go. You are my priority and mine to protect, not a throne or a kingdom."

She sucks in a sharp breath and rubs at her chest, squeezing her eyes shut as she shakes her head. Years of conditioning have taught her to view herself as someone to only give love and never receive it. She'll offer pieces of herself on a platter until she has nothing left to give, but it ends with me.

"A crown is an ornament, nothing more than a gilded lie. It's worth nothing against a sword, and only armies keep it on a ruler's head. I may have kept to the shadows, but I ruled from them, and I've never needed the validation of the world. Power isn't given, it's taken."

She sobs, and it breaks something in me I didn't know was whole. I step forward, risking her ire by framing her cheeks in my hands. She doesn't pull away, but she also doesn't move closer. "I conquered a kingdom to have you. It was the only way."

"You manipulated Eagor. You manipulate everyone around you to get what you want." She shoves at my chest, her anger returning despite it clearly exhausting her. "I must've been an easy target. A woman who never knew love aside from her best friend. You dangled the moon on a string, and I grasped for it like a fool." Her next words are growled through her teeth, "I will not close my eyes and accept treatment I don't deserve just because I want to be with you."

"You think I manipulated *you*?" I ask incredulously and drag a hand down my face. Elowen's anger is cold, but her heart is warm and light. She loves fiercely and hurts deeply because of it. I never want to change a damn thing about her, I just want to be the one to protect that heart. I want it to be safe with me. "If I was manipulating you, I would've demanded you marry me before we freed your dragons, knowing you would have. All hells, Elowen. If I manipulated you, I wouldn't have ruined myself in the process. I wouldn't be tormented every hour that passes by knowing it's another spent with this distance between us."

She keeps shaking her head, the frustration evident on her features. She's been told empty words all her life; I can't blame her for doubting whatever I say. I unsheathe the dragon dagger on her thigh and wrap her fingers around the hilt, keeping mine over hers and holding the blade against my neck.

"What are you doing?!"

"It appears we're at an impasse." Her hand trembles under my grip but I hold firm. "Kill me if you truly hate me so much for what I've done. I have no regrets when it comes to you, and I refuse to die by anyone else's hand. I've been slowly dying since the moment I saw you, so it seems fitting for you to be the one to deliver my end. For as long as I live, you will never be free of me and even in death I will do every-thing in my power to haunt you."

The blade stays pressed against my neck after I release her fingers, and I lean into the sharp edge. Elowen sucks in a sharp breath and her chest heaves as I lean down and slide my fingers through her curls as beads of blood begin dripping down my skin. Her eyes dart between the blade and my gaze, her brows knotting when my lips hover an inch above hers.

"Make your choice, sirantia, because all I have ever chosen is you."

Each tear that drips down her cheeks is like another blade piercing my flesh. "Do you want to know the worst of it? If you had told me you wanted to be king, I would've fought for you. I would've married you if it got you what you wanted. After everything you've done for me and my dragons, I would've."

"I didn't want it to be like this." My loyalty may be blood-soaked, but it has always been hers. Elowen is the light in my life, the only good part of me. She's the silence in the mayhem. "I'll sacrifice myself at your altar a thousand times over to be the man you deserve, knowing I'll always fall short because a man good enough for you doesn't exist."

She remains silent, moonlight illuminating the tears that flow like rivers down her cheeks. I hate tears, they've always made me uncomfortable, but these fill me with a feral desperation to make this right. She's the only exception, and I have no fucking idea how she managed it. Sorin curls around her, making sorrowful noises deep in his throat. It sounds like the tune Elowen hums to calm them on occasion.

She must recognize it because it makes her sob again as she drops the blade to her side. "You know I can't do it. No matter what's happened, I can't."

"Come here," I mutter before hoisting her into the air and wrapping her legs around my waist. She collapses against me as I walk us back to the house, clinging to me so tightly, like she's as desperate for this as I am. Her body continues shaking as I walk her through the hall and set her down on the bed. I add another log to the fire before riffling through my bag to find the tin I need and tilt Elowen's chin up. "I'm going to give you a few moments to get ready for bed while I make you some tea. Just call out if you need anything."

She nods, her eyes dry but vacant of the vibrancy I've come to adore, and I can't stop myself from pressing my lips to her forehead before leaving. I hang my head, wanting to throttle someone, something, anything, as I place the bronze kettle over the fire still burning from earlier. The tin clatters on the kitchen counter, and I drop my head into my hands. No matter how angry Elowen is, she can't hate me more than I hate myself.

A door down the hall creaks open and I straighten my spine, wiping the emotion from my face. Finnian saunters around the bend in his night clothes, glancing at my neck. "Do I want to know?"

"Even if you did, I wouldn't tell you."

He snickers while picking up the tin to read it. "Chamomile and lavender?"

"It's supposed to help anxiety."

"For you?" he asks, despite knowing the answer, so I don't dignify the question with a response. "You're in love with my sister."

Gods, does anyone in this group mind their fucking business? Love is the most selfish emotion in my opinion. You make someone love you and ruin them in the process. Love ruined both of my parents.

Fate wields love like a weapon, leaving only tragedy in its wake.

I turn away to find a mug, but Finnian doesn't disappear by the time I turn around. "Don't hold your breath if you're waiting for me to deny it. If that woman sheds another tear tonight, I'm going to have to murder someone."

Finnian laughs softly. "Strangely I'm happy she has someone like you. I'm surprised you didn't kill Ailliard before that night."

I shrug, wishing this fucking kettle would boil already. "I threatened to."

Finnian's brows shoot up. "He never mentioned it."

There aren't many men who would admit to being on the brink of vomiting while pinned to a wall. "It was after Elowen and I came back from Kallistar Prison. I told him I'd break his neck and make it look like a riding accident if he didn't start treating her with more kindness."

"That explains his change in behavior," Finnian mutters. "I should've done it years ago."

I hold back my retort, knowing Elowen would hate it if I were to upset Finnian. If he wants comfort, I'd rather wake Ryder up. He's by far the friendlier of the two of us and would deal with the situation a lot better than me. "She's in her room if you want to go to her."

"It's not me she needs." He gives me a pointed look. "Elowen is not vengeful by nature. She wasn't born with her darkness, it was made. One of the gentlest hearts beats in her chest, and once this war is over I look forward to living in a world that allows her to be herself. I don't think she ever would have picked up a knife had she not been forced to."

The kettle whistles, and I douse the tea leaves in steaming water. The most dangerous people are not those who are born with anger, it's those who became lethal to avenge something or someone. Motivation becomes the whetstone that sharpens you against the world. "I want you to be the commander of the Aestilian forces. Elowen is the only one with the authority to grant you that position, but you know she'll agree."

I'm already walking toward the hall when I hear his raspy whisper. "Why?"

"Elowen always tells me that she wouldn't have survived exile without you." I stop in my tracks and glance over my shoulder. "If anyone deserves to be named Commander of Aestilian, it's you."

Finnian blinks slowly and I leave him to digest the news. Elowen can speak to him about it, but Finnian's loyalty is unquestionable. It reminds me of the bond I share with Ryder and Saskia. I grew up beside them, struggled with them, learned their strengths. It's why I promoted them both when I became Commander of Vareveth.

I've hurt more people than I can remember, letting their faces fade into the darkness within me, but Elowen's remains. I push open the door and something pinches in my chest when I take in her red eyes and dark curls cascading around her as she sits up against the headboard.

"I'm—"

"The most beautiful woman to exist?" I hand her the mug, cutting her off. "Never apologize to me."

She brings the mug to her nose, her eyes slipping shut as she inhales the floral aroma before taking a sip. I kick off my boots and toss my shirt aside, taking a seat on the bed to face her. She traces the rim with her finger, looking into the water like she's searching for an answer.

"He kept some of my childhood belongings in the same compartment where he hid the pardons. I burned them along with his things." She sniffs. "He didn't love me, even if he tried."

"His inability to love you is a reflection on him, not you. Don't base your worth off of someone who couldn't have been half as good as you if they'd tried," I say. "He was a fool for not loving you."

She takes another sip, swallowing hard and licking her lips. "The irony is that he punished me when I couldn't make a kill once. I was a child, no more than twelve, and Ailliard arranged a hunting party where I saw a doe and her fawn. He raged at me when I put my knives down and told everyone I tripped when he slammed my head into a rock. He even convinced me. Finnian had to carry me home." My hands itch to grab a sword but there's no target. "He tracked the deer through the forest after that and bled them both in front of me before forcing me to eat them, not that I kept the meat down." She drags her eyes to mine. "I feel more remorse for those deer than I do for my own uncle, and when I think of everything he did to me, everything he said to me, my mind feels like a mess. My own memories aren't even a reliable source because I don't know what he manipulated."

"He deserved to die." When I greet death, I'll make sure to find Ailliard in hell and torture him for everything he's done. I slide into bed beside Elowen, pulling her against my chest and threading my fingers through her hair. She must be tired because she doesn't put up any fight, but the bed is too small for us to share without touching anyway. She drapes her leg over mine, and my skin burns every place she presses against. I've done nothing in life to deserve her, and yet I can't stop wanting her with a devotion that could rival religions. "Elowen, I swear to you, everyone in this world who has harmed you will die screaming."

She lifts her head to look at me, mindlessly tracing one of my scars. Gods, those eyes. It's like she's twisting a knife into my heart, and yet I feel no reprieve in her absence. "Don't betray me."

"My loyalty to you will never cease."

CHAPTER
FIFTEEN

ELOWEN

I'M TORN FROM THE CLUTCHES OF SLEEP BY A CLAP OF THUN-der. My eyes snap open, and I groan into the pillow when I note the sunlight peeking through the curtains and realize it's not thunder, but Saskia. "Get up!"

Her fist continues pounding into the door, and if she keeps this up, she'll probably break through the damn thing. I haven't slept this well since we overthrew Eagor, and my exhaustion continues to drag me down like chains are shackling me to my dreams. I've been plagued with nightmares to the point I avoid the meager sleep I'm able to get, but I didn't wake up once last night.

"Fuck off, Sas," Cayden grumbles while tightening his arm around me. His voice is even deeper and raspier in the morning, and memories of him kissing my neck while murmuring sensual promises against my skin flash into my mind. I should get out of bed; that's definitely the intelligent thing to do, but it's also something that I don't want to do. Cayden doesn't miss a thing, and though I'm not facing him, he knows I'm awake, and that I haven't moved. We must've switched positions sometime in the night.

I inhale deeply and arch against him, pretending to innocently stretch.

A delicious groan vibrates against my back. "Elowen," he warns.

"Hmm?" I press my hips back again, and his hard length digs into me. I clutch the blankets and try to focus on keeping my breathing steady.

"All hells," he hisses into my hair and splays his hand over my stomach. I've never craved the touch of anyone else, and it's impossible to resist him when he's close. One of the only times my mind quiets is when his arms are around me. Cayden touches me like he laments the moment we'll be parted and will fight for a few more seconds. He clenches my slip, unintentionally dragging the material up my legs. My thighs press together from featherlight sensation, and the anticipation makes a needy whimper crawl up my throat as someone bangs on the door again.

He uses his other hand to cover my mouth as he grazes his lips along the column of my neck. I tilt my head to grant him more access, and he loosens his grip on my slip to draw slow circles on my skin. "Stay quiet for me, love," he whispers, and bites down on the most sensitive spot, flicking his tongue over it as he leaves his mark. His hand muffles another moan, and my desperation for more grows impossibly stronger.

The pounding on the door resumes, followed by a frustrated growl. "I'll be back," Saskia states before stalking down the hall.

Cayden releases my mouth and nibbles on my earlobe. "Please." I keep my voice low, so the others won't hear through the paper-thin walls. "Maybe it'll be easier to be around each other if we stop denying ourselves."

His hand travels from my stomach to cup my breast, and the calluses on his fingers make me shiver. His movements are languid as he kneads and brushes his thumb over my nipple. His chuckle is warm and rich like a dollop of chocolate melting on my tongue. "Do you think it'll be that simple?"

No, but admitting that out loud sounds humiliating. "Yes."

"Elowen." My name is caressed by his voice, making each syllable sound like a secret he wishes to keep entirely to himself. "I wouldn't have fallen into madness craving more of you than I deserve if my feelings could've been erased by a simple touch, but we don't align on what we want."

His warmth is ripped away as he sits up and swings his legs over the bed. The morning light illuminates the raised red scars on his back and the smattering of stars that travel down his ribs. His back muscles flex as he stretches and runs a hand through his messy waves.

I clear my throat and press my back into the headboard, trying to ignore the sting of rejection. I just want to forget everything that's happened for just a few moments. "W-what do you mean? What do you want?"

"I understand why you doubt me. You made it clear last night that I hurt your trust and mending that is my priority." He looks over his shoulder. "Because I want everything with you, El, and I won't accept anything less than that, even if it takes years for us to get there."

"Years?" I echo, blinking slowly, but his face doesn't change from the unwaveringly serious expression as he nods only once. "You truly mean that."

He licks his lips and reaches forward to rest his hand against my cheek. "All I ask is that when your mind starts to wage war on you, you give me a place on the front lines."

A smile tugs my lips up and my eyes soften. I think most men would wish me to keep my thoughts trapped behind my lips, but never Cayden. He hangs on to my every word and emotion like they belong to him alone. "Okay, soldier."

A dimple deepens in his cheek as his mouth quirks up in one corner, and he leans forward to kiss my forehead before rising from bed. The floor creaks under his weight, and a chair scrapes against the floor in the dining room, followed by the sound of pounding footsteps again.

"Have you spent enough time gazing longingly at each other?" Ryder shouts, and Cayden tilts his head to the ceiling and sighs.

"I'll find a mirror so you don't feel left out," Cayden responds.

Shadows dance as Ryder stops behind the door, but he lowers his voice to whisper through the wood. "Please come out. Finnian isn't awake and Saskia is terrifying when she has a task list she feels behind on."

Cayden casts me a flat look while tying the drawstring on his pants. "We can sneak out the window."

I roll my eyes while throwing the covers off. "Oh, today is going to be so fun."

CHAPTER
SIXTEEN

ELOWEN

FRIGID WIND WHIPS DOWN FROM THE MOUNTAIN PEAKS, sprinkling us with a dusting of snow. The treetops sway, their limbs brushing together in an endless, winding labyrinth. Sorin roars, and the lonely sound echoes through the valley.

"Do you think he misses the others?" Finnian asks as we walk arm in arm down the road.

"Most likely. He hasn't been apart from them since birth." I recall Saskia's words from yesterday as I watch Sorin fly in uneasy circles. "Dragons are born from old magic; maybe he can sense whatever god magic remains within the land."

"I didn't think you believed in the gods."

"I don't worship them, but there is magic in the world." Before I was born, I'm sure people said the same things about dragons. They were myths lost in legends and tales, creatures that parents would tell their children about while putting them to bed. "The world changes every day, creating new possibilities that others deemed impossible. All it takes is one person to alter reality into something unrecognizable, whether for better or worse."

Finnian shudders. "I've lived in godly land all my life, but at least I got a break from all the rituals while I was here."

"I thought you hid in the barn during the ceremonies."

"When I was old enough to leave my mother's side." His eyes scan the surrounding trees. "Before that I was stuck listening to chants for hours."

I tighten my hand on his arm, knowing it's hard for him to talk about his past. The family he lost when a clan burned his home down. "I'll try to limit Asena and Ophir's chanting."

"Thank you," he sighs, sounding sincere. "Blade is coming with us. I helped him pack up the forge yesterday and he mentioned that he'd like to work in Ladislava. I imagine we'll be needing as many weapons as possible."

Blade took Finnian under his wing when he was no older than thirteen, and I imagine he eventually would've taken over the forge if we weren't evacuating. "He'll be swimming in syndrils before the month is over."

We stop at the target field where we've spent our lives training. I watched Finnian shoot his way through several bows, all different sizes to accommodate his growing form. We've spent nearly every day together since meeting over a decade ago, and I braved the world because it meant standing between him and whatever came our way.

Aestilian was where I grew up, but Finnian was my home.

He becomes somber, and I wonder if he's seeing a younger version of me standing in my place. "Did Ailliard's betrayal poison Aestilian for you?"

I've never truly felt content here. My need for revenge always outweighed the safety this place offered. Finnian nocks an arrow in his bow as I unsheathe a knife dangling off my belt. Red painted targets stand out against the hay bales, and I throw my first blade. "I've made my peace with this place, but I can't remain here now that I know what it's like to be part of the world I watched from behind a barrier."

"Do you miss him?"

"No." I needed to let myself grieve Ailliard's death to be done with it. It felt as if I were trying to hold a broken vase together with my bare hands, constantly being cut while taking on a hopeless task. I needed to let it break fully and accept that it would never be whole again.

"His actions led to his demise, and I'd never have kept him in a cell after a knife was held to your neck."

The second knife becomes a silver whirlwind glinting in the sun as it sinks into the center of the target. Finnian and I walk toward the hay bales to retrieve our weapons, and he nudges me with his elbow. "I've always loved when you get murderous on my behalf. It's like an angry kitten hissing."

"You know, you don't have to voice every thought in your head."

I wrap my fingers around the hilt, but an icy sensation slides down my spine. It's the same feeling I get while being watched. Rustling in the woods draws our attention, and we keep our weapons ready. It's too loud to be wind, and no patrols are guarding the perimeter since we're leaving soon. I didn't want to risk anyone being left behind when the portal opens.

Crack.

Crack.

Crack.

Finnian and I exchange a glance as Sorin lets out a mighty roar, sharply decreasing his altitude and flying straight toward me.

"Attack!" I call out over my shoulder. Something is wrong, I can feel it in my bones. "Draw your weapons!"

Bells begin ringing to warn soldiers to prepare for an ambush, and I command Basilius to burn the pyre beside the castle. I brace myself, preparing to face Imirath's army. Ailliard must have revealed the location. Garrick must have a spy in Vareveth that informed him of my movements. My nerves steady, and I don't risk a single blink. I refuse to die here.

"All gods," Finnian mutters.

It's not Imirath that bursts through the trees—it's netherwraiths. Their white fur blends in with the snow, but their red eyes stand out like twin droplets of blood. Venom drips from their exposed fangs as their feral snarls mingle with the screams of the people yards away.

"They're in the town," Finnian says, his head quickly whipping in the direction of the houses behind us. I command Sorin to burn the tree line in front of us as I throw my knife. It sinks into its skull as Finnian shoots an arrow at the second, but it keeps charging as the eruption of Sorin's flames shakes the ground. A wall of fire rises as he engulfs the trees that have stood here for centuries along with more beasts. I throw another knife, but the creature dodges, the blade only managing to clip its ear.

Finnian nocks another arrow in his bow, but there's not enough time.

I spring off my feet and tackle him as the netherwraith leaps for us, sending us tumbling into the snow as the arrow misses its mark. The beast doesn't turn back to us and continues running toward the town.

"I had it!" Finnian exclaims.

"And you would've died in the process."

Finnian locks his arms around my body and kicks another netherwraith in the side of the head. My lungs burn from inhaling the frigid air and smoke, but I manage to scramble off him quick enough to slice its neck open. Screams echo throughout the kingdom, and I command Sorin to continue burning whatever sections of the forest the beasts are coming from. My chest tightens as he rebels against the command, wanting to stay by my side, but I hold firm, issuing the order until he obeys. Blood stains the snow. Screams build and build until they mesh together, becoming one panicked cry for help as my ears ring.

Cayden.

I need to find Cayden.

"Saskia is still at the house. You need to get her to the wagons. That's where the portal will be, as well as Cayden and Ryder," I rush out. We don't have time for arguing—Saskia and the Vareveth soldier stationed to guard the house don't know Aestilian as we do. His unease matches mine as he presses our foreheads together. "Shoot straight."

"Throw true."

With the blaze at our backs, we sprint toward the town. A row of small cottages splattered with blood are nestled closely together, and Finnian and I dart into an alleyway. I leap over a corpse bleeding out at the center of it, and chaos erupts as soon as we make it through. I cast Finnian one final look before someone pummels into me. I hardly have time to register the throbbing in my shoulder before I'm surrounded by a mob of hysterical people pressing into me at all angles. Basilius successfully lit the pyre because the wispy portal shines like a beacon several yards away, and people practically claw their way to the front to get through.

Names are shouted, tears are shed, and pained screams are everywhere. The main road in town is packed so tightly with the surge of citizens that they can't move as the beasts begin running through the buildings to pick immobile people off. I jam my elbows into those surrounding me, making my way through them like wading through thick mud, and focus on keeping my feet beneath me. Queen or commoner, whoever trips will surely be trampled.

I can't breathe.

No matter where I turn, there's no reprieve.

There is no escape.

We jolt forward as one, and I'm forced to step on someone beneath me. Gods, I hope they're dead. I can't even manage to move my arm enough to put them out of their misery if they're still breathing.

Sweat slicks my skin, and I force the bile down my throat from the sensation of so many people touching me. Sorin flies right toward me, crying out as his green eyes lock on mine, and I manage to raise my hand high as he dives. He hovers above me, extending his claw as people begin grasping on to my shoulders, arms, any part of me to free them from this. They try climbing onto me, but I manage to stay upright. He uses his other claw to free me from them, and wraps his talons around my torso, carrying me above the crowd.

I take my first deep breath, rubbing at my ribs now that I'm safely with my dragon. "Thank you, my sweet boy."

My eyes water as his flames engulf another hundred trees, and from this vantage point I can see just how many beasts surround us. Too many to count. More than I've ever seen together. He swoops back toward the ground once I spot Cayden fighting back-to-back with

Ryder. The Vareveth soldiers who accompanied us fight with them as a unit, but the pair of them are formidable. I wonder how many times they've fought like this. Cayden and Ryder move as if controlled by the same mind, not only trusting each other wholly but knowing when to aid the other without looking.

Sorin lands in the snow, placing me down gently as I draw the sword at my waist and another knife. In a brief reprieve from the creatures, Cayden turns and rushes toward me, wrapping one arm around my waist while keeping a firm grip on his sword.

"Are you hurt?" he asks, scanning me for injuries I don't have.

Ryder runs toward us before I have the chance to respond. "Where is my sister?" he frantically asks. "Where is Finnian?"

"We had to split up, but he's bringing her here."

Houses along the perimeter have caught fire, and netherwraiths swallowed in flames run frantically through the village until they collapse. There is death and gore wherever I look. Claw marks mar the fallen, blood and ash decorating their demise. Sorin takes to the sky again to continue burning droves of them.

Cayden slices through another beast, splattering his boots and adding more to the crimson field littered with entrails. I throw my knife at one leaping for Ryder, giving him time to spin out of the way and stab another.

"There are too many," I pant. "We must get everyone through the portal and follow before we're killed. There's no end to this until we're home." Cayden glances at me, and I already know what he's going to say. "I'm not leaving you."

I defend my kingdom because it's my duty, but there is a feral need to protect my friends, to protect Cayden.

"I'll throw you through the portal if I have to," he says.

"And I'll return on dragonback."

I crouch low, slicing at a netherwraith's ankles in time for Cayden to shove his sword through its skull. He raises his voice to address our soldiers, keeping his eyes on me. "I will kill all of you myself if any harm comes to the queen."

"How sweet of you." An arrow spears the belly of a beast and relief trickles through me. Cayden spins into his next swing, decapitating another that was leaping for him. I narrowly dodge the head and kick it away when the tongue flops out of its mouth. "Gods, that's disgusting."

"Sas!" Ryder shouts as she and Finnian come into view. They're just as blood-soaked as us, but that doesn't stop Ryder from briefly wrapping his arms around her when she's close enough.

"A netherwraith has never made it through the mist," I tell Cayden. "Do you think Thirwen could be responsible for this?"

Thirwen has aligned with Imirath, and the mages born there hone their power through animal familiars. The most skilled magic-wielders can slip into their animal's mind and control them, but what if they found a way to control beasts? My blood chills. Could they find a way to control human minds? Dragons?

"We'll figure it out once we're home," Cayden answers. "Fall in!" The Vareveth soldiers respond immediately, as well as at least fifteen from Aestilian, ready to receive orders and follow Cayden wherever he demands. "We need to secure the perimeter around the crowd as they escape. Take the first chance you get to enter the portal."

"Yes, Your Majesty," they respond in unison.

"Stay close," Ryder says to Saskia.

We fight through, making our way to the back of the crowd. Netherwraiths flow between the buildings like several streams leading to a river. Did Sorin sense something amiss? Is that why he's been uneasy this entire time?

I shake my head, clearing my thoughts for now.

Cayden pulls something from his back pocket and rips a pin out of a black-and-silver orb while slicing through a beast. He tosses it as far as he's able, and fire erupts, swallowing at least fifty netherwraiths in the flames as the ground shakes.

Then, with blood trailing down his face and in the midst of battle, Cayden *smiles*.

I command Sorin to bring the flames closer, watching as what remains of Aestilian is bathed in fire. I can't build a pyre for every fallen citizen, but I can offer them this. These are my people, and Ailliard may have referred to me as the discarded princess of Imirath, but this is the kingdom that chose me, that will follow me to war.

We continue battling and inching back toward the portal as more citizens file through. Sorin's flames make my eyes water and ash sticks to the blood covering me. A creature rakes its claws down my leg, and I slam my knife through it, ignoring the blood and pain.

Magic pulses at my back, making me shiver. The beasts delve into a frenzy to get away from the flames, but Sorin roasts them. Ryder wraps an arm around Saskia's waist, casting one final look to Cayden before ushering her through the portal. Finnian fires his last arrow, but I shove him through before he has the chance to draw his sword, a weapon he has never favored.

Cayden throws an axe with so much force the beast he hits crashes into another rapidly approaching. It screeches when Sorin's fire grows closer, slowly melting the flesh off the bone. All I can see is fire and blood. The portal begins shrinking, and Cayden's arms are around me before I have the chance to warn him, and together we fall into a pit of whirling midnight wisps with Sorin.

Part II

AN HEIR
TO RISE

CHAPTER
SEVENTEEN

CAYDEN

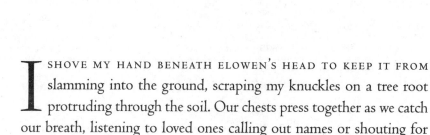

I SHOVE MY HAND BENEATH ELOWEN'S HEAD TO KEEP IT FROM slamming into the ground, scraping my knuckles on a tree root protruding through the soil. Our chests press together as we catch our breath, listening to loved ones calling out names or shouting for healers. It was a massacre. I've seen my share of gore and tragedy, have fought countless battles both honorable and not, but never have I seen beasts attack in such a frenzy.

I plant my elbows in the dirt to give Elowen room to breathe. "Your leg."

"Your chest." A netherwraith managed to sink its claws into me during the chaos of our final moments, but it's not fatal, and at least it wasn't a venomous bite. The bright red blood from where the wound pressed against her further ruins Elowen's blue-and-gold ensemble. I kneel and pull her up to a sitting position to inspect her injury, but she distracts me by pulling at my shredded shirt.

"I'm fine," I insist. "Once I wash the blood off, you'll see the wound isn't that deep."

She drops her gaze to her leg. "I'm the same, it's already clotting. They'll both scar though."

"Oh, the horror," I mutter.

"Was anyone bitten?" Elowen turns to our other companions slumped in the grass, all too winded to form words but they shake their heads. "I don't have healing supplies to stop the venom if anyone was."

"What about Nyrinn?" I was loading her trunks when the beasts came, and I shoved the woman through the portal before she could protest. Elowen would've been devastated by her death.

Elowen's head whips around, frantic until she sees Nyrinn amid her trunks, stuffing her belt with herbs and tonics and giving orders to Aestilian soldiers around her. "I should help her."

The sound of retching makes us turn in the opposite direction. Finnian is slumped over and violently trembling as he clutches his stomach. Elowen springs toward him, rubbing his back and pushing the sweaty hair off his forehead.

"Was he bitten?" Ryder shoves to his knees.

"It was like before," Finnian rasps through bloodless lips, wiping his mouth with his sleeve. "So many families lost. So many children now orphans. I couldn't save them." Finnian isn't with us, I realize. He's lost somewhere in his mind.

Dried blood flakes off his cheeks when Elowen frames them, unconditional love written plainly on her features. "Your mother, father, and sister, wherever they are, are thankful you weren't in the house that night. What happened to them was a terrible tragedy, but I believe they find solace in your heart still beating."

Finnian's eyes fill with tears, and he crushes Elowen to him, burying his face in her neck as his body is racked with silent sobs. We're all covered in gore, but Finnian holds her as if she's the only thing that can take his pain away. I offer Saskia a hand up, and then Ryder, the latter clapping me on the shoulder.

Where Finnian's eyes are water, Elowen's are pure fire as her anger burns. "If this was an orchestrated attack by Imirath or Thirwen, I want the people responsible dead before nightfall and their heads on pikes."

"Mage!" I call out, not remembering his name.

"I don't want a lesson on the gods from Ophir. I want to mount a dragon and burn their fucking camp," she growls as Finnian releases her. "If this was their first act of war I will gladly respond."

Elowen is capable of doing whatever is necessary to win, but she won't slaughter innocents. Families visiting soldiers on the front, healers working along the border, those people would stop her from following through. I've always thought fate to be a spiteful bitch, but Elowen being the person to share a bond with five dragons is a rare mercy.

"All magic has a signature that other mages can sense. It's like signing a letter. In rare cases that signature can be hidden but it's highly unusual. If Thirwen was controlling those beasts, the mage will be able to confirm."

Still, something is off. If this was an act of war, and our enemies were targeting us knowing we weren't protected by our army, they'd have made themselves known. They'd either have attacked us directly or run from the forest to escape the dragonfire.

"Your Highness, welcome ho—"

"Were you able to see through the portal?" I ask.

"Yes, sire. The portal is transparent to Asena and me because we conjured it."

"So you witnessed the attack?" He nods in response. "Were you able to sense any magic when you opened the portal?"

Ophir's brows furrow. "No, sire. Godly land has felt more volatile since the dragons have been released, but we all believe that's the cause of the imbalance. Dragons haven't existed since the gods left us."

Elowen huffs and looks toward the sky. "So you don't believe anyone was controlling the netherwraiths?"

"No, Your Highness, but they are known to live in the Sweven and Terrwyn forests. They must've followed the scent of blood straight to your kingdom."

"They don't travel through the . . ." She drums her fingers against her lips. "Would it be possible for you to open a portal where the Caleum River curves through the mountains? It doesn't have to be large, just enough for me to see."

Ophir nods, closing his eyes and muttering a spell in Ravarian. Sparks and wisps gather around his fingertips, swirling through them like snakes as he parts the air and creates a portal no larger than the length of my sword. He continues his incantation, and the black and purple fade, revealing a clear picture of a forest.

"Sunlight." Elowen's hand latches on to mine. "The mist is gone."

"You sense no magic with this change to the mist?"

"No, sire. No living person would be able to lift it. The barriers were made by the gods and cannot be undone."

"Why now?" Elowen mumbles, more to herself than anyone.

"The magic left behind by the gods grows weaker every year," Ophir answers anyway. "This could be a result of that."

"You can close it, thank you," Elowen says, still lost in thought. I nod to the mage, and he bows before turning away and finding Asena amid the rows of people waiting for care. Castle healers have also joined them, and servants distribute bread and water.

"You all right, angel?"

"I don't like how they speak about the events in our lives as if they're determined by gods I don't believe in," she mutters. "Ailliard swore the mist would never fade, so I suppose I'm glad to have been right, but Sorin was uneasy the whole time we were in godly land. He could barely tolerate landing."

"They're fanatics. It could rain and they'll say it's because a god is crying or pissing." The dried blood on her cheeks cracks when she laughs wearily. "But at least it wasn't an act of war."

She nods, still not looking fully convinced. "I'm going to write to the queen of Galakin tomorrow and have Asena send it with magic so it arrives instantly. It may not have been done by Thirwen's or Imirath's hand, but every day that passes is another pushing us closer to the inevitability."

CHAPTER
EIGHTEEN

ELOWEN

M Y DRAGONS WEAVE THROUGH THE APPROACHING storm clouds, their vibrant scales a stark contrast to the frothy gray domain, but they never go far enough to cross the Imirath border. Despite the impending war, the Vareveth war camp is just as relaxed as it's always been. Soldiers congregate around firepits while stirring pots of stew, sharpening their weapons, and laughing while trading stories and drinks.

"I received a . . . concerning report today from a spy," Saskia says, the wind carrying the scent of her jasmine-scented soap as she loops her arm through mine, which is probably for the best considering how exhausted I am. For the most part, the roads through the war camp are dry, but there are some muddy puddles I'd rather not step in. I spent nearly all night tending to the wounded with Nyrinn while the others oversaw settling my people in their new homes. The images of the attack haunted me as I tried to sleep. Not everyone who made it through the portal survived. The antidote for netherwraith venom doesn't always work depending on how far gone someone is. No matter how much people begged me as they faded before my eyes, I can't perform miracles, regardless of how much I wish I could.

"Where are they stationed?"

"Imirath," she whispers, her dark eyes scanning the area. My steps slow, and I huddle closer to her. "A border scout reported seeing large cages being transported throughout the kingdom."

"Cages?" My brows furrow. "How large? What was in them?"

"She couldn't get close enough. They're covered in tarps but there were no sounds to give away what's within. If they're hiding beasts or monsters, I imagine they used silencing runes as they did on the dragon chamber. The cages are under heavy guard and wheeled by ten soldiers each." She looks around again. "They're coming for you, Elowen. This war is personal."

Garrick knows he'll never be able to defeat me with ordinary swords. Whatever beasts he has, they will never surpass the power of a dragon. This war has been personal from the moment he dragged me away from them and forced me to listen to their screams. "Good. It saves me the task of seeking them out if they're brave enough to face me on the field."

"What if there was a way to see inside the cages?" she asks. "Would you be willing to try?"

"Of course." I reach beneath my cloak to tug my pendant along its chain. "But you know I can't sneak over again. Their defenses will be strengthened, same as ours."

"I'm not talking about that." She looks around again before pulling me into a tent filled with rows of shields and various weaponry but, thankfully, no people. "How old were you when you fled Imirath?"

"Eleven."

Her dark eyes sparkle. "Magic manifests in a person when they're twelve. What if there is more to your bond than we know? Mages in Galakin wield fire but are not bonded to five dragons. They don't have the same connection to the element as you do. And there are those in Thirwen who can see through the eyes of their animal companions that they *share a bond with*."

"You . . ." I hesitate. "You believe I have magic? Wouldn't I know by now? You know . . . accidentally light something on fire when I'm angry, which is quite frequent."

"I think your bond became dormant due to separation—not broken, just dulled. All I'm saying is maybe you're able to do more than just ride."

I take hold of Saskia's arm, dragging her farther away from the opening, nestling us in a dark corner filled with barrels of spears. "Whether it be weapons or creatures in those cages, they'll be targeting my dragons and I'd rather be prepared. Asena might know something. I've been reading about dragons but there are missing details within the texts, and I don't know anything about awakening magic."

"We'll talk to her together but keep the details as limited as possible."

I nod. "Have you told Cayden yet?"

"Only about the cages, not about my suspicions regarding your abilities. I thought it best for you to talk about that together."

"Thank you." It's not that I planned on hiding it from Cayden, but I like feeling important enough to Saskia that she'd bring this directly to me.

"You're welcome." She smiles. "I'll do more research today. I have an extensive library in my home; so does Cayden. Between the two of us, I'm sure there's something to be uncovered." Her braids sway as she shakes her head. "Gods, I wish I had access to my father's library, though he'd probably throw me out before I ever crossed the threshold."

I've never understood why people have children if their hearts are so full of themselves that they don't have the room to fit someone else. "Was he cruel to you?"

She laughs but it's bitter and so unlike her. "He sold me into marriage with a man twice my age when I was fifteen. Ryder ran away with me before the ink on the betrothal agreement was dry."

A child.

"If you give me his address, I'll pass along your retribution." Saskia ventured into enemy territory for me, and I'd do the same for her without hesitation. I'll mount a dragon this very moment if she asks it of me.

She sighs. "For a man like him, the worst punishment is letting him live in his empty home without an heir to carry on the Neredras name."

There are so many girls who don't have the chance to be just that. To enjoy their girlhood before someone tries to take it from them and turn it into something ugly and weak. "There is an undeniable strength that comes from existing in a world that wasn't designed for you, and I think it's time we changed the way things are."

She reaches forward to squeeze my hand, but a dragon landing shakes the ground beneath us, cutting off whatever she was about to say. Several swords clatter on the ground, and the shadow of their wings spreads on the canvas like a figment conjured from darkness.

"The king has returned!" a soldier shouts. It's probably Venatrix that landed beside the tent then. She preens under his attention.

I didn't know Cayden had left the camp. He and Ryder were supposed to be going over battle plans before we meet with the Vareveth generals to discuss strategies. We step outside, and even from a distance, I can feel the tension radiating off him. He looks like he's ready to head into battle right this moment.

"Where is Elowen?" The words come out raspy and rushed.

"I'm here!" I stride forward, taking pity on the soldier grasping the reins of Cayden's horse, gaping at him in fear. "I didn't think we were meeting the generals until later." His hands latch on to my shoulders and slide down my arms as his gaze rakes over me, almost like he's searching for anything amiss. "What is it? Where did you ride from?"

He shakes his head and loops his arm around my back, tucking me close as he guides us toward our tent. The same one we've shared since the night I tracked Cayden to the border while he was executing the soldier who had plotted my assassination.

He stops short of the entrance to address one of the soldiers standing guard. "Nobody is to interrupt us unless it's absolutely necessary."

I slip between the tent flaps while untying my cloak. We haven't been here since before the heist, and I must admit that I've missed it. The castle is beautiful, but this place is far cozier. It's much more spacious now that Cayden's bed has been removed from the front room, and his desk has been added back into the bedroom that once only belonged to me. Well, I suppose it was his first considering he vacated it to give me a safe place to sleep.

He didn't change any of the feminine decor, and when I made a comment about how his soldiers would tease him when they learned of their leader sleeping in a bed of flowers, he merely shrugged and said, *If they could sleep in a bed beside a woman as beautiful as you, I highly doubt they'd even notice the flowers.*

I sink onto the couch stationed beside the firepit and warm my hands. "If this is about the cages, Saskia discussed them with me."

"The fucking cages." He huffs a humorless laugh. "That report was worthless. We were already anticipating Imirath finding a way to target you. If they didn't have anything noteworthy to say then they should've kept their ink off the page rather than endangering an entire chain of communication."

His hand dips into his coat before shrugging off the heavy fabric, draping it over a chair and dropping two pieces of folded parchment into my lap. "I wanted to make sure you heard it from me first."

I thickly swallow. "Are these from one of your spies then?"

He nods, claiming the chair across from me. "I have a chain of spies stationed within Imirath. A report was due so I rode to my tavern to retrieve it."

I slowly unfold the first to take in the contents, and read it twice to ensure I haven't made a mistake. "My father is taking a new wife in the coming weeks." Garrick never remarried after my dragons burned my mother and there were never even rumors of any mistresses. He's paranoid and lets his fear of the unknown rule him. He may seem formidable to the eyes of Ravaryn, but to me he'll always be a grown man who feared a little girl enough to lock her up.

"Read the next."

I do as he says, bracing myself for whatever's put him on high alert. Ice slides through my veins, freezing me from top to bottom. I should've known something like this was coming, and I don't know why the first thing I feel is . . . anger. Not relief like I once thought I would.

"He's promised their firstborn daughter to Thirwen's heir. That's how they're solidifying their alliance."

"And he means to replace you as heir with his firstborn son," Cayden says through a clenched jaw.

"He's going to have more children," I echo in a daze. I'll potentially have siblings. Innocents being born into a war-torn kingdom. "Oh, gods."

Male heirs are favored, but in certain cases, like Eagor's mother, a woman can ascend.

"*You* are the princess of Imirath. Rightful heir to the throne with a bond to five dragons and a marriage secured to the king of their enemy kingdom. People will pledge themselves to your name no matter what your father says."

"We will be fighting an endless war if he has a son before we kill him." I rip the papers in half and toss them into the fire, watching as the flames curl their edges until they're nothing more than dust.

"Whoever takes the throne after Garrick will always be threatened by your existence. They will never stop hunting you. Even if you withdraw your claim, you'll still be the rightful heir reigning in their bordering kingdom."

I rest my elbows on my bouncing knees. "What does the conflict between Imirath and Vareveth stem from? I know it had to do with disputes over magic and land, but there must be something more to poison two peoples against each other."

Imirath is technically accepting of water magic; it's not hard to understand given their capital is built upon a series of isles, but most mages keep to godly land. Their use of magic was limited in Imirath, and it created tension with Vareveth rulers who predated Eagor and let earth magic run rampant in the kingdom. When reading the myths of Ravaryn, I saw illustrations of mermaids sunning themselves on the black beaches of Imirath, shining with gold foil beside the lengthy text.

"Hatred can be inherited. It passes through bloodlines just as physical features and religion," Cayden says. "Many Imirath and Vareveth people have lost loved ones to the ongoing conflict and harbor malice over time."

"But the Crimson Tide War had a *cause*, even if it's disputed by both sides. If I'm to unite two kingdoms with a strong, shared hatred, I need to know the true origins."

"There was 'The Slaughter of the Seven,'" Cayden begins. "About three hundred years ago a group of Atarah princesses and princes were traveling to a summer palace close to the Vareveth border. The queen at the time had a total of ten children, and the three heirs closest in line to the throne remained in the capital to study politics and swordsmanship instead of attending the holiday. However, the seven never made it to the palace. Every beach and forest was searched but there was no trace of them. Many blamed the abduction or murder on Vareveth soldiers sneaking over the border because a scrap of a torn green cloak was found on a branch not far from the road."

"Gods," I mutter. "That's awful."

Cayden nods. "There was also cause for Vareveth to villainize Imirath. After the battles between the two kingdoms began, a Dasterian crown prince was captured and fell in love with a lowborn woman from Imirath who healed him. He was too valuable for Imirath to let him die. One night, she set him free from his cell and smuggled him a piece of parchment. He pinned a letter to his cell stating he wanted nothing to do with the war and was running away with this woman. Imirath sent hounds after them, favoring his death over losing him entirely. Both were torn to pieces, and parts of the prince were delivered to the Vareveth castle. Their tale is called 'The Pauper and Prince of Parts.'"

"Well, whoever coined that certainly has a way with words. I'm beginning to think there are no happy endings in this world." I shake my head. "And you think I should take the throne of Imirath? You think I can erase years upon years of hostility?"

"I want to make your father regret every wrong he ever dealt you and return it a thousandfold." He licks his lips and moves closer, not stopping until he's kneeling before me and clasping my hands in his.

I hate that they're shaking. It makes me feel as weak as I look. I've always wanted to be strong when facing Imirath, but sometimes it's like the mere mention of it reverts me into the little girl splitting her wrists open on her shackles as she tries and fails to claw her way to her dragons.

My dragons.

They'd be hunted, too, not just me.

"You are not the flaw in the family line like he tries to make everyone believe; you are the pinnacle. You are the only ruler I have ever believed in, and I put faith in nothing. It's true that Imirath and Vareveth have been enemies for centuries, but you are the first person to have a claim to both. You will never be able to eradicate the past, but you can promise these people a future."

"Imirath." I can practically taste the blood in my mouth, can smell it, can feel it. My thoughts keep coming, pummeling me into the ground and making my limbs feel boneless. I'm both light and heavy. Clammy and freezing. I feel like I need to run and like I already ran a mile. "They humiliated me in that castle."

"The people who were complicit in your torture will die." His voice is raw and rough. "I will kill any enemy and do whatever it takes to keep you alive. If you don't want to rule Imirath, I understand, but I want you to think about it before declining. When I took you to the village where I was born it . . . eased something in me. The pain is still there, but there is also happiness. You did that for me, and if you give me the chance, I'd like to do the same for you."

It's nearly impossible to think with a clear head when it comes to Imirath. I want to leave this tent and spend several days in the forest, not thinking, not speaking, just existing. My words are stuck in my throat like thousands of bees buzzing within a hive, but I don't have the energy to let them out. I can't live with the constant threat of Imirath, and it's not only my life I'm fighting for.

When I was in exile, I was told I'd never have an army large enough to take on Imirath, but I do now. I was told I'd never see my dragons again, but I freed them from the castle where my father cowers. I was prophesied to either be the salvation or doom of Imirath, but maybe those two paths are actually one. Perhaps the only way to be the salvation of Imirath is to doom the Atarah line. I'm tired of being viewed as a discarded princess, unwanted by her own father despite being his only living heir. Putting limits on myself never seems to work in anyone's favor, and perhaps I should prove that to Garrick one last time by taking what is owed to me.

"What if—" I get to my feet and begin pacing, my boots silenced by the rug. My fingers press into my forehead, and then slowly slide over to ease the pounding in my temple. "What if *I do* want more?"

"Whatever you want, we'll see it done."

I dip my hands beneath my curls to rest on the back of my neck. "What about Feynadra and Urasos? They both rest on our northern border and I doubt they'd like the idea of Imirath and Vareveth becoming one kingdom. There would be no barrier between them and the largest army in Ravaryn."

"To deny your claim to Imirath would be contradicting their own, and they'd like Garrick overtaking Vareveth far less. You do not have the reputation of a tyrant, but Garrick does. He continues to oppress the southern isles, which were once an independent kingdom before your great-grandsire conquered them. Both Feynadra and Urasos are notoriously neutral. The landscape of Urasos makes it nearly impossible to invade and Feynadra has a good relationship with Galakin— who you know hates Imirath—because their queens are sisters. Though Nasha is the queen of Feynadra and hates Thirwen because of the sister she lost, she doesn't have as much power as Cordelia because she married into her crown; Cordelia was born for hers."

"Be that as it may," I begin, "no ruler in Ravaryn will support how we gained Vareveth's crowns. Even a spark can light their world on fire."

"It's best to ignore the mumblings of a mindless mob built on tradition," Cayden states, resting his hands on the hilt of his blade as he watches me. "You and I were not raised as these people were. The world is controlled by people who believe they're important and broken by those who know they're not. My worth was not given, I made it with my blade, and if they stand against us, they'll soon realize their mistake."

I thread my hands through my curls again. "The people of Imirath have been conditioned to hate me for years. I doubt they'll be secretly stitching banners with our sigil, waiting for me to return."

His gaze takes on that calculating gleam. "There is another matter I need to discuss with you."

"Well, it's not as if this one is resolved."

"No." He drapes my cloak over my shoulders. "But this could influence it."

CHAPTER

NINETEEN

CAYDEN

ORMALLY INTRODUCING ELOWEN TO THE GENERALS WAS
not the only reason I wanted Elowen to come here. Last night,
a group of four Imirath soldiers tried to sneak over the border.
It was reported that they never struggled. I've spent the greater part of
the last several years in a war camp, and most prisoners I've come
across will hurtle any insult with the hope of obtaining a quick death.
In some cases, they remain silent, but never have I known a guilty
party to lay down their swords the moment they're found.

I place my hand on Elowen's back as a series of freestanding cells
that serves as a prison looms into view. My expression is dark, my
glare sharp, ensuring none of the prisoners we pass jeer at Elowen as I
escort her. My boots sink in the mud when we stop at our intended
destination. The soldier guarding the entrance bows and tucks his
smoke between his lips before unlocking the door. The scents of
human waste and body odor sting my nose, but it's nowhere near as
pungent as the enclosed dungeon beneath the castle.

The captives quickly scramble to their knees when we step inside,
though their wrists are chained to individual posts, making their
movements awkward and sloppy. Questioning prisoners isn't exactly
what I want to be doing right now, but Elowen needs to hear this. The
Imirath throne is hers, and I won't let someone who will continue to
send assassins after her take it.

"I'm assuming you knew the consequences of trespassing in our land when you took this mission?"

"Mercy, sire."

I don't respond to his plea, utilizing my silence to heighten his fear. A shadow overtakes the cage as Venatrix lands behind it, an eerie clicking noise vibrating her throat as she lowers her face to the bars stretching across the top. The prisoners whimper, and my lip curls when the sharp tang of urine is added to the already abysmal aroma.

"We won't waste time dragging information out of infantry soldiers," Elowen says, her eyes dancing over their simple armor as Venatrix growls. Her crimson gaze is locked on the bars that separate her from Elowen, and I won't be surprised if she destroys it with her fangs. "Speak in this moment or die in the next."

"There has been unrest in the Imirath camp ever since the dragons were freed. Many of us believe their release to be a sign of favor from the gods. To fight against you would be to wage war on them."

I never thought I'd rely on religious fanatics to establish a point to Elowen, but I'll take it. "*State* your mission. I will not ask again."

"To—" The soldier hesitates, and I rest my hand on the hilt of my sword. "To kill the queen."

Elowen closes her eyes briefly, accepting the reality of our position. Her father will never stop. Whoever he appoints as a successor will never stop.

I've always been protective of her, and yet the anger that surges through me whenever someone levels an insult or a threat at her will always catch me off guard. It's a living thing inside me. An unquenchable need to eliminate the danger before it finds her.

I step in front of Elowen, cutting off her view of the captives, and bend down to whisper in her ear. "Walk down to the road. I'll be there in a few moments."

Her brows crease. "What are you planning?"

"Trust me?"

She purses her lips and hums while narrowing her eyes but spins on her heels and exits the cell. I gesture for the soldier guarding the entrance to unlock the prisoners from their posts while keeping my gaze on Elowen. Her presence is already growing a crowd. The cold chains bite into my flesh when I tighten my grip and escort the prisoners into the road, forcing them to kneel in the freezing mud.

More of my soldiers stop what they're doing to watch, forming a circle around the display. Ryder shoves his way through the crowd to stand beside Elowen, scanning the area to ensure she's safe.

"I'll allow you to keep your lives if you denounce your allegiance to Garrick Atarah." If I kill them right now, they'd be martyrs, their deaths inspiring further hatred, and if Elowen is to take the throne, we must be more strategic.

There is more than one way to fight a war, and yet manipulation is so often overlooked in favor of blades and blood.

"We denounce all allegiance to Garrick Atarah," the prisoners say in unison.

I unsheathe a knife from my thigh and slice their palms open one at a time. "Swear your allegiance through a blood oath. If you break your word, death will follow."

"We swear to you, my king, and to our queen. The rightful heir of Imirath," one of the prisoners says, and the other three press their bound hands to the ground to let their blood soak into the earth, repeating the same oath as the magic takes hold.

"Transport them for further questioning and surveillance," I command two soldiers. I highly doubt they'll know anything noteworthy but it's a waste to not inquire. "See to it that any part of their armor bearing the Atarah sigil is thrown over the border. Let their soldiers see how quick those in their army will betray King Garrick."

"Yes, my king."

The prisoners go without a fight, and the soldiers around us begin cheering. Word of this will spread; it's why I wanted them to offer their oaths in public. Garrick will most likely strengthen the security on his border, not wanting to let others slip through, but that will only inspire hatred within. He caged Elowen as a child, and soon he'll be forced to cage his citizens. It'll make him look weak and panicked.

The people of Imirath will relate to her through Garrick's actions. It'll make them favor her.

I'll utilize every advantage offered and remove the crown from Garrick's head myself. He will pay for all he's done, and he will regret the day he made an enemy of me.

Venatrix cries out, sounding impatient, and Elowen juts her chin to the dragon, a question in her eyes. Though I want her to stay so we can continue our discussion, she needs to form her own thoughts in regard to reclaiming her birthright, so I nod and watch as she disappears into the crowd.

CHAPTER
TWENTY

CAYDEN

A MASK COVERS THE LOWER HALF OF MY FACE AS I WEAVE through the streets of Verendus. Restless energy pounds through me and has only grown stronger as I await Elowen's return, knowing she's pondering Imirath's succession. I'd have gone mad if I remained in the tent or returned to the castle. In the past, I'd pick up extra jobs when darkness cloaked the sky, often fulfilling multiple assassinations within a night, but I haven't since I became commander. Well, at least not for profit.

Wind howls through the narrow roads, carrying a rotten smell with it. It's far worse in the summer, but it's still not pleasant in winter. The dilapidated buildings lean against one another to keep themselves standing, only adding to the unwelcoming aura this place gives off. Nobody who lives here wants to. I turn down the alley beside the tavern and reach for the key ring looped onto my belt, flicking through them until I find the small brass one.

The back entrance to the Demon's Den creaks open, and my boots vibrate with the cheers resounding against the basement ceiling. I roll my neck and crack my knuckles before forcing myself to turn in the opposite direction.

The place is doused in darkness, considering no worker has access to the upper floor, and I pull the matches off the shelf where I keep them and light the lanterns around my office. The shutters are still open from when I was here earlier today, and I pause only briefly when a dragon cries out in the distance.

A sharp, patterned knock brings my attention back into the room. "Enter," I say, turning away from the sky and taking a seat behind my desk. Alexus slips in, a bag slung over his shoulder most likely containing his servant uniform. He may have changed his clothes, but garlic and wine still waft off him. "What position did you secure this time?"

"Butler." He drops the bag to the floor and takes the seat across from me. "Nobles make it so easy. All I have to do is stand in the corner with a pitcher of wine while they bitch and moan."

"So they've been vocal?"

"Oh, they're opinionated, as all entitled people are." He gestures toward the whiskey I keep on my desk, pouring himself a glass after I nod. "But they're terrified to mobilize. They have hired guards, but everyone knows a sellsword's loyalty is to their coin first."

"Their arrogance will win the battle against logic, as it so often does with lords." I lean back in my chair. "Once they meet, it'll be all the proof I need to execute those who refuse to bend the knee without risking a rebellion."

Alexus nods. "I'll get word to you the moment I hear of them gathering. I imagine it'll be soon; their hatred grows by the hour."

Then it's my personal goal to increase that to every minute that ticks by. "If you have nothing else to report you can return to your position."

Alexus throws back his whiskey and I toss him one of my smokes. He lights it in the lantern before tucking it between his lips and slipping soundlessly into the hall. A sword isn't the ender of men; it's their mouths. The nobles have made the mistake of thinking they're invaluable to the kingdom, but I'll end them all if it suits my purpose.

Before I was king of Vareveth, I was king of the bastards.

I move to the window, raking a hand through my hair and down my face. *Fuck.* I can still smell her on the tips of my fingers from when I touched her hair earlier. In the midst of the slums, sweat, and smoke, she's there. The only life in an endless sea of death. A flower growing in a graveyard. The scent of her is enough to spark a need to find her, to pull her close until she surrenders her anger and gives me *everything*.

I grip the railing, deeply inhaling in an attempt to quell the pounding in my head. My patience is practically nonexistent, and I know I need to get ahold of myself before I see her again. I'm tortured by the memory of her beneath me, her curls fanning across the pillows and my chest in the aftermath. Her taste.

Gods, her taste.

The door slams open behind me, and the steel of my sword sings against its sheath as I draw it. A sharp yelp fills the air as Ryder homes in on the tip stopping an inch in front of his face. I roll my eyes, sheathing the blade once more. "Knock next time."

"Is that how you answer the door to your house? No wonder you don't get any visitors."

"Is there something you need?"

"Why are you angrier than usual?" he asks, draping his limbs over my desk chair and indulging in the whiskey. "Could it have something to do with a raven-haired woman who flew away?"

"Her hair isn't raven." When she steps into the sun it's clear that it's the darkest shade of brown.

"Right, well, can't say I've paid close attention to Elowen's features." He sighs. "I'm not going away until you tell me what happened."

"You never go away." I clench my jaw and tuck my tongue into the side of my cheek. "Garrick is getting remarried and means to replace Elowen as his heir."

Ryder's face sobers at that, sitting up straight and placing his feet on the ground. I think having a younger sister makes him naturally protective of Elowen, especially considering she and Saskia have grown close. "Her only option is to take Imirath. She'll never be safe if she doesn't, nor would any of your heirs, considering they'd also have a claim to the throne."

Gods, I don't want to think about heirs. My concerns begin and end with Elowen. There's no need to complicate matters. Not to mention I have the nurturing capacity of a rock. I can't risk a child—our child at that—being a casualty of my inability to love properly. "She knows that."

"The Vareveth army is unwaveringly loyal to you, and to Elowen by extension. You rose in ranks beside them, bled on the same fields as them. Give the command and the throne will be taken."

"Battles will be fought, and many will die no matter what Elowen decides. It's not a matter of succession."

"You could take the throne, birthright or not." Ryder rises from the chair to stand beside me, and his eyes that usually dance with mirth are unwaveringly serious. "We chose you as our leader long before you took Eagor's throne. Not because you were born into it, but because you were a person worth following. You never needed to tell anyone where you come from for us to know you were different. You are the first commander to bring war to Imirath and the first king in our history to take your crown through an act of rebellion. The soldiers—all the hard battle-worn bastards—worship you like you're some kind of god when you lead a charge that every other king would watch from behind their armies if they were even present."

I face the city again, overlooking the sloped roofs as smoke rises from chimneys, mingling with the snow and disappearing. As a boy I remember watching the same sight, the fires that would never warm me while I didn't know if I'd survive another night, wanting to become no more than a shadow. In the dark, my need for vengeance grew and festered like an untreated wound. In the absence of mercy, I became someone who would never need it.

I crack my knuckles and move to open the trunk in the corner to retrieve a mask, bandanna, and tonic. Ryder's statement hangs in the air, but I won't be another man to use Elowen to his advantage, and I will not plot the events of this war without her. I know Ryder means no harm in encouraging me to take the throne, but things are different now. I have someone to lose if I act only out of selfishness, and I don't want Elowen to be a casualty of my deceit. I lift the small vial to my lips and toss it back, letting the evidence of my past slashed into my flesh disappear. Violence is all I've ever known, and before Elowen it was all I had. The presence of pain became normal, and I don't know how to live without it.

When thoughts of Garrick surge, it drags up old memories I don't want to think about. I take one last look out the window in the direction of Imirath. By the end of this war, I'll hoist my enemy's daughter above the ruins of his reign and make him feel just as powerless as he once made me feel.

CHAPTER
TWENTY-ONE

ELOWEN

OCEAN SPRAY DOTS MY CHEEKS AS ANOTHER TOWERING wave crashes into the black cliffs beneath Delmira's talons. Moonlight dances on the ocean's unruly surface, and my dragons fly among the waves, dragging their claws through the frothy crests before twirling beneath the stars.

We've flown so far that I don't even know if I'm still in Vareveth or if I've ventured into Imirath, and yet I feel no different. There once was a time that the mere thought of Imirath would send me into a downward spiral. I still don't think of it with happiness or ease, but traveling to Zinambra softened something within me. I close my eyes, picturing myself sitting in a café beside one of the canals as the summer sun shines. My dragons love being close to water, and I think they'd love being in a city with so much of it. Cayden spent some of his childhood there, and I wonder if he misses it at all.

I suppose I never had the chance to love it, or to take pride in the kingdom where I was born. The people are not my enemies, only those who had a hand in the torture my dragons and I underwent. Garrick has attempted to kill me on numerous occasions. I don't even remember them all. There is nothing more important to him than his crown, so much so that he abused his only daughter because of a prophecy. His new wife may give him a son, but no matter how many children she gives him, I will not let him erase me. I will not let him take more from me than he already has.

Imirath is my birthright. He can make plans for the future of it, but so can I, because the throne is mine.

Beyond the sandy shore, trees stretch for miles and miles, and the same snowy mountain range I see through the windows in my bed-chamber pierces the sky. This could all be mine. I don't want to be the damnation of Imirath, but I never thought I could be its salvation. If I were to fly my dragons above their kingdom and burn it to the ground, I'd be no better than my father. Orphans would regard me as Cayden regards Garrick, a tyrant who killed their parent and made them brave the cruel world before they were ready.

I'm now the queen of Vareveth, betrothed to its king, and I want Garrick to understand the consequences of my rise to power. It means the downfall of his.

Delmira's wings flap impatiently, most likely sensing my change in emotion through the bond, and I click my tongue. Wind howls in my ears and slices at my cheeks as she dives off the cliff, veering to the left to fly just above the surface. My eyes slip shut as I command her to take me home, letting the sky embrace me like an old friend despite the biting temperature.

Fear and tragedy shape us just as much as love and happiness do, whether we wish them to or not. They force us to become wary and jaded toward a world we once viewed with innocent eyes. The world is beautiful. It's the people who inhabit it who make it unbearable at times. Finding the light in the dark is something I've done for years, looking for the silver lining no matter how minuscule.

Delmira lands, but before I open my eyes, the smell alone gives away that we're not at the castle. I don't recognize this part of Veren-dus. It's darker, cramped, and reeks of booze, garbage, and things I'd rather not identify. The sound of glass bottles breaking echoes throughout the curved streets, as do drunken slurring and unintelli-gible shouts.

"Delmira, my darling girl, have you lost your navigational skills? Perhaps your sanity?" Her blue scales that are as light as a summer day have shifted to black. It's probably the only reason people didn't scream as she dipped from the sky, but it's only a matter of time before someone spots her in the shadowed alley. "Home. Take me home."

She huffs impatiently and arches her back, causing my saddle straps to strain as I'm briefly thrust into the air. "Delmira! I will not give you any fresh meat—only carrots."

She bucks again, much more forcefully, and lowers her wing to the ground so I'm able to climb off. I roll my eyes and unhook myself, sliding down until my boots smack against the cobblestones.

"Just so you know, I'm not dressed for this." I gesture toward my outfit. It's like what I wore to Aestilian, made of dark blue fabric but embellished with a mixture of white and light blue beading, and trimmed in white fur to match my cloak. It flows behind my calves like a dress while still granting me access to my knife-clad legs covered in black pants to match my boots and waist belt.

Sighing, I yank up my hood and assess my surroundings, pointing toward a puddle a rat scurries through. "Is that my new bathing chamber? You really have an eye for decadence, Delly."

She stomps her feet and nudges me toward the back entrance of the building, and, accepting the task my pushy dragon is forcing upon me, I reach for the lockpicks in my boot. I hum to myself while slipping them inside the keyhole, utilizing the technique Cayden showed me. My breath puffs in front of my lips as I try to turn the picks but meet resistance each time.

Delmira huffs again and shoves me with her snout before sinking her fangs into the wood, biting out a huge chunk, and swallowing—doorknob included. The creak sounds more like a scream as the half-eaten door swings open, making me cringe.

"Subtle . . . and highly nutritional."

I pull one of my dragon daggers from the sheath on my thigh and hook a black mask over my ears while entering the dark stairwell. The door swings open again as I try to close it, but thankfully Delmira didn't eat the deadbolt, so I slide that in place and disregard the fact that more than half the wood is missing. It's someone else's problem.

She flies away as noise pulses against the bottom of my boots, so I turn in that direction to seek out the source. I can't see the bottom of the stairs through the darkness, but I keep my hand on the wall to steady my footing. A sliver of light bleeds into the opaque shadows along the floor, and I continue sliding my hand along the smooth wood. My eyes adjust given the meager light, and I wrap my fingers around a lever, yanking it up to pry open the hidden door.

The energy of the room swallows me like an oncoming wave I have no hope of fleeing. The mixed scents of blood and sweat hang heavy in the air, accompanied by smoke that casts a haze over the basement and rises to the cracked wooden beams above. Nobody notices me as I close the door behind me; they keep their focus entirely on the two men pounding their fists into each other in a single raised ring.

I step farther into the room, and my boots stick to the floor in what I *hope* is spilled ale. If I'm wrong, I don't want to know.

"I was wondering when you'd find your way here." A hand wraps around my wrist, and I jut the tip of my knife between the person's ribs. "Do me a favor, sunshine, and don't let him see you pointing that thing at me. I fear he'll throw me into the ring, and I quite like my face as it is."

I lift my gaze, staring into an unfamiliar pair of blue eyes shadowed by the brim of a cap. The man is also wearing a mask, which muffles his voice, but it's so . . . familiar. I retract the knife. "Ryder?"

He lifts a finger to his mouth. "No names. Why are you here? Did something happen?"

A tugging sensation sends my gaze back to the ring, and my shoulders stiffen further when I realize it's not simply two fighters in there . . . one of them is Cayden. This must be the business he owns. The tonic he told me about makes him almost unrecognizable at first glance. His hair and most of his face are covered, but he's still just as tall and muscular. His skin is free of the scars and ink I've become familiar with, the markings that make him the man I know him to be.

Home.

Delmira took me *home.*

"No, everything is fine."

The opponent slams his fist into Cayden's ribs, and I suck in a breath as if I'm the one who's taking the hit. He easily could have dodged it. I've seen him take on several soldiers at once and come out without a scratch. Cayden dodges the next hit, but leaves his bad shoulder open, letting his opponent take advantage of the vulnerability.

"Why is he doing this?" Blood beads under my nails from where I dig them into my palms. "You know he could easily beat this man."

"He could easily beat anyone who steps into that ring." Ryder wraps his arm around my torso to keep me from fighting my way to the ring.

"You both have made enough money."

"It's not only about the money anymore," he says.

"What do you mean?"

Ryder shakes his head while turning back to Cayden. "He could've stopped fighting once he became commander. I even brought up the possibility of selling this place to protect him from those who would pry into his past when he ascended in rank, but violence is how he copes. Cayden is always in pain and he's not the type to talk about whatever is happening in his head."

I cringe when Cayden takes another hit to his ribs. "But why does he take so many hits?"

"Coping isn't always pretty." He jostles me a bit in a brotherly way, pulling me closer into his side as the crowd becomes rowdier. "He's fine. He's much better since he met you. He'll probably love that you're watching once he realizes so take a breath and let him make a few more syndrils to pay for the ring he's going to put on your finger."

I take a deep breath despite the air having a bitter tang to it and laugh weakly. The white wrappings on his knuckles are splattered with blood, and sweat glides down his chiseled torso, making my body heat. Something else courses through me when I realize I'm not the only one who notices. He's beautiful in the ring, moving with a grace so few ever master.

Nearly all the women in the crowd watch him with desire written plainly on their faces. Do they linger when he finishes? Do they touch him as he walks through the crowd? Has he been with any of them before? I don't know this part of his life. I don't know this version of him. But I want to.

I take a step away from Ryder, submitting to the pull that has drawn me to Cayden since I met him, and it's as if that one movement triggered something in him because his gaze collides with mine. His eyes are unhinged and filled with so much malice that it sends a chill through me. Whoever he's fighting isn't who he sees in his mind. He can temporarily erase the scars from his skin, but he can't extract the memories that make healed wounds bleed. He does a double take, his brows coming together like he truly doesn't believe I'm here as he shoves his opponent back by the shoulders.

He makes his next move faster than I can blink, slamming his fist into the side of the man's face, sending him tumbling to the ground where he remains as Cayden ducks through the ropes. The roar of the crowd is deafening, but instead of flocking to him as I suspected they would, they do the opposite. His dark gaze never leaves mine as he stalks toward me like no force in this world could alter his course.

"That's five wins for the Viper! Collect your winnings at the window and place your bets for the next fight," the announcer calls out.

My stomach sinks.

Five fights.

Did speaking about the Imirath throne trigger this?

I barely have time to soak in the sight of him once he's close enough. He throws me over his shoulder and I'm hardly able to hear Ryder laughing over the blood rushing to my ears as Cayden carries me away. He slips through the hidden door and sets me on my feet before ripping his mask off. He crowds my space not a moment later, and my back presses into the wood.

"Why are you here? Did something happen?" His breathing is labored, and he carefully reaches forward to unhook my mask, not that it truly makes a difference. The most I can see is his silhouette, but I prefer it this way, considering he took the feature-altering tonic.

"I'm not hurt." I dig my nails into the door, tilting my head back as his breath fans against my lips. "Why did you come here?"

"I had to meet with Alexus."

"You know that's not what I'm asking." Ryder and I already spoke about this, but I need to hear it from him. "Why were you fighting?"

When he speaks his voice is a deep rumble that I feel in the marrow of my bones. "It quiets my mind."

I swallow. "Does anything else quiet your mind?"

He moves one arm above my head, undoing the clasp on my cloak with his other hand, letting it slide off my shoulders before wrapping his fingers around my throat. "It's quiet right now." His thumb settles over my jumping pulse point.

I try to find relief by dropping my gaze, but there's none. I can't see his eyes, and yet they still burn into mine. He's always been able to do that. To see me when no one else can. Cayden is bound to me in the same way the moon and stars are bound to the night: we remain together no matter how much darkness surrounds us.

"I—" My throat is so dry it's nearly painful to speak.

"You're trembling." His hand moves from my throat to glide down my arm. I've always hated how visible my anxiety is. "Are you frightened?"

"I think so," I whisper, and his hand stops moving as he stiffens. "Not of you, but of what I need to say to you."

He cradles my face, keeping me close as if it's impossible for him to let me go. His thumb brushes over my bottom lip, and my eyes slip shut. I can tell his mouth is so close, and I'm so tempted to close the distance, but his warmth is suddenly ripped from me as he links our hands and tugs me off the wall.

"We'll talk in my office." I yelp as he scoops me in his arms and begins climbing up the steps. "Did anyone see you without your mask?"

"No. I kept it on the whole time I was here."

"Good. Nobody would forget a face like yours if they saw it. Trust me, I know." I'm thankful he's not able to see the flush creeping up my neck just yet.

Oh, gods.

Delmira ate *his* door.

Cayden's steps slow when we reach the first landing, and I inspect my nails after side-eyeing the door and blowing out a breath. "You should really take better care of your investments. This place is falling apart."

"There are bite marks in the wood," he flatly states.

"Listen, I won't judge you if you got a bit hungry but perhaps next time you could try something with sugar in it."

He sighs as we continue our ascent. "What did I say all those months ago about that prissy royal attitude?"

That I've mastered it. "Something about it being one of your favorite things about me."

"You must not have very many good qualities to choose from then."

He laughs at my annoyed huff and opens a door at the very top. The narrow hall has a few other doors within it, but he guides me through the first. It's small but practical, with sparse office furniture in various shades of wood and a few ledgers neatly stacked behind the desk. The red-and-black rug underfoot has seen better days, but I can see why he designed this place as he did. Nothing in here aside from the whiskey reminds me of him.

He sets me down and I turn to face him, but suck in a sharp breath while stumbling into a chair. Noticing straightaway, his brows furrow above a pair of *brown* eyes. He moves to place his hand on my shoulder, but I'm unable to stop myself from flinching. I never imagined what his face would look like without the scar. I suppose it makes him look more classically handsome, but he's always been beautiful to me, and I prefer him with it.

"What is it?"

"You—" I shake my head. "You don't look like—" *my Cayden.*

His confusion clears and he turns away to pull a vial from the trunk in the corner, swallowing the orange fizzy liquid encased within. My lips part as the scars on his back slowly re-form, and when he turns back around my shoulders loosen. He throws a shirt over his head as I pour him a glass of water from the pitcher on a small table.

He regards me curiously. "What did you want to talk about?"

I look around, but there aren't many places to sit, and I'd rather not conduct this conversation from stiff chairs. I take the glass from his hand and take a few sips before handing it back. His lips quirk up in a familiar way that eases my nerves slightly, and I pull at the fur on my sleeve while walking to the open window.

"So this is your business?"

He raises his brows and tucks a hand into his pocket as he moves to stand beside me. "The Demon's Den."

I laugh softly, cutting my eyes to him before overlooking the city. "Subtle."

He shrugs. "Subtler than the way you're trying to stall."

My teeth sink into my lower lip, and I force myself to swallow through my tight throat. "I spent most of my life seeking love from a place of pain, so I think I stopped expecting it as a way to cope. But the more pain I experienced, the more I craved love, and the more desperate I became. I didn't realize how far gone I was. It felt as if I was constantly reaching out my hand and only realized the pain I was in when all my fingers were broken, my skin was marred with blood, and I had nothing left to give." It began before Ailliard. I remember clinging to the bars of my cell while I cried out for a mother who never came. "So when you hurt me, I thought shutting you out was the best way to protect myself. I've always been told the depth in which I feel things is a weakness and that it's best to keep weaknesses hidden."

"I don't want you to hide a single part of yourself from me," Cayden says, curling his hands over the window ledge. He tilts his head down so I'm able to look into his eyes. "I adore everything about you, even the traits you despise."

I nod, hanging onto his reassurance like a lifeline. "I miss you."

His features contort in pain as his gaze flashes to my lips. "I've always been here."

"But I need more." I briefly close my eyes to subdue the burning within them. "If I'm to be vulnerable with you again, I need you to do the same. If I'm to take the Imirath throne with you by my side, I need to be able to fully trust you. If you always wear a piece of armor when you're alone with me then I'll always expect a battle."

"I never intended to make you feel that way," he answers gently, his eyes softening. "I've just lived without vulnerability for so long that I don't remember what it's like to not be burdened by caution."

"You know what happened to me when I was a child. You tortured one of Garrick's guards, you heard the tales of the tortured princess, and you've pulled me through my panic." I take a deep breath, urging myself to continue. "You keep imploring me to communicate with you, but I won't be able to until you climb the wall you keep between us and meet me on the other side. I want to know you, Cayden. I want to know that you trust me enough to tell me the things that have shaped you into the man you are today. I don't ever want to be blindsided by anything when it pertains to you again."

"You want me to tell you about my past," he states without emotion. "You want to know why I hate Garrick aside from the scar on my face and him murdering my mother."

"Yes."

A muscle flutters in his jaw, and he tucks his tongue into the side of his cheek as he weighs my words. He's looking at me like I'm his favorite puzzle in need of solving, bright green eyes tracing my features and the fingers wrapped around my pendant. He nods more to himself than to me, like he's come to a conclusion within the confines of his mind.

Several beats pass, and though his face doesn't change, his fingers lace through mine.

CHAPTER
TWENTY-TWO

CAYDEN

I'VE NEVER FORGOTTEN WHO I AM, OR THE EVENTS THAT OC-curred that shaped me into the man I am today. If you always remember who you are, nobody can use it against you. Dirt and blood are caked beneath my broken nails from clawing my way to the top, to rise above those who would look down upon me, and time has taught them to fear my name.

After donning my cloak and a fresh mask, I lead Elowen down the steps and retrieve hers. I pull the hood up as she hooks her face covering over her ears and we exit the building through the half-eaten door.

"Get on the horse," I say, jutting my chin toward where Koa's tied to a post. My muscles are tired from the ring, but I hoist the hefty crates to block the gaping hole. Ryder will repair it before he leaves, but I don't want to leave it like this. I itch to grab a smoke as memories resurge, but I push the craving away and swing myself up behind Elowen. It's late, so the streets are empty aside from a few loiterers swaying as they walk, too deep in their cups to realize who we are. "What exactly do you want to know?"

"Why were your parents on the run from Garrick?"

Screams.

They blast through my skull whenever I think of my mother.

I don't remember the shade of blond her hair was or the dresses she used to wear. I only know the color of her eyes because they're exactly the same as mine, and sometimes when I look at my eyes in the mirror, all I can recall is watching the light leave hers.

Every other feature I have is entirely my father—and it sickens me. I was designed to hate myself.

"Me," I say without emotion. "My mother was a lady-in-waiting to yours, and my father was a palace guard assigned to her. They couldn't be together publicly; it would've been seen as a betrayal to Garrick and Isira because my father was well beneath her station. My mother was from a noble Imirath family, but they refused to take her in after she fled the castle pregnant with the bastard of a bastard from the southern isles without lands or a title."

"Did you try to contact your family when you were on your own? Either side?" Elowen asks quietly.

"No. No matter how cold or hungry I was, I was steadfast in my decision. My mother was the only person in this world who loved me, and I'd rather have died than betray her memory. She'd have wanted me to go to them if it meant getting off the streets and not succumbing to a life of crime, but even knowing that, I couldn't." The thought of sitting at the table of those who cast her aside seemed worse than killing someone for money. "This is something I should've told you earlier. Garrick wouldn't have cared about who I was when I was a commander because I ascended in rank through merit, but royals hate bastards because it shakes the foundation they stand upon. He will recognize my surname and try to turn people against us."

"Well, I've always found most people to either be entirely dull or entirely idiotic so it's best to ignore whatever they think," she says, and wraps my arm tighter around her when I chuckle. "Garrick won't remember the name of a castle guard—"

"I took my mother's name, not my father's." She gave birth to me and raised me, and I never wanted to be associated with my father once I got away from him. "I suppose my true name is Cayden—"

"Veles," she cuts me off. "You are Cayden Veles. That is who you will always be."

I've suppressed both feelings and memories for so long that they don't even feel like they belong to me anymore. It feels as if I'm telling the story of someone else's life. But something in my chest tightens when the adamancy laced within her tone pronounces words I never thought I'd hear.

"I can be an Atarah if taking a royal name makes this easier. The Atarah line has ruled over Imirath for centuries."

She cranes her neck to face me, though I can see only her eyes, considering the hood and mask she wears. "All you'd be doing is taking the name of a man you despise after forsaking your own father's."

I grit my teeth. "My pride is not worth your pain."

Her eyes soften and I grip the reins tighter. Eagor's father wasn't a Dasterian, just as King Erix of Galakin wasn't an Ilaria; they took their queens' names to prolong the legacy. Cayden Atarah. It makes me want to get back in the ring and punch someone until my knuckles are busted to the bone. But I'd do it . . . for Elowen, I would.

She strokes her thumb over my wrist. "I've never been my father's daughter, never belonged anywhere or to anyone, and I know I'll never meet your mother, but I'd like to keep her name alive to thank her."

My brows draw together. "Thank her?"

"Were it not for her, I never would have met you."

I don't realize how hard I pull on the reins until the horse stops in the center of the road bordered by snow-coated evergreens as we cross into Ladislava. If Elowen noticed our path leading away from the castle, she hasn't made it known. She pulls off her mask now that we're alone and my eyes fall to her lips as if they've whispered an enchantment to always command my gaze.

"What is it? I thought you'd be pleased."

"I am." I jostle the reins to command my horse to trot again. I don't understand how almost nobody in her life has held on to her. Her presence alone is enough to make me, a man I thought beyond redemption, grasp at morality just to have at least a sliver of my soul be good enough for her. "You are never getting away from me, *Elowen Veles.*"

Gods.

I'll never get over how good that sounds.

She smiles while facing forward again, taking a deep breath as she relaxes against me. I lick my lips, urging the horse faster as I continue wading through my memories, watching small flakes of snow slowly float down. "My father stood there while Imirath soldiers dragged my mother out of our house by her hair. She begged me to stay hidden when she heard them coming, but I remembered where my father hid his sword." The blade was far heavier than all the sticks I'd practiced with, but I was desperate. "I disarmed the man holding the sword to her neck, but another took his place. She died, choking on her own blood, watching while they sliced my face open.

"My father begged on his knees for his life while I killed the soldier who cut me." There was so much blood, I remember thinking they'd blinded me. I remember feeling the tip of the blade digging into gums. "They all turned on me then, but I kept hold of that sword. That's when my father bargained with my mother's killers and told them I'd be worth more alive."

Elowen trembles against me, but I continue because I'd rather just get this over with. "My father chained me and began entering me in fighting pits in Imirath like the one you saw, only I don't allow children in mine. I began throwing the matches out of spite, and the soldiers threatened to kill him if I didn't stop, so he began whipping my back as punishment whenever I lost." The words taste like acid in my mouth, and I rotate my wrist, momentarily removing my hand from Elowen. "He got more creative and booked me in fights to the death, knowing I burned with the need to avenge both my mother and myself."

"Please tell me you killed him," Elowen whispers.

"He stole a cage that belonged to a hunting hound when all of this began. That's how he kept me from running away. He'd only pull me out of the ring when I was so beaten or exhausted that I could barely walk." Elowen flinches but doesn't say anything, probably realizing our childhoods have far more things in common than she expected. I was at the mercy of my father from the ages of eleven to fourteen, and she was at the mercy of hers from the ages four to ten. It's why I can't stand being touched—I've been conditioned to kill anyone who comes too close. "After a series of wins over the course of two years, my father started getting sloppy. I pocketed the key to my cage when he was drunk and freed myself once he passed out." I chuckle without humor, dark and dangerous as we break the tree line and gallop down the hill leading to Ladislava. "I woke him up before slitting his throat exactly how they cut my mother."

Elowen tries to cover her sniffle by clearing her throat, but even if she had managed it, the tremors racking her slim frame would have given her emotions away. "Were you able to take any money from your winnings? Was that how you got your first apartment?"

Anytime I won, my father would blow it all on women, booze, and drugs. Fucking gods, I don't want to talk about this. "All I took was his coat before crossing into Vareveth."

"Your existence is not a mistake because someone wanted you to believe it was." Elowen shakes her head before swinging her leg over the horse, sitting sidesaddle to throw her arms around my shoulders.

I tighten my grip on the reins to slow the horse. "Do you even know how to ride sidesaddle?"

Her body vibrates with the sobs she's trying to keep contained as she pulls me closer, like she's trying to hug the version of myself I was when I was forced to fight in those rings, and I don't have the heart to tell her that he's gone. Maybe he's off somewhere with the ghost of who she used to be; perhaps they're having the childhood that was robbed from them.

The roaring in my ears quiets the longer she's with me. A river in the distance creates a soothing melody, and Elowen's softness manages to blunt the edge of the brutal memories. I keep breathing in her light floral and vanilla scent to replace the sharp tang of blood. There are certain aspects where she and I undoubtedly match, but it's moments like this, when I find the strength in her gentleness, that I realize how we're different. She's the life that stems from the death that's plagued me, and the light that breaks apart the darkness encroaching me. It requires a different kind of strength to remain kind in a world that has given you every reason to become jaded. Elowen has a vengeful streak within her and her bloodlust is prominent, but she loves with everything she's made of.

"I fought." I clear my throat. "Because I knew you existed. I kept telling myself to survive until I found you. The princess with a bond to five dragons who was wronged by the same man who ruined my life. I thought of you on my worst nights, and you kept me alive."

I lean forward to kiss Elowen's tears away, brushing my thumb over the sapphire ring she only takes off to bathe and sleep. "This belonged to my mother. It's passed down to the women in my family. I could never part with it, no matter how starving or cold I was." I pulled it off her finger as the soldiers yanked me away. It was covered in so much blood they didn't see it in my hand before I shoved it in my pocket. "She'd have loved you."

"You should keep it," she whispers, so much emotion in her voice it makes my heart ache.

"I don't want it." I bring her hand to my lips, kissing the jewel. "I want you to wear it."

She licks her lips, determination shining through her eyes. "You are Cayden Veles. You are not a bastard. You are Asterin's son. The greatest blessing in her life. You are a survivor. You are the bravest and strongest man I know. You are the king of Vareveth, and the only conqueror in our world."

My heart is beating out of my chest, and all I can do is look at her. I searched for her in every part of Ravaryn. I've been to all the kingdoms, the southern isles, and unmarked islands, and she was worth it. She's worth *everything*.

"I don't care what you've done to survive," she whispers. "I only care that you did."

"Thank you for being the reason I did."

Even when I had nothing.

I had the thought of her.

"We're going to take everything from Garrick," she says with a fierceness like no other. "We're going to take his throne and erase his name from this world. His legacy ends with us."

"You'll take the Imirath throne?"

The iron gates to Veles Manor creak open, but Elowen doesn't turn, never drops her eyes away from mine even as a guard greets us and lights a torch to alert the house staff of my presence. "Queen Cordelia of Galakin hasn't answered my letter, so there's a chance we'll be fighting two kingdoms for a throne that most won't want me to ascend, but it will be ours. I am the Princess of Imirath, and I will fight for my birthright."

CHAPTER
TWENTY-THREE

ELOWEN

I TRACE MY THUMB OVER MY RING.

Asterin's ring.

Nothing he has ever bought me could mean so much. My heart feels like it'll burst out of my chest as I make a silent vow to Cayden's mother, promising that I'll keep both this ring and her son safe.

My shoulders loosen as the long road bordered by a wintery forest littered with frozen streams ends, and Veles Manor stands in all its glory. The dark wood and stones that create the exterior are bathed in moonlight, and the stained-glass windows are illuminated by flickering candlelight within. Sharp turrets spear the night, topped with dragon statues that match the ones atop the fountain at the center of the circle before the main entrance, fashioned to look like all five taking flight with their tails wrapped around a pair of crossed swords. That fountain has been there since before we were betrothed, I realize. The statues atop the turrets are new, but somehow, I've always existed here even before we met.

"Why did you have that made?" I ask as his hands bracket my hips and he helps me down from the horse. "It resembles our sigil, but I remember it being there when I first came here."

"It served as a reminder," he says, drawing my eyes back to his. "That you were somewhere in the world, and I would not tolerate a reality where I didn't find you. I also perceived the dragons to be a symbol of Garrick's weakness. Brave men don't chain things they have the courage to face or tame."

He nods to the stable hand who takes the reins, but I continue looking up at him as the stars shine enough to emphasize the harsh lines of his face. His anger is like the sea; its power is evident even when it seems dormant, and once a storm comes, only he decides when the destruction will cease.

"Are you sure the Imirath throne is what you want?" he asks.

Claiming the Imirath throne isn't a matter of want, it's a matter of how far I'm willing to go to protect myself and the ones I love, and *that* is limitless. "My life has been a series of men putting me in cages or keeping me in the dark. They will have only themselves to blame when I burn their world to the ground and build a new one upon the ashes. Our enemies have ensured that peace will never be an option, so we must make them realize that all the years they've lived have been a mercy from us when we come to end their existence."

"You were never able to live in their world, and for that they will die in ours. I will not stop fighting until everyone who abused you is dead," he says, green eyes simmering with intensity. "Garrick will not survive the hell we unleash upon him, nor will anyone who stands with him." His fingers wrap around the back of my neck and I'm unable to look anywhere but at him. "I'm with you, Elowen. This is not another task you must accomplish on your own. Unload all your worries onto me so you don't have to bear the weight of them alone."

I hold on to the steadiness his presence offers, honing it like a blade and sheathing it on my thigh. The Imirath throne belongs to me, and I will claim it with my father's enemy at my side and dragons flying above.

Light pours down the front steps like spilled water as a servant opens the main entrance, but I latch my hand on Cayden's arm as he tries to step toward it. Rising to the tips of my toes, I press my lips on his scarred cheek, needing him to know that I see him, all of him, and I'm not leaving. His pupils dilate as he scans his eyes along my features, and my yelp bounces off the walls as he slides an arm beneath my knees and around my back and hoists me in his arms.

"Did you know my legs work? Because it seems you forget quite often."

"I'm exercising my husbandly privileges." I wave at the servant as we enter, and the warmth feels sublime after several hours of flying. "Carrying my wife over the threshold of our home."

I roll my eyes. "You're not my husband."

He shrugs, and I know he's doing this to move on from the topic of his past, but I'll go along with it if this is what he needs. "Semantics, Lady Veles."

I wonder what it would be like to be a lady, not a queen. "Until I have a ring on my finger so large and heavy it makes me lopsided, we are *not* married."

"Royals," he mutters, and I smack him on the back of the head.

The entryway seating area is bathed in the shades of our house colors, with a golden replica of our sigil hanging above the wide fireplace made of stones that match the exterior of the home. He snickers in response and carries me down the hall. An ornate blue rug runs the length of it, and the walls are lined in a mixture of the same stones and dark wood, illuminated by gold sconces.

Every room we pass is tasteful and elegant but still feels like home. When I first came here it was filled with only dark shades: brown leather; emerald, blue, and red ornate rugs with hints of black . . . but as he slows his steps, I notice lighter shades that have never been here before shining through new paintings of spring meadows, walls showcasing murals of twisting vines and starry skies, new rugs that now include hues of lavender and sage, and several vases of flowers at the center of a sitting room, on the dining table, and nestled by the floor-to-ceiling windows. Even the wood is carved to reflect the smallest hints of delicate decadence.

My heart swells as Cayden carries me up the curved double staircase, and I reach my hand out to caress the divots in the railing. We bypass several closed doors with the same amount of detail as the rest of the house, and he sets me on my feet to unlock an especially stunning one.

My hand smothers a gasp as the door swings open, and I step into another sitting room filled with more dark wood furniture upholstered in our house colors arranged around a double-sided fireplace. A scene of five dragons flying above a mountain range hangs above it, with Ryder's signature in the corner. Rich curtains with a lace overlay and golden tassels are pulled back on either side of a bay window to reveal a tea set with several books stacked on the tray.

I kick off my boots and walk through the archway that leads to the bedchamber, and moisture gathers in my eyes when I look up and see a replica of the night sky painted on the dome ceiling. My chest rises and falls unevenly at the sight of ... *home*. I've been homesick for a place I didn't know existed.

I don't realize any tears have escaped until Cayden steps up beside me and gently rubs his knuckle against my cheek. "When did you have time to do all of this?"

"When I couldn't sleep at night." My breath wooshes from me, not anticipating the relief I'd feel at the evidence of where he was. "Where did you think I was?" I don't want to answer, but he must notice something on my face because his shoulders drop. "Elowen."

I shake my head and step farther into the room. "You don't have to say anything."

"Yes, I do." His hand clasps around my wrist and he takes a seat on the bench at the foot of the bed, wrapping his arm around my waist to keep me between his legs. "Ever since we met have you so much as seen me look at another woman?"

"I've seen them look at you," I answer, hating how my insecurity sharpens my tone. "I think some may have swooned while you were fighting."

"Every man with a pair of eyes looks at you," he answers flatly.

"Only the ones with good taste." I've never cared enough about anyone to feel this way, but the thought of Cayden being with anyone other than me makes my stomach twist painfully and violence pump through my veins.

"I've never needed a ring to be loyal to you. You occupy every corner of my mind to the point that I can't even think about the possibility of another woman. You are all I want, and I'd be a goddamn fool to forsake the greatest thing in my life."

I look down at his lap, but he's so close there's no way for me to truly hide my growing smile. He grasps my chin to bring my eyes back to his.

"Allow me to make myself very clear. There will never be another for either of us, understand? I conquered a kingdom to have you, and my feelings will never change."

"Understood."

He rises from the bench and leads me to the bathing chamber where a giant tub sits in the center of the room and snow gently pelts the three arched windows that overlook the lake where my dragons rest.

"I'll get you something to change into," he says, kissing my forehead before departing. I press a hand over my chest once he's gone as I spin in place, taking it all in. If I told myself a year ago that this was where I'd be, I never would've believed it.

I turn the knobs on the tub before stripping out of my clothes and jumping into the bath, lathering myself with soap and dipping under the water. Bubbles float atop the surface and I drag my fingers through them while watching my dragons through the foggy glass. I hear Cayden return to hang the clothes on a hook, but he leaves me be. My fingertips resemble raisins by the time I finish, and I let out a pleased sigh while scrunching the water from my curls. The light blue night slip is so soft that it feels like a caress.

"Is there anything you haven't thought of?" I ask, taking a seat on the mattress that must be stuffed with clouds.

"No." Cayden turns away from the window, his eyes darkening as they scan me from head to toe. I wonder if he's dreamed of having me in his bed. My breathing deepens as he slowly walks toward me, not hiding the desire and lust pouring off him, filling every crevice and corner of the room. "Because I know what you need." He takes my hips in his hands, and my head presses into the pillows as I lean back, but he keeps coming closer until he's hovering a breath away from my lips, his biceps bulging against his shirtsleeves. "And I love being the one to give it to you."

He's gone in the next breath, leaving me flustered and needy as he disappears into the bathing chamber. I press my hands into my warm cheeks and thrust myself out of bed to find a spare piece of parchment to quickly pen a letter to Finnian so he doesn't worry. I went to check on him this morning, but he was already out on a ride with Ryder.

"Cayden?" I call out.

"Yes, angel."

"Can we stay here? Not just tonight." The castle is lovely . . . but it's not mine. Ailliard's ghost haunts me around every corner as do my memories of the Imirath castle.

"This is your home. You don't have to ask me that."

My eyes briefly shut as relief washes over me, and I soak in the details of the room all over again when I open them. *It's perfect.* I finish writing my letter to Finnian before digging around the desk for the seal with our sigil.

Cayden's body presses into mine from behind as I'm straightening up, and my pulse pounds throughout every inch of me. I feel the warmth of his bare chest through the thin night slip, and the loose pants he wears do nothing to hide the bulge contained within. "For Finnian, I'm assuming?"

The deep rumble of his voice sends sparks shooting through me. "Mhmm."

"I'll take it downstairs for you." He pulls the now slightly crumpled letter from between my fingers and strides from the room. I douse the lanterns and climb back into bed, sighing as my sore and tired body finds reprieve. Gods, even the sheets smell like him.

"No line of pillows this time?" he asks when he returns, removing a dagger from the drawer of his nightstand and setting it on top.

"It's entirely unnecessary. I've grown used to your hulking presence."

He flexes his muscles, smirking at me as he reclines and tucks an arm beneath his head. I turn away from him to hide my face, settling into the pillows and pulling the plush covers up to my chin. The hair on the back of my neck stands up, and the urge to turn back to him is so strong it's pulling me like the undertow of the sea.

I shut my eyes, trying to let sleep welcome me, but it's not darkness behind my lids. It's Cayden at different ages in his life, facing horrid things at the hands of our fathers. I don't care if the world thinks he's a demon. He's been better to me than they ever were.

I abruptly spin around, locking my arm around his torso and twining our legs together. He doesn't say anything as his hands come around me, one settling on my back and the other gliding through my hair. I rest my ear over his heart, taking comfort in the steady beating that so many have tried to silence, letting it lull me to sleep like a lullaby that was never sung to me.

"Goodnight, demon."

His lips press against my forehead. "Goodnight, mia sirantia."

CHAPTER
TWENTY-FOUR

CAYDEN

I'VE WATCHED ELOWEN FLIP THROUGH ONE HUNDRED AND forty-seven pages of a book she's clearly enthralled with. That her narrowed eyes have remained on me for the last fifty is a sure sign of enjoyment. I have no intention of stopping, and her stubborn nature prevents her from backing down. Here we remain, locked in a silent contest like we don't have other important matters to attend to.

"How was your morning ride?"

"Fine."

"And how's the book, sirantia?"

She dramatically flips another page. "Riveting."

"Are you going to continue answering me with only one word?"

"Perhaps."

Her dragons were restless just before dawn, and she didn't bother changing out of her slip before donning *my* coat and a pair of her boots. They circled the property for the most part, and I watched them through the windows while reading the daily reports I receive to make sure nothing went wrong during the night. The servants brought breakfast into the sitting room in front of the bedchamber, and Elowen threw off the coat as soon as she saw pastries and coffee, collapsing on the couch.

She looks like something that crawled out of a desire-drenched dream, sent into reality to be my undoing. It's a doom I'll happily accept, whether it be delivered by her lips or the tip of her knife. She's the only form of torture I'll never hold up against. I haven't stood a chance for months, too far gone to even try to deny the magnitude of the longing that pulses through my veins.

I place my elbows on my knees and lean forward, setting aside the sword I was sharpening. "Tell me about it."

She considers this for a moment before flicking her mussed curls over her shoulder, drawing the already short hem up her thighs. *Good gods.* "I haven't had enough coffee to merit a prolonged conversation with you."

I shouldn't love her attitude, but I adore it. If she were to stare at me with pity in her eyes after I revealed the details of my past, I'd find any excuse to leave the room, but this is exhilarating. Her defiance, the feeling of a challenge, all it does is make me want her more. I steeple my fingers in front of my lips to hide my grin despite my dimples giving it away and shamelessly drag my eyes along her reclined body.

She snaps the book shut and reaches forward to grab another strawberry puff, moaning as she bites into it. My gaze attaches to her lips as she licks some jam and powdered sugar off her fingers, dragging them along the plump surface. She hollows her cheeks and the image of her on her knees when she took me in her mouth causes my desire to amplify. She knows exactly what she's doing and grins triumphantly. I'm aware I'm wretched in this life, but I must've been an abysmal prick in a previous one to deserve this.

"Marry me," I state. "A week from today. Or sooner."

"Say please."

"Please marry me."

She drops her hand away from her cheek and scrunches her nose. "Not good enough."

We're already betrothed for fuck's sake.

"Elowen Atarah, my sweet affliction, the object of my obsession." I rise from the chair and round the coffee table filled with more trays than necessary for two people and get down on one knee as a flush creeps up her neck. "When I'm taken from this world, I will happily walk into hell knowing I've experienced divinity in your presence and tasted salvation from your lips. Will you please put me out of my misery and become my wife within the week? I will always choose you in any lifetime and all worlds, so please allow me to publicly proclaim that in this one."

I keep my tone low, the whisper of desire and honesty making her shiver. She sinks her teeth into her lower lip, and I curl my fingers to stop myself from reaching out. The urge to kiss her is so strong but by some miracle I will myself not to give in. I need her answer.

"Yes." She presses her lips together to try to hide her smile, but it's evident through her shining eyes. "I suppose there's no point in delaying it. I'll send for a dressmaker to come to the house tomorrow morning."

"Pay extra to have it done as quickly as possible."

"For a royal wedding dress, the fee will be substantial."

"I don't care," I reply. "Send me the bill and I'll take care of it."

She purses her lips. "I have expensive taste."

I lean closer so my mouth hovers an inch above hers. "So do I."

I've hoarded my money over the years, so she can spend as much as she wants. Elowen does have expensive taste, but I have deep pockets and a penchant for wanting her happy.

"We should invite the rulers of Feynadra and Urasos to begin fostering a relationship. Do you think there's any chance they'll align with us in the war?" she asks.

"I think the best we can hope for is neutrality. Ensuring they don't join forces with Imirath should be our main focus because fighting a war on two fronts is hellish. We stand between them and Imirath. They won't want to waste soldiers in our war if they have nothing to gain and everything to lose if Imirath invades Vareveth and pushes north. The princess married to the crown prince of Urasos is a daughter of one of the noble houses of Thirwen, so I doubt they'd be willing to break that peace."

"Galakin is the most essential alliance anyway," she answers. Their navy is what we need, not more soldiers from two minor kingdoms.

"Maybe the queen of Feynadra can put in a good word for us with her sister, Queen Cordelia."

"I'll find out what I can about the rulers and send out the invitations today. If there's anything useful, I'll be sure to tell you."

"You should be thankful we're getting married so soon." She giggles while propping her cheek on her hand. "If we summoned a royal gathering before our vows, rulers would be begging me to marry their sons. Queen Cordelia wasn't subtle at the alliance ball."

I stand and reclaim the seat across from her, taking a sip of my lukewarm coffee. "A pompous prince would never fulfill you."

"No?" She straightens up, sitting primly on a couch and making it look more like a throne. "If our lives were different, how would you have dealt with my many suitors in Imirath?"

"Sliced them open and thrown them in the canal."

"Do you think we would've been friends?"

"I could never be only your friend." She laughs, *and, gods,* her laugh. If I could bottle up the sound and listen to it on repeat, I would. It's unburdened, like it's meant only for me. I hoard this memory to store it with all the others I keep of her, separate from the other parts of my life so these moments remain untainted. "Firstly, I'd have stolen you away before you had the chance to walk down the aisle to someone else. Secondly, even if you were to smile at royals offering up their sons like gifts to a goddess, you'd still be crawling into my bed at the end of the night, and I'd remind you just how deeply you belong to me."

"And what if you're someone I can get out of my system with a few tumbles in the sheets?"

"Hmm." I quirk a brow. "Am I?"

She smiles brighter. "Completely."

"Come here." I widen my legs, knowing she's lying through her teeth. She rolls her lips together, straightening her spine, and I know I have her under lock and key. She'll never refuse a challenge. Her hips sway seductively as she slowly closes the distance between us and drops into my lap. Her scent surrounds me as she leans close, and her breasts push against my chest. My hand tightens on the arm of the chair as she trails her fingers over my shirt, tracing my scars through the fabric. I wonder how many times she's studied me shirtless to know their exact placements.

"Entirely unaffected," she says on a shaky exhale.

"So it appears." I hide my smile, slowly releasing the death grip on the chair, and slide a hand down her back. Her thighs press together as she shivers, and she tries to hide it by shifting. "Tell me the truth, beautiful."

Her throat bobs and hands tighten on my shoulders. She shifts again as I reach up with my other hand and wrap her curls around my fist. I've always loved how dark they are, and how they make her eyes shine with warmth. I pull her closer to me and she sucks in a sharp breath when I tilt her head to the side and glide my lips up her neck. A chuckle rumbles deep in my chest when she shudders. "I'll be so good to you, Elowen."

I lower my mouth over the spot she loves just below her ear, flicking my tongue, making her cry out and arch against me. She releases her hold on my shoulders and locks her arms around my neck, leaning into my hand, baring more of her throat to me. Lust mixes with the need to mark her as mine and courses through me like a drug.

I continue licking and nibbling all the places I know will make her moan, making my way down to the neckline of her slip and tugging it down with my teeth to expose the tops of her breasts. *Fucking gods*, this woman.

"Give me the truth, love."

"I did," she moans as she threads her fingers through my hair and guides me toward her nipple visible through the fabric. My defiant angel.

I wrap my lips around her peak, and she whimpers, dragging her hips over the bulge in my pants. "The truth is that if I parted these pretty thighs, you'd be dripping for me."

"You're delusional," she gasps.

I smirk against her, licking my way back up to her jaw and holding her in place as she squirms, wanting her closer, wanting to possess her.

My fingers caress down her back and thigh until I can dip them beneath the hem to push her legs apart with my fist. She whimpers again, a knot forming between her brows, and she tilts her hips forward, searching for the reprieve I won't grant.

"The truth—" Her eyes briefly squeeze shut when I trail a finger over the side of her panties. Her pants paint my lips, mingling with mine as our pulses pound together. I keep my finger where it is, rubbing back and forth to give her a hint of what I'll do once she gives me what I ask. All she has to do is tell me she wants me, but fuck if I don't love the fight.

The bell chimes at the foot of the steps, the servants signaling a visitor has arrived. "Ignore them. I'm not expecting anyone."

"W-we don't want to be rude."

"Yes, we do. We want to be extremely rude."

She abruptly stands up but remains between my parted thighs with a devilish smirk on her lips. She hooks her fingers through the thin straps on her shoulders and *slowly* slides the fabric down her body until she's left in nothing but the morning light that graces her skin.

"Fuck," I groan, resuming my death grip on the chair. "I'm going to kill whoever is at the door." She laughs, turning away from me to walk into the bedroom, her tits and ass bouncing as she does. I want to bury myself inside her and wring every ounce of pleasure from her until she's limp. I want to capture her moans in my mouth and bury my face between her thighs. "I'm not joking."

I run my hands through my hair and drag them down my face before tilting my head back against the chair. If this is the game she wants to play, so be it. She can push me all she wants; all it does is make me want to return the torment. She walks through the door again with innocent eyes, looking breathtaking in a lavender velvet gown in her favored style with delicate embroidery.

"Let's go greet our guests." She slips her hand into mine and tugs me from the room.

"Let's murder them."

CHAPTER
TWENTY-FIVE
ELOWEN

"N o," CAYDEN STATES BY WAY OF GREETING WHILE glaring at the towers of trunks stacked throughout the entryway with more still attached to the wagon beyond the door. I'm the culprit for the majority of the clutter considering I requested several pieces of jewelry, gowns, shoes, and other items to be transferred here, but Finnian's, Ryder's, and Saskia's trunks join the chaos. Hinges squeak when I crack one open and run my fingers over a clothbound book embroidered with pink roses.

"Elowen invited us," Ryder answers. "Who am I to deny my queen's request?" He throws an arm around my shoulders, and I force myself not to stiffen from the unprompted touch. I'm doing better with expecting this while in everyone's presence, but I think there will always be a part of me that rebels against having a person close to me at first. Cayden yanks me from his best friend's hold, wrapping both arms around my waist and pressing my back to his chest.

"Go home."

Finnian raises a hand. "I don't have a house."

"I'll buy you one," Cayden answers. "The other two have houses of their own to return to."

I reach up and shove my palm over Cayden's mouth. "I'm happy you're all here."

Cayden peels my hand away. "I won't judge you for your lapse in judgment."

"Cayden was born with a stick up his a—" I smack his hands away when he pinches my sides to tickle me and turn to face him.

"Keep running your mouth and I'll find a much better use for it," he whispers before straightening up. My desire from earlier hasn't dissipated, and he smirks as he regards my features. He pulls out his pocket watch and glances down at it. "I have an appointment in Ladislava shortly, but I expect your belongings will be removed from my house by the time I get back."

He kisses my forehead and steps around me without looking back. I narrow my eyes on his retreating form. "Cayden."

"Hm?" He removes his coat and boots from the closet close to the main entrance and puts them on.

"Look at me."

"I'll see you later, love." He cuts a direct path to the door, dodging trunks with ease. I hurry to catch up to him, stepping into his path and framing his face to drag his gaze down to mine.

"I don't want to leave Finnian on his own after losing Aestilian and having Saskia here will help me plan the wedding more efficiently. It makes me happy to have the others close."

He groans as he looks into my eyes and grumbles his answer. "Fine."

Ryder's laugh bounces off the walls. "Gods, this is too good. We should've had Elowen around ages ago."

A wide smile parts my lips as Finnian whoops triumphantly and Cayden's exterior cracks slightly. "How do the wards work here? I remember you mentioning the manor is protected but I'd like to invite Asena over to ask some questions about the dragons."

"As long as she doesn't mean you harm, she'll be able to get through. The wards included you once I put your name on the deed." He moves toward the door, glancing over his shoulder as he opens it. "I won't be long. Don't leave the estate without me or a dragon."

"What do you have to do in Ladislava?"

His only answer is a smirk before he disappears from sight, leaving me alone with our friends and some servants carrying their trunks down the hall. I'm assuming Finnian will claim the room he had when we were here last, and Saskia and Ryder will do the same. Not only do I want them close for personal reasons, but each has a role to play in the battles to come, and living together will prevent sending sensitive information through letters.

"I stopped into your chambers to ensure everything you requested in your letter to Finnian was packed," Saskia says, coming closer to lower her voice. "And I already informed Asena to come here midday. She doesn't know why. I'll leave that up to you, but it's best if we figure this out as soon as possible."

"Agreed." But I don't say anything further as a servant approaches with a pleased smile on his face, deepening the age lines around his mouth. "Welcome home, Your Majesty. My name is Cyrus, the head of the staff. They're so pleased you and the king are taking up residence here."

He has a kind, round face and short stature. He's the type of man I'd pass on the street and wouldn't be suspicious of, which is a rarity. "I'd love to introduce myself if you'll escort me. I'm still learning my way around."

"Of course." His smile widens as the others make their way down the hall to get settled. "His Highness informed us of your love for gardening and ordered you some equipment. We've stored it in the stone shed at the back of the home. The greenhouse is also nearly done being built."

My heart flutters in my chest, and I have the same urge I did last night to pinch myself to make sure this is real. I didn't think he'd remember our conversation at the inn. Most promises I've received have been empty, but Cayden finds a way to fill each oath to the brim and spill over the top.

The morning passes quickly with Cyrus introducing me to the staff and showing me around the different wings of the house. All equally beautiful, mixed with light and dark, wood and stone, gothic and delicate.

I finish off in Cayden's office on the upper floor. He keeps the key in his nightstand because it's the one room in the manor servants aren't granted access. It's both for his privacy and their safety, so they don't see something not meant for them. Unlike our shared chambers in the castle, being in this room makes me feel as if I'm surrounded by Cayden wherever I turn. Dark leather furniture is complemented by deep shades of blue and black, matching the stained-glass imagery of the night sky at the center of several paneled windows overlooking the river that runs behind the property.

A portrait I sat for hangs above the fireplace, and the only mercy of staying put for several hours was that Ryder made me laugh through-out the painting process. I didn't know it was meant for Cayden's of-fice; I thought it was going in the royal gallery. My ornate gown fashioned in the colors of House Veles matches the equally decadent crown on my head, and a silhouette of a dragon spreads its wings be-hind me. Unable to resist snooping, I stride toward the large desk that faces the room, and I wonder how often Cayden's eyes drift to me as he works. My fingers grace the polished surface, and I yank open the top drawer, jolting back as if struck by lightning.

A tremor travels through my hand as I reach forward, not caring if Cayden never meant for me to see this. The first thing I grab is a stack of letters I wrote to him while he was at the border. It's tied with a ribbon I had discarded after untying my hair—thinking nothing of it—and at the center is the now-dried flower he tucked behind my ear at the bakery. The flower I did miss. I thought one of the servants threw it away when cleaning my room. The ink on the letters is smudged and creased in a way that makes me believe he folded and carried the parchment in his pocket.

Beside them is a sharpened and cleaned knife I never thought I'd see again after throwing it at a netherwraith for him. A chill rocks my body when I think of him in the darkness, those chilling eyes locked on my blade, laced with the unrelenting promise of finding me.

He kept it.

I can't believe he kept it.

I keep rummaging, unable to resist my curiosity, and pull out a second stack of papers riddled with smudged ink. *They're music sheets.* Several notes are crossed out and written down the margins as if he didn't want to waste time finding a new piece of parchment.

The door abruptly opens, and I shove the items back inside before shutting the drawer and smoothing my hands down my gown. Asena enters with Saskia, glancing in awe around the room as she comes to a stop in front of me to curtsy. "Your Majesty. It's an honor to be invited into your home."

"Priestess." I smile, escorting her toward the seating area. She claims the chair closest to the blazing fire, and Saskia and I sit on the couch across from her. "Would you like anything? Tea or food?"

"No, thank you, Your Highness." She smiles shyly and brushes her tight coiling curls behind her shoulders. "Lady Saskia told me you have some questions regarding the gods."

"Can I count on your discretion?"

"I will not betray you, blood oath or not. You were born from the fire of the gods, and my loyalty is to you."

I exchange a glance with Saskia, who subtly nods. "What do you know about dragons during the time of the gods?"

My education was less than limited while growing up, and it's one of my largest insecurities. It's also something Ailliard never failed to hold over my head, reminding me I couldn't venture out into a world I knew nothing of. But perhaps he's the one who should've stayed locked in his cage of cowardice. Maybe then he'd still be breathing.

I've always known there are ten gods in Ravaryn Legends, but I didn't know the vastness of their power. None of them simply presided over one thing. Five of them were dedicated to the elements among other things: the God of the Sun and Light, the God of Earth and Harvest, the Goddess of Air and Storms, the God of Water, Death, and the Moon, and the Goddess of Flames, Life, and Stars. The latter two are the gods Asena and Ophir believe blessed Cayden and me. The other five gods are the Goddess of Souls, Mercy, and Destiny, Patron of Seers; the Goddess of Love, Marriage, and Fertility; the Goddess of Grief and Sorrow; the God of War and Strategy; and the God of Illusion, the Mind, and Memory.

"It's said the first dragons were born from the stars to light the world when the night became too dark. I worship the Goddess of Flames but not the God of the Sun, although his power is fire. There are four forms of fire: sunfire, starfire, dragonfire, and earthly fire. The God of the Sun wields his power from the sun, obviously, and the Goddess of Flames can wield the other three, hence the triple flame symbol I wear around my neck. Only gods can conjure elements from nothing, while mages and priestesses like myself can merely wield what's around us."

"Why couldn't they wield all forms of fire if they're fire gods?" Saskia asks.

"Because they're entirely different elements. That's like asking why the earth god can't wield water. All fire is unique and incomparable." Asena's dark eyes flash to the flames when a log cracks. "People think the gods disappeared."

"But you don't think that?" I ask.

"Nothing that exists on this earth is ever truly gone. Life and death are inseparable. When a body is buried, it's absorbed by the soil that life sprouts from. The God of the Sun was cruel to the dragons, and the Goddess of Flames challenged him to relinquish his claim as a fire god. Their feud is what doomed the gods. There aren't winners in war, only survivors."

"If nobody won, what was the outcome?" My palms moisten as I glance out the window to where some of my dragons are soaring above the trees, and others are sprawled out in the snow, their colorful scales creating a stark contrast. Nobody will take them from me. Not a god or a mortal. I'll rip apart anyone who challenges me with my bare hands if I must.

"We speculate, but nobody knows."

"But what do you think?" Saskia presses.

"I don't think the end has come to pass. I think it's been brewing for centuries."

I flinch as thunder claps in the distance, and swallow the ridiculous sense of pending doom, focusing on the task at hand. "You say that I'm blessed by your goddess. Do you think that might give me abilities beyond the bond I share with my dragons? So that I could do more than simply ride them and command their loyalty?"

Asena weighs my words, pursing her lips and glancing into the fire again as if she's searching for an answer within. "I think there are many possibilities that can come from being blessed by a god, and I don't think you should dismiss any."

I glance at Saskia again and shake my head. I'd rather not reveal unnecessary information despite her swearing she won't. I'd be long dead if I trusted every person who gave me their word. Waking up dormant magic is a subject we can find in a book; godly lore is far more limited. "When you opened the portal for us you were speaking Ravarian."

"The forgotten language of the gods." She nods. "It's passed down through members of the cults, but written accounts are rare."

A talon-like sensation scrapes against my mind, urging me to ask my question. "How do you say dragonfire?"

"Zayèra."

"Zayèra," I respond, rolling the R as she did, and a pleased smile forms on her face when I pronounce it correctly. "Thank you, Asena, you've been very helpful today."

"Of course, Your Majesty. I'm happy to help you in any way I'm able."

"To repay you," I begin, rising from the couch to escort her out of the office. "I'd love for you and Ophir to officiate the royal wedding. Your people are also welcome to attend."

Her eyes widen and lips part before breaking out into a wide smile. "Y-yes, Your Majesty. We would be honored."

"Asena, if you could just wait outside for a moment, I'll walk you down," Saskia says in a kind tone, and doesn't continue until the priestess takes her leave and shuts the door behind her. "The nobles will be in an uproar if you let a mage and a priestess officiate the ceremony. You've only just lifted the bans on magic."

"Oh, I'm counting on it." I drum my fingers over my lips. "Sometimes when a snake slithers into your garden, you have to seek it out before it bites you."

Saskia's brows rise, and a smirk lifts her full lips. "I like the way you think."

"We have a week to prepare."

"A week?" she shrieks. "You tell me this now! You don't even have a dress." She places both hands on her forehead, groaning as she looks to the ceiling. "The wedding of the century and you give me a week to plan it."

"The dressmaker is coming tomorrow!"

"Oh, yes she is." She rips the door open in a huff and stomps into the hall.

I slide my pendant along the chain, still laughing softly as I glance toward my dragons again. Born from the stars. Maybe that's why I've always been so drawn to them.

Footsteps patter closer, but it's not coming from the hall, it's coming . . . from behind the wall. My palms prickle with nerves. I know the house is warded, but that doesn't stop me from pulling a knife from my thigh sheath and gliding through the room without a sound. My back presses into the wall. I follow it and hold my breath as the gold-framed painting of a churning ocean with a stormy sky swings open, and a blond man dressed as a servant steps through.

The tip of my knife is pointed at his neck before he gets far, and his throat bobs as he swallows. He's taller than me, but I latch my hand on to his shoulder, pressing the blade farther into his skin. "If I nick you right here, you'll bleed out in seconds."

"You move like an assassin." He sounds far more impressed than a man in his position should be.

"Perhaps I am."

The door to the office is shoved open and Cayden strides into the room. My heart swells at the sight of him. "Don't make me jealous, angel. Alexus is a good spy, and you know I don't act rationally when riddled with that emotion."

"I'm your *best* spy," the man . . . Alexus, answers.

I retract my knife and hoist my skirts to sheath it on my thigh again before rounding Alexus to get a better look at him: fair hair on his head and jaw, and light green eyes. Not a deep shade like Cayden's, closer to a lily pad floating atop a lake. "You snuck in here so I'm not going to apologize."

His eyes scan me from head to toe, widening slightly when they return to my face. Not in a way that makes my skin crawl. He's too earnest in his perusal. "That's enough," Cayden says, tucking me against his side. "I'm assuming you're not here to gawk at my betrothed."

Alexus clears his throat, his cheeks reddening. "Yes, sir." He pulls a small silver key from his pocket, swinging it around his finger. "Lord Xantheus is hosting a dinner at House Baelyn, which several lords are invited to. I stole the spare key to Lord Xantheus's office from the head butler's chamber, and you'll want to come with me tonight."

CHAPTER
TWENTY-SIX

CAYDEN

"I STILL HAVE NO IDEA WHY YOU'RE WEARING THAT," RYDER grumbles.

"Because it's pretty."

"We're going on a stealth mission. You don't have to dress *pretty*."

The sweet smile is evident in Elowen's voice. "No need to tell me. Your choice in attire makes your beliefs apparent."

"Cayden," Ryder growls. "Can you please step in here?"

I rest my head on the back of a tree, looking to the sky for a bit of strength. "I've been ignoring this entire conversation and will continue to do so."

"Your betrothed is wearing light blue!" Ryder exclaims.

"Would you calm down? There's *black* embroidery and beading."

"And she looks beautiful," I reply without looking at either of them, scanning the back of the Baelyn estate we'll be infiltrating once Alexus gives the signal. From the corner of my eye, I see Ryder look to Finnian for support, but he wisely raises his hands and shakes his head, also wanting no part in their argument. *Smart move, Finnian.*

"Anything yet?" Elowen asks as she moves to my side, and I hook an arm around her waist to pull her back against my chest. It's like a reflex at this point.

Elowen could wear the brightest shade possible and still keep to the shadows better than someone dressed in all black. Her skills would be unnerving if we weren't allies. She can move without sound and stand directly behind someone without them being any the wiser. She changed before we left so it would be easier to move while on the mission, but Elowen is always dressed in something feminine and elegant. I doubt I'll ever see her in anything that doesn't complement her. The light blue tunic trimmed in black fur to match her cloak hugs her frame perfectly. A panel of fabric stretches just below her knees, and another in the back, leaving her knife-clad legs on full display and the waist belt adding more definition.

"No." I don't remove my gaze from the servants' entrance. "Alexus is probably waiting until they're deep in their cups before slipping from the room."

"I think we should split up once we're inside."

Not happening is the first thing that flashes in my mind, and even though she can probably sense where my thoughts have gone when my arms tighten around her, she doesn't say anything. "Why?"

"Because if the nobles are gathered and drunk then they might voice some thoughts about us. Maybe they'll reveal something useful. You don't need me to infiltrate the office, and you'll know what to look for better than me." She cranes her neck, but I don't look down. "We've been in worse places than a lord's house, and you know I can handle myself."

She can do more than handle herself. It's me that's the fucking problem. Not having her by my side is unnerving and divides my attention, which is something that's never been an issue before. My missions have always been the most important things in my life, and clearly that's changed. Everyone has strengths and weaknesses, and she's told me she prefers spying and taking down a target from a distance. The thought of not being there if she gets overpowered makes me wake up in a cold sweat some nights.

"Keep Ryder and Finnian with you." The words taste like acid. "It'll be easier for me to navigate the halls without them."

All those working in the household will be focused on keeping the lords happy and won't be bustling around the halls as much as they normally would, but it's still best to limit our exposure.

The back door opens, and I monitor the sight like a hawk, releasing Elowen once I see the white cloth waving from the small crack. "I'll find you inside once I've completed my search."

Her lips quirk up. "Don't you always?"

"Damn right."

After making sure nobody is watching from any of the windows, the four of us creep from the tree line and slip into the dining area reserved for the servants. Alexus presses a finger to his lips, jutting his chin toward the archway leading to the kitchen. The pots and pans clanging along with orders given in raised voices is a dead giveaway. We keep quiet, following him up a staircase at the end of the hall, and pause on the landing.

"The office is on the top floor, but I've cracked open three windows in the dining room. If you want to spy, you'll have the best luck hiding in the room directly above it," Alexus mumbles.

Elowen looks back at Finnian who steps closer to her. "Go with them," I say.

Ryder nods, not looking pleased but knowing I've taken on far more dangerous tasks than looking through a lord's correspondence.

Alexus pops his head into the hall before holding the door open for them. "It's the first door on your left."

I keep my eyes on Elowen's back, gritting my teeth as the door shuts behind her, and turn to walk up the second staircase that leads to a much shorter hallway displaying a dark crimson-and-black theme as in the rest of the house. It might've been a decent place if it wasn't so gaudy. Alexus quickly unlocks the office and lets me inside.

"This is where I leave you." He tosses me the key. "They'll notice my absence when they need more wine, and I'd rather not have the mission fall apart while we're all inside."

"Collect your things tonight if you have anything here," I say while scanning the room. "If we don't find anything now, I'll handle them in a different way."

"Are you not worried about an internal rebellion anymore?"

"I always have another plan." It's better to control them and keep them in my back pocket, but either they'll bend, or I'll break them.

I walk toward the large oak desk set in front of a wide fireplace. Xantheus must've just been in here because the heat is stifling. I don't waste time removing my coat, but I do pull the hood down. The plush rug absorbs my steps, but I still step lightly enough to ensure anyone in the room below won't hear. The lockpicks are cool in my grip as I pull the smallest one from my pocket and drop to my knees, making quick work of getting the first drawer open.

I filter through the parchment, making sure to keep everything in order when I return the useless stack and relock the drawer before moving on to the next. It reeks of bergamot in here, and I wouldn't be surprised if Xantheus burns the incense because he thinks it smells like wealth. There's some kind of vase or gold piece wherever I look. It seems every inch of the house is crammed with trinkets.

The next drawer slides open, and I repeat my earlier actions, flicking through page after page until I pause. Dropping the stack of financial records on the desk, I scan a letter from a lord of Thirwen letting Xantheus know that there aren't enough ships left in their kingdom to continue trading throughout the war. Thirwen lacking ships makes no sense. They're an island kingdom, same as Galakin—their navy is far superior to their armies.

Fuck.

I knew Thirwen would be offering reinforcements to Imirath by sea, but I didn't anticipate the magnitude. It's a risky move considering it leaves their own kingdom unprotected . . . but there must be a reason. Something more than just a marriage between future heirs securing their alliance. I find a piece of blank parchment and place it atop the letter to trace the words and signature. I fold the letter and commit the sigil on the seal to memory—a ship's helm. Ryder will be able to re-create the simple design in hot wax before it dries. We've been forging documents for years.

Before slipping into the hall, I make sure nothing is out of place. The last thing I want is Xantheus running from the kingdom before I have the chance to bring him to heel like the bitch he is for what he said about Elowen alone. I'd rather not waste my time tracking him down. I love a chase, but only when the reward is worth it.

"Did you find something?" That voice. That sweet fucking voice. That'll always be worth it.

The sitting room is just as obnoxious as I anticipated. Moonlight bounces off the gold-plated furniture as well as every vase and relic propped on various podiums. Jewels in varying shades speckle the walls like the skirts of a hideous gown, and my nostrils burn from all the damn incense. The three of them could've heard whatever the lords were saying downstairs if they stayed on the couches, but I wouldn't be surprised if they decided to sit under the windows for some fresh air.

"I did." I crouch in front of Elowen who has her back pressed against the wall, and a half-eaten pastry held up to her mouth. "What did you hear?"

"A load of bullshit," Finnian growls, biting into the soft bread in his hand.

"Foolish men running their mouths," Elowen adds. "I'd have stopped listening if I weren't on a mission." I raise a brow, jutting my chin toward the food. "Spying takes awhile sometimes, so Chef Leonardo made some pastries." Leonardo, the chef at Veles Manor, was all too excited when I informed him the lady of the house has a love for sweets and baking. I lean forward before she has the chance to react and take a bite. "Hey!"

"Thanks, angel." She narrows her eyes. Elowen would hand over her meal if she knew I hadn't eaten, but this woman does not share her sweets. She could be stuffed after four courses and still manage to make room for dessert. "Are you going to tell me what they said? Because I'll happily go down there and ask myself."

"Oh, I'm sure," she mutters. "If I spent my life crying over what men said about me, I'd never leave my room."

"Yes, you would because I'd kill them."

"They're a bunch of rich pricks who haven't gotten the shit kicked out of them enough," Ryder grumbles.

Elowen pats my chest and shoves herself to her feet, finishing off the pastry and walking to the door to peek into the hall. "I'm not telling you here because we didn't spend all this effort spying just for you to reveal our presence by losing your head and going down there with blades drawn."

My anger pulses under my skin. They can lose *their* heads for all I care. "It was that bad?"

"Their hatred can be weaponized if we wait for the right moment to wield it." She turns away from the door, crooking her finger at the three of us ready to storm down there. "Men say spiteful things about women and yet the world keeps turning. Don't mistake my calm for complacency. I'll silence them, but you're all going to follow my lead and let me do what I do best." She swings the door open and steps into the hall once we're close. "Outsmarting those who consistently underestimate me."

CHAPTER
TWENTY-SEVEN

ELOWEN

AYDEN'S HARDLY SAID A WORD TO ME SINCE WE LEFT the estate, more than likely keeping his temper reined in by a thin leash. Insults made by cowardly men who would tremble in fear if forced to say it to my face don't bother me. It's easy for them to follow one another's opinions like mindless sheep, to view themselves as untouchable gods. What's difficult is knowing how to sink your claws into the minds of the masses to control their perception. The tragedy of language is how few people have the ability to string together words that actually mean something. The lords can spew whatever vitriol they want. All it does is provide me with more ammunition to use against them.

Ladislava is packed with people spilling out of taverns and congregating along the roads. Verendus was too, but the citizens who live in the inner city don't idolize Cayden as the soldiers in Ladislava do. Cheering echoes off the buildings as Cayden slows the horse on which we both ride, and pints are raised in honor of the king and queen. Ale splashes onto the cobblestones and turns the fresh snow to slush as tankards slam into each other. They revere Cayden because unlike most kings in Ravaryn, he fights alongside them, and unlike all Ravaryn kings, he was one of them.

I tug my pendant along the chain, knowing Cayden will recognize this as one of my anxious ticks. His temper has been stewing like an oncoming storm, and I intend on wielding it.

"What did they say about you?" The words are forced through his teeth. He's probably thinking the vile things the lords said have begun to sink in, but they hate me because I have more power than them. Their insecurity is transparent, and they're not worthy of influencing my emotions or self-perception.

"It was nothing, Cayden," I sigh. "It means nothing to me."

He releases his hold on my waist to tilt my chin toward him. "It means something to me." *Oh, I'm counting on it.* I'd feel bad for manipulating him if it weren't for our benefit. He's smart enough to know what I'm doing, but his anger overpowers logical reasoning.

He turns toward Ryder when he realizes I won't talk. "Tell me what they said."

He's forced to raise his voice, causing several curious soldiers to glance our way. I make sure to lean closer to him when they do. Playing the part of the wounded woman even if it couldn't be further from the truth.

"Too much," Ryder sneers, his face distorting in genuine disgust. "I will not repeat the things they said they'd do to her body. Elowen can tell you if she chooses, but I'm sure you can guess."

The shudder that rattles my bones isn't faked. Violence against women is so normalized among men that they can sit around a table and jest about it as if we're worth less than waste on the streets. I'll never understand how they can look into the faces of their mothers, daughters, sisters, wives, or ordinary strangers who deserve to live their lives unscathed by misogynistic malice and proclaim happiness in the face of female suffering.

I also can't understand why some men are so threatened by strong women. When they can't fathom female power, they display the vilest of intentions to deface her, to diminish her, while women are too often taught that our strength comes from what we survive at their hands. And I hate that. I despise that our power is linked to how they defile us. Strength comes from so many places, but for women, it comes from within us.

We are not defined by what is done to us, and we are made of more than the abuse we suffer.

"They made several treasonous statements aside from those. One lord even revealed that they're searching for any bastard sons of Eagor to support his claim to the throne."

A soldier unabashedly staring up at us as we pass hears Ryder's statement.

"They won't touch you," Cayden vows menacingly. "I'll cut every finger off their damn hands if they so much as reach for you."

The soldier's lips turn down, and I watch as he heatedly speaks to others in his vicinity, pointing in our direction as we round the corner. All it takes is one drop to create a ripple throughout a pond. There's little people love more than gossip, and news of the lords' treason will spread throughout Ladislava like wildfire.

"Not that I disagree with your tactic, Elowen, but aren't we trying to avoid a rebellion?" Ryder asks once we're far enough from the commotion.

"We're avoiding a rebellion against the crown," I respond. "But if the army chooses to revolt against the lords for their treasonous statements, then Cayden and I can dust our hands of it until we step in to diffuse the situation."

"They will be painted as the villains, and the crown can show power," Finnian adds.

"Exactly." And I highly doubt their heirs and wives will stand by traitors as they're sentenced to die. "I sparked the fire, but I'll also put it out when the time is right."

Two guards push open the tall wrought iron gates of Veles Manor and we continue down the road. I feel more at peace just having crossed the property line. "I know why you waited to tell me," Cayden says. "You needed the soldiers to see my anger, and you played it well, but I meant what I said."

"I know," I softly answer. I won't be at the mercy of another man again, and they will beg for clemency before I'm done with them. "We'll end them together."

"That we will."

All four of us bound up the front steps and through the main entrance, removing our cloaks and boots for the servants to hang in the closet. Someone rushing down the hall catches my attention, and I crane my neck just in time to see Saskia round the corner and latch her dark eyes on mine.

"I found something!" she exclaims while carrying a several-hundred-page book in her arms. "I think it can be achieved!"

"You do?" I meet her halfway, ignoring the mumbled confusion behind me.

"We can test the theory tonight if you're up to it."

"What are we doing now?" Finnian groans.

Saskia threads her hand through mine and leads me to the sitting room while the other three follow hot on our heels. Cayden takes the spot closest to me on the couch, Finnian and Ryder sink into the chairs across from us, but Saskia paces in front of the fire, her dark purple gown dragging behind her. "Elowen and I spoke to Asena earlier today to discuss Elowen's potential ability to possess magic."

"Oh, yes, let's trust the woman who chants in a circle around a fire," Ryder mutters.

Saskia glares at him but continues speaking, "I scoured through whatever stories I could find regarding magic in Thirwen, given the bonds they share with animal familiars. There are prominent families mentioned in there whose magic dates back for centuries, but when someone born into that family lacks abilities by the age of twelve, they perform ceremonies to awaken dormant magic."

Cayden sits forward to rest his elbows on his knees. "What magic of hers are we trying to awaken?"

"The ability to enter my dragons' minds," I say. "To see through their eyes."

"For what purpose?" Finnian asks.

"The cages on the border," Ryder responds, and Finnian's face pales. "There was a report by one of our spies in Imirath, and we all believe whatever is in those cages will be targeting Elowen and the dragons."

"To give the ritual a higher chance of success, Elowen will have to deprive her senses," Saskia says. "She needs to entirely focus on her bond with the dragons and give in to it, but she's unpracticed in magic. In many cases, an anchor is used, which is a person deeply tethered to the potential mage who will keep their hands on them throughout the ceremony."

"Young mages in Thirwen are sometimes transported to the ice fjords to awaken their magic. Some believe it has something to do with magic in the water and others think it has to do with the freezing temperatures," Cayden adds. "I've heard of this tactic before, but I don't know anything about anchors."

"They provide a pathway back once she's not in her own mind. If Elowen can't find her way back to her body, then she could become . . . stuck. Asena will be returning with Ophir shortly to aid in the ceremony, since they'll know more regarding the topic."

"*Stuck?*" Ryder questions. "We have a war to fight and my queen might be *stuck* inside a dragon?"

"She can't risk herself like this!" Finnian exclaims.

"Elowen will make up her own mind," Cayden cuts off their hysterics in a stern voice and turns to face me as the other three bicker among themselves rather than projecting their doubts onto me. "When did you start speculating about your abilities?"

"Saskia and I were discussing the matter when you returned to camp to deliver the news of Imirath's succession. I was going to tell you," I insist. "Everything happened so fast."

"It's fine. What do you want to do?"

I dryly swallow. The idea of being unable to return to my body is unnerving, but I have a duty to my dragons, and I can't let them down again. "I have to try. I know it's a risk, but I won't be able to live with myself if my inaction tonight harms my dragons."

He nods like he expected me to say this and darts his eyes to the side to glare at the others. Their bickering still fills the room. "Don't listen to their doubts. Everything you need to survive this lives within you."

I reach forward to squeeze his hand and open my mouth to thank him for his reassurance, but something entirely different overtakes my thoughts when I look down. "Is that my name?"

"Yes," he states evenly.

I gape at him, unsure whether to kiss him or question his thought process. "How are you so calm about this!"

He lifts a brow. "Because I'm the one who put them there."

"*Them?*" I lift his hand so I'm able to get a better look at it, and sure enough, the same tattoo is mirrored on both sides. "You permanently inked my name on your finger, Cayden! *Twice!*"

"I had to do it twice. I can't see your name on the outside of my finger. This one is for me." He holds the inside of his ring finger in front of my face to showcase *Elowen* written in my delicate handwriting. "There may be times I have to take my wedding band off so I don't damage it, but I did this so you know my vows will always be upheld."

I drop my face into my hands. "You're insane."

"Stop acting like you don't love it." He tugs at my wrists until he can see me again, and a devious smirk slides across his lips when I can't hide my smile any longer. This must've been his appointment in Ladislava a few hours ago. But his ease disappears when he turns back to the group, raising his voice above theirs. "Elowen will perform the ceremony, and if the three of you don't stop bickering like children, I will forcibly remove you from my house and bar you from entering for the foreseeable future." Silence cloaks the room immediately, and Cayden leans his head on the back of the couch, slipping his eyes shut as a sigh escapes his lips. "Fucking finally."

CHAPTER
TWENTY-EIGHT

ELOWEN

I STEP OUT OF MY BOOTS BESIDE THE RIVER THAT CURVES
throughout the property, cringing when my bare foot hits the
frosty ground. A small waterfall spills into a pool at the base of it
before thinning out and continuing its path through the trees.

"Elowen," Asena says, timidly speaking my name despite me ensuring her titles would only complicate matters unnecessarily. "Saskia
told me she informed you of the concept of an anchor."

"She did."

"Due to the gods blessing your union, we believe Cayden to be
your strongest option."

I lift my brows while untying my cloak. "And if I don't believe in
the gods?"

"The tides flow for him as the flames blaze for you. You feel the
pull between the two of you. Don't deny it where your safety is concerned." And quickly adds, "My queen."

I laugh softly, my gaze flashing to Calithea when she flies overhead.
Even if I were to mount a dragon and fly over the border, their eyesight
is much sharper than mine. What looks like a speck to me is fully visible to them. My presence would only endanger them because they'd
have to fly closer to the ground for me to see what's within the cages.

Cayden wordlessly kicks off the tree he was leaning against and
begins disarming himself. I'm sure Finnian would've been a successful

anchor, but I don't know enough about magic to ignore Asena's advice. The place Finnian holds in my heart is warm and bright like a summer's day and being with him makes me feel like the child I never had the chance to be. Finnian refreshes my soul, but Cayden calls to it. There is something both unusual and familiar about my connection to Cayden. I feel it in my bones when he's near and wear his gaze like a gown. We fall into each other so naturally, like a lush garden in full bloom where the flowers grow into and around one another.

I look to Finnian to apologize, but he shakes his head and holds a hand up. "I'm relieved I don't have to freeze in that water, Ellie, and I thank the gods for their consideration of my comfort."

I place my hands on my hips. "I'm not staying with you next time you drink too much at the tavern and vomit up the contents of your stomach."

"That was *one* time."

I give him a flat look.

"It was much more than one time," he amends, pulling his cloak tighter around him as a gust of wind shakes the forest. The treetops sway and sprinkle us with snow. I cross my arms over my chest, already freezing in my thin slip as Cayden stands beside me. He nods only once, and it's all the reassurance I need to face Asena and Ophir on the other side of the pool.

"You'll both need to add a few droplets of blood into the pool," Ophir instructs.

"It's always a blood payment," I mutter. Saskia hands me my dragon dagger, and I rub my thumb over the design before pricking the tip of my finger, letting the red droplets disappear in the shallow depths. Ice coats the surface of the rocks beside the falls, as well as several dotted along the shore and down the river.

Basilius appears when I summon him, circling above the towering evergreens. He's gentler than the others despite being the largest. He has two sides to him, and the switch flips effortlessly. Basilius can go from ripping apart an enemy to whirling through frothy clouds with bloodstained claws in a matter of seconds.

Though the dragons listen to me, I don't control them. If Sorin or Venatrix were to fly over the border, I don't trust them not to engage with the enemy. The dragons suffered for years, and when the memories of their tortured cries in the night resurge, it's like rubbing salt in a wound that'll never heal. Basilius's lavender scales switch to black, camouflaging him against the night sky, and I send a loving stroke down the bond to him.

"What now?" Cayden asks.

"You must enter the pool with Elowen. Keep your hands on her as she floats in the water. It will give her a physical tether to her body," Ophir says.

I feel as if I've stepped on a bed of nails rather than the smooth rocks that make up the riverbed. My teeth clatter together no matter how hard I clench them, but I trudge into the water until we're at the center and lie back. Cayden places his arms under my thighs and back, keeping me as close to him as possible. I call to Basilius through the bond, pulling on the strand within me that connects us.

"You must find a way to slow your heartbeat and let the magic overtake you. Let the water coax what lies within you to the surface," Asena says, lighting a few candles and spreading them along the embankment. She hums a low song in her throat and Ophir glides his fingers through the water.

"How long does she have to be in here?" Cayden asks, our mixed discomfort making his tone harsher than usual . . . which is saying something. "Can I carry her out once the magic takes hold?"

"She can't break her connection to the water, but we'll make a fire once she mindwalks. You can guide her to the edge of the river, but she cannot leave it until she's back in her body," Asena answers.

Their voices grow fainter, and my body becomes numb to the cold. The needlelike sensations cease prodding every inch of my skin, and my ears stop throbbing. I lock my eyes on Basilius, watching his rhythmic circles as his lavender eyes meet mine.

It's just us, sweetling. You have nothing to fear from me, I say through the bond.

The flames within my soul roar inside me, heating my skin and slowing my heartbeat. Basilius breathes comfort into our connection with every flap of his wings and every glance.

I press my head to Cayden's chest to listen to his pulse and spread my fingers, letting the water flow through them, pretending they're my thoughts being washed away until only the shell of me remains.

Basilius flies as if he's nothing more than a feather. I imagine the freedom of what it would feel like to take to the skies at will, to the realm no mortal can claim because it's ruled by the dragons.

Cayden gently strokes my hair. "You were born to ride dragons, now let yourself become one."

Thump.

Thump.

Thump.

The flames of the dragons anointed my existence. Through them, I am immortal. I am limitless. I am the might of the beasts no one can tame.

A crack snaps through me and all sound disappears.

I'm nothing more than a wisp of smoke rising through the air until I'm fire encased in flesh.

The scene before me is created entirely of lavender wisps. A curved bridge stretches over a river, and I peek over the side as shades of gold, light blue, and silver are added to the current. Our auras twine together like hundreds of stars have fallen from the purple sky but hover around me. They stretch as far as I can see instead of crashing into the ground. We're nothing more than souls until I'm thrust into the forefront of his mind, watching the world through the eyes of a dragon.

Basilius turns toward the border, flapping his wings hard enough to take us above the clouds where no one will be able to see us. From this height, I'd never be able to see anything more than specks, especially at night, but for Basilius the world is a vivid landscape.

We soar over Ladislava—familiar sounds of songs, chants, and clattering steel rising from below—and continue onward. It all fades away as we cross over into Imirath. Something restless coils in Basilius, but I calm him with my presence, keeping a hold on his mind without hurting him.

"Stay high," I command, though I'm not sure how. "They can't know we're here."

Basilius doesn't make a sound and slows his pace, decreasing our altitude in minuscule amounts as we stake out a cage. At least fifteen Imirath soldiers stand guard around it, all with spears or swords in hand. I don't spot any others, but I suppose they'll be spread out. We continue monitoring from our vantage point, not wanting to risk landing within the territory. Time slips away from me as Basilius cuts smooth circles through the wispy clouds, a feeling of pure contentedness encompassing me.

I sense a tug, making me feel like I'm late for something, but I shake it off as a spiked tail blasts through one of the tarps. The silencing rune must've been rendered useless once the beast inside broke through the steel because a sharp shriek follows, as do claws raking down the walls of the prison. Basilius is immediately alert, all senses homing in on the potential threat. An Imirath soldier cries out as the tail curls around his neck, but his pained pleas die out quickly as his head is removed from his shoulders. Soldiers rush forward with spears, shouting for aid as they slam the sharp tips into the scaled flesh to tame it, but the beast doesn't react meekly. It continues swinging its tail, sending soldiers flying through the air and puncturing their stomachs with the spiked end.

I've seen a tail like that, I realize. Wyverns. A distant cousin of the dragon. I read about them in one of the beast books I've recently acquired, and seen their likeness drawn within the pages. In most cases, they can't blow fire. The spiked venomous tails are their main weapons against foes. They're smaller and not as fierce as a dragon, but something volatile churns in Basilius as we look down at the scene.

"Not yet," I command. His temper continues mounting now that we've identified what we'll face on the battlefield. "You'll have your chance, but not today. We can't face them alone."

Basilius snarls, but there's too much commotion on the ground for anyone to hear. He begrudgingly turns away, carrying us back to Vareveth when something pulls at the center of my chest again.

A beacon to follow to return home.

CHAPTER
TWENTY-NINE

CAYDEN

THE FOREST IS QUIET, ELOWEN'S BREATHING EVEN MORE so. I've spent the last two hours in this freezing river, clutching her body to mine and counting her breaths. Ophir said I'd probably be able to step out of the river as long as I kept my hands on Elowen, but I can't let her suffer alone. I sent the others back to the house after Asena said it might help if I spoke to Elowen while she's in this state. She can't hear me, but she might be able to feel me. I'd never be able to speak to Elowen about anything deeper than the weather if others were listening.

She's deathly still in my arms with only the whites of her eyes visible and her hair floating around her. It's unnerving. The fire Asena lit is dying, and I won't risk removing my hands. I need to get Elowen inside. My head jerks up when I hear Basilius roar in the distance, close enough to be over the border.

"Elowen," I murmur, my voice strained from the cold. "Wake up."

Nothing.

Not even a twitch of her fingers.

"Elowen." I shake her in my arms a bit. "*Wake up.*"

Panic begins to claw its way up my throat like a beast threatening to breach the surface and overtake me. She looks dead. There is no warmth to her, no vibrancy. I lock my eyes on her steady, albeit slow, pulse. Gods, I can hardly look at her. This ritual is fucking with my head by shoving the image of what chases me from sleep most nights in my face.

"Elowen!"

I hiss when her limbs thrash, splashing my arms and chest with water. Her brown eyes are back, soaking in the sights around us as she reaches up to clutch her forehead. "Are you all right?"

She looks up at me, pressing her hands into her face, shoulders, and heaving chest as her shivers send ripples throughout the water. "Y-yes."

I hoist her in my arms before she even finishes the word. She continues looking around as if she's seeing the world for the first time. Snow crunches under my bare feet, but I can't be any colder than I already am. I grab her cloak from where Finnian hung it on a branch and wrap it around her shoulders, using my coat to cover her front and rush toward Koa. Mounting him while keeping her balanced in my arms is a difficult feat but I manage. I keep her pressed to my chest as I jostle the reins, urging Koa to sprint to the house.

My mind is filled to the brim with questions, but I force myself to save them for later. I need to get her inside and bring her body temperature back up. The wind slices into my cheeks and biceps as we ride, and I shove her face into the crook of my neck.

I dismount once we make it back, and the back door slams against the wall when I shove our way through. A staggering breath of relief rushes from my chest as the warmth wafting through the house surrounds me. The servants must have all the fires burning.

"Is there anything you need, Your Highness?" Cyrus asks, rushing into the hall and practically running to keep up with my steps. "I've already lit a fire in your chambers."

"Send soup and tea up," I respond without turning. "Thank you."

Saskia, Ryder, and Finnian spring off the steps when they see us, and Asena and Ophir turn away from the window.

"What did she see?" Saskia asks.

"Not now." My tone is final, and though Ryder and Saskia have pushed me on a few occasions over the years, they know when not to cross that line. "I have her, and she will give you a report when she's ready."

"Is she okay?" Finnian calls out.

"She will be once she rests."

I kick the door to our chambers shut and set her down in front of the fire, tugging the soaked slip up her body and tossing it aside. I do the same with my pants and return to her with several thick blankets. She presses herself into me, sitting between my covered legs as I wrap another around her shoulders. I messily pile her hair on top of her head to get it off her back and secure it with the leather strap I always wear around my wrist in case she ever needs it.

She keeps looking around the room like she's trying to reorient herself with reality, still not entirely in her own mind. I'm sure it'll get easier the more she utilizes her abilities, but the first time must be the worst. I'd be in awe of her if the image of her white eyes and unresponsive body in my arms hadn't brought my worst fear into reality.

Her wide eyes are locked on my face, looking at me like I'm the only real thing in the world. There's a desperation I've never seen laced within her gaze.

"You're back with me, sirantia. You're home," I murmur, rubbing my hands along her arms.

Her shivering begins to calm down, but she still trembles slightly as she reaches forward, pressing the tip of her finger into the top of the scar on my face, slowly dragging it down before repeating the motion three times. Nobody has ever touched me like she does. I'd cut their hand off if they tried. She sags against me and presses her forehead to my shoulder, nuzzling into my neck.

I place my fingers against her pulse, keeping an arm banded around her as I watch the flames consume the log. Elowen possesses magic. I'm not surprised, considering she shares a bond with five dragons, but I'm curious to know what other abilities she may have.

"How bad does my hair look?" she mumbles.

I chuckle. "*That's* what you're worried about?"

"My hair is very important to me."

"It looks like you threw out your comb five years ago and never bought a new one."

She groans. "I'm calling off the wedding."

"Good luck with that."

We return to silence while watching the fire. Cyrus and another servant carry up trays filled with what I requested along with several sweet options for dessert. They're trying to charm Elowen, and from the way she smiles softly while looking at the spread, I'd say it's working. We polish everything off, and when I'm sure her body temperature has risen enough to get into a bath, I hoist her in my arms.

I don't make the water too hot, just in case the normal boiling temperature she bathes in is too much for her to handle right now, and settle her between my legs. "What did you see?"

Her chest presses into mine as she continues resting her head on my shoulder, still tracing the scars on my chest and arms. She touches me like every detail of me is worthy of being remembered. I've been deprived of her body for weeks, and having her pressed against me is an addictive kind of torture. Thoughts of her plague my mind like a curse I never wish to be freed from.

"Wyverns." She matches my quiet tone. "They'll be bringing the battle to the skies it seems."

My hands tighten on her hips. "Training with a bow and arrow could be beneficial. We don't know if they'll have riders."

She huffs. "I hate that weapon. I'll be fine with my knives."

I tuck my tongue into my cheek, not responding to her statement, opting to untie her curls and begin washing them. She moans when my soapy fingers massage her roots, sending a wave of want through me. I suck in a slow breath, forcing myself to think of strategy and not what she looks like under me.

Finnian is a skilled archer, and I don't doubt he's tried to train her over the years. I'll need to think of something different, but she'll need something with more power behind it than just a throw. Thank the fucking gods wyverns don't breathe fire or else we'd be having a much more heated conversation.

"How do they have wyverns?" she asks. "Where did they come from?"

"I once read about a mage from Thirwen who lived about one hundred years ago. Some say that she used necromancy to raise two wyverns from the dead, but others say she captured them in the wild, though they were believed to be extinct at the time. She kept them in cages, forcing them to breed, and then forced the hatchlings to breed when they came of age. It was a deplorable and cruel practice, and the wyverns were controlled by mind magic. They were never let out of their cages while having free will. That's why the world held its breath when it was revealed you have a soul bond to your dragons. Nobody has ever possessed your power."

"That's terrible." When Elowen mounts her dragons and kills the wyverns she faces, their death will be a mercy to the beasts. "I just . . . I can't think about that right now knowing what I'll have to do during the battles. What did you find earlier in Xantheus's office?"

"Thirwen is sending more naval reinforcements than I anticipated," I say. "I sent orders for a chain of scouts to keep watch along the coast. We'll be alerted when each of them lights their beacons."

"I hope we hear from Galakin soon." I clench my jaw. I'll find a way to manipulate Galakin into this war if they don't come willingly. She pushes away from my chest to meet my eyes. "I'm assuming you have a plan of attack?"

"Always. I also forged the letter so we can use it to charge Xantheus with treason since he didn't report an enemy's movements to his rulers."

"I'll be glad when he dies." Her eyelids are heavy with exhaustion as she falls forward again, and I suck in a breath through my teeth when her hand glides over the head of my cock. She laughs softly. "I won't bed you before my wedding. I'm a lady."

"Oh, yes," I mutter. "A lady of the night."

She lightly smacks the back of my head and climbs out of the tub while wrapping herself in a towel, swaying her hips as she walks into the bedchamber. I chuckle under my breath as I finish up in the bath before following her path. I'm surprised to find her already fast asleep when I slide into bed.

The fire from the hearth dances over her features, making it impossible to tear my eyes away as I lie on my side to face her. When I look at her, it's like I know what it is to see my heart beating outside of my body. I twirl one of her damp curls around the finger that now has her name inked onto it.

After living on the streets, not even being in a house could fully eliminate the cold within me. Not until I met Elowen and had her in my grasp. Love is supposed to be something light and beautiful and pure, but what I feel for the woman sleeping beside me could lay waste to armies and end worlds.

I've never cared about anyone like this, never wanted or had the urge to. It feels as if I've never truly seen anyone now that I see her everywhere. I know this path is dangerous, and yet I can't stop following it. She makes a noise of irritation, scrunching her nose a bit as she blinks her bleary eyes open, wrapping herself around me without saying a word.

Gods, I'm fucked.

I'm well and truly fucked.

CHAPTER
THIRTY

ELOWEN

"IT NEEDS MORE DETAIL," SASKIA SAYS BEFORE TAKING A sip from the dainty cup in her hand. "A royal wedding is more than a ceremony, it's a statement to the entirety of Ravaryn. Elowen has a penchant for enjoying finery given the extravagance of her everyday attire, so we can't scrimp on adornments."

"I wouldn't call it a *penchant*. I simply have particular taste, and my eye just so happens to gravitate toward more expensive items entirely coincidentally."

Saskia laughs as she tucks her feet up on the couch beside her. "Of course."

Gazing at myself in the trifold mirror, I scrutinize the white fabric pinned to my body. A team of three dressmakers buzzes around me like busy bees, their various pins acting as stingers. I've been poked and prodded more in this single session than ever. The woman behind me abruptly tightens the fabric along my spine, straightening my back and pushing my breasts up at once.

"Much better," I say through a strained breath.

The seamstress pinning the hem smiles up at me from the base of the box I'm standing upon. "The bodice will be adorned with thousands of tiny gold beads that will trail down your skirts."

"We know you prefer flowing sleeves, so how about we do split sleeves just beneath your elbows with a sheer blue layer of fabric as another ode to your union?" The seamstress behind me adds. "We could also embroider small blue flowers along the vines on your skirts. Forget-me-nots are an option given their deep blue hue."

"And blue dragons on the backs of her arms!"

I nod. "That sounds—"

My head jerks up at the sound of the door opening. Everyone in the room gasps. Saskia abruptly stands, and the women lurch for the dressing screen to hide me, but it's all for naught.

"I believe brothers are allowed to see the gown prior to the wedding," Finnian says, his voice thickening the longer he looks at me.

Everyone aside from me lets out a collective sigh of relief. Finnian shuts the door behind him and slowly walks toward me. His throat bobs as he takes in the panels upon panels of ivory fabric. "Ellie."

"Finny." My lips quirk up on one side as my eyes grow warm. "Can you give us a moment?" I ask the woman who pulled my bodice tighter. She's the leader of the three despite them working as a unit.

"We could help you out of the dress if that's easier, Your Majesty. We've done as much as we can here, and the sooner we get it to the shop, the sooner we can start sewing."

"I'll be done in a minute," I say to Finnian as he offers me a hand down from the platform, nodding silently as he continues looking at me. "Don't cry." My voice is as thick and wobbly as his.

"I'm going to look out the window." He walks like there's a fire beneath his heels, and I force my eyes to dry as the women help me out of the gown without giving me another cut. I feel like their personal pin cushion. They leave me behind the screen, and I remove the slip I left on, unable to stomach the idea of being completely bare with strangers, and don the lavender gown I wore yesterday. The thick velvety material isn't a foolproof defense against the cold, but it helps.

Finnian's red tunic is rumpled from riding, and his cheeks are wind-kissed from the cold. "How'd it go with the Aestilian soldiers, Commander?"

"They're prepared to fight for their queen," he says, finally tearing his eyes away from the property and giving me his full attention. "Now, tell me, what can I do for *my* queen?"

"Walk me down the aisle?"

His arms drop to his sides and his eyes widen. I'm a daughter with the heart of an orphan, but I've always had a brother since the moment Finnian entered my life. We made our own family.

"I need you to know that it always would've been you I asked to do this, even if Ailliard were still here. You're the person I've loved longest."

He loses his battle with his emotions, muttering a curse as tears stream down his cheeks. His arms wrap around me, sweeping me off my feet as he swings me in circles. I laugh into the crook of his neck, wet with tears of my own, before he sets me on my feet.

"Of course, Ellie. I'd be honored."

His reaction eases something within me. I've been on edge since I woke up, knowing I'd be fitted for my wedding dress. I don't recall ever dreaming of a wedding, even when I was a little girl. When you don't believe you're destined for or deserving of love, it seems pointless to dream of it. Saskia follows me out of the sitting room, accepting a stack of letters tied with a ribbon from a waiting servant in the hall. Finnian doesn't remain with us. He's due to meet Cayden and Ryder to give them insight into his soldiers' numbers and skills. I could've done it, but I'm glad it's Finnian. Appointing him as commander was one of the easiest decisions I've ever made.

I was informed that Chef Leonardo takes a nap between breakfast and lunch, and I'm relieved to find that to be true. The kitchen is vacant. Wooden beams that match the counters and island at the center run along the stone walls and ceiling. I throw a pale-yellow apron over my gown and sink to my knees to light the fire beneath the oven to bring it up to the desired temperature as I work. It's quaint but has everything you could need for either baking or cooking. Copper pots hang from shelves filled with potted herbs and spices, and sacks of flour and sugar line the wall beneath a large window. Saskia gets settled at the breakfast nook in the corner, and I put the kettle on for her.

For loving baking as much as I do, I haven't done it much. I mainly learned by watching bakers through their kitchen windows while I perched in a tree, swearing to myself I'd one day be able to have food I wanted, not just food I ate because it was available. Sitting still has never been a skill I've mastered, and with the current state of my mind, I'd probably create a trench in the floor with all of my pacing.

I like to bake because it's one of the only things where I can control the outcome. I garden because I want to know that my hands can create life, not just take it away. I read because sometimes the confines of this world seek to strangle me, and the words grant me a haven.

"Urasos and Feynadra have responded," Saskia says when I place the teacup in front of her. "The king and queen of Feynadra will attend, but the crown prince and princess of Urasos will come in place of the king. He's gravely ill and can't risk the journey."

I blow a rogue curl out of my face while dumping flour into a bowl. "Tell me what you know about them."

She sets her letter aside, fixing her dark eyes on me as I bustle around the space. I know basic information from tutoring myself, but I need more. "Queen Nasha of Feynadra is the sister of Queen Cordelia of Galakin and they are rumored to be quite close. She may be able to put in a good word with Cordelia since she won't be in attendance. The king of Feynadra, Lycidias, is extremely reserved, and known as the frost king. I don't believe it'll be challenging to get either of them to recognize your claim as heir to Imirath or secure neutrality. They're extremely traditional. Queen Nasha has earned the title she-wolf due to her protective nature of her children; they're her only happiness in her marriage. Lycidias doesn't concern himself with issues in other kingdoms and will want to keep his soldiers close in case Vareveth falls."

"My letter to Cordelia has still gone unanswered so let's hope Nasha has some sway over her sister." I finish mixing my dry ingredients and begin mashing raspberries in a separate bowl. "What of Urasos?"

"They're a bit more complicated." Saskia sighs, gliding a hand down her crimson skirts and taking a sip of tea. "Princess Lethia is a noble woman originally from Thirwen, and I don't know how close she is with her family. Her father is the richest in the kingdom and married her off to Prince Hale with a substantial dowry. Apparently, she hated Prince Hale in the beginning, but they seem to have resolved their issues. He adores her now. Urasos has the same reputation as Feynadra for remaining neutral, but I don't know if Thirwen's involvement with Imirath will influence that."

A crease forms between my brows. "If they can't assure their neutrality and refuse to support my rightful claim to the Imirath throne, we'll be forced to regard them as enemies. I suppose we'll see how deep Prince Hale's admiration for the princess runs when dragons are flying over their kingdom."

Saskia nods. "Let them speak first. Both of us know firsthand how women in our world aren't valued by their fathers."

"I will." I scoop the raspberry mixture into my shortbread tarts and place them in the stone cavern. The scent of cinnamon surrounds me when I begin my next recipe, not bothering to clean the island since another mess will be created. "Anything noteworthy in your reports?"

"No news of the lords yet, but you only just planted the seed last night," she responds, adding the opened letter to her pile and opening another. She blinks slowly, her eyes skimming over the words several times as her lips part. "There was a revolt in the southern isles."

My spine straightens. "The southern isles?"

"Yes." She glances up at me in disbelief. "It was quickly quelled, but my spy reports that the tension is palpable in the streets. A group of fishermen threw their nets around Imirath soldiers patrolling the docks. At least four drowned, but it's said they called for the rightful king." She shakes her head. "I don't understand. House Vellgrave was slaughtered years ago. None of the heirs survived your great-grandsire."

"Cayden," I whisper, realization washing over me.

"Cayden? Why would they be calling for Cayden?"

Saskia doesn't know Cayden's parentage. "His father was from the southern isles. Cayden may not have royal blood, but he's the only king alive with their blood."

"That's perfect!" She abruptly smacks her hands against the table, and clumps of brown sugar fly through the air as I squeal. "It strengthens your claim. Why hasn't he brought this up?"

Cayden hates his father—that's abundantly clear. He probably doesn't want anything to do with him, even if it makes his life easier now. He'd view it as a favor from him. "I'll talk to him when he gets home."

"I guessed he was part southerner years ago, and he lied." She scoffs. "He probably didn't want Ryder and me to have another win against him after Ryder figured out his birthday."

"How did Ryder manage that?"

She laughs while glancing out the window to the snowy forest. "He wished Cayden a happy birthday every day until he pissed Cayden off enough to reveal it."

I laugh softly, but it's weighed down by insecurity. "When is his birthday?"

"The ninth of November." It passed weeks ago. We would've been in Imirath on that date . . . but I didn't even know. The lump in my throat doesn't disappear when I swallow. It stays lodged there like a rock. The rolling pin clatters on the ground, the abrupt noise causing Saskia to jerk her head. "El? What's wrong?"

"I just wasn't expecting to know him on the date you said."

"He hates his birthday anyway. Don't feel bad."

I shake my head, dusting the rolling pin off with my apron and setting it on the counter as Saskia steps toward me. "We're getting married, and I didn't even know that about him. It's something so basic."

Saskia reads my emotions easily. "Have you talked to him about what you're feeling? It's all right to be nervous."

We start out in life completely defenseless, but time draws its blades against us, and only those who don armor live to fight another battle. "Think about how many people get married and then wake up one day and don't recognize the person they've bound their life to."

I don't know why my mind works the way it does, making the words I hear become twisted like prickly brambles in a dark forest. My emotions battle with logic, but there's never a winner, rendering my thoughts a wasteland of casualties. I don't want to second-guess Cayden, but I feel like it's my last defense against him.

"I'm fine," I assure her quickly while removing the raspberry tarts from the oven, not wanting to truly dissect my fears. "Maybe I had sex with him on his birthday and unknowingly gave him the best present he ever received."

"I think you might've made his life." I throw a pinch of flour at her, and it paints her dark cheeks that get rounder as she laughs. "He's not like everyone else. I told Cayden he should marry you to solidify the alliance before I met you, and he was adamantly against it. He said he would never subject himself to the hell of marriage." I flinch before I can stop myself. "The man you know is someone nobody has ever met, not even me or Ryder. He broke the Dasterian line not because he wanted the crown, but because he was terrified of losing you. There is darkness in Cayden, and it's made so many people run from him, but I've always thought that was why he was running to you all his life. You're his light."

I press my lips together, dragging my pendant along its chain. "You truly mean that?"

"I know it." She squeezes my wrist before letting go and stealing a tart from where they're cooling.

"When are yours and Ryder's?" I ask, not wanting to miss anyone else's. Finnian's is the fourteenth of July, and we always do something to celebrate, same with mine.

Saskia's eyes soften. "I'm the fourth of September and Ryder is the tenth of December. Yours?"

"The fifteenth of January."

Her smile widens. "I'll start planning."

We pass our time in comfortable silence, and I realize how nice it is to be with someone without having to be present the entire time. I lose myself in the recipes—kneading dough, sprinkling powdered sugar, making icing. Not stopping until the counters are covered in various baked goods and heavy footsteps pound down the hall.

"You owe me a debt, angel." Cayden's deep voice echoes through the corridor, and my stupid, hopeless heart kicks in my chest at the sound of it.

"You must be thinking of someone else," I say. "I owe you nothing."

Cayden steps around the corner, filling the doorway with his large frame clad in his familiar black tunic and loose pants with a sword strapped across his back ... but it's what's on top of his clothes that makes the tin slip from my fingers and clatter loudly on the counter. "I've come to collect."

He lunges for me, and by reflex, I sprint around the island, but it only seems to encourage him. My tongue feels like dead weight in my mouth while I blink slowly. Not truly absorbing the sight in front of me. I must be dreaming. "Oh, my gods."

"You don't remember," he says the words like he's accusing me of a crime. "During your first dinner in Vareveth you told me you'd kiss me if I wore the pinkest and frilliest apron."

Laughter bubbles in my throat, spilling out of me until my stomach hurts. "How the hells do you remember that?"

"I remember everything about you." He curls his finger toward him. "Pay up, princess."

I scrunch up my nose, keeping the island between us as I slowly move in time with him, wanting to force him to catch me. "Are you that desperate?"

"Determined." He lunges around the counter, and I yelp while quickly rounding the corner to keep him across from me. His green eyes scan the full counters piled high with cinnamon rolls, honey buns, bread loaves, and the raspberry tarts. "Are you baking for the entire army?"

"Aestilian," I correct. "I wanted to make something for the children before the war takes me away."

He lifts a brow. "I don't think any of this will make it farther than the front door."

"Not even for children?"

"I was a child once."

I throw my apron at his face and book it for the door, pumping my arms as my legs carry me down the hall. My heart thunders in my chest as Cayden's long strides soon catch up with me and he grabs me around the waist, spinning me in his arms before pressing my back into the wall. His heart beats in time with mine, slamming against his rib cage as he pulls me flush against him.

"Easy, demon," I whisper, pressing my fingers into his mouth hovering inches from mine. It's a punishment for myself as well as him, but his determination is addictive.

"You are playing a very dangerous game, angel," he states in a low tone.

"That is the best kind." I love having this power over him and adore making him ache for me. He drops his forehead to mine and looks at me with so much yearning that I can feel it like a tether between us. "I think pink is your color."

"Don't get used to it." His gaze remains locked on my lips like they're the only thing he can see as he removes the pink fabric. "I have something for you. Are you almost done?"

"Fuck me, this is good," Ryder groans from the kitchen, and I push away from Cayden and run back from where I came, finding Ryder at the small breakfast nook by the window with a plate piled high. "Elowen, if it doesn't work out between you and Cayden then I'm—"

"Sas, grab your letters," Cayden warns. Water flies over my shoulder, drenching Ryder and his ample pickings. Cayden loudly tosses the bucket that I was using to wash dishes to the floor. "I've been meaning to get that leak checked."

I cover my mouth with my hand to try to suppress my laughter while Ryder sputters and wipes his eyes and Saskia clings to the wall like a lifeline. "That was highly uncalled for!"

"What did you think was going to happen after you said that?" Finnian manages to ask through his boisterous laughs. "He's threatened people for looking at her."

"Not that!" Ryder shouts.

Cayden shrugs, unlatching the window and tossing a honey bun to

Delmira. My heart tightens in my chest, knowing that years ago he watched me do the same thing. I throw a cloak around my shoulders before putting my boots on.

Cayden shoves a honey bun into his mouth as he waits and grabs a cinnamon roll for the brief walk outside. The wind slams into my face as he unlatches the wooden door, carrying away the flour and sugar speckling my cheeks. My boots sink into the snow when I stop dead in my tracks, spotting a quiver filled with arrows and an array of red targets in the distance.

"I told you I hate shooting with a bow."

"Which is why I brought you something different," he replies, pressing a hand into my back to keep me walking, and plucks a sleek, polished weapon from the table he must've set up. "A crossbow."

I take it from his hands, surprised by how much it weighs, and envy Cayden for how effortless he makes it look to hold this thing. "I've never used one of these."

"You have this wonderful thing called a husband who is well-versed in many weapons." I roll my eyes, not bothering to correct him again—it won't get through his thick skull. He pulls my back to his front, covering his hands with mine to show me how to properly hold the weapon. "Remember that if your eye ever wanders." He kisses my cheek. "Now, you're going to keep this finger on the trigger and aim at eye level. It's best to keep both eyes open to get an accurate shot."

He keeps his lips close to my ear, maneuvering the crossbow into the correct position and pressing down on my finger, letting the arrow fly and absorbing the kickback as it hits the center of the target. He releases me to grab an arrow from the quiver lodged in the snow and twirls it in his fingers as he shows me how to reload it. "Is this why you couldn't sleep last night? Were you thinking about me fighting the wyverns?"

His lips remain shut, and his face gives nothing away as he juts his chin toward the target. I roll my neck, keeping my feet shoulder width apart and taking the shot. The arrow zings through the air, landing several inches away from the center.

"When you're using it in a battle, you'll feel when the aim is right. The more you use it the easier it'll become." He moves behind me again, correcting my stance with his arms wrapped around me. He fires again, splitting the previous arrow he shot down the middle when the other lands in the same place. I lower the crossbow, tilting my head back as he straightens to his full height. "Show every bastard on that field what you can do, El. Show them what it means to be your enemy."

"There's something you need to know," I say. His brows furrow, but he doesn't release me. It's better he hears this from my lips. "There are revolts in the southern isles. The people are calling for the rightful king. You're the only ruler in Ravaryn with the blood of the southern isles with a claim to the Imirath throne. I think they're calling for you."

His eyes narrow as he runs his tongue over his teeth. "Okay."

I drop the crossbow to my side, turning to face him as he twirls one of my curls around his finger. "Okay?"

He shrugs. "Imirath soldiers knew who I was when my father entered me in fights, and he had the deep tan complexion of most people in the southern isles, same as me. I don't have any royal blood, so if they're calling for a bastard to be their king then so be it."

"You're not bothered?"

"Of course I'm bothered," he says. "I don't want a damn thing from that man." He grabs the crossbow from my hand and points it at the farthest target that's no more than a speck in the distance. "But this will gain us an advantage because if they're calling for me, they're calling for you. It further weakens Garrick if people in his territory are calling for a bastard and a displaced heir to take his throne. Let them scream our names loud enough to reach Garrick in the tallest tower of his castle as an omen of what's coming."

He pulls the trigger, hitting the target dead center.

CHAPTER

THIRTY-ONE

ELOWEN

CALITHEA SHARPLY DOWNTURNS ALONG ONE OF THE CAS-
tle spires, twirling around the tower effortlessly. Instead of
taking hold of the saddle horns, I spread my arms wide, reveling in the feeling of being weightless while my saddle straps keep me
attached to her. It's a high I've never experienced and know I'll never
find elsewhere.

She evens out, swooping up again and carrying me to where I'm
needed. I unhook myself and slide down her wing into the meeting
room that's open on all sides, with only a few ivy-covered pillars to
offer some semblance of a barrier from the staggering fall to the bottom. The magic within the castle must keep the plants alive, considering the Dasterians were once linked to earth magic.

Basilius shoves his head between the pillars Calithea vacated, nuzzling my stomach with his snout as I pull my glove off with my teeth.
I kiss him between the eyes before he turns away, taking to the skies
with the others to stand guard over me.

"How is it that it takes you longer to get here on dragonback than
it does for us on horses?" Ryder asks as I stride toward the long table.

I slide my coat down my arms and hand it off to a servant. The
room is enchanted to stay heated despite the open concept, but the
cold nips at my exposed shoulders and clings to the crown resting
across my forehead. A dark blue sapphire glimmers in the center and

matches my off-the-shoulder corset top embellished with gold bro-
cade along the bodice, draping sleeves, and panels of fabric that reach
just below the backs of my knees. "If you could ride a dragon, you'd
never want your feet on the ground."

"Fair point," he responds.

I take a seat beside Cayden in one of the upholstered chairs at the
head of the polished dark wood table and wrap my fingers around a
cup of tea awaiting me. Two crystal decanters of wine rest on either
side of the table, and candlelight from the chandelier hanging in the
center of the elaborate ceiling dances like the flames are trapped
within. I take a moment to admire my surroundings.

When I first arrived, the Vareveth castle looked like it was an enchanted forest, and though it retains certain elements, it's now kissed
by the night. House Veles is the only house in Ravaryn history that
will possess the ability to touch the sky, and the regality cloaking our
castle certainly reflects that fact. Dragons are chiseled into the pillars
surrounding the perimeter of the room, always serving as a reminder
of the power I possess.

I stand beside Cayden as across from us Braxton and four battle-
worn generals step through the double doors bordered with banners
bearing our sigil. Cayden's gold crown glints as he moves, and the thick
velvety material of his quilted tunic hugs his biceps and shoulders. He
looks strong, imposing. I don't understand how Eagor looked at him
and only saw a commander. Cayden is a king, not because it's in his
blood, but because it's in his soul.

"Generals," Cayden says. "May I present my queen, Elowen Atarah."

"The woman who brought dragons into the world. It's an honor,"
a man with shoulder-length auburn hair says. He's not particularly
tall, but he's built like a mountain. I smile at him, grateful the mention
of my parentage doesn't seem to inspire any animosity in those gathered. "General Killian."

"It's lovely to meet you," I reply as he takes the spot beside Finnian.
Cayden told me bits about them over breakfast this morning. All of
them were infantry soldiers that Cayden promoted after he became

commander. They've all fought by his side in various battles. Their positions were hard-earned.

The blond woman introduces herself next, a soft smile lifting the scar that cuts through her lips. "Ren." A woman with hair chopped below her chin, a shade of red so deep it's almost purple, takes the spot beside her and introduces herself as Autumn, a fitting name really. Both women are quite tall and muscular, but Autumn has warm, golden skin whereas Ren is fairer.

Braxton smiles warmly at me before coming to stand at my side, a hand resting on his sword. There's only one man I don't yet know. His hair is golden blond and tumbles down his broad shoulders. "Gryffin," he says.

I repeat the names several times in my head, willing myself not to forget them. Unease twists my gut when I think of past guards: Ailliard, Zander, Nessa, Esme . . . Lycus, who I couldn't save, the others that I killed. But I shove it down, forcing myself to move forward.

"May I present Finnian Eira," I say. "Commander of the Aestilian forces."

Quite like Cayden, none of the finery they wear can mask the danger that wafts off them like a smoke signal. It serves as a warning. I know Cayden would never have become the demon commander of Ravaryn had he not had those loyal to him ready to do his bidding.

"Before the lords get here, there is something you all need to be aware of and it is not to leave this room," Cayden begins. "Thirwen has mobilized its naval fleet, and I've stationed scouts along the border to alert us when they're spotted." He stands from his seat, pulling the map of Ravaryn closer to him. "They won't travel through the center of the Dolent Sea and risk being spotted by Galakin's naval patrols, so they'll be closer to us." The rings on his fingers glint as he smooths the map's surface. "General Ren and General Killian, ready your forces to march at a moment's notice. We'll be attacking when they dock."

"When they dock in Imirath?" Killian asks. "What if they dock on the southern tip of the peninsula? We'd have to travel through the entire kingdom to reach them."

"They'll be bringing provisions for the army stationed at the border, and presumably off-loading foot soldiers. The only port deep enough for ships like that to get close to shore is Port Celestria. We'll move under the cover of darkness and board our ships after Thirwen passes to keep up with them. The army will have to finish the journey by marching, but we'll dock in a cove close by." He juts his chin toward me. "Elowen will burn the ships, and we'll handle the army."

Port Celestria is said to be one of Imirath's most beautiful beaches. It earns its name because the stars shine so bright that they're reflected perfectly in the water. Waves upon waves of stars crash onto beaches bordered by obsidian stones, making it entirely night-kissed.

"Yes, sire," they both answer in unison.

"Once we claim the port, we should be able to hold it, considering it rests on our border."

"It'll make Imirath look weak, and though it won't cut off their trade route entirely, it'll complicate matters," Ryder surmises.

Cayden nods in response and lifts his gaze to the door as more footsteps approach. "Not another word about this."

We sit down as three lords escorted by castle guards strut through the double doors. All look to be in their fifties, and their richly colored outfits laden with jewels create an interesting contrast to the generals in armor, leathers, and cloaks. The three men bow and occupy the remaining seats.

"Your Majesties," the first man says. He wears a purple-and-gold coat with fur around the collar. I take note of his features, black hair sprinkled with gray and equally dark eyes. "My name is Lord Xantheus. Accompanying me is Lord Caspian." He gestures to the dark-skinned man in red. "And Lord Drystan." He finishes by pointing to the slim man with white-blond hair.

Cayden's hard gaze remains locked on Lord Xantheus, and I recognize his voice. He was the most vocal about his hatred for me . . . and my skin crawls when I recall the vile threats masked by laughter.

Saskia clears her throat. "As I'm sure you've all heard by now King Garrick is taking a new wife with the intention of fathering more children to displace Queen Elowen as heir. This has now become a war of succession. Elowen is his firstborn, and the throne is hers by right."

"But Her Majesty is not a son. If King Garrick manages to have a son before the war is over, many will support his claim, even as an infant," Drystan says in a nasally voice. "What are the plans for the child or children if they're born before the war is over?"

"They will be welcomed into our home," I state.

Drystan must not catch my tone because he continues, "They would be the offspring of Garrick Atarah. All his offspring should be slaughtered."

My fingers grip the arm of my chair. I have no doubt he includes me in that statement, and the thought of children—*innocents*—being murdered for political gain sickens me. If I cannot hold a throne without utilizing mindless butchery then I don't deserve to be on it.

"Mind your tongue, Drystan," Cayden states in a low voice, not addressing the man with his proper title. "The next time you speak of the blood that runs through Queen Elowen's veins, I'll throw you off this tower. If she's feeling merciful, she can send a dragon to retrieve you before you hit the ground, but I'll leave that up to her."

Drystan's cheeks redden, and he waves a servant over to pour his wine. "I meant no offense to Her Majesty."

Xantheus speaks next, interjecting in a much more cheerful tone. "Many speculate there is an alternative reason for the rushed wedding. Can we expect an heir to be produced in the upcoming months?"

"You can hope, but it will go unfulfilled," I reply. "I have battles to fight, and I will not bring a child into a war-torn kingdom."

"The dragons are untested. What Vareveth needs is an heir, not a queen riding off into battle and potentially dying in the process."

"I wasn't aware you were so privy to Vareveth's needs." I pierce him with my eyes, urging him to shrink in his seat. "I will have the Imirath throne and Garrick Atarah's head, and I will not achieve either while sitting in a castle. The next person to insinuate my place is on the ground or in the birthing bed will regret it. Though I should thank you for your concern. If any of you are truly worried about my dragons' capabilities, I encourage you to face them yourselves and see how quickly steel and flesh melt."

"I do not doubt your capability, Your Highness," he practically snarls, his cheeks taking on an ugly ruddiness. "It is merely known that the gentler sex is best kept within the house."

"And yet you've expressed such bravery by leaving yours today. I applaud you." I stand from my chair, pressing my palms into the table in front of me, moving without the haste or anger he exudes. "You're welcome to try to take the crown off my head should you succumb to the stupidity coursing through your veins like a disease. Draw your sword and see which of us walks away from the duel."

His eyes flash to all those in attendance other than his fellow lords. Hands rest on the hilts of swords, ready to slice him open should he make a move against me. "The other lords know where I am, and they will know who to blame if you kill me."

"One of the wisest decisions I've made was killing someone who tried to control me." I quirk a brow. "I've gotten quite good at it."

"You have no idea what's coming for you in this war," Xantheus sneers.

"I'm prepared," I calmly state, which only enrages him further.

"No, you're not!" He shoves to his feet so quickly that the chair falls back and clatters on the ground. Cayden squeezes the back of my thigh in silent encouragement.

"I've been preparing to face Imirath my entire life, and a few ships from Thirwen won't deter me."

"A few?" He laughs incredulously, spit flying from his mouth as the vein in his forehead throbs. "You will face far more than a few."

I remain silent, saying nothing as a smirk grows on my lips and Cayden slowly stands at my side. "How do you know that?"

Xantheus blinks, looking down at the floor before pinging his gaze between us. "Imirath's alliance with Thirwen is public knowledge."

"The magnitude of their aid is not." Cayden rests his hand on my back. "Failing to report any knowledge you have regarding an enemy's movements is treason."

"I don't have any knowledge."

"You trade with several Thirwen nobles and write to them regularly."

"Are you having me followed?" he growls. "I am loyal to Vareveth! I have always been loyal to Vareveth!"

"You're loyal to your profit," Cayden replies while reaching into his pocket to pull out the letter he traced in Xantheus's office, watching as horror floods the man's features as he shakes his head in disbelief. "I granted you the courtesy of a warning, a privilege I don't dole out regularly, and you have squandered it."

"No," he mutters, scrambling sloppily toward the door to escape, but the castle guards cross their spears. "No! You stole from me! Nobody in my house would betray me. You're nothing more than a fucking thief from the slums!"

"Better a thief from the slums than a lord with minutes left to live," Cayden says as he gestures for the guards to return Xantheus to his place. He turns to me. "Aso es tesis tasuri nunti cytore vos?" *Who is the man that threatened you?*

"What is he saying?" Xantheus demands, the other two lords looking just as frightened. Cayden is both unpredictable and ruthless. He's just as likely to stab someone through their back as he is while looking at them in the eyes. Though they were all present during the banquet, it's Lord Drystan's voice I remember.

I smirk while answering Cayden in the ancient language, just to unnerve them even more. "Tesis sosta addi." *The small one.*

"Por vos, mia sirantia," Cayden says as he shoves his chair back and tucks his hands into his pockets while strolling around the table. *Por vos* translates to *for you*, but much to my dismay, I still don't know what *sirantia* means. I'm sure I could ask Asena, but I want to figure it out on my own. Whatever it is, he added *my* in front of it.

None of them dare to move. They're hardly breathing as Cayden's boots slowly thump against the floor. Whimpers escape from their sealed lips. I reclaim my seat, leaning back and propping my chin on my hand while I watch the show.

"Your servants are far more forthcoming when it comes to relaying treason." He stops behind them and slowly unsheathes his sword, letting the steel sing until the room falls silent again. And then he moves, striking as quickly as a viper as he fists Drystan's blond hair and slams his head against the table, placing the pommel of his sword beneath his eye. His scream rings through the air as Cayden yanks his head back up. Blood drips from his eye socket, splattering against the table and mixing with his tears. Xantheus and Caspian try to flee again but are restrained by the guards at the door as they plead and beg. "Did you think there would be no retribution after you said you'd bend my woman over a table while your friends watched you defile her?"

He tightens his hand in Drystan's hair, making him scream louder. "Now they will watch as I demonstrate what happens to those who threaten my queen."

He hits him hard enough between his shoulder blades for a crack to echo through the space, mingling with the flames popping in the hearth and inspiring the same warmth within me. Drystan falls forward. His cheek presses against the table, entirely at Cayden's mercy as he slowly shoves his sword between Drystan's ribs. The man thrashes and spits blood. Cayden's face is cloaked in vengeance and without an ounce of pity as he looks down at the dead lord, his body in the same position he jested about putting me in.

He wipes his blade on Drystan's expensive clothes before sheathing it and looking to the remaining two. "Seize them and attach a cage to General Braxton's horse. We'll be taking a ride together."

CHAPTER
THIRTY-TWO

CAYDEN

B Y THE TIME WE MAKE IT TO THE WEALTHIEST PART OF
Vareveth a mob of townspeople and soldiers follow in the
shadows of Elowen's dragons. All the lords live on large estates
outside the city limits, but I sent a battalion of soldiers ahead to escort
the remaining lords and their heirs to an open field along the main
road that winds for miles through the countryside. Elowen's plan
worked. It seems the citizens are more bloodthirsty than either of us,
shouting insults and calling for heads as I slide down from my horse
and unlock Xantheus's cage. I grip his heavy chains in my fist, dodging
his spit, and yank him forward for all the other lords to see.

"No, wait!" he cries out, losing all trace of the brief spark of rebellion. "I didn't think anything of the letter. I would have brought it to
you had I known."

I continue dragging him behind me as he collapses, muddying his
fine clothes as he descends into hysterics. The sharp tang of urine in-
filtrates my senses, and I don't hide my revulsion as I look down at
him. Sorin lands and leans close to the ground so Elowen is able to
slide off, but he doesn't return to the skies where the others circle. He
keeps his head low as he bares his fangs, placing his front claws on
either side of Elowen.

I hold up my hand to silence the crowd before speaking. "Lords of
Vareveth, I bring forth a traitor in your midst. He had written infor-

mation from an enemy that he did not reveal. Had I not been fore-warned, countless Vareveth lives could've been lost." The crowd is in an uproar again, calling for his death as Xantheus begs his friends for aid. "Who is his heir?"

"I am, sire." A man who looks to be around my age steps forward and drops to his knee. His clothes are simpler than his father's but extravagant nonetheless. "I renew my oath to the crown and denounce my father for his crimes. You are the one true king of Vareveth by right of conquest."

"You are no son of mine," Xantheus sneers.

His son slowly looks up, disgust written on his features. "Thank the gods for that."

I nod, accepting his renewed oath. He stands, offering a bow to Elowen before taking his place beside a heavily pregnant woman I assume is his wife, resting a hand on her stomach to soothe her. She looks close to tears as she grasps the lapels of his coat. I don't care if he renewed his oath out of true loyalty to Vareveth or hatred for his father. His emotions matter little as long as his promise is kept, but I'd respect him more if he renewed the oath in order to see his child grow up.

"Take her home, Lord . . ."

"Sillas, my king." He gives me a grateful nod, and his wife smiles timidly. I watch as he presses a hand into her back and escorts her into a carriage. A small part of me envies the fact that they'll go home to their normal life. That Sillas won't have to take his wife to war. My path was determined years before I met Elowen, when I had nothing to lose, and now I must fight for a life I'm not willing to sacrifice.

"I sentence Lord Xantheus to die for his crimes, along with Lord Caspian for his complicity. Lord Drystan met his end within my castle for threats levied against your queen." Ryder ushers Caspian forward while Finnian drags Drystan's corpse, discarding him in the grass without a care.

The lords in front of me wisely remain silent as I unsheathe the knife from my thigh and turn to Xantheus, forcing his mouth open by pressing my fingers into his cheeks. "I told you to keep my woman's name out of your fucking mouth." I slice his tongue out, letting the piece of flesh thump on the grass and use his hair to keep him in place as he flails and cries out. I tighten my hold, imagining the things he said about Elowen that Ryder wouldn't repeat. She told me enough but couldn't get through it all without disgust overtaking her. I don't have to know everything; I just have to remove him from this world as punishment. "The gods have let you live long enough, and I'm here to remedy their mistake."

I slice his neck, spraying my boots with blood and stepping out of the way to toss him down as he chokes. The cut wasn't deep enough to kill him instantly. That would be too easy. I want him to suffer. Keeping my bloody knife in my hand, I execute Caspian as I walk past.

Elowen steps over Lord Xantheus's body as if he's no more than a fallen branch and addresses the onlooking nobility. "Renew your oaths to the crown or refuse and die."

Six of the remaining nine lords and heirs fall to their knees, some looking happier than others. I'll continue to monitor the situation, but there's no sense in killing all of them. Lord Caspian's son bends the knee, declaring his loyalty, but Drystan's son remains standing despite shaking worse than his father did.

"Round them up," Elowen orders some of our soldiers. They react instantly, separating the traitors from their families. Most of whom are stone-faced as they bend their knees, watching their patriarchs be escorted to an empty section of the field. Elowen's eyes glow gold as Sorin's flames engulf them. Piercing screams echo throughout the surrounding area until they fall silent, leaving behind scorched grass and the smell of burning flesh.

Sorin cranes his head in the direction of those kneeling before us, letting out an earth rumbling roar that causes them to cower and pull their loved ones closer. Once he's satisfied by their terror, he looks to Elowen once and rejoins the others in the sky.

"It's a better result than I'd hoped," Elowen remarks.

"A large dragon certainly helps."

Elowen's eyes shine whenever she looks at them, like they're the most precious things in the world. "That they do."

The image of Lord Sillas and his wife being able to flee and live a normal life is still stuck in my mind, and a burning sensation floods my chest. I could never let the crimes committed against Elowen go unpunished. I will have my vengeance for the scars carved into her mind and wrists. The inevitable has surrounded us from the moment we met, but I need to take control of this narrative before other kingdoms try to make it a weakness.

I turn toward the crowd of citizens and soldiers who followed us from Verendus, ready to address them despite not being one for speeches. My victories have always spoken for themselves, but as king, I need to do more.

Anything I've needed to say has been communicated through blood and blades, but that was when all I worried about was myself. Not because I had some grand life planned or the vision of a future, but because I fueled myself with hatred and used it as a life source. Things are different now . . . for the first time in my life, I want a future. I don't really know what it looks like, but Elowen is there and I'm uninterested in any version of reality without her in it.

I turn toward the crowd, raising my voice above the demand for more blood. "You want blood? Turn your swords on Imirath, not those within our kingdom. Weakening Vareveth will do nothing but give Garrick Atarah what he wants." Swords are unsheathed and raised above the crowd. "You do not yield! You do not falter! You show no mercy and place your queen on Imirath's throne!" I unsheathe my blade to mirror their actions. "To war!"

"To war!" the crowd echoes at a deafening volume.

CHAPTER
THIRTY-THREE

ELOWEN

"STOP GLARING," I HISS.

"This is just my face."

"You're making a point to scowl at any man in our vicinity."

"When, pray tell, have you known me to not do that?" Cayden balances a smoke between his lips, and I ignore both his words and the jolt it sends through me as he flips my hood up to fend off the wind.

Finnian reaches into the basket looped on my arm to pull out another honey bun, eating half of it in one bite and throwing his head back while groaning. "I still think you should open a bakery once the war is over."

"You'll be my taste-tester in exchange for new knives when you take over for Blade."

"Deal." He drapes an arm over my shoulders, tucking me into his side as we climb up the hill that leads to where most people from Aestilian have settled. Snow-topped stone cottages line the road, their shutters open and smoke rising from the chimneys. Children throw snowballs, some even going as far as to climb trees to get a higher vantage point, while adults buried in blankets sip steaming mugs on the porches.

"Queen Elowen!" a little boy calls out, bounding toward me on his tiny legs. He's swallowed in a coat two times his size. I sink into a squat and open my arms for him just before he slams into my body.

"Hi, Ollie."

Two years ago, I was traveling through the Terrwyn Forest during a terrible storm when I found him. The rain was so bad that I could hardly see my hand in front of my face, and sought shelter in what I thought was a vacant home within one of the unnamed villages. But Ollie was there, starving, freezing, and crying in front of a hearth he didn't know how to light. His parents abandoned him, claiming several days prior that they'd return from the market in a few hours. I brought him to my house to make him soup and tea before taking him to the orphanage. He took to the other children quickly, and his smile is something I'll always be thankful for. He's probably about six years old now, but he didn't know his birthday so that's just a guess.

"You've grown since I last saw you."

"Three inches," he proudly states, dragging his fingers through my curls like he did when I carried him on my horse. He has freckles across the bridge of his sloped nose and curly blond hair. His brown eyes slide to Cayden, and he tilts his head. "Is he your husband? Everyone keeps saying you're married now."

"Yes," Cayden says at the same time I say, "No." I glare at him over my shoulder. "We're getting married in a few days, and you are more than welcome to attend with Lady Marigold and the other children."

He beams like I just told him the sun will never stop shining. "Will there be lots of food?"

"More than you could imagine," I whisper it like it's a secret, and his eyes brighten as I reach into my basket. "And I made your favorite."

He squeals, jumping in place when I hand him the cinnamon roll, squishing it a bit when he holds it to his chest. His little dancing fit lands him directly in front of Cayden, who looks down at Ollie like he's another species, while Ollie looks up at him with wide eyes.

"Is it true you drink blood?" he innocently asks, and Finnian's laughter flies freely.

"Yes."

"No!" I exclaim as other children begin to swarm me, and I lower the basket to let them pick whatever pastry they want. Ollie remains staring, and Finnian continues to vibrate with barely suppressed giggles.

"Yes?" Cayden lifts a brow and addresses Finnian over my head. "What do I do with it?"

"Oh, Ryder is going to be sorry to have missed this," Finnian mutters, stepping forward to greet the children.

"How many people have you killed?" Ollie asks.

"How high can you count?" Cayden replies.

Ollie scrunches his brows, counting off on his fingers silently. "One hundred and seven."

"Let's go with that." Cayden looks to me for help, seeming more uncomfortable than I've ever seen him. I glance at Finnian, unable to control my laughter any longer. For months, Ollie has said he wants to be a soldier, and Cayden's victories aren't a secret.

"I never liked the men who hung around Elowen. Well, some were okay, I guess." He picks at the button on his jacket. "Finnian is the best. Everyone knows she loves Finnian."

"Right you are, little man," Finnian calls out.

Cayden's eyes light up at that, and he sinks down to Ollie's height. "Do you remember their names?"

"Okay!" I exclaim, and step between the pair, hauling the basket off my arm. "Ollie, can I trust you to bring this to Lady Marigold to ensure all the children get one?"

He puffs out his chest as much as he can. "Of course."

"You are the bravest little soldier." I ruffle his hair, sliding it onto his arm as he turns back toward the orphanage. He only makes it a few steps before Cayden calls out for him, stepping around me while reaching into his pocket to procure a few coins.

"There's a sweetshop down the road. Don't go without an adult," Cayden speaks without emotion, like he's giving a soldier a set of orders, but I think Ollie likes it. He nods, jutting his chin out and instead of running away, he marches. Cayden turns back to me, the confusion still evident on his face. "He's a strange child."

"Mhmm." I take his outstretched arm. "Planning on including him in your spying ring?"

"He talks too much to be a spy." He rolls his eyes. "And besides, I don't care who's in your past; I'm the only one in your future." I raise my brows at that before he tacks on, "As long as they don't breathe around you or think about you."

"Cayden, I wanted to run something by you," Finnian says, catching up to us while I stop at some of the street vendors' booths, handing over some coins in exchange for a tin of cookies I think Ryder will like, and some gold beads for Saskia to braid into her hair. "The Aestilian army is trained to take enemies by surprise, and I think they could be useful in the upcoming battle."

"It's your call," Cayden responds as we step into Blade's shop. Expertly crafted weaponry decorates the walls: war hammers, axes, scythes, swords, and more. It smells of smoke and steel but brings me comfort. "If you get me a list of soldiers, I can arrange a ship to be made available for them."

Finnian seems taken aback. "That was easy."

Cayden looks him over carefully. I pretend to be engrossed in a selection of knives while Blade retrieves my order, having noted my presence the moment I crossed the threshold. "Make a decision, don't ask for permission. An army is only as steadfast as its commander. You will always teeter on the edge of chaos and control with your army. Never lose the latter and know when to utilize the former."

Finnian nods, standing a bit taller than he did before, and my heart skips in my chest. Finnian doesn't give himself enough credit for how intelligent he is. I buy a new wrist guard for him to protect himself when he shoots, which he enthusiastically puts on before dipping around me to speak with Blade. Cayden escorts me to the alley beside the shop and I place two small pouches in his hand.

"What are these?"

"Presents."

"For the wedding? I'm already getting everything I want."

"No." I close his fingers around it. "You didn't tell me your birthday had passed so the red one is to make up for that, and the blue one is just because."

His brows furrow as he looks down at them, and I wonder if anyone's ever bought him something just because it reminded them of him. Realizing he won't do it himself, I uncurl his fingers and open the first pouch, pulling out a gold signet ring with the House Veles crest at the center. In the wake of all he's revealed to me about his past, I wanted him to have something he could wear every day to remind him that he has a home where he's wanted. He still doesn't move, so I open the second and dump it into his palm. The obsidian arrowhead pendant and gold chain glisten in the sun, as does the small gold hoop earring to match.

"You buy me presents all the time," I say, trying to wake him up from his trance.

"That's different."

"No, it's not."

"You deserve good things, and I want to give them to you." It's the way he says the words that makes me pause. They're wholly earnest, as if he doesn't consider that he also deserves good things.

He slowly blinks, and my pulse picks up. "Obsidian is a stone associated with protection, and I still remember the arrow you shot for me when you found me in the forest before we traveled to the temple." His eyes flash to mine when I unlatch the chain's clasp and fasten it around his neck so it rests slightly lower than the other chain he always wears. "And the hoop is because I noticed your right ear is pierced but you never wear anything in it."

He smirks, his eyes becoming lighter. "Did I ever tell you why my ear is pierced?" I shake my head. "I lost a bet to Ryder when we were teenagers. We were drunk as hell and I bet him that I could steal a knife off a guard without being noticed."

"Oh, gods." I cover my mouth with my hand. "What happened?"

"I stole the knife and got away but kicking the poor bastard in the balls definitely got me noticed." He presses his lips against my forehead while I brace my hands on his chest to laugh, imagining a younger version of him striding up to a guard with an overwhelming amount of confidence. "Thank you, love."

He hooks it through his ear, and I force myself to look away from how handsome he is. I step around him as Finnian leaves the shop, needing to use the cold air to drench my burning cheeks as his gaze drills into the back of my head. The bright signs along the street flap in the snowy wind, and fires are lit every few yards to give citizens a chance to warm their hands in the stone pits. We stop at a street stand for hot cocoa that tastes like magic, and the scent of roasted caramelized nuts makes me breathe deep.

"Nyrinn!" I call out, spotting the woman I was looking for. She stops in her tracks, and her face splits into a pretty smile when she sees me. She meets me halfway in the center of the road. "How are you settling in?"

"Better than I expected. I've been to your cottage on healer's row, and it's beautiful. I'm going back there later but had to finish up a few house calls."

I'm glad she's been using the residence. I'd love to get back there, but there are too many things to deal with right now. Once things are calmer, maybe she'll take me on as an apprentice again. "If you have the time, I want to invite you to my wedding feast. I could send General Braxton to escort you to the castle."

Her cheeks flush a bit, and she grasps the front of her cloak. "General Braxton? He's the tall one with the amber eyes?"

I twist my lips to hide my smirk. "That's the one."

Nyrinn hasn't looked at a man since she came to Aestilian. She hasn't looked at anyone for that matter, but I saw her dark eyes following him as he guarded me. Braxton is a fine-looking man, with a sharp jawline and broad shoulders honed after years spent wielding a sword.

"Of course I'll come." She glances at Cayden over my shoulder. "Be good to my girl."

"I swear it," Cayden evenly responds.

CHAPTER
THIRTY-FOUR

CAYDEN

BELLS CHIME IN THE TOWER AS GILDED CARRIAGES COAST down the road leading to the circle in front of the castle. Guests climb the steps, decked out in elaborate outfits of rich tones and billowing fabric. I tuck my hands into my pockets and lean against the window that overlooks Verendus. As far back as I can see, streets are draped in strands of light and dark blue flowers. Their fallen petals speckle the cobblestones. The city is alive with people reveling in the merriment of the royal wedding.

A party of six soldiers astride white horses leads the path of a decadent silver-and-white carriage. The first two riders carry the banners of House Duskbane: a snarling silver wolf stitched onto dark gray fabric. A squire announces the royals and opens the door for King Lycidias and Queen Nasha. She resembles Cordelia. The sisters share the same deep brown skin, but Nasha's hair is so black it soaks up the sunlight around her. Lycidias is a stark contrast with pale skin and short white hair tied at the nape of his neck.

"I knew I'd find you lurking away from the crowd," Ryder says, striding down the hall and mirroring my position on the opposite side of the window. "Do you think they'll be a problem?"

"Not with five dragons flying overhead and my army surrounding them."

As if summoned, Sorin dips in front of the castle and the guests jerk their heads toward the sky to see his green scales on full display and his wings spread wide. A mixture of wonder, awe, and fear coat their faces. Soldiers gather around the royals despite knowing steel is nothing compared to dragonfire. It's a testament to their loyalty, I'll give them that.

"The fact they're here is a positive sign." Ryder pulls out a flask from the inside pocket of his jacket, taking a swig before handing it to me. "They are publicly acknowledging the transfer of power in Vareveth despite it stemming from an act of treason. It strengthens your claim to the throne in the eyes of other kingdoms."

I take a swig knowing Ryder's choice of poison is also whiskey and twist the signet ring around my finger.

"It doesn't hurt that he looks the part," Saskia says, gliding down the hall in her dark blue-and-gold gown, complete with dramatic skirts and sleeves that loop over her middle fingers. She's woven the beads Elowen bought from the market into her hair, and pulled the majority of it away from her face but left two braids to frame her features. Her eyes drift to the golden crown atop my head with the House Veles sigil at the center, shining with pride.

Ryder and Saskia are the closest thing I have to a family. Before them, I had absolutely nothing in this world and nobody to care if I died. Ryder loved life enough to remind me I was human, and Saskia was always there to rein us back in when we were too reckless. We became a unit, banded together by nothing more than the need to survive, and realized that somewhere along the way we began offering our backs to one another to take on the world.

They began calling me their brother before I viewed them as anything more than a liability and waited for me to figure my head out. Thank the gods I did.

"Be happy today, Cayden. For both your sakes," Saskia whispers.

Ryder nods, clearing his throat. Unspoken emotion lines his eyes as he sticks his hand out, a gesture we do before every battle, a symbol that we'll take on whatever comes by each other's side. I clasp his forearm, and he steps closer to slap me on the back as I squeeze Saskia's shoulder with my other hand. That's the end of my rope when it comes to showing affection.

"She's by the lake," Saskia says.

I quirk a brow in response. I tried to see Elowen earlier and Saskia threatened to scoop my eyes out with a spoon if I saw her before the ceremony. "Despite my earlier remarks, I think it would benefit her to see you."

I'm hustling down the hall before she even finishes the sentence, and Ryder's laughter follows me down the spiraling stone staircase. My heart slams against my ribs and anticipation makes my chest feel so tight it would crack if I tapped it. The servants bustling about the castle grant me a wide berth as they ready the chambers for guests and prepare the feast. I straighten out my cloak before shoving the glass door leading to the lake open.

The sun glistens along the surface and bathes the snowcapped mountains and forest. Elowen stands along the edge of the icy shore, watching her dragons as they twirl through the air. The idea of salvation in the underworld is a mockery now that I have her in my sight, knowing there's nothing sweeter than this woman, nothing that comes after this that could compare.

The wind carries her floral scent toward me, and I inhale it like a drug, letting the high of her presence encompass me. Her curls are perfectly structured and adorned with sparkling blue jewels, and her dress leaves her shoulders bare and is made of a mixture of lace and silk so delicate it's like water flowing around her. It shimmers as if starlight were woven into it. The dramatic train and hem are embroidered with delicate golden vines dotted with small blue flowers, and two embroidered dragons decorate the back of her upper arms, matching the blossoms on her ample skirts.

Her shoulders stiffen when she's alerted to my presence, but she doesn't face me yet. "It's believed to be bad luck to see the bride before the wedding."

My pulse picks up to the point where I can't form words as she turns around. A wave of adoration slams into me so hard that my knees weaken. It's a miracle I remain standing. Elowen is the ivy that consumes me. Her vines are strong and latch on to me, as they have for years, but now she's not only wrapped around my mind but also embedded into the soul I didn't know I had until I met her.

Gods, I'm so in love with her.

"*You.*" I shake my head, my fingers reaching toward her cheek but never making contact. "There aren't words, Elowen, for how beautiful you are."

I don't recognize my voice, this guttural, breathless tone.

Her brown eyes, lightly lined in black, shimmer with emotion as she soaks me in. The front of her dress is even more beautiful than the back, with lace peeking above the corset top to grace the swells of her breasts with a star sapphire set between them. Her gown is a mixture of draconic and celestial elements all fashioned in the colors of our house. The golden beads on her bodice and hips are so small I'm surprised blood doesn't mar the fabric, given the amount of time and work it must've taken to create this. Sheer dark blue fabric spills from the split sleeves and drapes elegantly at her sides, dotted with more golden beads that resemble stars.

Instead of a traditional crown, she wears the golden circlet I sent to her this morning. It rests across her forehead with several teardrop-shaped sapphires and blue-flashing moonstones along the elaborate band. Five thin chains droop from the back of it, all with a dragon at the center. The front pieces of her hair are braided back with small blossoms woven into them, and I'm glad a veil doesn't cover her face; instead, translucent gold fabric hangs from two chains at the back of her head, laced with the same blue jewels that decorate her hair.

"I'm convinced you're not real." I shake my head, tipping her chin up to drop my forehead against hers. "You must be a figment of my imagination because nothing as perfect as you could exist in a place as wretched as this world." She gives me a watery laugh and blinks rapidly. I brush the curls off her shoulders and trace my fingers down the column of her throat. It's sacrilege for my hand, sullied beyond redemption, to be touching something as divine as her. "And if I'm dead, and this is the afterlife, then I'll kill whatever creature comes to drag me away from you once the universe realizes I've done nothing in life to deserve this."

"You have," she whispers, a shaky hand stretching up to cup my cheek. "You found me. You have searched for me since you were seven years old and carved out a place for me in this *wretched world.* One day you're going to realize that you deserve happiness."

I curse again. The distance between us is as small as it can be without wrinkling her dress and yet it's too far. Jerking my chin toward the place below the cliff where our guests are waiting, I ask, "Are you ready for this?"

"I am." She lets out a shuddering breath, nodding against me. "I'm better now. It was just nerves from thinking about the crowd."

I tighten my hand on the base of her neck. "You keep those pretty eyes on me. These people don't mean anything. It's just us, angel."

My love.

My wife.

My Elowen.

CHAPTER
THIRTY-FIVE

ELOWEN

AN ANGELIC BLEND OF STRING MUSIC CARRIES ME UP THE
hilly forest, signaling it's time to begin the procession to the
clearing. The castle on top of the mountain looks even more
impressive from the base. The spires are so tall that they kiss the
clouds. I tighten my hold on Finnian's arm as we pass under a white
stone archway cloaked in vines of ivy. His presence at my side keeps
me calm as hundreds of eyes settle on me, but I force myself to disregard them and keep my shoulders straight, floating down the aisle with
elegance and grace. Dark blue petals are crushed under my jeweled
slippers and are swept up by my dramatic train.

With each step, I bring myself closer to a future I've chosen for
myself, a life I've finally taken control of. My dragons fly overhead and
dance above the forest in the distance, never too far and always within
my sight. As Saskia said, this wedding is not merely a ceremony, it's a
statement that will ring out like bells throughout Ravaryn, a message
shouted from the southern isles to the northen tip of Thirwen.

Cayden is the most dangerous man in Ravaryn, without possessing
any magic, and the enemy of the man who sired me. Everyone here has
heard the tales of Cayden's ruthlessness on the battlefield and his various victories. It doesn't surprise me he's not blessed by the God of War
but by the God of Death, because wherever Cayden points his sword,

death follows. There is no warrior like him, nobody in the Legends of Ravaryn who compares to the king who rose from nothing and conquered everything.

If my enemies didn't want to face the monster they created or watch me align myself with another, then they should've tightened my chains. I was beaten by men who will face me on the battlefield, and they will cower under the might of House Veles. I was born from the ashes of the fires they tried to burn me with and built a kingdom with my bare hands. I am everything they never thought I'd be, and I hope they hear my name—Elowen Veles—and look to the sky with fear so overwhelming they feel it in their bones.

Candles drip wax onto the black stone sprinkled with snow along the aisle and rocks surrounding the small pond at the base of the staggering falls, casting Cayden in a golden glow. He stands with Asena and Ophir; but all I can see is him. Souls don't meet by chance, and once I encountered his, it was like I found something I didn't know was missing. A wrong had been righted. Being with him feels like light spilling into the dark cracks in my heart, as if the stars themselves were meant to live in my body.

To anyone else, Cayden would look unmoved where he stands with the flames and falls at his back, but I see the reverence cloaking his unwavering gaze. His black tunic is fashioned to look like dragon scales along his chest and arms as an homage to me, and the rest of his finery is of the same rich night-spun fabric. The only pop of color comes from the signet ring on his finger and the golden crown sitting within his messy chocolate waves. Pride shines within me as our sigil glints in the sun.

Finnian stops at the end of our journey as the music builds to a crescendo and Cayden strides toward us. The pair exchange a heavy glance as Cayden extends his hand, and Finnian clasps it before leaning down to kiss my cheek. "You are the most beautiful bride."

My eyes moisten further when I meet his gaze. "I love you."

He clears his throat and nods, taking one final look at me as I hand my bouquet off to Saskia. They take their place beside Ryder at the front, all decked out in blue, black, and gold. The crowd gathered holds their breath as Cayden places his lips on my knuckles, staring at me with unyielding devotion, and butterflies erupt in my stomach. He's the perfect picture of a man who stole the crown to have me and would steal theirs if they tried to take me away. He leads me closer to the water and positions us to face each other as Asena begins the ceremony.

"Welcome, esteemed guests, to the Kingdom of the Dragon and Demon. We are here today to celebrate the union of Cayden Veles the Conqueror, the demon of Ravaryn, king-ender and queen-maker; and Elowen Atarah the Dragon Queen, the firestorm made flesh, the queen of fire and daughter of flame, princess and rightful heir to the Imirath throne."

Ophir raises his arms, causing the thick blue robes to bunch around his elbows. "The gods are with us and have granted their favor."

Asena rubs her hands together before shooting them toward the candles nestled under our house banners that hang on either side of the waterfall, pulling the element from the several candles surrounding us but never too much to extinguish any flame.

The string instruments are replaced by deep drumbeats as the cults begin humming and singing in Ravarian. Ophir hunches over a stone slab, muttering over a bowl while throwing herbs into it. I look up at Cayden, no longer fighting my smile once a small one spreads on his lips.

Ophir produces a blade so black it absorbs the sunlight and hands it to Cayden. "With this knife forged from the flames of the goddess, cut your left palm as an offering to the God of Water, Death, and the Moon, and willingly give your blood to the blessed bowl." Cayden does as instructed, and I watch as crimson drops plummet into the water, then take the knife and do the same.

"Now repeat with your right hand, in an offering to the Goddess of Flames, Life, and Stars," Asena says, bringing over a bowl made of volcanic stone and filled with fire. The embers at the base hiss and the pair of them stare down at their individual elements like they'll reveal some grand secret. "Lastly, you must both cut the tip of your ring finger and paint a line down each other's lips. This is an offering to each other, to seal your union."

Cayden tilts my chin up with his other hand, careful not to get any blood on my dress and keeps his voice low as he glides his finger down my mouth. "I vow that my soul will never be parted from yours in this life and to find you in all the lives that follow, no matter the world or distance, because one life with you isn't nearly enough. However, if I have the mercy of dying before you, merely grasp the hand of my corpse and I will find a way to return to you, for you alone command my heart. You have my name to bind us, my sword to slay anyone who wishes you harm, and my body to shield you."

I take the knife from him with a shaking hand while blinking back my tears. I hardly feel it when I prick my finger, reaching up to add my blood to his lips. "I vow to be yours in every life, and to wait for you in all of them. When my soul enters the underworld, I will not cross the river until you find me again, because only then will I know peace. Every part of me belongs to you, even the broken shards, and I never want them back."

I pull my hand away, never taking my eyes off his as Asena calls for the rings. Ryder and Saskia step forward, each of them handing us the bands we commissioned for each other. "We stand here to witness man and woman joined in the light of the gods. Look upon each other and state the vows of Ravaryn, knowing that these will tether you to each other now and forever."

Cayden slides a gold band onto my finger, fashioned to look like ivy growing around an oval amethyst bordered by small diamonds. It's the most beautiful ring I've ever seen, and the only reason I'm able to hold myself together is knowing there are hundreds of people staring at us. He doesn't look down as I slide his obsidian band with crushed sapphires over his tattoo and onto his finger. We clasp our hands as Asena instructs and Ophir dumps the blessed bowl into the volcanic one, dousing the flames.

"I pledge myself to you in an oath that can never be broken," we say in unison. "I am yours, and you are mine, from this day until my last day. Amito evidani." *I am yours.*

Power I've never felt blooms in my blood, unfurling like the first blossoms of spring. I can tell Cayden feels it too from the faint trace of surprise on his face. The flames around us burn higher, and the rushing water grows louder. The feeling within me grows stronger, zinging through me like lightning, but it doesn't hurt. It makes me feel *alive.*

The earth rumbles beneath our feet and the pull I feel to Cayden grows stronger.

The cults' singing becomes more powerful.

My heart feels as if it'll burst from my chest.

My palms burn where our cuts press together and the world around us goes dark.

Asena steps forward to pull our hands apart. Our cuts are healed, and no blood remains on our skin, but in its place are markings. Thin, golden swirls trail around my fingers and meet at the center of my palm like a star. The same design is reflected on the back of my hand and stops just above my wrist. Mine are more delicate than Cayden's thick black markings in an identical design, and his seem to travel around my name inked on his finger.

"You didn't tell me the ceremony would mark us," I say, not that I'm complaining. They're beautiful.

"It wasn't supposed to," Asena mutters, looking to Ophir in disbelief before dropping my hand to address the crowd. "A divine union!"

"An eclipse!" someone calls out.

"The gods have spoken," Ophir shouts. "To be an enemy of House Veles is to be an enemy of the gods."

I recall what Asena told me about the God of the Sun and Light—his possessiveness of dragons and hatred for the goddess she believes blessed me, and Ophir believes Cayden to be blessed by the God of Death, Water, and the Moon. An uneasy feeling settles within me as sunlight splays around us again. I may not worship the gods, but the markings . . . and the eclipse . . . they unsettle me.

I shove the feeling aside, needing to complete the task at hand with the eyes of Ravaryn on me. There is no room for mistakes.

"You may kiss the bride," Ophir says.

Cayden places his hands on my cheeks to tilt my head up and presses his lips to mine.

Gods, I've missed this.

He cradles my face as if I'm the most precious thing in the world and kisses me as if he longs to taste my soul. The crowd cheers wildly, tossing flower petals while Cayden keeps a firm hold on me. When his lips are on mine, I know what it is to be craved by a person. It's like he's starved for my touch whenever we're apart and savors every second he has me like it'll be his last. He parts my lips slowly, kissing me like we have all the time in the world, but pulls away far too quickly. Our eyes meet, and it becomes apparent to me that though people have looked at me before, they've never *seen* me. He sees all that I am, and all I can become, and wants it all.

"It is my honor to present King Cayden and Queen Elowen Veles of Vareveth! Long may they reign," Asena cheers.

"Long may they reign," the crowd echoes.

CHAPTER
THIRTY-SIX

ELOWEN

Y DRESS SHIMMERS AND FLOWS AROUND ME AS
Cayden leads us through the steps of our first dance. He
moves as he always does, practiced and controlled, and he
lifts me off the ground so easily that I feel weightless. Our hands lock
in front of my face when the final note is struck, and he slowly lowers
them to meet my gaze as couples flood the floor. My heart pounds
within my chest, not from the dance but from the intensity within his
eyes and the dominance that has cloaked him since he slid the ring on
my finger.

The power that thrummed inside me during the ceremony has
faded, but the markings haven't. Mine glisten in the lantern light,
whereas Cayden's absorb it. Quite like the blade we used to cut our
palms, which is now sheathed on Cayden's thigh.

"Elowen Veles," he murmurs in a gravelly tone, one dimple deepening when his lips quirk up on one side. He drags his tongue along his
lip as if he loves the taste of it.

"The title of your greatest accomplishment."

"Damn right."

"Who should we deal with first?" All lords and ladies of Vareveth
are present with the full horde of their houses, as well as several who
accompanied the royals from Urasos and Feynadra, but we have no
reason to converse with them aside from a polite greeting. After doing

more digging, I've learned that for the past two years Prince Hale of Urasos has made most of the decisions for the kingdom. I suppose he must find a balance between ruling in his father's stead and remaining faithful to his wishes.

"Feynadra," Cayden answers. "They don't have any ties to either Imirath or Thirwen."

I slide my arm through his, turning in the direction of the Feynadra party. They're gathered at the base of the platform our thrones sit on, created by a team of stonemasons under the guidance of Asena and Ophir. A paneled window stretching behind them overlooks the snowy Seren Mountains. Mine is chiseled from moonstone with stars carved into it, and five dragons cut from the same stone branch off the chair. One takes flight above my head, and the other four are mirrored on either side. Cayden's is made of obsidian with golden swords crossing at the top and a crescent moon at the center. They're stunning on their own and made even more so by the two massive stone dragon heads mounted on either side, spilling water from their open mouths, lined with fangs, that collects in a pool beneath them.

A squire steps in front of the royals before we have the chance to introduce ourselves. "May I present King Lycidias Duskbane and Queen Nasha Duskbane of Feynadra."

"I'm afraid we don't bother with additional titles as you do," King Lycidias says, and though he attempts to laugh at the end, the jab is clear.

"There is always time to acquire some," Cayden replies in the same tone. "May I present my wife, Queen Elowen Veles."

Nasha steps forward and threads her arm through her king's. The train of her gown made of silver fur and gray velvet drags in her wake. She exudes a regality I've recognized in her sister. "We offer our sincerest congratulations on your union."

"And we thank you for making the journey to attend," I respond.

"It's not every day a king conquers a kingdom on your southern border." Lycidias rests his chilling blue eyes on Cayden. His white hair is streaked with gray, and his bone structure is as harsh as winter nights. Nasha's smile strains when looking at her husband from the corner of her eye, and the fabric in the crook of his arm ripples as she tightens her grip, perhaps in warning.

"It's not every day a king's decisions lead to his own demise," Cayden flatly states, daring Lycidias to say something in favor of Eagor, but the cold king merely grins, seeming to appreciate Cayden's retort.

"My sister sends her regrets for being unable to attend," Nasha begins, thankfully changing the subject. "However, she's due to send invitations for her Winter Solstice Ball today and mentioned your name being on the list. With all the festivities I doubt you've had time to monitor your correspondence."

I tighten my grip on Cayden but keep the anticipation surging within me hidden. She may have disregarded my previous letter, but an invitation to her kingdom must be a positive sign. We'll have to face the Thirwen fleet before we depart and weaken our enemy enough to delay a counterattack. If we leave sooner, it could be detrimental.

I wonder if Nasha misses Galakin. It must be heartbreaking to leave a place you love knowing you'll always long for it.

"I'm sure we'll be able to attend, as long as tension in the south doesn't spike."

"Yes." She offers me a curt nod. "Although we were thankful to be included in your day, we assumed there was an alternative reason for requesting our presence."

"We will not send aid," Lycidias cuts in. "Feynadra is much smaller than Vareveth and will need every sword fighting for our land if you lose your war and King Garrick pushes north. While we acknowledge Queen Elowen is the heir to the Imirath throne—to deny her claim would discredit mine—we will not fight for it."

I've never been happier for a man to open his mouth.

"I don't recall asking for your aid," Cayden says. "And did not plan to."

Lycidias and Nasha exchange a glance. "If you don't want anything from us, why have you asked us here?"

"To foster a relationship between our kingdoms, given we share a border." I smile easily, feeling like a spider watching a fly get tangled in her web. Their reputation for neutrality precedes them. They played right into my hand.

Lycidias nods, the air of superiority slightly dissipating, but it's Nasha who speaks next. "If what you say is true, all I ask is that you don't turn your dragons north."

I scan my eyes over the party they traveled with, noting the absence of her children. She's come here wanting something from me: a promise that I won't conquer her kingdom and slaughter her heirs in the process. I wonder if they realize how lucky they are to be loved by their mother, to have someone willing to stand between them and any threat.

"Do not intervene in my battles, and I will bring none to your door unless given a reason."

"Then we have an understanding." Lycidias dips his chin and removes himself from Nasha's side before immersing himself in the company of his lords. Her pained eyes track him, and I can't help but pity her. Royal marriages are often arranged and unfeeling. Women are sold to the highest bidder to secure an alliance or further the agendas of men. All it does is lead to a life of unhappiness. I force myself to look away when Nasha returns to her ladies.

Cayden waves a servant over. "Did either of us receive a letter from Galakin today?"

"Yes, Your Majesty," he responds, and the relief is so strong my knees weaken. "Queen Cordelia sent Her Majesty an invitation to the Winter Solstice Ball."

"There was no response to my previous letter?" I ask.

"All we received was the invitation, Your Highness."

"Thank you." The servant bows and returns to his earlier position by the table filled with flutes of sparkling wine. "Both Queen Nasha and the servant said Cordelia spoke only of me."

"Then I suppose I'll be a happy surprise." Cayden leans against one of the pillars lining the room, wrapped in wisteria vines that are also draped across the ceiling alongside House Veles banners. "I'm sure that's something along the lines of what my father said when he learned of my conception." I laugh before I can stop myself but feel less guilty when Cayden follows along. "I anticipate that Thirwen's fleet won't be far. We'll prepare to leave for Galakin after the battle, since we'll be along the coast."

CHAPTER
THIRTY-SEVEN
ELOWEN

THE HAIRS ON THE BACK OF MY NECK RISE, AND WHEN I glance over my shoulder, the princess of Urasos has her brown eyes locked on me. Lethia's brows rise when she notes my gaze, and she must tighten her grip on her prince because Hale pauses his conversation to grant her his attention.

I slide my arm through Cayden's again and take a sip of wine a servant offers me. "Urasos is approaching."

"After today we're taking a break from hosting and attending gatherings."

"We were just invited to a ball," I flatly state.

"We'll secure the alliance before it occurs and then I'll happily keep you occupied in a dark corner after making a brief appearance."

I pinch his bicep and subtly press the cool chalice into my neck to quell the flush creeping up.

"I don't believe I've had the pleasure—Prince Hale Warthorne and my wife, Princess Lethia," Hale says, but Lethia remains silent beside him. Her unwavering attention is fixed on me as if she's seeing a ghost. Her emerald-green gown embellished with brown embroidery matches Hale's tunic adorned with a chain across his chest to depict his sigil: stag antlers framing a mountain.

"Queen Elowen Veles." I extend a hand to Lethia, and this seems to shake her from the trance. Her pale hand is slick and shaking slightly when she wraps her fingers around mine.

She clears her throat, pushing a strand of straight blond hair out of her face. "My apologies. I'm not normally so . . ."

She clears her throat again.

"Would you like to get some air?" I ask, jutting my chin toward the double doors that lead to a pavilion. Not only am I asking for her benefit, but I'd like to take a break from the festivities as well—and it'll give us all the opportunity to speak privately.

"That would be lovely." Her shoulders lower slightly, and the four of us make our way outside. Though it's freezing, the breeze swooping down from the snowy mountaintops caresses my heated skin. My dragons sense me now that I've ventured outside and alter their course to fly above the forest stretching for miles. Hale stops in his tracks when he spots them, and drags a hand through his wavy, raven hair that stops just below his chin. It's shaved on the left side, and a tattoo of a stag is inked onto his scalp.

"You don't remember me, do you?" Lethia asks. Cayden takes a step closer to me when he notes my unease. I tilt my head, doing my best to analyze her features. She has a band of freckles across the bridge of her nose, which has a small bump in it, and she's quite tall for a woman.

"When would we have met?"

She smiles softly. "I don't take offense. You were so young."

I take another sip of wine to wet my dry throat. "Imirath. Before my imprisonment."

"I'd travel with my family to visit Zinambra in the summer," she says. "My father is good friends with King Fallon, who is obviously close with your father, given their alliance."

Bitterness sours my stomach, and I look to my dragons. Cayden drags his fingers down my spine to soothe me, taking over the conversation. "If you've come to my kingdom to speak fondly of my enemies then you should've remained in yours."

"I hold no loyalty to either Imirath or Thirwen, despite my wife's heritage," Prince Hale states. "Nor does she."

Their union hints to that being untrue. If Lethia's father is close to Thirwen's king, he'll expect his son-in-law to support them in the war. I stride toward a table and chairs positioned beside thick greenery and bordered by torches, like the ones lining the streets of the kingdom, fashioned to look like dragons spitting fire. The others follow and we take our seats across from each other.

"Then why are you here? It's clear you have something to say," Cayden continues.

Hale drags his thumb down his stubble-covered jaw. The golden rings on his fingers complement his dark complexion. "I'm not the king of Urasos yet, so I have to act within limits, but I'm here to offer information."

"Why should we trust it?"

"Because I want revenge on those who harmed my wife. I'm sure you can understand how it feels." Hale narrows his blue eyes.

Cayden's hand pauses on the nape of my neck. "If it were my wife, I'd press a pillow over my dying father's face to join the war and avenge her myself."

"He's my father," Hale hisses.

"It was merely a suggestion. We all have our priorities." He resumes his movements, gliding his fingers along my skin. "Tell me what you know."

"Urasos has remained neutral for centuries, and with my Thirwen heritage, we cannot join your war, but we will not act against you. If Hale's father were dead, it would simplify matters, but we must work within our limits," Lethia says, her gaze flashing to mine again. "I mourned you. I was told you died of a fever, but as I grew older, I realized that couldn't be true. The dragons were never heard of again and there was no funeral. You all vanished as if you never existed."

"I'm sorry for any sadness that might've caused you." I'm having a hard time finding words beyond those. What do you say to someone who remembers a version of you that you don't? That no longer exists?

The girl she remembers died in those dungeons, and I am all that remains.

The pair of them keep speaking and yet say nothing, and my patience is wearing thin. I glance to my left, noting the added presence of Finnian and Ryder along with two soldiers from Urasos. They're close by, but far enough for our conversation to remain private.

"What do you want in exchange for the information?" I raise my brows. "My guarantee that the dragons won't lay waste to your kingdom?"

"Is that so preposterous to request?" Hale asks.

"Predictable," I correct. "I don't act without motive. Don't give me a reason to make you my enemy and you won't share the same fate as mine." I gesture with my hand for them to proceed.

"We won't be attending the upcoming ball in Galakin, so I won't be able to introduce you myself, but Prince Zarius Liluria of Thirwen is believed to frequent the gambling dens in the kingdom. It's rumored that Fallon murdered his first wife, Zarius's mother, and then tried to kill him. He hasn't been home since he was ten. Though he was disinherited by his father, the people of Thirwen haven't forgotten the late queen and how she loved her son."

I've never even heard of Prince Zarius. I thought all Thirwen's heirs were under the age of three. *That's* Thirwen's motivation in this war. I knew there had to be an ulterior motive. No matter how close Garrick and Fallon are, comradery doesn't come before a kingdom. Both Garrick and Fallon have children they're trying to erase from their lineage. It unites them in the same way shared hatred for Garrick unites Cayden and me.

This could potentially sway Galakin in our favor as well. Galakin has poor relationships with Thirwen and Imirath. They stopped trading with Imirath after Garrick refused to send them a native plant that was vital for medicinal production during a plague. Those with healing magic couldn't save everyone due to the highly contagious nature of the disease.

Their rivalry with Thirwen was sparked by the events leading to the Crimson Tide War.

If I claim the Imirath throne, and Zarius claims the Thirwen throne, Galakin can have an ally in both kingdoms instead of enemies.

"Thank you," I say. "I won't forget this kindness."

Lethia smiles and I run my hands down my skirts, standing from the chair and gesturing for her to walk with me. Our heels click on the stone as we stride back into the party with Cayden and Hale just a few steps behind.

"I love your dress," I say. "It complements your hair beautifully."

"Yours is incredible," she replies before wrinkling her nose, looking down at herself. "I don't miss Thirwen, but I do miss wearing red to parties."

"Purple is my favorite color, so I suppose we're both unlucky with where we ended up in the world." She laughs, and I join her, thankful for the tension slowly uncoiling within me. "I am sorry . . . that you mourned me."

She shakes her head. "I'm merely glad that it was fruitless. It's hard for women to find happiness in a world designed by men, and security in a world where it feels like they take every step to make it treacherous. And I know you don't remember me, but I'm glad to see you happy."

"It's also hard to find good people in this world, as I'm sure you know, but Urasos isn't far from here." I bite my lip. "Perhaps Cayden and I can visit once the war is over, or we could exchange letters?"

She smiles down at me. "I'd love that."

CHAPTER
THIRTY-EIGHT

ELOWEN

Y VOICE IS HOARSE FROM LAUGHING AND MY FEET
ache from all the dancing Finnian and Ryder led me
through. I even shared a dance with Braxton, who blushed
through the entire song, and I spun around a few children from the
orphanage who tugged on my skirts.

As I stumble off the dance floor, I tilt my head to the far side of the
room where Cayden is watching me from the shadows. The hair on
my arms rises when I note the heat laced within his eyes. I take a step
to my left to duck behind a pillar, peeking around it to watch him kick
off the wall and take a step to his right. He's always carried an aura of
danger and mystery, warding all others away, but it pulls me toward
him. Maybe it's because I've experienced pain where love was supposed
to be, and love where it never should've existed.

I slip behind another pillar, but when I peek around the side, he's
nowhere to be seen. Exhilaration shoots through me, knowing he's
watching even if I can't see him. I keep moving until I stride out of the
throne room and find the nearest exit from the castle. I can't see or
hear him, but I can feel his presence. My lips still burn from our brief
kiss during the ceremony, and the promise of more weakens my knees.

Hurrying down the path I walked several hours ago, I follow the
trail of dying candles into the forest that leads to the base of the castle.
The sleeves of my gown flow through the trees like woodland spirits

dancing for the moon as I hop over a stream and quicken my pace. My curls whip around me as I swing my head in all directions, seeing nothing other than snow-coated pines and icy rocks. My heart pounds in my chest when I make it to the base of the mountain where the ceremony was held. I fist my dress while running down the abandoned aisle, trampling the flower petals as snow crunches close by.

He wouldn't let me hear him unless he intended it. Like a predator homing in on their prey and wanting them to know a collision is imminent.

A small ledge curves around the edge of the pool, and I squint into the darkness as the wind blows, taking some of the falls with it. There's a dark cave behind the base of the waterfall. I've always obeyed my curiosity, unable to ignore the nagging voice that tells me to explore an unknown place. It's strange because I'm almost never curious about people. They're usually disappointing when you peel back their layers, but nature has a way of surprising you even with its smallest details.

The stone is slippery underfoot, and I grasp more of my skirts to save them from tumbling over the ledge and dragging through the surface. Ice crackles beneath me, creating weblike cracks as I step. Sharp peaks press into my palm as I lean on the wall beside me and climb up the incline, keeping my footing while ducking behind the gushing falls and rounding the corner. I'm submerged in darkness and listen to my surroundings to paint a picture in my mind. It's obvious there's a river splitting through the center of the path based on the echoing sound of rushing water. The ledge I'm standing on grows thicker as I continue around the curve and spot a faint blue glow at the end of the narrow cavern.

My hair becomes heavier as the air grows thick and moist. I drop my dress and reach one hand behind me to sweep the tresses off my neck, but it does little to offer me any reprieve, considering my discomfort grows with every footfall.

But my grip slackens on my curls when I step through the archway in a daze, my gaze tracing the enchanting sight. Pools upon pools of crystal water spill into each other, staggering in size and height, with steam wafting off their surfaces. They're built into the rock, and I'm forced to crane my neck to see the top. The misshapen ceiling is speckled in blue glowing splotches more vibrant than any night sky I've ever seen, with shards of rocks piercing between the clusters.

"Hello, wife." Cayden's hands snake around me. "Following you always leads me to the strangest places."

"Well, at least you'll never grow bored," I answer. "Did you know this was here?"

"No. I don't think it's common knowledge."

I slip out of his hold and spin to face him, slowly unlacing my corset while kicking my shoes off. "Then perhaps we should take advantage of our discovery."

"Leave that on," he commands, a look of pure hunger flashing across his features. He stalks toward me and presses my back into a wall. Dampness bleeds through my gown, and his lips skim over mine as he tilts his head down.

A crease forms between his brows, and his throat bobs. "I didn't chase you with the expectation of anything more than your company. It doesn't matter that it's our wedding night. I don't want to do this if you're not certain."

I reach up, resting my trembling hand on the nape of his neck. However awful the world may think he is, Cayden has never pressured me for anything, no matter how blatant his desire is.

"I want this." I smile faintly, and he traces it with his finger. "I want you."

His mouth descends upon mine in the next second.

I stand on the tips of my toes to get closer to him as he wraps an arm around my waist and threads his hand through my hair. He parts my lips and presses me to him like I'm a flower between the pages of a book, but the only word transcribed within the novel is his name. I'm completely and utterly consumed. He's all I can think of as the world fades around me. He kisses me like the world is ending and he's desperate to memorize the taste of me before we're torn from each other.

I'm breathless when he pulls back, and his pants mingle with mine. "Gods, I've missed you," he murmurs.

My heart skips in my chest, and he looks at me for a long moment before lacing our fingers together to lead me up the slope, not stopping until we're nestled beside a small pool somewhere in the middle. Whatever is causing the ceiling to glow is reflected on some of the rocks bordering the path. Cayden turns to me, and my eyes slip shut as he glides his fingers down my neck and across my collarbone. I lean into his touch, craving more than a gentle brush. It's been so long since we've been together. I want him to make me feel like I'm his again.

"I've watched you all day, unable to tear my eyes away, imagining the moment when I'd finally be able to take this gown off you," he whispers, and I force my gaze back to his. "Wanting you is the sweetest torture I've ever experienced. Not even sleep grants me mercy. You're always there when I close my eyes, in my mind, whenever you're not in front of me."

I thought he'd be ready to rip my gown off once he caught me, but he handles me with reverence, caressing the beading on my bodice and raking his eyes over my frame like he's assuring himself that I'm truly his bride. He takes a step closer, and I lick my lips when our chests press together as he loosens my corset. He never detaches our gazes when the bones slacken and he hooks his fingers into the sweetheart neckline to slide the gown down my body, sinking to his knees as he does. His jaw clenches as he stares up at me. I bite my lip when he cups the backs of my thighs, dipping his thumbs beneath the lacy strap attached to my garter belt.

His breath dances across my torso when he leans forward to place a kiss. "Did you wear this for me, beautiful?" The deep timbre of his voice makes my thighs press together. I nod, not trusting my voice as he rises and walks around me in a slow circle. A rough breath rushes from him when he looks at my face again, and he tosses his crown and tunic aside. "I must've been a fucking martyr in a past life."

I smile softly and step out of the puddle of skirts at my feet to undo the laces on his pants, though he doesn't remove my crown or the veil attached to it. His eyes burn with unrestrained desire as he abandons them, making me shiver from the anticipation of what I know he can do. This feels different from any other time we've been together because Cayden is no longer just my ally, he's my husband. A sly grin coats his features as he hoists me in his arms, and a needy whimper climbs up my throat when his hard length presses into me.

My pulse flutters in my neck, and I roll my hips forward to glide against the bulge.

He groans, and I drop my forehead against his shoulder while repeating the same movement, but his hands latch on to my hips before I can do it again. "What kind of man would I be if I didn't take my time on you after you put this on?"

I tighten my legs. "An intelligent man."

He chuckles while walking us into the pool and a pleased hum vibrates within my chest as the warm water rises over my hips. I trail my lips up his neck, needing him closer, needing to feel him. He walks to the front of the pool and sets me on the ledge. Fear stiffens my spine when I take in the steep drop to the next pool below, and the edge is so thin I'm not even fully on it.

"Which you clearly are not! Put me down."

"I've never kept my desire for you hidden, and I won't let you rush me through this, Elowen. If I want to stand here and admire my wife, I will. If I want to wrap your legs around my head while I fuck you with my tongue, I will. And if I want to bury myself deep inside you and make you cry out my name like a prayer, I will. In fact, I look forward to it." His words wind me so tight I feel like I'll break from the simplest touch. "Is that understood?"

"Yes," I breathlessly say.

He keeps one arm around my hips while reaching forward with his other to cup my breast, and despite the trepidation of our position, I spread my legs wider. "Always so responsive for me." He wraps the scrap of lace covering my aching core around his finger, each brush of fabric sending jolts of pleasure through me, but it's not enough. He snaps it, leaving me bare aside from the lacy bands on my thighs attached to my garter belt and a matching band across my breasts that leaves little to the imagination. "It's been too long since I've tasted you." He presses his lips just below my ear, and I weave my fingers through his hair as he continues dragging his mouth down my body, driving me to the point of desperation when he focuses on my breasts next. My nipples are visible through the lace, and I arch into his touch when he wraps his lips around one.

"Cayden," I plead.

"Are you finally going to let me take care of what's mine?" He presses his cock against my clit, and my toes curl beneath the water. "Are you going to keep these pretty thighs parted so I can properly worship my wife?"

Good gods.

I manage to separate myself enough to kick up and extend my leg until my ankle rests on his shoulder, and I lower him to his knees. "Much better."

"If you take your eyes off me, I'll stop. You're going to remember exactly just how well I know how to give you what you need, and I meant what I said earlier. I want to hear your screams echoing through this cavern." He licks up my slit, groaning at his first taste, and my eyes roll back in my head before I force them back to him. "Fuck," he groans, throwing my other thigh over his shoulder. Gods, it's been too long. "You get more perfect every time."

He sucks my clit into his mouth, flicking his tongue over it as he delves into a ravenous frenzy. I can't catch my breath, can hardly manage to say anything other than his name as my body heats up. Damp curls stick to my forehead and tickle my hips when my head falls back, and Cayden chuckles against my core as he tightens his hold on me. I'm too lost in what he's doing to my body to care about the potential fall. He reaches up with his other hand, sliding it beneath the lace band and running his thumb over my nipple.

I move my hips against him, and he growls his approval. "That's it, angel. Fuck my tongue and give me what I want."

"I'm so—" My shaking worsens. "Oh, gods."

"I could do this every damn day if you'd let me." He slides two fingers into me and curls them and I swear I see stars. "When you get pissed at me, you sway your hips while you storm off, and all I can think about is lifting your skirts, bending you over, and fucking you with my tongue until the attitude is gone."

"Do it." The thought of him stalking toward me with determined eyes after a verbal spat nearly sends me over the edge.

He chuckles again, licking the wetness off my thighs as he continues to finger me. "And what about my cock? Will you let me smother your screams if I want to take you in a dark alcove during the day?"

"Yes!" I choke on a sob as he sends me over the edge, the mixture of him between my legs and the image he's painted in my mind overwhelming me. Wave after wave of pleasure washes over me as he continues, wringing every ounce of ecstasy from me before he catches me when my body slumps forward.

He hardly gives me time to recover before flipping me on my stomach, my knees resting on the stone shelf beneath the water. I look over my shoulder, combing my fingers through his hair and bringing his lips to mine. His tongue dips into my mouth as he spreads my legs with his knee and unloops the satin buttons keeping my top secured.

He begins sliding into me and our lips part in tandem. "What am I?"

I crack my eyes open as he gives me time to adjust while fingering my overly sensitive clit. He groans when I clench around him. "Mmm." I arch my back, feeling the familiar sense of a challenge rising within me. "A prick?"

He presses farther in but doesn't fill me yet, and his hand latches on to my jaw to keep my chin tilted and our eyes locked. The hold exudes the same dominance and possessiveness as him. "Try again."

I shake my head, not giving him what he wants since he's doing the same to me. He rears his hips back and slams them into me. "Cayden!" I cry out as he releases me, and my breasts press into the stone ledge I'm practically hanging over.

"That's who I am." All hells, *his voice*. He holds me here for a moment, placing a hand on my stomach to feel him deep within me before sliding out and driving back in. "Tell me *what I am*."

He stretches me as he did all those weeks ago, and I'm too lost in him to care about anything else. "My husband."

"Now was that so hard?" He rewards me by quickening his pace as he keeps me pinned beneath him. Pleasure shoots through me, and I don't dare move, not wanting to ruin this beautifully torturous rhythm. "You were made for me," he groans, pulling out just enough to flip me over and wrap my legs around his waist. I'm practically boneless in his hold, and he presses his lips to mine again while carrying me through the water. I don't care where he's taking me, just as long as he doesn't stop. My back presses into stone and water trickles between my breasts and over my nipples, heightening my pleasure as Cayden finds his rhythm again, fucking me relentlessly with each thrust.

"You're mine, Elowen." He tilts his hips forward to press into my clit while sheathed inside me. "I want to hear you say it."

"I'm yours."

"Such a perfect wife." He tightens a fist around my curls to pull my head back, dragging his tongue up my neck. "Taking every inch of my cock, begging for it."

"Fuck, you feel so good," I moan.

His gaze darkens as his thrusts grow frantic, frenzied, and I latch my hands on to his shoulders. The small trickling waterfall from the pool above slides down his biceps, and wet waves stick to his forehead. "I know you're close, beautiful." I frantically nod, desperate for the imminent high. "Call out my name again when you come undone."

The familiar wave of ecstasy rolls through me, and I fall apart with his name on my lips. He grinds his hips while spilling into me, keeping us in this position as he slows down and presses his forehead to mine. Our rapid breaths mingle together as he gazes at me, and a small smile curves my lips in time with him. He slips out of me and eases us back into the water, stroking his hands along my back.

I feign sadness. "We can't go back to the party; you got my hair wet."

He dunks us under the water and bubbles stream out of my mouth as I laugh beneath the surface, and continue when we rise above. He slicks his hair back and a handsome grin splits his mouth, water droplets curving into his dimples. "Pity."

Our laughter fades, and he looks at me with a softness he'll never show the world. I don't know why it makes my eyes burn. I tighten my arms around him and bury my face in his neck. "I've got you, El."

"I just . . ." I swallow. "I knew I missed you, but I didn't realize how much. I'd miss you while we slept beside each other."

"We have time to figure everything out."

I shake my head. "We don't live the kind of life where I can be mad at you today and not know if it'll be my biggest regret tomorrow. I don't want to take anything for granted. I want to *live*, no matter how awful the circumstances may be."

"Then it's my honor to live with you." He tightens his arms around me. "Elowen Veles."

"If you keep saying it, you'll grow tired of hearing it."

"Not a chance in all hells."

I dip my fingers into the water and flick them at his face, wiggling them as the gold markings swirling around my hand shimmer. "Do you want to address these?"

"What's there to say?" He unwraps an arm from around me, examining the markings on his left hand.

"You know just as well as I do that these were not some trick conjured by Asena or Ophir. You felt it. Not only did it absorb our blood, but it healed our cuts."

He sighs. "Please don't run off and join a cult." I narrow my eyes in response. "You've proven you have some kind of magic in your blood when you slipped into the mind of Basilius. It could be a result of that magic sealing our vows when our blood met."

"That's logical."

"Thank you for noticing I'm not a complete imbecile." I splash him with more water, unhooking my legs from around his waist and swimming away. The jewels in my hair shimmer and stay locked along the wet strands. "You look like a siren sent to lure me to my death."

I swim between the small streams, sticking to the darkness of the cove. "Maybe I am."

"As long as I die with the taste of you on my lips, I'll consider it a life well lived and a better end than I deserve."

CHAPTER
THIRTY-NINE

CAYDEN

I SLIP BACK INTO BED AS GOLDEN LIGHT PAINTS THE ROOM, and brush Elowen's mussed curls off her back to kiss her spine. I know she hates when her hair gets like this, all unstructured and messy. She'll probably pout in the mirror when she sees herself, but I adore it. Probably because I know it was my fingers running through it, and the possessive part of me loves that. She hums in her sleep, arching into my touch as her pretty brown eyes blink open.

"Good morning, love," I murmur, the rough edge to my voice making her arch again. Her wedding dress is draped across one of the chairs, and we somehow managed to make it home to the manor with her wearing my tunic and me wearing my pants as we stumbled into a carriage. Guests from the wedding definitely saw us, but I couldn't give less of a fuck. She climbed onto my lap once the doors were shut, riding me with her face buried in my neck. The night was spent claiming her in every way, on all pieces of furniture in our chambers.

She yawns, looping her finger through the chain around my neck and pulling me back up to her, causing the plates on the bed to clatter. She pushes herself up, clutching the sheet to her chest as her gaze pings around the room. "H-how? When?" I pull her between my legs, settling her back against my chest and pouring some coffee into a dainty cup on the tray, sweetening it the way she likes. "There are so many bouquets I can hardly see the floor."

I press a lingering kiss to her neck in response. She's not wrong. It smells like a flower shop, with bouquets in varying shades of her dragons' scales, both dominant colors and markings. She turns to face me, running her eyes over my features. I'm no stranger to people staring at me, but it's different when Elowen does—it's not with a shred of fear or hatred. No, when she looks at me it's like she's trying to see into my very soul.

"Thank you." She kisses my cheek, and by reflex, my arms tighten around her. "I have a present for you, too."

She slides out of my arms and hisses as she hobbles to the en suite dressing room. "Don't even think about having sex with me today."

"Sorry, love." I chuckle. "I won't go anywhere near you, but I make no promises about what my mind will conjure up."

I shove down the initial unease at the notion of her buying me something. It's the same feeling I had when she bought me the jewelry. It's not that I've never received gifts—my mother used to do her best with what little we had, and Ryder and Saskia have bought me things over the years—but like everything else, Elowen is different.

She returns with a square box in her arms, looking far more hesitant as she claims her earlier position and pulls the blankets over our legs. "If you hate it, you can throw it into the fire, and we never have to speak of it again."

My brows rise. What could she have possibly—

But my mind goes silent when I flip open the lid, staring down at the cake I haven't had since I was eleven. The scent of blueberries and sugar wafts toward me, memories of autumn leaves tumbling to the ground and my mother complaining about me growing up too fast. Elowen sucks in a sharp breath. "I know it won't be exact since I don't have the recipe, but I tried several before I think I managed to get it close to the one you described." Something cracks in my chest at her anxious tone, but it's like I'm frozen in place. "I didn't mean to overstep."

Waking up from my trance, I place the box on the bed and pull her face to mine, quieting her rambling and thoughts in one move. I keep the kiss slow, wanting to pour every ounce of what I'm feeling for her into it because saying it out loud will feel too much like a goodbye. Experiencing love is nothing more than waiting for tragedy to strike, and telling her I love her will be like getting to the peak of the mountain we've been climbing and waiting for someone to push us over the edge.

"I love it," I murmur, placing my forehead on hers and swiping my thumb over her lips. "I pity those who will never know this side of you and yet I am grateful they never will."

She smiles at me, and that same sense of foreboding doom deep in my gut doesn't dissipate, it strengthens. I've never been scared before a battle, but I'm fucking terrified now. I manage to keep it all off my face as she cuts into the cake and hands me a slice. She eats some pastries from the tray and sips her coffee, pouring one for me as well.

"*Fucking hells,*" I groan around the fork and her eyes shoot to mine again. "I hate to say that I agree with anything Finnian says, but you'd put all other bakeries in Ravaryn out of business." She laughs, tossing a strawberry at my face. "I'm not joking. I'd be too frightened to tease the dragon queen."

"I'll add that to your list of lies." She waves a hand through the air. "I'm happy to bake for the people I care about and leave it at that."

I finish off the slice she gave me and reach into the drawer of my nightstand, pulling out a velvet box. "I have something else for you."

"No." She shakes her head, latching her hand around my wrist to push it back toward the nightstand. "You've already given me too much."

"That's a matter of perspective and I'm more than happy to inform you that you're wrong."

"I'm never wrong," she states, dipping a strawberry into the whipped cream and looking up at me through her lashes as she licks the remainder off her fingers. "Maybe I don't want another gift. Maybe I want something else."

A rough breath escapes my chest as I shove the box at her, brushing my fingers along her thighs as she opens it. Her face lights up as she stares lovingly at what's inside. "Still want something else?"

She pulls one of the two identical and intricately made wrist cuffs closer to her face: a dragon with its wings spread wide enough to meet on the underside of her wrist with a long tail that curls around her middle finger. It's made sturdy by a second band that locks around her wrist in the perfect position to hide the scars left behind by her shackles.

"El." Her eyes flash to mine again. "You're perfect in my eyes, and you don't have to conceal a single scar either internal or external, but I know how it feels to wish to hide them sometimes."

Hardly a moment passes before she closes the gap between us, and I twist her until she's flat on her back beneath me, writhing and panting exactly how I want her. My tongue presses into her neck, trailing down the valley of her breasts as she moans, and gods I love that sound.

A knock pounds against the door as I'm kissing her stomach, and she stiffens.

"I thought you said we'd be undisturbed."

"I did." Saskia, Ryder, and Finnian said they'd stay at the castle while Elowen and I celebrated our wedding however we wanted to, and the servants were told to leave us be. I climb off her, throwing on my black robe and leaning down to press my lips to her forehead. "I'm sure it's nothing."

By the time I make it to the door in the sitting room, that same familiar sense of dread latches on to me again. My instincts are telling me not to open it, to ignore the world and keep Elowen in here, but that's just a dream. Quiet mornings untouched by war isn't our life yet, but it can be. *It will be.*

Braxton stands on the other side, an apology he doesn't voice lining his amber eyes. "Thirwen has been spotted. We still have time, but if we're to follow through with the plan—"

"We'll have to leave by nightfall," I state with no emotion. "Summon the others. We'll meet in a half hour to discuss strategy."

He dips his head before retreating down the hall and I softly shut the door again. I feel Elowen's eyes on my back, knowing she heard the whole interaction, and turn to face her leaning against the doorway in one of my shirts. "And so it begins."

I nod. "To war, my love."

Part III

THE
WAR OF FOUR
KINGDOMS

CHAPTER
FORTY

ELOWEN

I LEAN BACK ON VENATRIX'S CHEST, KEEPING ONE BOOT crossed over the other as I watch the dark water lap against the shore. Our anchored ships bob in the rocky cove, and soldiers continue flooding the beach in black-and-blue armor. They shove their rowboats far enough up on the sand to keep them from being taken by the tide. With the cover of darkness and the distance between us and our target, we won't be spotted, but we need to strike quickly.

This is the first battle in the war I've been fighting since the day my dragons and I were put in chains. I'm not fighting this war for validation. When history is written, it rarely favors women. I don't care how I'm perceived; all I care about is survival and retribution. I want a better world, and the only way to achieve that is by anointing the earth in the blood of my enemies.

Two crossbows are attached to my saddle with capped quivers of spare arrows alongside them. I'll always prefer knives, but I've come to enjoy the feeling of firing the weapons. Finnian approaches first, and I take a moment to trail my eyes over him in full armor. Like the rest of the army, quilted blue velvet covers the steel on his chest, and the House Veles sigil is imprinted on the plate that attaches his shoulder guards. I've seen many versions of him over the years, but never a commander, and I think it suits him. His shoulders are stiffer, his chin higher, and he's packed on a bit of muscle from training with Cayden and Ryder.

"The battalions are ready to march," he says.

Nerves prickle my palms, not for me, but for him. "Are you going to be leading the charge?"

"No." He looks down for a moment. "Cayden advised against it since I've never been in a battle of this magnitude. He told me to find my footing on the field before I rush to the front."

Relief is prominent, but not enough, knowing Cayden has the experience and that he'll be on the front lines. Similar to my approach regarding my dragons, Cayden won't send soldiers into a battle he doesn't lead—especially not when the revenge he's chased for years is finally within his grasp. The urge to ask Finnian if he's ready for this burns through me, but I shove it down for his sake. "You were given this position because you deserve it. You're a fearsome fighter, Finnian. I wouldn't be leading a charge if I was fighting on the ground either. I don't have the experience."

He nods, seeming relieved by my faith but not replying as Cayden approaches in a set of entirely black armor aside from the House Veles sigil on his chest. Cayden is already larger than most men, and the armor emphasizes that fact and even makes him taller. Dragon scales cover his chest and upper thighs in two short panels, and shine above the chain mail that separates his shoulder guards from the spiked gauntlets that cover his wrists and hands. He wears a helm resembling a dragon with wings flaring away from his face and two curved horns jutting from the top. It hides his features entirely aside from his eyes, and the ominous sight is enough to inspire fear in any foe.

Finnian looks over his shoulder quickly. "I'll be getting to my post."

I throw my arms around him, murmuring into his chest, "Shoot straight."

His arms tighten around me, pressing me closer to him. "I suppose I should tell you the same thing now."

I laugh softly, patting my knife-clad thighs. "I might still get a few throws in."

"You always do." He nods to Cayden as he retreats, making it back to the Aestilian soldiers.

Cayden stops a few feet away and removes his helmet, soaking in every detail as he always does before a battle. He starts low, dragging his eyes up my leather coat also covered in dragon scales with high double slits for my blades to be easily accessible. The fur lining the interior keeps me warm, and two panels of dark blue fabric hang down from the dragon heads on my shoulders. I didn't want to wear full armor, knowing I'll need to move with Venatrix. My hair is styled as it always is when I fly, with several small braids along my skull leading to one large one that falls to my waist, and a golden House Veles sigil rests along a golden band at the center of my forehead.

"No flower?" he asks, and as a response I offer him the back of my head where I tucked a few of the flowers he gifted me. It's hard to believe mere hours ago we woke up in bed, eating pastries and trading gifts. A faint smile blooms on his lips, but there's an intensity in his eyes that can't be drowned out as he steps closer, grasping the back of my neck. "Hit them hard and fast. Don't linger. Don't yield. Don't show mercy. You do whatever you must and come home to me. It doesn't matter if the wyverns have riders, you're better than any of them. Fire burns in your blood. Your dragons are faster and fiercer, but you're the most fearsome of all."

I nod, soaking in his words, letting them pound through me like a war drum. I dip my fingers beneath my neckline to pull out the two rings I added to my necklace beside my moonstone pendant. "Against my better judgment I seem to quite enjoy your presence." I tuck them back where they were. "Keep your eyes on the field, not the sky, soldier."

He kisses me before stepping back, resting his hands on the hilt of his blade. "I've mastered keeping an eye on you while people are trying to kill me. It's an enviable skill and one I take pride in."

He puts his helmet back on, making him a nearly seven-foot-tall demon, and meets Ryder in the distance. I turn back to Venatrix, pressing my forehead to hers as she bends down, and slide my fingers over her scales. I open the bond, letting it flow through me, consume me. Golden light illuminates my soul as I become one with my dragon. I breathe when she does, and our hearts beat as one.

"We ride to war, my sweetling."

Her crimson scales morph into black, and the other dragons follow suit, mirroring the darkness blanketing the sky. The only vibrancy comes from their eyes. They're restless and eager to begin their quest for blood, their claws stomping on the ground every few seconds. I wonder if they can sense the savagery pounding through me, if we're linked even in our vengeance.

"Solka," I say while mounting her, tightening my hands on the saddle horns as she sinks her claws into the sand to get a running start. It's the command for *fly* in Ravarian. One by one, every set of eyes on the beach turns to watch a sight nobody thought possible. The air crackles with my power as a melody of unlimited might is created from the wind rushing through the dragons' wings. I lead them silently into the sky, high enough for the night to conceal us. The firestorm made flesh sitting atop her shadows of death and ash.

Following the plan we discussed, I fly away from the shore, toward the back of Thirwen's fleet. It's massive. Hundreds of ships bear the sigil of House Liluria, setting their force apart from the Imirath ships closer to the coastline. A black kraken with its tentacles wrapped around a ship adorns their dark red sails, not one ship suspecting that they'll meet their end tonight.

Water laps against the hulls and torches flicker on the decks, illuminating the provisions Thirwen brought with them. Crates of food and weapons are sifted through by soldiers. If there was a way for me to raid the ships, I would, but victory is more important.

War cries shatter the silence on the beach, and I close my eyes, muttering a prayer for my dragons, my friends, and my husband despite my prayers going unanswered throughout my entire life.

I let the flashback of my past overtake me, push it all to the forefront of my mind. I think of the frigid and sweltering days in the dungeon; I think of my blood coating the floor as it gushed out of my body. I think of the hands that touched me without my consent, when I was far too young to even do so. I think of the humiliation, the shame, the look in my father's eyes as I was beaten in front of his throne. *My throne.* I think of my dragons being chained and ripped away from me, and the earth-shattering pain that consumed me when Garrick tried to break my bond.

"Zayèra." *Dragonfire.*

Though the dragons respond to my commands when I speak the common tongue, there's something that feels right when I speak to them in Ravarian. Venatrix shakes her head as if awakening from a long slumber.

Venatrix sharply dives, and a battle cry forged in flight and fury rips free from my throat as the wind screams in my ears, doing nothing to drown out the echoing roars of my dragons. They unveil their vibrant scales as blazing flames swallow ten ships in one breath. The hulls crack and splinter, and soldiers in full armor jump into the water unless caught in the crossfire. The steel will drag them into the depths of the Dolent, fleeing flames only to be swallowed by the tide.

My lips part as I look around me. My dragons' flames are different from those I've seen them blow previously—their fire reflects the color of their scales. Flames as red as the ripest cherry spill from Venatrix's mouth, streaked with pink and gold. The heat that accompanies them is overwhelming, so much hotter than earthly fire. Sorin cuts a line down a ship with emerald flames as black dances within, and Basilius does the same with lavender. Calithea's flesh-melting silver flames shimmer like stars, and Delmira's burn like a blue sky with the sun at the center.

I recall Asena telling me dragonfire and earthly fire were two entirely different elements, but I didn't expect them to look vastly different. Dragonfire is so beautiful that an onlooker would burn themselves trying to bottle it as a keepsake.

Screams drift up to me, twining together with the essence of their demise as smoke stings my eyes. Venatrix blasts another ship, spitting fire as she glides just above the water, setting more ablaze as she turns her head side to side. Sharp shrill shrieks rise in the distance, and I spot leathery, scaled bodies thrashing through the air.

Wyverns.

"*Don't show mercy,*" Cayden's voice echoes in my mind. It's them or us, so I harden my heart and push forward.

"Venatrix, Sorin, Calithea," I command. "Vetàs tesis wyverns!" *Attack the wyverns.*

Venatrix tips her wings up, an answering roar echoing through the other two as Basilius and Delmira stay behind to continue burning the fleet. Imirath will spend ages removing the graveyard of shattered and splintered ships. No one will be able to sail into this port once we're done with them.

We sharply upturn, and I jolt in the saddle as Venatrix's jaw unhinges and latches around a wyvern's neck. She takes the beast by surprise as her fangs slice through the flesh like warm butter, splattering the pair of us in blood. The rider's eyes are entirely white as she tries to keep hold of the mental connection to the wyvern, but they clear once the beast goes limp in Venatrix's hold. Her face ripples with pure terror as Venatrix unlatches her teeth and I fire my crossbow, hitting the rider straight through the chest before Venatrix lets the pair of them fall to the sea.

I hook the crossbow onto the saddle again, looking toward the sandy shore soaked with blood and littered with bodies. Sorin kills two wyverns flying close to the ground, flaying several enemy soldiers in the blast. Calithea isn't far behind, shooting up beneath a wyvern approaching me and decapitating it.

The battle continues as entrails and flames descend, and the clattering of swords rises.

I bare my teeth, continuing to shoot commands down the bond and letting all of Imirath and its allies see what happens when you wrong someone more powerful than you.

CAYDEN

I leave a trail of corpses in my wake, dodging the entrails Elowen drops from the sky and arrows aimed at me. Blood slides down my armor and though I've never had a problem instilling fear in the enemy, the dragon helm certainly helps. All it does is solidify the image Ravaryn has of me: not entirely human, but some kind of monster ruled by a demon lurking within.

Someone charges me, and I spin away from their strike, impaling the back of his skull with one of my swords. Blood pours from their opened mouth as I yank my blade back through it, immortalizing his final battle cry. I'm an artist, but not in the way Ryder spends hours blending paints for the perfect shade. My blade is my brush and the only color I see is red.

I need more.

I crave more.

A flash of silver catches the corner of my eye, and I jam one of my swords in the sand, pulling a knife from the sheath on my thigh and spearing the enemy rushing toward Ryder through the side of his neck. He didn't become my second in command because he's my best friend. He earned his position, but it's instinct to look out for him. Sometimes when I look at him, I see the lanky boy begging me to help his sister who didn't know how to hold a sword. He's not my brother through any blood we share, but through blood we've spilled.

"I had that!" he calls out, slicing through the stomach of the soldier he was fighting.

"Oh, I'm sure," I drawl just to piss him off.

Eight men form a circle around me, and I wrap my hand around the hilt of my discarded blade, twirling it as they close in. My chuckle is smothered by my helmet. Imirath can send eight men or eighty—I'll cut them all down. When I was fourteen, I once ripped out a man's throat with my teeth in the fighting pits; after that, most confrontations seem tame.

I slice through their armor, pivoting and maneuvering around their blades as they try and fail to take me down. One aims for my leg, and I stomp their blade into the sand and break their jaw with my other boot. Their bodies join the corpses surrounding me, serving as a warning to anyone who decides they're brave enough to fight me.

I'm not a king or commander on the field.

I'm a god.

Flames blaze from my left, and the heat slams into my face as the scent of burning flesh stings my nose. It draws the eyes of everyone on the beach. Elowen is a beacon on the battlefield, haunting the mind of every soldier as she sits atop Venatrix, making sure every person can see that the dragon queen is here to take what was stolen from her. The blast of pure red flames swallows all the Imirath and Thirwen soldiers firing arrows from the ramparts of the fort. The purple banners framing the entrance with a golden trident spearing a crown are victims of Elowen's wrath, as are the docks jutting into the ocean. The sight of Elowen destroying the symbol of House Atarah after taking my name is something I'll never forget.

I step to the side, quickly dodging a sword swiped at my face. The soldier growls, and though their armor indicates they're from Thirwen, I don't sense any magic. It seems all of Thirwen's magical efforts are focused on the wyverns, but I expected more. It keeps me on edge. He aims for me again, but I grab his wrist, twisting it behind his back and bringing him to his knees.

"You shouldn't have gone for the face. My wife likes me pretty." I slice his neck open, shoving him down with the others as I continue pushing against the enemy. My father once told me I destroy everything I touch, and rather than fight it, I became destruction. Steel clashes and separates as boots slosh in the wet sand.

Another soldier approaches and grits his teeth while tightening his hand on the hilt of his blade as if it'll save him. I twirl my twin blades, widening my stance and waiting for him to advance, not for any reason other than the fact that I prefer defense. When I take the offensive route too quickly, the fight ends before my muscles even have the chance to burn. He cranes his blade back as the ground rumbles beneath our feet. The soldier glances down, and I end him for his hesitancy. The ground rumbles again, and blood ripples in the puddles along the beach.

"Retreat!" I hear in the distance. "RETREAT!"

All around me, Vareveth soldiers begin cheering as a mixture of Imirath and Thirwen forces rush back toward the port town. Ryder looks to me, but I shake my head. Something is wrong. They wouldn't give up the fort this easily.

"Stand your ground!" I command. "We take no prisoners!"

Rocks along the cliffs framing the bay tumble into the water, and though the fort hasn't completely collapsed, it soon will. Dust and stones rain down from the top. Asena and her cult accompanied us, while Ophir stayed behind, needing to prepare for the journey to Galakin, but I know this isn't her. Her task has been wielding fire to cut through enemies, nothing worthy of this reaction from the landscape.

A blinding light shoots up behind me, and sparks burst through the air as it dissolves. Everyone holds their breath while the air around us becomes heavier, as if it's weighed down by humidity and being pulled away from us. Screams make my ears ring as a transparent arch—a ward—forms high behind us, even higher than Elowen where she flies on the other side. It's longer than the beach and begins closing inward. Ryder and I are deep in their territory having led the charge.

"All hells," I mutter. "Fucking mages."

A stampede of soldiers plows through the sand, delving in a directionless frenzy as they fight to reach their respective sides. Anyone on the wrong side of the ward once it closes will be executed or taken as a captive. Someone slams into my bad shoulder, and I grit my teeth, quickly righting myself as I fight my way to Ryder, not caring who I'm plowing down. I hardly see my surroundings as I swing my blades, dodging both the enemy and my soldiers trying to run to safety. The sky above me is coated in the dome. It's growing farther into their territory as the gap for us to leave grows smaller by the second.

"Ryder!" I call out, catching glimpses of him through the chaos.

"Get out of here!" he shouts, farther into Imirath territory than I was, but I keep killing my way toward him.

They swarm around us like black flies in search of blood, but I make my way to him, cutting down the last soldier between us. He looks at me, splattered in blood and chest heaving, relief clearly written across his features. We don't bother saying anything as we turn around and push through the masses, painting our path in entrails and corpses. The closer we get to the dwindling gap, the tighter the space becomes. Swords have no use anymore, and we use our height and size as an advantage, elbowing and shoving our way through, keeping our footing as we step over bodies, both alive and dead.

There is no good and bad in war, only those who survive and those who die.

I'm not fucking dying today.

I keep my eyes locked on Elowen flying toward the gap in the force-field, fighting my way out of hell, finally having a reason to do so beyond selfishness.

CHAPTER
FORTY-ONE

ELOWEN

ENATRIX TEARS THROUGH ANOTHER WYVERN, AND I
command her to fly up the beach and make for the closing
gap. Cayden and Ryder lead the charges, so there's no possible way they're on our side. I have to find a way to at least slow the
magic to give them a greater chance of escape. Soldiers are packed so
closely together the mass of them hardly moves. Most of them will be
crushed to death before the gap even closes. The only small mercy is
knowing that Finnian isn't with them.

My saddle straps strain as she flips around, offering her back to the
ground as the shimmering walls creep closer. "Zayèra!"

Venatrix blows her flames toward the wards with a new vigor, sending the magic back to grant the soldiers below a bit more time. I turn
away to give my eyes some reprieve from the heat and watch Sorin lock
claws with a wyvern. It slams its tail into him, but his scales hold
strong against the venomous spikes. He bathes it in green flames,
melting the flesh from its rider and dropping them into the sea. He
bares his bloody fangs and lets out a vicious roar, calling out to any
others that may be lurking in the distance. Challenging them to come
find him and face their doom.

Basilius comes to us, mirroring Venatrix and bathing the wards at
my back in dragonfire. I can feel their power, feel something awakening

in me through them. It's like remembering the thing you forgot moments ago when it was on the tip of your tongue.

But the wards grow stronger, they keep coming at us, and the dragons are forced to keep descending. Venatrix jolts as arrows are fired at me, letting them bounce off her scales. My blood chills the lower we get. The scent of sulfur is heavy down here. It conjures memories from the day my father tried to break my bond with my dragons. I look over my shoulder, trying to find Cayden once I'm close enough to the ground to make out faces, but it's impossible to spot him.

Venatrix and Basilius are forced to abandon their efforts. Their bodies are too large to keep fighting within the small space. Heat slams into me as a large boom resounds through the air. Venatrix tips up, blocking the brunt of the billowing flames that weren't conjured by any of my dragons. Severed limbs and scalded bodies fly away from the remaining gap. The dome stretches as far back into Imirath as I can see, and I search our side for any sign of Cayden.

If he's stuck in Imirath, there's not a thing I won't do to break through this barrier.

With the surviving soldiers thinning, and corpses lining the beach like grains of sand—close together and impossible to differentiate—I see Cayden. Like a phoenix rising from the ashes, or a monster ascending from an ocean made of blood, Cayden stands from where he covered Ryder's body with his. His eyes blaze with a hatred six hundred men couldn't possess if they tried. He tosses his helmet aside, baring his teeth, covered in blood, and raises two swords against the enemies surrounding him.

Oh, gods.

Blood pours from the corner of his mouth, and as I fly down to him, I note the pieces of glowing metal jutting out of his armor. His exertion will only make it worse, but he thankfully finishes off the wounded soldiers quickly. Ryder pushes up from the ground unscathed but a little unsteady on his feet. I unfasten my saddle straps before Venatrix lands and slide down her wing, free-falling my way to the beach when she's close enough and running over to the pair of them.

Cayden spits out blood, wiping his mouth with the back of his hand before resting it on my cheek. "Are you hurt?"

"I'm fine." Shards from whatever the bomb was made of continue to glow in a sickly green color, jutting out of the right side of his chest and arm in harsh pieces. "Cayden—"

It was forged from magic.

I don't know how to heal magic-induced wounds.

My panic begins surging.

"Don't worry about me," Cayden insists, but Ryder cuts him off while removing his helmet.

"The bomb was poisonous. There is a mage in Thirwen who creates them, and he must be here. His name is Nykeem. His signature is the green metal."

"What kind of poison?" I demand. "Nyrinn is at the encampment with the other healers—"

"He won't survive that long," Ryder interjects. "He makes the poison himself and experiments in dark magic."

"Stop being so dramatic," Cayden drawls. "It's a fucking scratch."

"There are several pieces of metal jutting out of you," Ryder growls.

Cayden shrugs, looking toward Ryder with glassy eyes. "Many scratches."

My stomach roils and breathing quickens. I twist my head in all directions searching for the one person who can help me. "Asena!" My voice is shrill, and my emotions tighten my throat. I do my best to shove them down, but it's nearly impossible. "Asena!"

She possesses fire magic, as do many in Galakin, and the mages there are known to channel their magic into healing abilities.

She must be able to help.

Someone must do something.

Cayden rests his other hand on my face, bringing my gaze back to his as Asena appears in leathers streaked with blood and a red undershirt as an homage to her goddess. "I'm here, my queen."

"You have fire magic, does that also mean you have healing magic?"

"I'm fine, love. I just have to take out the pieces and take a counter-active tonic."

"You fool," Ryder cries. "You fucking fool!"

"Thank you would also suffice."

"I can't heal a poison I can't identify," she says, her face grave as she looks Cayden over.

"Who can?"

"The goddess," she says, and I shake my head, refusing to believe it. Her brows crease, and she rolls her lips together as she looks at the markings on our hands. "There are limits to mortal magic, but per-haps there is another way."

She begins chanting in Ravarian as she opens a portal. Cayden's legs give out, bringing him to his knees, and I fall with him. Venatrix takes a protective stance over us, clawing the dead bodies away to clear a space amid the gore. Ryder forces Cayden onto his back, and I man-age to find a clean part on my clothes to wipe my hands.

"Can I start removing the shards?"

"I don't know!" Ryder throws his hands up.

"Yes. I will be right back," Asena answers before rushing through the portal.

"Okay." I shove the stray pieces of my hair behind my ears and take a deep breath. I've healed countless wounds. I can do this. I can't let him die. "Cayden, this is going to hurt."

"Do what you must," he says.

I don't waste time before wrapping my hand around the first shard, careful to avoid cutting myself, and yanking it out. Cayden doesn't so much as blink, and I'm worried his body has become numb until I look down to where his hand clutches the hilt of his blade. I yank out another shard trailing down his right side, and once again, *nothing*. I wonder how much pain he's experienced in life to perfectly mask it when anyone else would be screaming. If I could kill his father myself, I would, and I'd make it slow. Only years of training keep me from losing my head. I know I can't heal him, but I can at least prepare him for whoever Asena is bringing to us.

He meets my eyes. "You can't hurt me."

"We both know that's a lie," I whisper.

I swallow through my tight throat, continuing my actions until all the shards are out, and begin unhooking his armor. Why can't love find a way to untwine itself from tragedy?

Oh, gods.

I'm in love with him.

I think I have been for a while, but how could I have been so blind? Love is the swelling feeling in my chest whenever he's near, like I'll burst if he doesn't wrap his arms around me. Love is how he kisses my tears and scars to replace my pain with adoration. It's the catch in my breath from both intimate and simple touches, and the weakness in my knees when he stares at me with intense eyes.

Love is woven into our daily lives so completely that we don't realize it when it's right in front of us because it's always present.

Cayden's been scaling the walls of the fortress I keep my heart locked in for months. I am entirely his. Trying not to love him is like attempting to survive without breathing.

I unlatch his armor and cut through his undershirt until his chest is bare. I press my lips together to keep from crying out. Ryder looks away, pressing a fist in front of his mouth as his nostrils flare. He's covered in blood and bruises from the retreat.

"Remind me to get hurt more often if it results in you ripping my clothes off," Cayden slurs.

I force a laugh for his sake, knowing he'd be keeping me calm if the roles were reversed. "It's the only time I find you tolerable."

"I can think of some other times." More blood trickles from the corner of his mouth. "Some very good times."

"ASENA!" I scream toward the swirling portal, no longer able to keep my fear masked. I'm wholly inadequate to treat him. My uselessness is so potent I could choke on it.

The veins in his neck, chest, and arms on his right side are turning black, spiderwebbing through his skin. A female mage cloaked in purple robes steps through the portal with Asena. The pair of them rush toward us and drop to their knees on Cayden's other side.

"Your Majesty," the woman says, her tone grave as she looks down at the wounds.

"No." I can't hear that tone. I can't listen to her pity. I can't lose him.

"A poison of this nature is extremely deadly. It pollutes the blood until only the poison remains."

"I didn't ask what it was," I hiss. "I'm commanding you to heal him."

Finnian finds us, his eyes sticking to Cayden as he remains rooted in place. I think it's strange for all of us to see Cayden like this; out of all of us he's the one who seems unbreakable. Asena and the woman delve into a heated discussion, but my heart is pounding too fiercely to absorb more than every other word. *Please don't take him. Please don't take him. Please don't take him.*

"Let me see those pretty eyes, sirantia." Cayden reaches a hand up to cradle my face. "The marriage clause is fulfilled. Nobody has the right to challenge your claim to the Vareveth throne, even if I'm not ruling beside you."

Finnian kneels beside me, but doesn't reach out, just lets me know he's here for whatever I need as I shake my head. "Stop talking."

"That word. It means—"

"No."

"*Starlight.*"

I suck in a sharp breath.

"*Sirse* is *star*, and *veantia* is *light*. I call you that not only because you love the stars, but because you guided me to a home I didn't know existed, and shone like a beacon through the darkness that's plagued me for years. I would relive every moment of my life, all the pain and suffering, knowing it would lead me to you. I don't belong to death, I'm yours, and I will find you in every life."

"Don't you dare say goodbye to me. Don't you dare break your promise to me." The pain piercing my heart is unfathomable. If Cayden is taken from me, there is not a ward strong enough that will keep me from getting into Imirath.

He tightens his fingers in my hair. "Being married to you for even a day has brought me more happiness than any bastard like me deserves."

Tears trail down my cheeks. "I want more."

"It was worth it, El. All of it. Never forget that."

I look to the woman again. "What can you do? I'll give you anything. I'll do anything."

"There is a ritual that can be done only *once*," the mage says. "But I cannot stress enough the danger of it, and also the pain you will experience."

"I don't care."

"Elowen, no," Cayden commands, but I ignore him. This is my choice. All I need is a chance. One minuscule shred of faith, and I'll hang on to it like a lifeline.

"Slice both of your palms open, his as well. We'll need to tap into the godly magic within the markings. The magic will pull some of the toxins from his blood and put it into yours, and you'll have to fight through the poison together. He'll feel better, but you'll feel . . ."

I'm already slicing open my palms before she finishes and move on to Cayden's despite him trying to rip his hand from my grip. The poison has made him too weak to fight me, and he especially can't escape the hold Ryder has on his shoulders.

"Let me do this. He's my brother," Ryder pleads. "Don't make her take this pain."

"You may be bound, but your souls are not," the mage responds. "The only reason a ritual like this can work is because of who they are to each other, but the queen could still die if the poison is too strong for her."

"Do it." I ignore her strange wording, just wanting to get this done. She begins muttering prayers in Ravarian to the God of Death, Goddess of Life, and Goddess of Souls.

"Get her away from me," Cayden demands, his glassy eyes branding Finnian. "If she dies, it'll be on your conscience."

"Shut up," I command, and Cayden turns his attention back on me.

The skin on my palm already burns from his blood as he tries to pull away, but I know this is only the beginning. "Don't risk yourself for me. Let me go, my love. My body can fight against this."

My hands start shaking but not from the pain. "Don't ask me to do something you would never do. You've promised to die beside me many times; now I'm promising to do the same."

"Elowen," he slurs, his blinks slowing as the mage finishes her prayer, and I lean down to press my lips to his as he murmurs my name one final time before falling unconscious. "My Elowen." His pulse still beats, but it's weak.

Golden wisps surround where Cayden and I are joined, creating an unbreakable barrier as I watch his chest rise and fall unevenly. I keep our fingers locked tight just in case, not wanting to take any chances with breaking the connection.

"There's no taking back your choice once the poison enters your blood, Your Highness. You will be cheating death, and there is always a price to pay," the mage says. "This is my final warning."

Whatever the price is won't compare to losing Cayden. I nod, just once, and pain like I've never experienced sinks its claws into me. It's like walking through fire. Having a thousand knives piercing my skin at once. It's like my flesh is slowly being peeled off my bones. I clench my teeth and drop my head, not wanting anyone to see the agony this is causing me.

I will not die here.

I will not let Cayden die here.

I choke on the copper taste in my mouth.

My whole body is shaking like there's an earthquake within me.

Red swirls begin crawling up my arms like the poison is burning me from the inside and trying to force its way out. More red splatters on my arms, running down my cheeks, and I realize I'm crying tears of blood. My chest is heaving, my throat is burning like the air itself is poison. I throw my head back and scream, no longer able to keep the pain contained.

Finnian wraps an arm around me to keep me upright as I'm burned alive with no fire in sight. Sweat drips down my back and he cuts off my sleeves to help cool me down. My remaining dragons land in the grass around us, Sorin coming close to nudge my leg with his snout, and the other three dip their heads and close their eyes.

Imirath will take nothing more from me.

I am made of fire, and nothing will burn me.

Magic sings in my blood, and I command it to consume the poison instead of my skin. I turn it on the foreign substance coursing through me like a blade. I build a dam against the pain and force it to become power.

I open my eyes and watch the red swirling marks that stop just above my elbows become lavender, pale blue, silver, and gold. They swirl together like vines and extend to where my gold markings end. The same swirling pattern is reflected on Cayden, but he's marked in black and one streak of dark blue. His markings travel up the ribs on his right side but leave his stomach bare, swirl across his chest, halfway up his throat, and down his arm.

The golden wisps fade along with the pain, and I can finally take a breath without it feeling like needles are in my lungs. When they're fully gone, I collapse on Cayden's chest, listening to the faint sound of his heartbeat that's become my favorite song. Our hands are healed and though the wounds on his chest aren't, they've stopped bleeding. I only let go when I know for sure that Cayden will be all right. I can clean his wounds later. All that matters is the poison is gone.

The mage is looking between us and our markings like she just witnessed a miracle. "I've never seen such markings."

I take the waterskin Finnian offers me as he brushes my hair back from my sweaty forehead and swish it around my mouth to spit out the blood. "This has never happened when you've done the ritual before?"

"No one has ever survived it," she responds, glancing between

Cayden and me like we're a puzzle in desperate need of solving, but I don't have time for her curiosity. Whatever magic coursed through me during the ritual doesn't dissolve, it grows stronger, pressing on my skin like it needs to be shed. "Your *eyes* . . ."

Finnian grasps my chin, and his lips part in surprise. "They're swirling. It's like they're molten gold."

Rage courses through me like a drug and I lose myself in the high as I get to my feet, still covered in blood and ash from the battle. Vareveth soldiers who witnessed the ritual are kneeling between the corpses in the sand surrounding us; even some soldiers from Thirwen and Imirath follow their actions.

"Where is the mage who created the bomb?" I demand, walking toward the wards. "Bring me Nykeem!"

I stop a few inches away from the glowing wall as the soldiers on the other side begin parting.

"I have refrained from burning your kingdom to the ground, but my mercy goes only so far," I begin, my voice raspy and raw from screaming. "Zayèra."

All around me, my dragons' fire blazes, colliding with the wards as I watch who must be Nykeem breach the crowd and struggle to combat them. His black hair is cropped just below his chin, and his armor is without a speck of blood. It's clear he didn't take part in the battle. Other mages from Thirwen join Nykeem, wide-eyed as they watch me. My smile is all bloodstained teeth as I glare at the man, pointing right at him so he knows what's coming for him.

Death.

"You tell Garrick that his nightmare has returned with a demon at her side."

Several Imirath soldiers behind the wards drop to their knees, and chaos quickly ensues as those loyal to Garrick spot them. Fights break out, soldiers push into the mages trying to hold the wards, and I laugh.

"Cower behind your wards all you want, but there will come a day when you will not be able to run, and there will be nobody to protect you when you're slaughtered by either myself or my king who you failed to kill."

Another wave of power rushes through me, and I clench my jaw as I thrust my hands out on either side of me, staring into the dragonfire as I pull it toward me. *Wield it.* A mixture of all my dragons' flames flickers in my hands and snakes up my arms in circles, answering to me.

I become the flames. Giving in to my power and owning it so nobody can take it from me.

More beyond the wards drop to their knees as I open the bond in my chest, commanding the fire as I command my dragons, and then I join them, shooting fire into the wards as the mages' struggles worsen. The flames transform into talons at the tips of my fingers, one color for each dragon on both hands. I begin to pry the ward apart like wet clay, tearing strips out of it as the mages' worried cries flood my ears. I sink my claws into it, thinking about ripping into them. Their hearts could beat in my palms after I tear them from their chests and shove them down their throats.

Not yet, I tell myself.

The wards don't only keep us from getting in, they also keep them from getting out until they're down. We arranged to leave for Galakin tomorrow morning once we heard of Thirwen's movements, and they've just sealed themselves within Imirath.

I command the dragons to stop, but they stay close. Sorin and Venatrix hover above, Basilius protects my back, and Delmira and Calithea stand on either side of me.

"You will never be safe again. I'll always be lurking in the shadows with my blades drawn and flames ready."

The flames curl up my arms, and in my reflection, I see them form a crown around my head. I slowly release my hold on the power, watching the talons fade away but forcing the crown to remain as I stand my ground with my dragons and face our enemy.

"I am Elowen Veles, and I'm coming for my throne."

CHAPTER
FORTY-TWO
ELOWEN

I REMAIN STANDING BY SOME MIRACLE, EVEN AS MY LEGS burn while trudging through the bloody sand. The wards didn't include the destroyed fort set on the water, and charred stones continue dropping into the waves as the walls crumble. The world blurs along the edges of my spotty vision as the magic leaves my body, the fatigue hitting me so fiercely it's as if I fell through the surface of a frozen lake, unable to move as I sink into the dark depths.

I wielded dragonfire.

My brain isn't moving as fast as my body, and I don't have the energy to theorize.

The soldiers remain kneeling as I return to Finnian and Ryder so they'll be able to issue orders. They rise from their knees, both sets of eyes full of questions I don't know how to answer. Every time I've experienced magic, it's made me feel untouchable and invincible, but I can never hold on to it. It always slips away, leaving me hollow and exhausted.

"I need healing supplies." Venatrix returns to standing guard over Cayden's body, and I bite the inside of my cheek when I take in all the blood and grime covering him. Ryder waves someone over and hands me the satchel they're carrying. "Assemble the soldiers and prepare them to return to Vareveth. There's no sense in leaving anyone behind. The dragonfire destroyed the port enough to render it useless and their supplies are buried under the rubble. Hang our banners from the ramparts. They won't risk dropping the wards, so they'll be forced to remember what happened today and fear the battles to come."

"We'll be quick and will have Asena portal us to the inn. Sas will be going out of her mind by now and Cayden needs to get somewhere safe while his body recovers," Ryder says. "What should we do with the enemy soldiers on our side of the wards?"

Something heavy weighs on my chest, but I keep my shoulders rigid, not wanting anyone to see me falter. "Give them the option of taking a blood oath. If they swear to fight for us, let them live, but execute them if they refuse. Imirath and Thirwen's loss could be our gain."

Ryder nods, a crease forming between his brows. "*How?*"

One word can hold so much weight depending on how it's asked. His question doesn't refer to the prisoners, it refers to everything else.

"I don't know." I shake my head. "I'm going to talk to the mage who performed the ritual before I depart."

"Be swift."

"You too. I'll order three dragons to remain until you're safe."

Ryder takes another look at Cayden and his throat bobs after he sucks in a sharp breath. His guilt is so apparent, it radiates off him, but he's stalking down the beach before I have the chance to say something. Finnian squeezes my hand before following Ryder, and the blood crusting our skin creases, making me long for a bath. I hate the feeling of dried blood.

Remaining here puts me on edge, so I shove my concern aside for the time being and find Asena standing on the shore with the other mage. The smoke wafting up to the sky is so thick it makes my throat raw. Burning wood juts from the water like a sea of broken bones stretching as far back as I can see.

Asena notices my pursuit and closes the distance quickly. "Your Majesty, what you just did—" The curls she piled on top of her head sway as she shakes her head, staring at me with wide, awestruck eyes. "No mage has ever wielded dragonfire."

"No mage has ever been bonded to five dragons," I answer. It's the only possible explanation I can think of. Even Asena herself said not to put limitations on the bounds of my abilities. "Can you introduce me to your friend?"

"Of course." She reaches behind her to tug the woman forward. "This is Sage. She's a soul mage who has dedicated her life to the Goddess of Souls. Her cult resides within the Etril Forest."

A chill snakes up my spine when I think of the eerie woods Cayden and I traveled through while fleeing Imirath. The perfectly symmetrical trees . . . the silence aside from the whistling wind and branches hitting into one another.

Sage offers me a shy smile and a curtsy. "Your Majesty."

"Thank you for what you did for me," I say. "I don't know how to repay you."

"No payment to me is required. You survived because the gods willed it, and my life is dedicated to serving them."

I clear my throat. "What did you mean when you said that Cayden and I are bound?"

She sinks her teeth into her lower lip and shoves her hands into her pockets. Her robes shift, and I note the burn scars on the column of her throat. "Before I performed the ceremony, my powers sensed a bond between you and King Cayden. I never would have performed it if it didn't exist; there would have been no chance of survival. It's an invisible tether between you two that only the Goddess of Souls can create."

"Cayden and I are bonded?"

"Yes," Sage states. "A soul tie. It weaves your fates together, makes you destined to cross paths, but how you feel about each other is entirely up to you. Some soul ties lead people to their enemies."

I blink slowly as I absorb the information. I've always felt a pull to Cayden, but any mention of the gods having influence over our lives makes me want to rebel against that fact. "And the new markings?" I glance again at the swirling lines traveling up my arms.

"They are evidence of the bond. We refer to them as aura markings because their colors reflect your souls. As I said, a ritual of that magnitude can be performed only once. It alerts other soul mages that they won't be able to tap into that magic should either of you be gravely injured again."

I sway on my feet, and Asena shoots a hand forward to steady me. "You should leave, Your Majesty. You need to rest."

"I'll see you when I return to Vareveth," I tell her, and she smiles in response. "And thank you, Sage. I am in your debt. If you ever change your mind about receiving payment, please don't hesitate to find me."

Her lips turn down. "It is not I who will collect the payment for the ritual, Your Highness."

My smile pinches, but I manage to keep it on my face as I turn away. Another wave of fatigue washes over me as I walk toward Venatrix. She lifts Cayden more tenderly than I've seen her hold anything and sets him gently on Calithea, who bends as much as she can so I can climb onto her. I weave the saddle straps around myself and Cayden before clipping them to my harness. There's no way I'll be able to bear his weight, but I keep his reclined form pressed between my knees and the saddle horns. Calithea is tuned in to my senses and knows this isn't an ordinary flight. I don't think the dragons would take so calmly to someone else being on their back unless the situation was dire.

She climbs up a cliff a few yards away and spreads her wings for an even takeoff, slowly gaining altitude but never tipping up enough to jostle us. Cayden's wounds need to be bandaged. I slide the satchel off my shoulder and pull out a clean rag and waterskin, needing to clean his torso first. It's always been easier for me to heal strangers—healing even a small scrape on a loved one riddles me with unwanted emotion. Cayden sucks in a breath, groaning when I press the rag over the largest gash on his side. His eyes blink open and focus on my face as best as they can. I command Calithea to glide. It'll slow us considerably, but I can't stitch him unless she keeps us steady. Ryder and Finnian will probably finish with the soldiers and portal to Avaloria, the oceanside town in Vareveth, before us. There was no sense in us traveling back to the manor when we'd have to travel to the docks before first light, but part of me still wishes we were able to.

I thread the needle and get to work. "One day you'll stop getting hurt to gain my attention."

His lips quirk in a dopey smile I've never seen on him. He's not fully conscious yet, but I know he's fighting his way toward it. "It's worked like a charm since the first night I kissed you, and I don't plan on stopping."

He falls asleep again and I finish stitching. Calithea gains speed every time I finish a gash, covering more distance while I thread the needle. Thankfully not all his wounds are that deep, and once the blood is cleared, I take a moment to admire his markings and trace them with my finger.

The trees fade away, and Avaloria takes their place. It's a small town within Vareveth made of curved roads and old stone bungalows along the coast. Ships are anchored in the distance and smaller boats bob along the docks with fishermen hauling in nets of their daily catches. Calithea and Venatrix land in front of the inn. Every quaint house along the street has wreaths made of colored sea glass and sea-shells. It's clear they're homemade, which only adds to the charm, as do the weathered painted shutters in shades of various blues, greens, and corals.

I use the lull of the surf crashing against the shore to drown out the pained screams that surrounded me moments ago. Our accommodations are set on the water, and I'm hoping we can still hear the waves through the closed windows. I'd love to come back here in the summer, but I'm eager to get out of the cold.

Saskia bursts from the entrance with Finnian and Ryder hot on her heels. Ryder is still caked in blood and quickly overtakes Saskia in her pursuit. "What took you so long?"

I unhook the straps attaching us to the saddle and slide down. "I couldn't stitch him if Calithea flew at full speed."

"Cayden!" Saskia shouts.

"Not dead. Hate to disappoint." Cayden sits up and mirrors my actions, using Calithea to steady himself and patting her scales. "Thank you for the ride, pretty lady."

"Let me help you inside." Ryder steps forward, but Cayden presses a hand to his chest to halt him as he pushes on without assistance. He shouldn't even be awake right now, let alone walking, and my temper rises at his stubbornness. He shoves open the door made of green and blue sea glass within a shell-covered arch. The innkeeper by the front desk screams and drops the stack of linens in her arms.

"I have that effect on people." Cayden leans against one of the white pillars that support the ceiling. "Room?"

"U-up the stairs and to the right, Your Majesty. It's our finest one."

"Thank you," I say, ducking under his arm. If anything, it'll help him keep his balance. He doesn't look at me, and the dopey smile is nowhere in sight. I know I did the right thing. I didn't do anything he wouldn't have done for me.

CHAPTER
FORTY-THREE

ELOWEN

MY HAIR IS STILL DAMP FROM THE BATH WHEN RYDER finds me at the small dining table. Similar to the entry-way, the tabletop is made of broken sea glass sanded by the waves, proving once again that even broken things can still create something beautiful. His dark eyes are shadowed with regret as he finds Cayden's sleeping form sprawled out on the bed.

"Are you hungry?" I ask, gesturing to the trays of food a servant brought up. All I've managed to do is pick at some bread while watching the waves through the arched windows and the rise and fall of Cayden's chest through the seafoam canopy. I may physically be at the inn, but mentally, I'm still in the battle. I can't stop thinking of the wyverns and the white eyes of the mages as they controlled the creatures. I will always choose my dragons, no matter the enemy, but watching the beasts fall from the sky twists my heart in the aftermath.

"I ate a bit before I bathed," he says, claiming the seat across from me. His gaze remains on Cayden as he drags a hand down his face. "Is it all right if I sit here? I should've asked."

I give him a half smile while blinking away the moisture in my eyes. "You're his best friend, Ryder. Of course you can."

"They'll get easier." He gives me a knowing look. "The battles."

I nod, clearing my throat and taking a sip of tea.

"I didn't know what he was doing when he tackled me." A muscle twitches in his jaw. "Everything happened so fast. We finally managed to get through the gap by some miracle. We were still packed together when the bomb went off, but he grabbed me to cover me before the explosion launched us through the air."

"None of this is your fault, and he wouldn't want you to blame yourself."

"He would've died had you not tortured yourself," he snaps before squeezing his eyes shut. "I'm sorry. I don't mean to lose my temper."

"I understand." If Ryder thinks *that* was losing his temper, he should've witnessed an episode from Ailliard. When I was fourteen, he destroyed the bookshelf I made myself in a fit of rage.

"He'd do the same thing when we were younger because I had Saskia and he had no one. I just want him to stop viewing himself as expendable and invincible."

I look to the waves again, remembering Cayden telling me about how they calm him. "What were you two like when you were younger?"

I've always had a hard time picturing how they became friends, but maybe reminiscing will help Ryder through his emotions. Ryder is the type of person who could befriend a rock, and Cayden is the type of person to throw a rock at someone.

"The first thing Cayden ever said to me was *Leave before I kill you for interrupting my dinner.*" Ryder finally gives a weak laugh. "Gods, if you think he's bad now, you should've seen him back then. He was so *angry.* I'd never seen anyone with that much rage. So, naturally, I attempted to befriend him and ended up with a black eye and busted lip."

"I give you credit for approaching him."

"I did it for Sas. We couldn't take any money with us when we left home because my father would've pressed charges, and I couldn't be a sellsword because I'd never used one. I was a shit thief, having been born into wealth. She got sick soon after we left home, and I carried her into the dingiest tavern I've ever seen during a stormy night and approached the worst-looking person in there."

"Did he turn you away then?"

"Oh, he tried, but I was a protective older brother who needed his sister to survive the night. When I brought her into it, Cayden handed over his keys and told us to be gone in three days. I still don't know where he stayed while we occupied his room, but hot soup and medicine were delivered to the door every night."

My heart thaws for the jaded boy from the past. Knowing what I do about his father, I wonder if he helped them because he didn't want to be the catalyst for someone losing a loved one. Cayden has killed many people without remorse and was even paid to commit murder, but maybe he saw himself in Ryder's desperation.

"So you were friends after that?"

"Absolutely not." He snickers. "I kept hanging around the tavern, and somewhere within that time he stopped punching me for stalking him, then he stopped threatening me for annoying him. We didn't become friends until he returned one night completely drunk and asked me if I wanted to help him hide a body, and even then, I use the term loosely. He called me Rykus for a solid year."

Ryder's shoulders shake along with mine as I laugh. He goes on to tell me about how he and Saskia moved in with Cayden soon after, how they began acquiring wealth through the fighting pits and smuggling, and how Cayden taught Ryder to wield a blade and pick a pocket.

"He sounds exactly how I thought he'd be," I say.

"No matter how much of a bastard he was, I felt more alive living in the slums than I ever did in my family estate," Ryder says. "I left for Saskia, but I also left for myself. I would've died in that lifestyle—it was too soulless."

I understand the feeling all too well. "We're all on borrowed time, and I intend to know that I truly lived when I close my eyes for the last time."

"That sounds like a decent plan, sunshine." Ryder gets to his feet, looking between Cayden and me. "I'll check back in the morning, but you should try to get some sleep."

"Oh, wait!" My slippers press into the cold wooden floor as I walk to my trunk and flip it open. What I need is right on top, and I return to Ryder, handing him the green tin with a white bow. "I know you had a pint with Cayden before the battle, but I wanted to wish you a happy birthday."

A broad smile parts his lips as he lifts the lid. "Did you make these?"

He devoured the cookies I bought him while visiting the Aestilian neighborhood in Verendus, and I figured food is always a good gift. "I did. It's a mixture of lemon, sugar, and shortbread cookies."

I have a tendency to bake when stressed.

And I'm stressed a lot.

"Thank you." His warm eyes settle on me. "Don't tell the others that I have these. They'll steal them when I'm not looking."

"They sniff out baked goods like bloodhounds, so I wish you luck," I say, and he chuckles while walking to the door. "Night, Rykus."

He glances over his shoulder, tapping his fingers along the door-frame as he watches me walk back to my trunk. "Welcome to the family, Elowen Veles."

The door softly shuts behind him, and I rummage through my belongings to find the vial of oil I bought several weeks ago. At some point Cayden turned to lay on his stomach, leaving the scars on his back bared to the faint candlelight in the room. Rage fills me at the sight, especially knowing it was his father who put them there.

I climb onto the bed, straddling Cayden's hips as I tug the sleeves of the sweater I stole from him up to my elbows and pour some oil into my hands. Even though I'm exhausted, I doubt I'll be able to sleep until he wakes up. I doubt he'll even remember getting here. Even if he was on his feet, I think it stemmed from years of self-preservation rather than him actually healing.

I glide my fingers down the red lash marks carved into his back, some raised and others sunken gashes, before digging my palms into his muscles to ease the inevitable aches. His skin glistens as I work, trying my best to undo decades of knots, but just when I think I'm getting somewhere, the world flips around, and I'm flat on my back with a knife pointed at my throat. Cayden's eyes are open and alert, glaring down at me with an emotion they never have. It's gone in a blink, disappearing quicker than my fear has the chance to appear.

"El." His chest heaves, and he throws the knife to the ground. "Fuck, I'm sorry. I'm so sorry."

"It's all right," I say through my racing heart, and his eyes flick to my glistening palms. "I was just trying to lessen your aches in the morning." His eyes dart to the window before looking around the room in confusion. "We're back in Vareveth. We're in Avaloria. The battle is over. We're leaving for Galakin in the morning as planned. I got you back here on Calithea."

He wraps an arm under me and crushes me to him, burying his face in my neck and inhaling deeply. His heart crashes against mine as I wrap my arms around his shoulders. He flips our positions, pressing his back into the headboard and placing me on his chest. "You should be sleeping," he murmurs.

"I needed to know you were okay." My throat tightens now that he's awake. His voice. I knew I craved his arms, but didn't realize how desperate I was to hear him speak. "There was so much blood."

"I know, but I need you to rest, love." He runs his hand through my hair and massages his fingers into the nape of my neck when I start shaking. "I'm all right, El. You're not getting rid of me after only a day of marriage."

I don't say anything, just hold him tighter as the mixture of fatigue and relief pummel into me. I want to stay awake, to soak in his presence, to talk to him about everything, but it's impossible to keep my eyes open. Guilt burns my throat when I think of the wyverns again. It's so much simpler killing humans. They're partaking in the battle consciously, but the wyverns are trapped under a spell. They must not even know what's happening to them until the mage dies and loses their hold on their minds. The greed of humanity harming innocent creatures, it's a timeless, wretched tale. "How do you sleep knowing what you've done will find you in your dreams?"

"Beside you," he answers. "You're a reminder that everything I've done is worth it." He kisses my forehead and runs his hands over my body like he's reassuring himself that I'm unharmed.

"Never," he whispers. "*Never* choose me over yourself."

"I chose myself when I chose you."

CHAPTER
FORTY-FOUR
CAYDEN

THE WIND WHIPPING OFF THE WAVES ISN'T LOUD ENOUGH to drown out my father's voice booming through my skull.

You ruin everything you touch, boy. My life was so much better before you came into the world, and I wish you'd died in your mother's womb. She would've mourned you, but she'd still be here.

I'm fucked in the head in a way that can't be undone. I'm sure the old man is smiling up at me in triumph after being proved right yet again. I hate that he would be happy that I'm king. I hate that he would be happy the people of the southern isles are calling for me to ascend the conquered throne. I hate that he would've said utilizing the marriage clause was wise.

I hate when it feels like I'm looking in a mirror and seeing my father.

We have the same skin tone, the same wavy hair, the same broad frame, the same facial features. Thank the gods I didn't get his eyes, even if it made him give me an extra lash when he saw my mother within my gaze.

The only damn thing that separates us is that I would never stand idly by while Elowen was harmed.

I never fell asleep after holding a knife to Elowen's neck. It was a sight too chilling; I knew it would be awaiting me in my nightmares. The last thing I remembered before passing out from the poison was

Elowen's screams, and I was still in my battle headspace when I woke up on my stomach with someone touching my back. I didn't know it was her, but if there was ever a moment when I wanted to grant her the favor of removing myself from her life, it was that one.

"Raise the sails!" Vale, the captain of the vessel shouts, and the crew scurries around the deck in response. Several water mages along with Ophir joined their ranks and are able to wield the water to get us to Galakin quicker.

Waves crash against the steep cliffs bordering the cove, the spray dissolving into the air filled with squawking gulls. We can't portal to Galakin because the distance is too vast and would risk burning out the mages, but if something goes wrong in Vareveth it's a risk we'll have to take. The ship lurches beneath my feet as wind fills the dark blue sails. I transfer my weight to keep from stumbling, something Elowen and Finnian haven't mastered, if their thumping and giggling streaming from somewhere on the deck is any indication.

My eyes remain on the endless horizon speckled with clouds as the dragons fly forward. Saskia steps up beside me, her gloved hands gripping the railing. "The five of us need to have a meeting now that we've left port."

Ophir cleaves a wave in two, allowing us to sail through it. "Is Ryder in the cabin?"

She hesitates for a moment. "He is."

I crack my neck and fill my lungs with the salty air, knowing the inevitable argument that's coming will only add to my exhaustion. "I'll see you down there."

I sneak one final glance at Elowen from the corner of my eye before climbing the steps to the upper deck and shoving the door to the meeting room open. Nautical-themed decor adorns the walls, but nothing overly extravagant. The whole ship is made of dark wood, including the furniture that's nailed to the floor—aside from the chairs.

Ryder glances up at me when I enter, his lips turning down as he looks me over. "Let's have at it," I sigh, claiming the seat across from him. "You've always worn your emotions on your face."

He shakes his head, a sneer contorting his features. "What's to say, Cayden? You saved my life, and I feel like a liability again, just as I did when we were younger."

"You've defended me on several occasions."

"I never took a bomb for you."

"There's always another day if that's what made your mood so sour." I shrug. "There was no sense in both of us dying. I knew what was coming, so I covered you."

"You have a wife!" He slams his hands on the table, rattling the lantern at the center. "*A wife!* I had to listen to that woman scream as tears of blood ran down her cheeks while I prayed to every god I've ever heard of to spare both your lives. You were dying right in front of me, and so was she."

It would have been less painful if he'd forced me to swallow glass. Gods, her screams. I'll remember them for as long as I live. The helplessness I felt in that moment disgusted me, and I've never hated myself more, knowing I couldn't rip my hands away from her.

"You should've taken her away from me."

"No, I shouldn't have." He shakes his head. "What she did was a miracle."

"What she did was suicidal," I growl, rising to my feet.

"Then you're perfect for each other." He mimics my position. "Where would your death have left her? Think of Elowen. She may have married you but there's no heir to secure the line of succession."

Flames fill my veins at the mention of fatherhood, something I've always rejected entirely. "All I have done from the moment Elowen came into my life is think of her! Dragons will secure a throne much more than a child, so I suggest you stop speaking of *my wife* as if her worth is entirely based on what comes from between her legs. Insult me all you want, but do not bring Elowen into this. You're acting like an immature prick, reprimanding me as if I ran toward the bomb when all I did was limit the death toll from an inevitable attack."

His face drops as he collapses back into the chair. The walls feel like they're closing in on me, but I clench my jaw and claim my seat as well. Saskia will be here with Finnian and Elowen shortly, and it is smart to have a meeting now that we're en route to Galakin for an alliance.

I pull up my sleeves and glare down at the new markings on my arm. I hate that I can't stop loving her, but I sickeningly never want to be freed of this cursed torment. Her screams continue echoing in my mind, and I'd already be halfway to the pit beneath the Demon's Den if we were back in Vareveth, needing to take my anger out on something. Fear is a pitiful emotion, but I could practically taste it when Elowen sliced her palms open. It was the only thing stronger than my self-loathing.

I'm deeply selfish, and my actions throughout my life reflect that. I kill when needed. I steal when needed. I lie when needed. I can generate some degree of feeling if prompted, but I don't navigate life with emotions.

Elowen has always been the greatest flaw in my logic.

It perplexed me to no end in the beginning. I'd lie awake trying to pinpoint the reason her happiness and safety began to matter more to me than freeing her dragons. I'd step off the battlefield or out of the fighting ring and pick through flowers with blood-coated hands and imagine her smile when they arrived in her room. She's the only good part of me, but when I think of the pain I caused her, it makes me want to bury my emotions so she'll never know the true depths of them. All my life I've been taught that love is a weakness, that all it does is spawn misery, and I wish I could be different, but I'm not.

Elowen crashes into the room like a storm as the ship lurches over a patch of rough water, and I manage to stand and wrap my arms around her before she slams into the table. "You'll find your sea legs eventually."

"I much prefer my land legs," she huffs.

"My lap is still available if you're scared of the sea monsters swimming below."

She groans, looking up at me over her shoulder. "I'll send you to them if you continue reminding me of their existence."

I pull her down next to me despite the dark emotions churning within, or maybe it's because of them. Her presence has always had a way of making the darkness bearable. She's the center of my universe and everything else revolves around her. I wrap my hand around the back of her neck, my thumb rubbing over her pulse point several times, and if she notices what I'm doing she doesn't comment on it.

"First thing," Saskia says, shrugging off her thick fur cloak and throwing it over a chair as Finnian takes the spot beside Elowen. "Since we're on our way to Galakin, let's discuss how we'll get Prince Zarius to join us."

"Kidnapping."

"Blackmail," Elowen says.

"Threats," Ryder adds.

Saskia drops her head into her hands as Finnian laughs. "You're the royal family of Vareveth. You must be able to negotiate with rulers properly, without blackmail. Even if he's a disinherited prince."

"Gaining the upper hand by any means necessary *is* negotiating properly," I say. The ship lurches again and Elowen squeezes her eyes shut and reaches for my hand. I pull her chair closer to mine and wrap my arm around her waist, kissing the side of her head. She grabs the wine bottle beside the lantern and tosses back several gulps before I rip it from her. "You haven't eaten."

"I'll get drunk faster, and time will go by quicker."

"Not when you're vomiting into a barrel." I give it a solid day before she's singing a different tune and falls in love with sailing. "We'll deal with the prince when the time comes. The best plans are born from improvisation anyway."

"You planned for several years before finding Elowen," Saskia points out in a prim tone.

"That was different."

"She was also a disinherited royal."

"With a bond to five dragons, the daughter of my enemy, and extremely beautiful."

"You didn't know the last part."

"My hope was fulfilled."

A flush creeps up Elowen's neck as she clears her throat. "Putting Prince Zarius on the Thirwen throne will benefit both us and Galakin. Not only will it provide us with another ally in the world, but Cordelia must crave answers about her sister who went missing and sparked the war between their kingdoms."

"No matter how much he wishes to hide, a royal can't remain a ghost forever." Finnian gestures to Elowen as proof.

"Zario is known for its gambling dens. It's just outside of the royal city. We'll check there before moving along to the castle," I say.

"Won't it be seen as an insult for us not to go directly to the royals?" Saskia asks.

"We've gone on stealth missions before," Ryder answers. "We'll lower the sails that have the Veles sigil on them. Elowen can command the dragons to stay out of sight, and we can be in and out of the city before the royals know. It's not as if Elowen and Cayden have visited here as king and queen before. Nobody will know their faces."

When the others aren't looking, Ryder offers me an apologetic glance, and I nod in response. I know he regrets his earlier words, but I'm not one for sappy apologies.

A servant carries in a tray of beef stew filled with sweet potatoes, carrots, onions, and other vegetables. The hearty scent fills the cabin as he sets it down. Finnian turns even greener than before, but I don't waste time before ripping into a warm loaf of bread and dipping it into my bowl.

"How are you eating right now?" Finnian grumbles.

"With my mouth," I flatly state.

"Galakin holds the gods in high regard, especially the Goddess of Flames. Their society is built around fire and light magic," Ryder begins. "You were both marked during your wedding, the ritual, and with Elowen's newfound ability to wield dragonfire—"

"Why didn't any of you start with that? Who gives a fuck about the prince?" I turn to fully face Elowen. "You wielded dragonfire?"

Elowen's mouth opens and shuts several times, and a nervous laugh escapes her as she glances around the room. "Sort of?"

"How do you *sort of* wield fire?"

"Listen, I don't know how I did it. I sat beside a candle for several hours last night and tried to pull the flames toward me but didn't feel anything. It could've been a fluke or a result of the ritual. I remember my rage amplifying after I knew you were healed, and the power felt like it would make my body combust if I didn't expel it."

"Try again." Ryder shoves the lantern toward her where a single flame flickers through the glass. "Or we could go up to the deck if you'd like to use dragonfire, and we'll cheer you on while you get to it."

"What a brilliant idea," Elowen drawls. "Let me just pull magical fire to me as I stand on a wooden ship in the middle of an ocean."

He snaps his fingers. "Noted. Not my best plan, I'll admit that."

"What happened after you wielded it?" Fucking hells, I can't believe I missed this.

"I was able to pry into the wards, and I would've kept going if we hadn't been planning to leave Vareveth, but the wards will help keep them out of our territory. I couldn't hold on to it, though. I'm hoping to be able to observe some of the Galakin mages and practice their techniques. In the meantime, I'll continue strengthening the connection to my dragons. Seeing through their eyes can't light the ship on fire and the more I do it the easier it'll become." She inhales deeply. "Soldiers on both sides knelt to me. It caused chaos within the Imirath and Thirwen ranks. I declared that I'm coming for my throne."

"You're . . . incredible," I say, unable to tear my eyes away from her face. Her blush deepens, and she sits forward in her chair to escape my intense gaze. I'll see her wield it one day. She may think it was a fluke, but I'm convinced this woman is made of magic.

"Has there been any news of the southern isles since the initial rebellion?" Finnian asks.

"No," Saskia responds. "All is quiet for now, but silence can shatter in a second."

CHAPTER
FORTY-FIVE

ELOWEN

DELMIRA SPIRALS AND SLIPS DOWN FROM THE CLOUDS, dragging her claws through the glittering sea beside the ship. Sailing has provided me with an excuse to slip away at all hours of the day to fly. I spend more time on dragonback than I do aboard the vessel. Part of the reason for that is how strange Cayden has been the past few days, but I don't need much convincing before mounting one of my fiery beasts.

He's not avoiding me exactly. He's never too far, and we share a cabin on board, but he's noticeably quiet. Volatile. Like a dormant volcano or a storm churning on the horizon. I can tell he's working through something within his mind, and I want to grant him the same patience he's given me, but I feel as if I'm tiptoeing along the edge of a cliff.

I still haven't asked Cayden about the sheet music in his desk, but given how closed off he's been, I don't think it's the time to admit I snooped through his belongings.

Delmira cuts above Sorin, camouflaging herself within the sky to ambush him, but the menace himself is never one to turn down a challenge. He roars when he notices her, locking claws with her as they tumble and twist toward the water below. I laugh as butterflies erupt in my stomach, and they separate only inches from the surface. They fly in a wide arc and nuzzle their snouts once they meet in the middle, much calmer than before.

I blink the dizziness away as Delmira evens out, keeping pace with the ship as I pull a book from the satchel I threw over my shoulder and lie on my stomach. I trace the gold-foiled mermaid on the cover as it shimmers before diving into the story. The gloves covering my hands make it a bit hard to flip the pages, but the weather is slowly starting to warm as we get farther into our journey. The first two days were nothing but rain. I still managed to fly above the clouds to avoid the storm but also spent time indoors playing drinking games with Finnian and Ryder while Cayden begrudgingly played the rickety and out-of-tune piano for Saskia and me to swing each other around the tiny cabin.

I repeat the same actions the next day but need only a sweater, and by the sixth day into our journey, I'm wearing a light pink gown made of flowy chiffon with cutouts along the sides and drooping fabric that leaves my arms bare but cuffs around my wrists. I trace one of the lavender lines swirling around my arm as I sun myself on Sorin's scales. The sky is painted in shades of fire as its last rays burn the day away. If I could have dinner up here, I would, but considering I packed both breakfast and lunch along with several snacks, I suppose it's best to show my face at some point.

I command Sorin to drop me off on deck, but he does the opposite and increases his altitude. "Sorin." I draw out his name like I'm scolding a guilty child, and he huffs before complying. "Goodnight, my sweet boy."

I slide down his extended wing and my slipper-clad feet smack into the deck as I find my balance. My eyes are on the sky when I hear him. "You're avoiding me."

Cayden is leaning against the railing beside the bow, wearing a white linen shirt that billows in the wind. The arrowhead necklace he's never taken off rests within the shirt's deep V neckline, and the markings swirling along his muscles are visible through the semi-translucent fabric. His loose black pants are tucked into boots, the same style he's worn every day since I met him, and a bandanna holds his hair back from his face. The sea suits him.

"Have you ever thought that perhaps I'm busy?"

"In the middle of the ocean?" he kicks off the wood, his heavy steps eating the distance between us. "You've read three books and take two out of three meals in the sky, and you're a terrible actress because you *giggle* into your pillow while you pretend to be asleep."

"I am a phenomenal actress." I flick my curls over my shoulder and cock a hip. "And it's frowned upon to stalk people."

He crosses his arms. "You're my wife."

"Congratulations, that was almost an intelligent observation." He tucks his tongue into the side of his cheek to keep from laughing. "Is there something in particular you've sought me out for or were you just craving the pleasure of my presence?"

"More like the punishment."

I shove him in his chest, which vibrates with his chuckle, and turn in the direction of the dining cabin. His eyes rest heavily on my back with every step, and I know each second ticking by is bringing us closer to an inevitable conversation.

After a tense dinner, and an even tenser night, I spring out of bed. Though I know my dragons want me to ride them, I stay on the ship and perch on a barrel while I sip chilled lemonade and stubbornly stare at Cayden, who isn't shy about meeting my eyes across the deck. It's another sweltering day beneath the sun, and Finnian is hiding in the shade of the sails as he rubs lotion on his reddening skin.

"I'm never going to survive this kingdom," he grumbles.

"You'll be fine." I smirk as I sharpen another knife. "If you find someone attracted to strawberries you'll have an ardent admirer."

He sticks his tongue out at me in response, and I giggle while popping another raspberry into my mouth. Cayden and Ryder discard their shirts and lift their fists as several soldiers cheer them on. The pair circle each other, and I'd probably be able to hear the taunts they're firing at each other if I wasn't so focused on Cayden's sculpted torso. *Good gods.* Fruit juice dribbles down my elbow, and I don't even realize I've squeezed the raspberry I'm holding until Cayden winks at me, breaking my trance.

Saskia scoffs from where she cools herself with a red satin fan that matches her off-the-shoulder two-piece set. It's in a similar style to mine, sheer flowy fabric cuffing around our ankles and wrists, but mine is lavender and encrusted with pearls instead of jewels and shows off more of my stomach. "You'd think they'd use their free time to behave as something other than brutes."

"I think you set your expectations too high."

"My turn!" Finnian shouts, shooting up from the shade and crossing the deck as the soldiers cheer when Cayden pins Ryder face down on the wood.

"Get him, Finny!" Finnian is the clear underdog of the fight, but I increase my cheering the more Cayden stares at me. There's a challenge in his eyes, and even Saskia joins me. Finnian strips himself of his shirt and I try not to cringe while looking at his sunburned skin. How did he manage to get burned *under* his clothes? Cayden easily dodges Finnian's punch and twists his arm behind his back before locking an arm around his throat. "Oh, Finny."

"Elowen, your husband is trying to kill me!" Finnian shouts, clawing at Cayden's arm despite him not utilizing even half his strength. Finnian just survives on dramatics.

Cayden rolls his eyes. "You asked to spar with me."

"Spar doesn't mean strangle."

"You annoyed me."

"That's surprisingly easy," Finnian huffs as Cayden releases him and takes a tankard of chilled ale from a chuckling Ryder.

I hop off the barrel and stride toward the sparring circle, stepping past the soldiers and standing toe to toe with Cayden. His glistening chest rises and falls, nearly pressing into mine with each breath. He seems lighter than he has the past few days, but the darkness lurking beneath the surface—which wasn't there before the ritual—is still present. I wonder if a foreign power thrums in his veins, building and choking him from the inside since he wasn't able to expel it. If he's also blessed by the gods, I wonder in what ways it'll manifest.

"You want to spar with me?" he asks.

Up close, it's even harder to ignore the pull I feel toward him. He's all hard lines and dark ink, and the memory of him pressed against me . . . pushing into me . . . my mouth goes dry. What I truly want is to guide him back to our cabin and lock the door.

"I do." He licks his lips, calling for two dulled practice swords, and I wrap my fingers around the hilt, testing the weight of it as I slowly circle him. "But I want to make it more interesting."

"A bet?"

I shrug, looking up at him beneath my lashes, the picture of innocence he knows I'll never be. "That's your area of expertise, is it not?"

I don't mention the tavern, given we're surrounded by people hanging on to our every word, but Cayden catches my meaning and looks even more intrigued. "What do you want?"

"A favor at a later date."

"Fine." He chuckles, stepping closer to me so only I'm able to hear his prize. "If I win, I want you to wear another one of those lacy sets for me."

"Deal," I whisper, my body heating from his raspy tone. "The winner is whoever disarms the other first."

Cayden won't hit me, which is why he called for the swords, and most likely won't fight at his full strength for fear of hurting me. Even when I first met him all those months ago, he only disarmed and restrained me. He'll be looking to do the same, just as he did to Finnian. Cayden is one of the greatest fighters Ravaryn has ever seen, and when the history books recount his life, it won't be the tales of his crown that come first, it'll be his sword. He fights like a god and has the mind of death itself.

Not even a breath later, he cuts the distance between us and strikes.

I shoot my sword up to block him, and our eyes lock over the blades. The clang of steel vibrates my bones. Using all my force, I shove him back, wasting no time in advancing. I strike once, twice, three times—he blocks them all. I feign frustration, baring my teeth, wanting to make him pay for his little actress comment last night. The soldiers around us chuckle as we repeat the same movements again.

He forces me back with his blade, and I stumble over the foot he wedges behind mine and throw my weight to the side to keep from falling. His blade twirls in his hand as he tracks me like a predator, and I know I've done enough to make him believe I have no ulterior moves up my sleeve. His sword cuts through the air and I pretend to be more tired than I am, letting the set of dulled blades slam into my side. I knot my brows together and drop to my knees, forcing myself not to smile as his sword clatters to the ground.

"Fuck, angel, are you—"

I keep a firm hold on my sword as I pivot on my knees, swiping my leg beneath his ankles and sending him crashing to the deck. I climb on top of him and point my blade at his throat. The deafening cheers vibrate the boards beneath us.

"You little cheat," he says, but his dimples are deep in his cheeks as he looks up at me.

"I believe it was you who told me to never fight fair." I drop the sword beside me and lean down to his ear. "But if you behave, I'll still give you what you asked for."

And with that, I'm off him and blowing a kiss over my shoulder as he drags a hand down his face and gets to his feet. Green eyes drill into me as I walk back to an ecstatic Saskia.

CHAPTER
FORTY-SIX

CAYDEN

THE WHISKEY BURNS MY THROAT AS I TIP THE BOTTLE back and rest my head against the couch while I listen to the ebb and flow of Elowen's footsteps. Our cabin is located at the back of the ship and split by a set of dark blue drapes that are usually pulled back but remain closed tonight. A paneled window stretches the length of the far wall, a feature I made sure to add with Elowen's fear of confinement in mind.

"You're out of practice, little shadow," I say, putting an end to the steady pattering. She mutters a curse under her breath and steps through the drapes, clad in nothing but a night slip. My hand tightens around the bottle, and I slowly release it one finger at a time to keep it from shattering.

She sits between my parted legs, and I grit my teeth to refrain from groaning when the scent of her perfume surrounds me. The scrap of fabric grazes the tops of her thighs and leaves next to nothing to the imagination. "How much have you had to drink?"

"Not nearly enough."

"I can put on a robe."

"I can burn a robe."

She laughs, and fuck if it's not one of the most beautiful things I've ever heard. In her hand rests a small bowl containing some kind of oil with herbs floating at the top. "I figured I could try again at alleviating the pain in your shoulder now that you're awake."

I dryly swallow and wet my throat with another drink. "You don't have to do that."

"I know." She dips her fingers in and rubs her palms together before latching her hands on to my left shoulder and digging into years' worth of aches. I drop my head on her shoulder as I grip her hips. Her pulse jumps, and goosebumps rise on her arms. Her touch hurts at first, but soon feels *so damn good.* She continues her tortuously pleasurable pattern, and I'm putty in her magical hands.

"What are you doing to me, angel?" My lips skim her skin as I speak, and she shivers again. It's a loaded question because what I feel for her threatens my very existence. There is nothing left for me in this world if she leaves it. I never realized how little I had until the magnitude of her presence became apparent. She is everything. She is both the knife that pierces my heart and the healer who mends the mortal wound.

"Taking care of you, since you refuse to."

"You're not inspiring me to start."

I draw my head back, but my eyes snag on her new markings, the delicate silver, gold, lavender, and pale blue swirls. Markings that will forever solidify what she did for me, and how I put her in harm's way. The darkness that's always lurked within me has been more forceful since the ritual. I want to keep it away from her, but it calls out to her, sings for her, dances to the tune of her voice.

Guilt.

It brands me and burns within my blood.

I tighten my hands on her, wanting to be here, not in my head, but it's holding me hostage. She digs her thumbs in again, and in this moment, if she told me she was an enchantress I'd believe her. "If you learned this from Nyrinn, I want a list of who you used this oil on."

"Why?"

"I just want to talk." I'm going to kill every bastard who had her hands on them like this. Truthfully, I'd kill whoever had her hands on them in general. She finishes the massage but neither of us moves as she continues trailing her fingers across my shoulder and down my back. She's inches away, but instead of feeling the usual peace that accompanies her nearness, I feel like I can't get enough air into my lungs.

A knot forms between her brows and my heart painfully pumps against my ribs. *You ruin everything you touch, boy.* I release her hips.

"Cayden?"

All hells, everything I feel for her wraps around my throat and cuts off my air. I'm drowning in her, but I've stopped trying to kick to the surface. I know this is going to kill me and I've accepted my fate. To be surrounded by her is exactly how I want to die.

"I'll be back in a second, love." I lean forward to kiss her forehead and throw on the black linen shirt draped over the arm of the couch. "I just need some air."

I slip into the narrow hall and stride down a staircase, locating the small private deck at the stern of the ship that rests beneath our cabin. The door shuts behind me as I rush toward the railing. I dip a hand into my pocket to pull out a smoke while rubbing at the never-ending ache in my chest. Quickly lighting the smoke, I inhale deeply and rest my elbows on the railing, dropping my head to stare at the water. However, even the symphony of the sea can't calm me.

I'm losing my gods-damned mind.

The door bangs open, and if Elowen's temper could start a fire, the ship would be incinerated. I don't even have to turn to know it's her, and I'd place a bet that she's swaying her hips while she stomps, like she always does when she's pissed.

"Stop running from me," she states. "I can't keep living like this. We have to have it out like we always do, not tiptoe around the issue like we're children. I know what you're thinking and it's not fair."

"Oh yeah?" I whip my head in her direction, stubbing out the smoke given her proximity. "What am I thinking?"

"I knew the risks when I agreed to the ritual." She stubbornly sets her chin. "I know that if I died I wouldn't be able to fulfill our deal, but—"

"Go inside."

"No."

"Keep pondering those thoughts of yours if you think I'm lamenting over a deal."

"You tried to manipulate Finnian into dragging me away from you. Do you think I could've moved on from watching you die, knowing there was something I could've done?" She pushes at my chest before fisting my shirt.

My nostrils flare when I note her rings glinting in the moonlight, but I keep my hands at my sides. "You would've lived a very long and celibate life."

She releases me and throws her hands up. "You were ready to accept death!"

"Is that what you think?"

"You said goodbye." Her voice cracks but her eyes are still filled with rage.

"What did you want me to say, Elowen?" I ask incredulously, tipping my head back to the stars before looking at her again. "Would you have preferred I told you exactly what I was thinking in what I thought were my final moments?"

Her throat bobs as I take a step closer, forcing her to tilt her chin up as I tower over her.

"Did you want me to tell you how bitter with regret I was knowing I searched for you longer than I've known you? That there is some sick irony in surviving all the years I wanted to die and dying when I finally had something to live for other than revenge? Because I wouldn't let myself look away from my reason, Elowen. You are it. Everything doesn't encompass what you are to me; you are infinite. You were all I let myself see as I was dying because I wanted to keep the memory of your face with me. Did you want me to tell you how I prayed to the God of Death to leave my soul with you if he truly gave me his blessing?"

"Then why are you pushing me away?" she helplessly yells. "You claimed that I've been avoiding you, but it's obvious you needed space.

I got us the time you say you wished for and you're acting as if you wish I'd let you die."

"You should have."

"Don't say that."

"Your screams echo in my skull every second of every day. If there is ever a choice between you or me, I always want you to choose yourself, even if it kills me."

"I know that Ryder was angry with you for doing exactly what I did, and that makes you a hypocrite."

"The situations are entirely different," I snarl.

"Then not only are you a hypocrite, but you're a fool as well! Your life is worth no less than mine, even if you believe it to be."

"That's what you don't understand! It is!" I fire back, my voice raspy and enraged. "Not because you're the dragon queen, or the heir to Imirath, or whatever other fucking title you acquire. My life is worth less than yours because *you are* my life. I'm a dead man walking without you."

Her face crumbles and a few tears spill from her eyes that she angrily swipes away. I would've married her if she had nothing to her name, the dragons didn't exist, and all she had were the clothes on her back.

I can't do this.

I can't look at her.

She'll be better off if I keep my damn mouth shut, a skill I've never mastered around her. I never expected her to love someone like me. It's not her fault I can't be worthy of her; that's been years in the making.

"Stop pushing me away. Stop walking away. Just stop!" She latches her hand around my wrist, but I don't turn around and keep walking even as she tugs. My sanity is holding on by a fucking thread, and my patience is so far gone I'm convinced it never existed. "Why can't you look at me?"

All hells.

"Because I love you!" I roar while forcing myself to look at her, the statement dripping in the anger accompanied by an unwanted confession. "I feel as if I've said the words in a thousand ways but if you need to hear them plainly, there they are. I love you. I am in love with you. Don't ask me when I began because I don't have an answer. All I know is that somewhere between meeting and marrying you, I realized I can't live without you."

The words race off my tongue, ripping open the bars on the cage I've locked them in for months. Elowen reels from them, stumbling back.

For a moment there's no sound other than the waves below, singing a symphony with my pounding heart.

"I love you," I say again, softer since she's never responded well to yelling, "and I'm not mad at you. I can never stay mad at you, but you nearly died for me, and I don't know how to live with that."

My blood pumps through me so fiercely that I hardly hear her gasp. Her brown eyes stare at me as if I'm not real. It's clear her first reaction is disbelief, which isn't surprising. She's spent a lifetime feeling un-loved, but I'll remind her every day if needed.

Even if I do nothing else right in my life, I'll love her like she de-serves.

"And— And I'm not worth it, Elowen." A lump forms in my throat but I fight past it. "I'm not even worthy of you. I spent my life walking in the darkness, loving nothing, not even believing myself capable, but then you came along. This ember of hope, of light. I was damned before I even realized it and have been in agony for months, loving you in silence. If that scares you then you'll have to find a way to live with it because I'm selfish to my core and will never be able to let you go. I would sooner forsake this world and reduce it to ash than ever live a day without you."

"You . . ." She steps forward, and her hands return to grip my shirt right over my heart. "You love me."

"My feelings have never had any stipulations. Even if you don't feel the same, or feel even half of what I do, I'll never stop." I'll accept anything from her, even crumbs. I'd rather starve for the rest of my life than be without her.

"You love me," she repeats in a daze, staring up at me with wide eyes.

"The only time I let myself feel anything is when I'm with you. Don't ever let anyone tell you that I'm incapable of love because you're living proof that something beats within my chest, and it beats for you."

I feel like I can't breathe. I place my hands on her hips, reassuring myself that she's truly here. In my arms. Sometimes I feel like I'll wake up, all of this will be a dream, and I'll have to go back to searching for her. I've never considered myself to be a kind man. I don't concern myself over the feelings of others . . . but Elowen is the exception to all my rules. When I'm with her, I feel like a different person. A better person.

I lightly drag my knuckles down her cheek, savoring the feel of her while keeping a tight hold on the silk she's wearing, terrified she'll slip away. I've never done this, never felt this. I have no fucking idea what I'm doing. "There is nothing that I want more than you. There is not a single thing I wouldn't do for you. There is nothing that I love more than you."

"What if I change over time?" She licks her lips. "What if you wake up one day and resent me because I'm no longer the person I was when you made that decision?"

"If you change then I'll spend the rest of my life finding new reasons to love you."

She nods and tightens her hands on my shirt. "I love you, Cayden."

I suck in a breath like she punched me in the gut—because that's what it feels like. "Don't say that if you don't mean it."

"I do."

I shake my head. "Elowen, I'm not right in the head. You can't say something like that lightly. All it does is feed my addiction."

"I love you, Cayden Veles."

"I don't deserve it."

"You don't have to be a perfect person to be loved. You have my heart, and you guard it as fiercely as you guard my body. I will never love anyone as I love you." Her hands weave through my hair and she yanks me down to slam our lips together. I tighten my hold on her hips and set her on the railing, stepping between her legs as she wraps them around me. She kisses me with a passion that sets my skin on fire. I run my hands along her body, doing anything to bring her closer.

This isn't real.

I must be dreaming.

"I love you," she murmurs against my lips, and I hang on to every syllable. "Even when our souls are forgotten wisps in the wind and the world ceases to exist, I'll love you. Amito evidani."

"Amito evidani, mia sirantia."

"You are so easy to love, Cayden Veles, and I'll spend the rest of my life trying to make you believe that."

"Then I'll take it upon myself to ensure you have a very long one."

She softly smiles up at me as the sea air dances through her curls and if I could live in this moment forever, I would. I kiss her again and keep her pressed against me as I part her lips. *She loves me.* It sounds too good to be true, and I hate that suspicion rears its ugly head. I shove it down, forcing myself to trust her in this unknown land we're navigating together, and deepen the kiss while lifting her off the railing.

She hums against my lips and slides her fingers through my hair. My steps falter when she shifts her hips against mine as I walk. I press her back into the wall of the dark corridor, and grind into her, unable to make it back to the cabin without giving her a hint of what she wants. I cover her mouth when her lips part against mine as she moans.

"Those are all for me, angel." She nods, her eyes rolling back in her head when I repeat my movements. She has no idea how much worse I'm going to become now that I know she loves me. She's never getting away from me. Another soft moan escapes her lips, and I chuckle against her neck, sucking on the sweet spot just below her jaw to torture her a bit more. She arches off the wall, pressing her breasts into me, and I bite her to stifle a groan.

Her hands roam over my shoulders as I walk us up the staircase and into our cabin, locking the door behind me. "You're always so needy for me, beautiful."

"So give me what I want," she answers as I set her on the desk beside the door and sit in the chair.

"Patience is a virtue."

"When have I ever given you the impression that I'm virtuous?"

I hook my finger into the neckline of her slip before bringing my other hand forward and ripping the garment down the center. I lick my lips while taking in the sight of her heaving breasts and open legs and lean forward to kiss her chest. She arches into my mouth as I kiss down her soft flesh and take one nipple into my mouth while using my fingers to play with the other.

Any piece of furniture is an altar with her on it.

I push her panties to the side and slide two fingers into her dripping center. She moans my name like it's the answer to anything she'll ever need as I begin slowly pumping my fingers. Every time I touch her, the unrestrained urge to make her feel so good she forgets any others that came before me strengthens. I want to be the only man in her mind. The only name to grace her tongue.

I press the signet ring she gifted me to her clit, and she throws her head back against the wall in answer. Something primal rises within me knowing our sigil is pressing into the most intimate part of her. I always take my time with her, wanting to savor every moment and each moan, knowing I could spend hours between her thighs. Her legs slip off the arms of the chair when I swirl my fingers, and she looks down at me with pleading eyes when I slide my fingers out of her and suck them clean.

"Why'd you stop?" she pants, one of her curls swaying in front of her lips.

But I don't answer as I reach for what's left of her night slip, ripping it down the back, and use the scraps that fall down her arms to tie her feet to the chair. Her eyes widen and throat bobs as she swallows.

"Is this okay?"

She nods slowly. "I think so."

"If anything changes, tell me." I slide my fingers inside her again and curl them. A desperate moan falls from her lips, and she widens her thighs. "You trust me to take care of you?" She nods. "You're making such a mess for me, my love."

I'm painfully hard, which isn't out of the ordinary when I'm around Elowen, even when she isn't doing anything sultry, but seeing her sprawled out before me makes me ravenous. The need to claim her, possess her, pounds through me. It's always lived like an insatiable beast under my skin, but it worsened after the ritual. I press my tongue to her clit, sucking it into my mouth as she fists my hair and her thighs shake.

She's mine, the darkness within me whispers, and I lock my arm around her back and drag her closer as a knock pounds against the door. I ignore it, keeping my head between Elowen's legs, not caring about anything beyond her—which also isn't uncommon. The taste of her is like a drug that renders me mindless. She tries to break away, but I don't let her, and she presses her lips together to smother a whimper as her shaking increases.

The knock pounds again, and I pull away from her just enough to state in a rough voice, "Unless you have a death wish, I suggest walking away from the door." I press my ring into her clit again, and she slaps a hand over her mouth as I move it in quick circles. She pleads with her eyes, and I know she's seconds away from finishing. The familiar blush creeps along her breasts and curls around her neck. "Do you like it when I use our sigil to make you come?" I murmur, low enough for only her to hear. "Does it remind you who you belong to?"

"Z-zario is on the horizon. We'll begin searching for an uninhabited place to dock," someone rushes out beyond the door before sprinting down the hall.

Like I give a fuck.

I yank her farther off the desk and lick her like a man drugged by her taste until she's choking breathlessly and shatters completely. I don't stop as she covers her mouth to scream my name, riding the waves of pleasure until she's limp, not yet willing to let go and wanting every last drop for myself.

I lick my fingers clean again and lift the glistening ring to her lips. "Kiss it."

She does as I ask, keeping her eyes on mine as I untie her ankles. She drops to my lap, her wet center soaking through my pants as she leans forward to lick a trail up my neck. My head falls back against the chair, giving her access to do whatever she wants to me. She grinds down on my cock, and all fucking hells, I'm never going to survive her. Jolts of pleasure shoot through me as she dances on me like she did in the brothel, and the memory of that night almost has me spilling into my pants. I'd never undress her in a room full of people, but knowing everyone there had their eyes on her, who only had eyes for me while begging for me to touch her, it was the most erotic thing I've ever seen.

Everything about her is overwhelming—her scent, her skin, her. Just her. Her fingers slowly trail down my chest as she continues rocking against me and undoes the laces on my pants. I fist her panties behind her ass and snap them off, wanting nothing between us. My length springs free and I groan against her lips as she coats me in her wetness, sliding against me until I line myself up with her entrance and she slowly lowers. She works her way down, moaning against my lips while adjusting to every inch, and pausing once I'm fully sheathed inside. Her eyes squeeze shut as she rests her head on my shoulder. I take over and thrust up into her, and her teeth sink into my neck. I prefer being in control. I love focusing on her pleasure.

She tears at my shirt until it's torn in two and glides her hands over my scarred torso while I place her on the desk again, thrusting into her at an unrelenting pace that has her sinking her nails into my back and locking her legs around my waist. I capture her lips with mine when she tightens around me and fuck her into a second orgasm. She screams against my lips and gazes at me with hazy eyes after her pleasure peaks.

"You're going to give me another," I say, slowing my thrusts, but never pulling out. She nods lazily, rocking her hips into mine at the promise of another high. "Are you going to let me fill this perfect pussy?"

"Yes." I quicken my pace again, slickening our heated skin with sweat. Another knock pounds against the door and Elowen breaks our kiss to whisper, "Send them away. Whatever you do please don't stop."

"If you think I'd stop fucking you for whoever is beyond that door, you don't know me very well."

I kick off my boots and discard the rest of my clothing as she continues moving on me, and I lift her into my arms. The dresser beside our bed has a small mirror, and I set her on the edge of the bed and flip her onto her stomach, dragging her hips up. She moans when I take her swollen clit in my mouth again, lapping at it for a few moments and feeling her grow wetter when she looks at our reflection. I give her one last lick and wink at her before getting to my feet, dragging my cock through her center as she locks eyes with mine again. I wrap her curls around my fist and rock into her, feverish and frantic, causing the headboard to crash into the wall and send a very loud message.

A cocky smirk forms on my lips. "Do you like watching me fuck you, angel?"

"Mhmm."

"Tell me what we look like." I kiss down her spine. "Because I think you look so pretty when you take all of me."

"You look like you'll never get enough of me," she gasps.

The headboard slams against the wall even louder, my thrusts becoming sharper from her words. "You're mine for eternity and it's still not enough time."

She loses control beneath me, calling out and sighing my name, uncaring of whoever can hear. Too lost in the pleasure I'm giving her.

"That's it. Make sure whatever bastard stands on the other side of the door knows you're mine." I flip her onto her back, kissing her breasts, neck, lips, and wanting to see her when she finishes. "Say it again."

"Cayden," she moans.

"Not that."

Her eyes are heavy with desire but spark with awareness. "I love you."

I slow my thrusts, and she whimpers. "Say it again."

"I love you."

I stop moving but stay buried to the hilt. "Again."

"I love you," she pleads. "I love you, Cayden."

Gods, that's intoxicating. "You really never should've told me," I echo my earlier statement. "I've been addicted to you for longer than you can fathom and now I'll never let you go."

I give us what we both want as I chase the high. I'm trying to hold on, but she's moaning my name and gripping me like a vise as she comes undone. I increase my thrusts to prolong her pleasure, and euphoria I've only ever found in her courses through me. I slow my movements as the haze clears, gently pressing my lips to hers. Kissing her cheeks, her forehead, the tip of her nose. She's the most precious thing in the world to me.

"I love you, Cayden," she says again, her voice riddled with emotion instead of pleasure. Something about the quietness of her tone, the gentleness, it tightens my chest.

I press my lips to hers again. "I love you, too. Always."

CHAPTER
FORTY-SEVEN

ELOWEN

ESPITE IT BEING WINTER IN GALAKIN, THE KINGDOM IS the embodiment of summer. The docks are bustling and the scents of spices and sweet tropical fruit create an intoxicating combination. I lace my fingers through Cayden's as the five of us hustle into the city. Zario is vibrant with revelers for the winter solstice dancing to music performed by street musicians.

We were able to find a covered cave in which to dock the ship after sailing along the coast of an unpatrolled beach. I thought the dragons would be upset when I commanded them to stay behind, but they dove into the shallow water, flapping their wings in the tiny waves as they relaxed. They didn't show signs of fatigue on the journey, but I'm sure they're enjoying their rest.

Zario is built along a steep hill with curved roads framed by white stone homes no taller than two stories with domed roofs in varying colors. My hair tickles the back of my arms as I tilt my head, gazing up at the staggering palm trees, heavy with coconuts. Wherever we go, the ocean is visible and it's just as crystalline at night. Cayden tugs on my hand, stopping us at one of the street vendors selling slices of some fruit I've never seen while Finnian and Ryder try on extravagant masks embellished with feathers and jewels.

"What is this?"

"Just try it," Cayden answers above the music and holds one of the slices sprinkled with red powder up to my mouth. It's sweet, savory, and a bit spicy all at once. He chuckles when my eyes light up and I reach for another piece. "The fruit is a mango, and it's sprinkled in a mixture of lime, chili peppers, and salt."

"Why don't we have these at home?" I ask incredulously.

"Mangoes only grow in the southern isles and Galakin, and they're expensive to import. This dish comes from the southern isles. Many people fled here when Imirath conquered them because it most aligned with their lifestyle. The winters in the isles are cold, not as bad as on the mainland, but in Galakin the people could make a living on the ocean and not have to worry about freezing while hauling nets."

It's nice to hear him speak positively about the isles. He rarely does, and I can't blame him. "When we win the war, I promise to eat mangoes with you until we hate them."

"Sure thing, princess." He throws an arm around my shoulders as a warm breeze ruffles my skirt and we turn down another road.

The entire row is made up of gambling dens, all in close proximity for people with deep pockets to hop from one to the other. Shutters on all establishments are open, and the sounds of cheers accompanied by cards being slammed down and chips raining drift into the street.

"Yes, I'd say we're in the right place," Ryder muses.

"Where do we even start?" Finnian asks.

"In the worst one possible," I answer. "It's the people nobody notices who know the most about everyone."

I snag a bottle of rum off a table surrounded by unsuspecting patrons and take a swig before passing it along. Though I've seen flame-wielders in action at home, it's different being here where they've worshipped fire for centuries. They pull the element from the lanterns lining the road and send sparks shooting through the air. Some even go as far as to create a flock of fluttering birds or a slithering serpent coiling around the sun. Neither my nor Cayden's godly markings draw unwanted attention despite our arms being on full display because various citizens have covered their bodies in colorful, swirling paint. Bowls of discarded shades spill onto the white stone road, and footprints create faded paths as whoever ran through it found something to capture their attention.

A deep bout of shouting draws my attention away from the paper lanterns hanging above. A clearly drunk man is thrown down a set of steps leading to one of the gambling halls by a sellsword far larger than him, made even more threatening by the burn scars covering half his face.

"This place looks perfect." I grab the rum from Finnian's hand before he has the chance to tip it back while I lead the group to an alleyway beside the small building. "You four wait here and I'll be back in a few minutes."

"Why do I have to wait out here?" Finnian whines.

"Because you blush when you lie." I take another sip before pouring some into my hand and dabbing it on my neck and the tops of my breasts, which are pushed up by my white band top with a star sapphire at the center. The matching skirt hangs low on my hips along with a jeweled chain, and I dab more alcohol on my stomach to ensure I smell like I crawled through a tavern.

Cayden leans down to lick some off my chest and I shove his shoulders. "No interfering with the performance."

"Can I have a private one?"

"I'm very expensive."

He shrugs, leaning his back against the wall across from me and devouring me with his eyes. "Name your price."

"You can't say anything sarcastic for an entire day in response to any of us."

"I said price, not miracle."

"And he failed already," Ryder says, claiming the spot beside Cayden. "I bet she gets what we need in twenty minutes."

"Ten," Cayden replies, shaking Ryder's outstretched hand and jutting his chin toward the entrance. Pride zings in my chest and I alter my walk slightly when I make it to the front steps, not wanting to seem obviously drunk. Subtleness is what sells a performance. If I were truly drunk, I'd be doing everything in my power to make people believe I wasn't.

The dragons push against the bond, wanting to disobey my command to stay out of sight and find me, but I dig my heels in and issue the command again, closing my eyes so nobody sees them glow gold in the dim light. I knew their complacency would be short-lived, but I didn't think it would end this quickly.

There's hardly anything noteworthy in here aside from the chipped mosaic of the sea crashing along the domed ceiling, but it's faded, same as the mismatched tables strewn about haphazardly. The air is hot and thick with pipe smoke and sweat, and I shove my way to the bar, catching myself on the wooden surface. I laugh to myself as I hop up onto a stool and smile at a pair of women who make brief eye contact before returning the gesture, giggling into their glasses.

"What are you drinking?" I ask, dropping my head onto my fist and kicking my legs.

"Rum and coconut water," the one closest to me says. "Would you like to try?"

"Why not?" I give my order to the woman behind the bar and thank her when she slides it in front of me. I don't love it, but it's not the worst thing I've tasted.

"Are you from here?"

"Oh, no." I laugh. "I'm just passing through on my father's merchant ship."

"Well, there's certainly enough entertainment for a young woman in this kingdom in case you haven't noticed." She glances over her shoulder where I don't doubt several men glance in our direction, not just for me, but for them as well. They may not be dressed in ornate gowns, but the lack of calluses on their hands makes me believe they're highborn ladies looking for an escape. Highborn people mostly keep to the more expensive part of the city, the Light District, so they'd have a better chance of not running into anyone they know here.

Beneath the bar, I transfer my wedding ring to a different finger.

"Perhaps I should take advantage. My father plans to marry me off to the highest bidder once we dock at home. I fear I won't be getting out of any arrangement unless I step back onto his boat with a prince on my arm."

The woman on the left laughs, sympathy lining her eyes. "Well any prince of Galakin will be locked in the palace. They never come into the city. Prince Zale does on occasion, but never outside of his favored places—mainly artist piazzas or the theater."

"Pity," I slur and finish off my drink. "I heard that the prince of Thirwen is here? Is that true? I've always wanted to meet a prince."

Both of them giggle as I smack my lips and huddle closer to hear their lowered voices. "There are rumors Prince Zarius frequents The Oracle. It's a gambling den a few blocks over and much more expensive than this."

My eyes light up. "Tell me more."

The one closest to me leans in again, her brown eyes alight with mischief. "He's allegedly an awful drunk and even worse when he's sober. He has no inheritance but somehow has money despite his father disowning him. I'd steer clear if I were you. He's not known for his kindness and his red eyes are said to be quite unnerving. It's like looking into pools of blood."

"Then wish me luck trying to find a different rich man who will please my father." I sigh and hop down from the stool, reaching over to pat their hands that rest on the bar.

They raise their glasses to me and I make sure to stumble over a chair leg as I wave over my shoulder. The scary bouncer at the door glares like he's ready to throw me out if I linger too long and annoy him. I fist my skirt as I strut down the steps and around the corner to greet my friends again.

Cayden's eyes light up at the sight of me and Ryder groans as he tosses a sack of syndrils into his outstretched palm. I drop into a curtsy, share the information I acquired, and the five of us make our way to the unknowing prince.

CHAPTER
FORTY-EIGHT

CAYDEN

RYDER AND FINNIAN HAVE POLISHED OFF ELOWEN'S STO-
len bottle of rum by the time we make it to The Oracle. The
streets are slightly less crowded, but still packed. I walk behind
Elowen, glaring at every man whose head she turns, which makes my
sneer nearly constant. Not only do I do it for my own selfish reasons,
but Elowen's also having fun, and she'd become defensive and wary of
her surroundings as soon as a man approaches her. I want her anxiety
to leave her be for just one damn night.

We claim an empty high-top table across the road from the gambling den, but a little far off from the main entrance so we're able to
observe the side door as well, the only other exit.

"What's the plan?" Finnian asks. "I *humbly* sat out while Elowen got
information despite my cheeks *not* reddening when I lie, so I volunteer
to venture inside."

"Have at it, Finny," Elowen responds, waving her hand toward the
building.

"Saskia and I will also go," Ryder adds. "You two can monitor the
exits, but since we're in a more expensive part of the city, you and
Elowen should stay out of sight as much as possible. We managed to
slip under their radar, but let's not push it."

I raise my brows. "*You* don't want to push luck?"

"Maybe I'm maturing."

"You cartwheeled into a melon stand on our way here."

"I said maturing, not changing."

"Maybe one day I'll be blessed with you experiencing both," Saskia grumbles while following him, the gold beads Elowen braided into her dark locks glinting as they sway. They're all dressed in the summery attire donned by the locals and will hopefully blend in . . . I don't have much hope for Finnian, though.

I tap a finger between Elowen's creased brows as I claim the stool beside hers, pulling her between my legs to keep an eye on the gambling den. "What's going on in that head of yours?"

Her lips quirk to one side. "Thoughts far too dirty for your ears."

"If you can't voice them, you could always just show me. I'm more of a hands-on learner anyway."

"Mmm." She scrunches her nose and shakes her head before looking down to twist her wedding ring. "I can't make the fire on the torch move. I was trying to pull it toward me like I did the dragonfire. It's like the power flooded through me and then went dormant in my body."

Gods, what I would have given to see her melting Imirath's wards, summoning all that dragonfire like a goddess reborn. I've forced her to recount the events several times, but it never gets old. I love watching her instill fear in our enemies; it really is a beautiful sight.

"Slip into Sorin's mind," I command, wanting to show her not all her abilities are dormant.

She cracks her knuckles, glancing from side to side to ensure nobody is looking at her face. My back is to a curved seawall overlooking the ocean, and the other white tables with painted orange and yellow tiles are filled with rowdy drunks too deep in their cups to notice if someone slapped them across the face.

Her irises disappear, and her hand tightens on my thigh as she spends time with Sorin. He's by far the most mischievous, but I know she loves it. She returns after a few moments, her brown eyes lighter than before. "I practiced slipping into their minds while we traveled so it's a lot easier for me to mindwalk, but that ability has never left, un-like the fire-wielding. Did you feel any different when you woke up after the ritual?"

I run a thumb down my stubbled jaw. "I don't know."

"What do you mean by that?"

My knife glints as I twirl it around my fingers, contemplating the best way to answer her question. "Death and darkness have shaped my life, and I've always felt them following me like a shadow. The mark-ings that I got through the ritual prove just how much darkness has infiltrated me." I gesture to my arm and neck where mainly black lines swirl around my skin, but the singular blue line is so dark it may as well be black. "It's always lived within me, been a part of me, but I feel as if something inside me is pulling me toward you. I've always felt like that, but it's stronger now. More of a volatile pull. I'd kill for you with-out question since the moment we met, but now it's like I can't sleep because taking my eyes off you even for a moment puts me on edge. Something in my blood pushes against my skin and bones to keep me vigilant, and it's not a peaceful force. Your presence has always quieted the voices in my head, but now it's like something has been awakened and it calls to you, but I don't know what."

"Oh." She ducks her head.

"It's not a bad thing," I add, drawing her eyes back to me. "Just—"

"Different?"

"Yes."

"There's something I didn't tell you about the ritual." She swallows, and I twirl one of her curls adorned with the same gold beads as Saskia's to calm her. "I spoke with the soul mage who performed it after I melted Thirwen's wards because I wanted answers. She told me that our souls are bound. We were destined by the Goddess of Souls to cross paths. Without it, the ritual wouldn't have been successful."

"And you believe that?"

"I don't know what I believe anymore." She blinks her eyes and locks her jaw while looking toward the ocean. "But I know you would've died without that ritual."

"Sirantia." I tilt her face back to mine. "I searched for you because you were the daughter of my enemy and bonded to five dragons. The pull to you wasn't as strong back then, it wasn't desperate."

"You're letting your feelings cloud your thoughts," she whispers. "Our lives are so much bigger than just us. Have you ever wondered if you have powers? Some kind of magical ability? If I'm able to mind-walk, ride dragons, and wield fire *on occasion*—what if you're able to do something as well?"

I shake my head. "Aside from being uncommonly good with my tongue and a blade—" She scoffs at my cockiness. "I'm afraid I'm entirely ordinary."

"I don't believe that." She looks at me for a long moment as she tugs her pendant along its chain. "Something lurks within you, Cayden, and whenever it manifests, make sure it's felt across the world."

I don't want to disappoint her, so I keep my mouth shut. Magic manifests in people when they're twelve. Elowen is an exception—whether her abilities were stifled as a trauma response or from being separated from her dragons, she was able to awaken them. I'm not bound to any creature and was entered into several fights by my father where I was beaten enough to entice some kind of magical ability to reveal itself . . . but all I had were my fists—and broken bottles if glass was thrown into the ring. When he whipped my back, and the urge to kill him was stronger than any force in this world, something would've happened.

I'm pulled out of my thoughts when the side door slams open and a man stumbles out, kept upright by whoever escorts him.

"That is no way to handle your prince," the slim one slurs.

Elowen and I exchange a glance.

"People in there are sniffing around for you like bloodhounds," the guard growls, the hilt of the broadsword strapped across his back glinting as he keeps the man upright by his shirt. "Do you think your father has stopped looking for you? Unless you want to be slaughtered, I suggest you keep walking."

"You knights are always so dramatic. If you'd just revoke your vow of celibacy, I'm sure you'd be much more agreeable."

"A knight?" Elowen whispers. "A knight of Thirwen is with the prince? I thought the king made all of them take blood oaths."

"That was a recent development," I mutter, and wonder what sparked the change. It was around the time that Ser Rhys Froydin went missing. He was a legend in the Crimson Tide War, known as the vulture for his ruthlessness when he fought in Thirwen's navy, and later knighted for his bravery. It's how he lost his left eye; he covers the evidence with a patch. It's rumored he had an affair with the former queen of Thirwen and that he's Zarius's true father. King Fallon tried to have him killed, but here he stands: gray hair, lines etched into his face, but still a warrior.

"Get the others," I mutter. "I'll follow them."

"Don't do anything stupid." She hops off the stool and parts from me when we cross the road. The street sharply slopes after I make it past the gambling den, and I keep to the shadows the buildings offer. I thought Zarius's hair was blond when I first caught sight of him . . . but it suddenly looks white. The strands blend in with the buildings, but his red shirt is easy to spot through the throngs of people. They stop in the road, and Ser Rhys looks over his shoulder. I dip into an alley and press my back into a wall while watching them around the corner, waiting for them to keep moving.

The crowds thin as I continue tracking them. I tuck my hands into my pockets, not bothering to keep my steps silent when it's just the three of us left. The prince is so drunk he doesn't seem fazed when Rhys draws his blade and turns to face me.

"Don't use your blade prematurely," I state. "It'll give me an incentive to kill you."

"I'd like to see you try." He keeps a firm hold on the prince's collar as he squints through the darkness, trying to make out my features as I lift my head. And there it is. The recognition when his eyes track the scar on the right side of my face.

I take another step closer. "Still believe I won't end you?"

"Demon."

"Vulture." His grip tightens on both the man and the hilt. "Though I can't say I know the name of your companion."

"Prince Zarius." He hiccups. "A pleasure to meet you, demon."

It's clear he has no idea who I am, and it almost makes me want to laugh. Rhys growls, pulling Zarius up again, and I have to respect his patience. No amount of loyalty could make me babysit a drunken man as if he were a child. "What do you want?"

Saskia and Ryder move to stand on either side of me as Elowen and Finnian jump down from the buildings bordering the street, surrounding Rhys and Zarius. Finnian nocks an arrow in his bow for good measure while Elowen circles to face them.

"Ah, fuck," Zarius mutters, glancing between me and Elowen. "They've come for my crown."

"You don't have a crown," Rhys sighs.

Zarius gasps. "Have they taken it already?"

Elowen looks him over. "I must say exile looked much better on me. Do you not have some water for the princeling?"

"I'm older than you, dragon queen."

"Could've fooled me." She steps forward, paying no mind to the drawn blade of the legendary knight. "No blood needs to be spilled if you cooperate."

"Are we your prisoners?" Rhys asks, directing his words to me.

I tilt my head as I regard the pair. Silence is just as effective in unnerving someone, sometimes even more so, especially when they know who I am. "That remains to be seen." The knight takes in each of us and accepts the fact that he's outnumbered. If he didn't have a drunk prince to look after perhaps he'd fight, but he throws his sword to the ground, baring his teeth in a feral snarl. "Pick it up, vulture. I'm not your squire, and I do not fear the end of a blade."

CHAPTER
FORTY-NINE

CAYDEN

I PERCH ON A RAILING AND LEAN MY BACK AGAINST THE STAIRS
that lead to the upper deck, twirling a knife on my bent knee
while listening to the waves lap against the ship. The salt in the
water smells stronger in the cave, so thick I can nearly taste it.

"This is ridiculous," Saskia huffs. "We're sitting around here like
we're waiting for a baby to wake up from their nap."

"Well, it's clear he nursed a bottle," Elowen replies, turning away
from where she strokes Venatrix's snout. The dragon returns to the
water at the loss of attention, sinking so deep only her head breaches
the surface.

"What were we supposed to do?" Ryder throws a card down on the
barrel between him and Finnian. "Negotiate with a drunk?"

"He's slept long enough," Saskia replies. "We're wasting time. The
matter needs to be resolved before we sail to the castle."

Finnian stands from the wooden crate and dunks two tankards into
the freshwater basin, striding to where Zarius passed out on a pile of
sacks filled with grain. Rhys rests a hand on the hilt of his blade.

"Stay your hand," Elowen warns, and growls echo through the cavern, creating a symphony of promised retaliation and ruthlessness.

Rhys's shaking fingers loosen, and Finnian throws the contents of
the first tankard at the prince. Zarius sputters and coughs, jolting up
as he pushes his hair back from where it sticks to his face.

"Welcome back," Finnian says in a cheerful tone, setting the other tankard beside Zarius and slapping the prince on the shoulder. Even Rhys can't manage to hide a small smirk. "Problem solved."

The dragons' low growls continue echoing throughout the cave, but they remain out of sight. I wonder if they sense the fear in Zarius and Rhys and wish to exploit it. Elowen moves to rest her back against my thigh and crosses her arms in front of her as Rhys offers Zarius a hand up. The pair of them make their way toward us, perching on two crates close to our section of the deck.

"Call off your beasts, queen," Zarius says. "I'm awake."

Elowen shows no outward sign of vexation, but one by one, the dragons emerge from the darkness at our backs with bared fangs, surrounding us with their heads as water droplets sizzle on their scales. "I suggest you never advise me on how to command my dragons."

A crew member hands Zarius a roll to soak up some of the alcohol sloshing around in his stomach, but he hardly notices it, unable to pull his crimson gaze away from the dragons. "I meant no offense."

"In order for you to offend me, I'd have to care what you think." Elowen shrugs, unsheathing the knife at her waist, pointing to the bread with the tip of it. "Eat."

"Why should I trust you enough to eat what you serve?"

"Because you're currently worthless," I respond.

His nostrils flare but he accepts it, biting off a chunk and washing it down with water as he flicks his eyes between us. "The bastard loves the princess and the world bleeds because of it." He chuckles dryly. "Oh, I've heard lots about the two of you."

"What else have you heard?" Ryder asks.

"The lovely Elowen is believed to be the most beautiful woman in Ravaryn, with a face that brought a kingdom to its knees. A woman blessed by the Goddess of Life, married a man blessed by the God of Death—it's all quite poetic if you ask me. Life and death, fire and water, stars and moon. Some say you're cursed, not blessed, and others say Elowen is a witch or an enchantress who bewitched Cayden." He turns to where Saskia stands beside Ryder. "Though I'd love to get to know you more so I can figure out why exactly you're staring at me as if you hate me."

Her lip curls and Ryder reaches for his sword, growling his warning. "Watch yourself."

He's always been protective of Sas. Not that I can blame him, but Saskia has proven time and time again to be able to hold her own against men. I've seen her tear them down with nothing but words and a condescending sneer. "I'd sooner pitch myself off the side of the ship than learn a single thing about you beyond what we need."

Zarius lifts his hands and pulls the top half of his wavy white hair back with a leather strap. He shifts uneasily under my gaze but tries to hide it with humor. "I'm still waiting to find out what exactly that is."

"For you to take the Thirwen throne," I say, not bothering to ease him into the topic. Rhys straightens, his interest clearly piqued though suspicion lines his brown eyes. Now that I'm able to get a better look at their faces under torchlight, I try to find similarities between the two. Though they both have white hair, clearly for different reasons, there isn't a single feature shared aside from their angular eyes. Rhys is pale where Zarius is lightly tanned. Even their builds are different—Rhys has the muscular build of a soldier whereas Zarius is slim, not scrawny but not bulky either.

"The throne?" Zarius echoes. "I'm not sure if you noticed, demon, but we're not exactly in Thirwen, and though Rhys is good with a sword, he's not an army."

"We're going to war against your father, unless you didn't hear that between tales of my wife's beauty," I state the obvious.

"I don't see what this has to do with me. I want no part of the throne. All it has brought me is death and despair."

"The throne didn't bring that to you. It's an inanimate object," Elowen interjects. "It's the person who sits atop it who gives it life."

"The greed woven within the very stones that construct it has brought me enough grief to last a lifetime."

"Then resist it," I state.

"Is that what you did when you conquered Vareveth?" he spits. "I watched my mother die right in front of me because she stopped being useful to *the crown*. You have no idea what that does to a person."

His self-pity grates on me. Yes, I do know what that does to a person, and though I've nursed my demons with alcohol and violence, I didn't let myself fall apart as he clearly has. Anger held me together like mortar, fortifying me against the world. I dryly chuckle. "I didn't know it made you into a spineless prick."

Elowen pushes off the wall and sinks onto a crate across from Zarius, gliding her dragon daggers against each other. "Given you know who we are, I'm sure you know we don't shy away from doing what we must to get what we want. You don't need all your fingers to sit on a pretty chair, princeling."

Rhys reaches for his sword, but Finnian steps forward. "I suggest you reconsider drawing a weapon against my queen. You're severely outnumbered and won't be able to protect your prince in death."

The knight growls as he shoves the blade back into its sheath and I exchange a glance with Ryder. Finnian's certainly come into his own since becoming Commander of Aestilian. He's packed on more muscle and there's a hardness to his voice that wasn't there a few months ago.

"She threatened my prince."

"A prince who—as he reminded us—has no army and no support regarding his claim to the throne. As of right now he's worth no more than any individual walking the street," I say. "We mean you no harm as of right now—"

"That's comforting," Zarius grumbles.

"But we will be taking you to the palace tomorrow, and you're going to be on your best behavior and prepare yourself to take your father's throne once we kill him."

Zarius and Rhys exchange a long look filled with a silent conversation, but it's the former who speaks first. "You plan to kill my father?"

I quirk a brow. "That is usually how wars end."

"So you want me on the Thirwen throne because you think it'll be easier to manipulate me than my father?"

"It's not manipulation if you know our plan," Saskia sneers, drawing Zarius's attention again. She lifts her chin under his scrutinizing gaze.

"You're not our enemy despite being born from one. I believe we both can understand that," Elowen begins, and Zarius slowly nods, a muscle fluttering in his jaw when he clenches his teeth. "Answer me this: do you want to waste away in gambling dens in a foreign kingdom for the rest of your life while your father hunts you?"

He shakes his head, seeming like he hates to admit it, but Rhys looks relieved.

"Have you thought about avenging your mother?"

His nostrils flare and his shadowed eyes look to his boots. "Yes."

"Our terms are simple: open trade between my kingdom, Galakin, and Thirwen. Fight with us on the battlefield so your people can see you still live." She sheaths her knives and gets to her feet, waving a crewman forward. "You'll be taken to a cabin. Think on my offer, for I assure you a better one will not come along."

Saskia stares at the ocean as Zarius and Rhys are escorted below decks, as does Zarius until the moment before the door closes behind him and his red eyes find her one last time.

Five.

Four.

Three.

Tw—

Ryder storms toward me. "I hate that fucking bastard."

"Technically he's legitimate. Might I suggest you alter your insult to make it factually correct?"

"I don't want to hear it."

"Saskia is a grown woman who will cut off his balls if he pisses her off," I say, knowing the root of his anger lies within Zarius's attention settling on Saskia more than once.

"Drinks on the beach," Elowen cheerily says, looping her arm through Saskia's and gesturing for Finnian to take the other. Saskia honestly looks relieved to be getting off the ship as the pair cart her away with a bottle of liquor in each hand.

There was a point years ago when Ryder spiraled after his lover was killed. He's the one who found her after searching all night. I never saw him cry as he did then, never saw his eyes so broken and dull. He began drinking more and eventually moved on to taking lovers night after night. I spent more time sleeping on my floor than in my bed and took jobs nearly every night to let Saskia have my room to herself. Whenever anyone is remotely interested in Saskia, Ryder chases them away. He's never said it aloud, but I think he's always trying to spare her any possible pain this world has to offer. He's taken on the role of a father in a way, and sometimes I think he still sees her as the little girl with bows on the ends of her braids.

"You need to pull yourself together," I say once the others are out of sight. "We need Zarius as an ally."

"I know," he bites out, taking a steadying breath as he shakes his hands. "I know."

"He's a prick." I shrug. "I don't like him—"

"You don't like anyone."

"And I still stand by that philosophy being the wisest," I add. "You don't have to make things pleasant for him. You don't even have to speak with him. Just stand by while we solidify the deal to secure Galakin."

He drags a hand down his face and nods. "Elowen mentioned drinks?"

I slap him on the shoulder. "I'll hand you the bottle."

He laughs weakly as we stride down the gangplank and cross the rocky cove. Laughter floats through the air as soon as we exit the cave. Palm trees conceal us in this oasis, and I kick off my boots where Elowen discarded her sandals. She stands ankle-deep in the crystalline water, plucking seashells from the sand and dropping them into her bunched-up skirt.

Her eyes light up when she spots me coming closer, swaying slightly when a wave crashes into her ankles. I look back at Finnian and quirk a brow. He holds up a half-empty bottle of rum and points at his best friend with a proud grin. *Good gods.*

"Cayden, look at these! They're like little treasures," she slurs.

"Very nice, love." I gently steer her away from the water, and she drops beside Finnian. They give each other cheeky smiles as they twist their arms together and take drinks from individual bottles before handing them off to me and Ryder. Saskia claps, looking much lighter than she did on the ship.

"I'm not getting that close to you to take a drink," Ryder says.

"How you wound me," I flatly state, making him snicker.

The next hour goes by quickly, all of us taking turns with the bottles while Elowen and Finnian teach us the drinking games they grew up playing. We must guess which of three statements is a lie, and whoever doesn't guess correctly has to drink. It gets harder as the game goes on, and it seems everyone but me can't keep a straight face when they lie.

"I've never swam in the ocean," Elowen slurs, her head dropping to my shoulder.

I chuckle, bringing the bottle to my lips again. "You need to drink water first, and I'm not getting naked with any of these people so—"

"Truth!" Saskia shouts.

"Lie!" Ryder adds.

"That wasn't part of the game," I respond. "And that's the fucking truth." Elowen shoots up from between my legs and begins sprinting toward the water like fire licks at her heels. "Why does alcohol give her more energy than usual?"

"Go, Ellie! You've got this!" Finnian shouts as I get to my feet.

Her hair and skirt whip behind her as I close the distance, throwing her over my shoulder while the other three drunkenly cheer. Her fists lightly pound against my back. "You didn't run this fast when we were fleeing Imirath."

"I'm open to debating that," she states, pointing to the ocean. "You just told me I need to drink water."

"Not saltwater." I smack her on the ass, and she laughs again as I turn back to the others. "Don't follow us."

Ryder gags in response and Finnian makes a series of kissing noises.

All hells, how did this become my life? I take us to a section of beach hidden by a lush forest filled with palms and hibiscus flowers and set Elowen on her feet. I tug her skirt down her legs and lean forward to playfully bite her thigh. She squeals and smacks me on the shoulder as she tugs her top over her head.

"I am a married woman, sir." She gasps, swaying her hips as she walks into the sea.

"Damn right, you are." I remove my pants, and catch up to her, wrapping her legs around my waist as a warm wave crashes into us. She shrieks, tightening her limbs around me as it barrels past, and I swim out past the break far enough that she's able to enjoy the swells without being pummeled by them.

"Do you miss the ocean when we're in Vareveth?" she asks, gliding her arms across the crystalline surface.

"Sometimes," I answer truthfully.

"What's Imirath like in the summer?"

I think back to blurry memories from childhood. "When I would venture into Zinambra, the ocean was a lighter blue than it was in the winter and a lot warmer. Some beaches had towering waves and others had small ones. People would fry fish on the docks for only a few syndrils and others would sit along the streets eating dishes of various seafoods and rice, washing them down with fruity wine. It was cooler in the mountains, but wildflowers grew all over the forests and in some places the tree cover was so thick you couldn't see the sky."

Elowen sighs, looking to the horizon. "I've been thinking about what comes after all of this, and I know you love the sea . . . so I was thinking we could spend the warmer months in Imirath. I . . . I don't think I'll ever be able to live in the castle again, but we can build a new one right on the water."

I know she's drunk, but the sincerity is real. "I'd like that."

She smiles softly, resting her hand against my scarred cheek and pressing her lips to mine. I dip us under the surface, keeping us locked together as the tide blocks out the world around us.

CHAPTER
FIFTY

ELOWEN

I STAND AT THE BOW OF THE SHIP, LETTING THE SEA AIR CA-
ress my cheeks and whip my curls behind me. There's something
so calming about being on the water, and when I look at Cayden
sharpening his sword while gazing at the shore, I wonder if he gets the
same freeing feeling aboard a ship as I do on dragonback.

We leave Zario behind and cross the river that splits it from Zraka
and spills over steep cliffs into the ocean. My skin prickles with awareness, and the hairs on the back of my neck stand. I feel like I'm being
watched. I look over my shoulder, but nothing is out of the ordinary.
Finnian, Ryder, Saskia, and a few crew members pile breakfast onto
their plates. Cayden's gaze still hasn't found mine, but my eyes drift to
the river and the mountains in the distance. Something tugs in my
chest like someone tied a string around one of my ribs, and Cayden's
eyes flick to mine.

"Did you feel that?" He nods while setting his whetstone aside,
granting me his full attention. "What's in those mountains?"

"They're uninhabited for all I know, infested with venomous snakes
and other reptiles, not to mention the monsters native to this kingdom."

Venatrix screeches as she glides closer to the river, only spreading
her wings wide to alter her course when I get too far away for comfort.

"Hmm." I keep my eyes on the falls as we continue sailing past, not moving until they're out of eyesight.

Ser Rhys escorts Prince Zarius onto the deck, and I dig my fingers into my throbbing temples in an attempt to alleviate the dull headache before he gives me another. A water mage ventured into the city to collect the remainder of their things from Zario early this morning, so at least the prince looks more presentable than the previous day. Nothing fancy, but his red linen shirt isn't wrinkled or reeking of rum, and he's donned some silver jewelry to add a bit of regality.

"Queen." Zarius nods to me, seeming much more formal than last night. "King."

"Have you thought about our offer?"

"Do I have a choice?"

"Everyone has a choice. It just depends on whether you're able to live with the consequences," I answer.

"I have terms," Zarius states, and Cayden gestures for him to proceed. "As I mentioned yesterday, I do not have an army, and my father has other heirs from his new wife who citizens may favor. After this is settled, you will sign a treaty between our kingdoms, opening trade to both Galakin and Vareveth as you requested, but I require you to fight with me as I will join you. If there is rebellion in my kingdom after I retake the throne, I need the demon king and dragon queen to help quell it."

I exchange a glance with Cayden, but it's a fair deal. Seeking Zarius out to place him on the throne so we can secure an alliance with Thirwen will all be for naught if he can't hold it. "Yesterday you said you didn't want the throne. Why the sudden change?"

He rolls his lips, tilting his head to the side as he contemplates. "Perspective."

I look to Ser Rhys standing stone-faced by his side and wonder how much sway he has over the prince. Whatever his influence, I'm grateful for it as I clasp my hands behind my back to avoid a handshake. "Very well."

Strands of white hair brush against his sharp cheekbones as he nods and bows his head slightly to glance at the markings on my and Cayden's skin.

"What is it?" I ask, and Cayden narrows his eyes in suspicion.

"I've never seen godly markings, only heard tales of them," he says, stepping toward the spread to pour himself a cup of coffee. "Tragedy follows the gods' involvement in mortal lives. News of your ability to wield dragonfire traveled over the Dolent, but I have to say I didn't believe it until I saw the markings. People don't survive the ritual you performed."

"How do you know all of this?" Saskia asks.

He looks at her, but his impassive expression doesn't change. "Just because I'm a discarded prince doesn't mean I didn't receive an education in my formative years."

No matter how I feel about the gods, and how many unanswered prayers I muttered over the years, the markings at my wedding . . . the ritual . . . it must mean *something*. I don't ponder their presence out of piety, but I'd be a fool to deny the shadow I've walked beneath since the eclipse.

The ship cuts through the sea, bypassing staggering mansions set on sprawling tropical estates as the island the castle is built on looms into view. Crew members hustle around the deck to slow our pace as we glide beneath an extravagant golden archway made to look like two serpents shooting up from the sea and plunging their fangs into a burning sun between them. The port is vast, and deep enough for vessels like ours to dock.

The shining rays spilling from the sky caress the white stone spires, and I blink, forcing my eyes to adjust. A mixture of blue, red, orange, and yellow domes top every tower, and all are connected by bridges, with waterfalls spilling down the steep hill and into the ocean. Palm trees stand tall in the open spaces, as do several types of tropical flowers, their sweet scents carried by the wind.

My dragons fly onward, circling the various buildings that make up the structure, and a mixture of servants, ladies, and lords flock to the open spiral staircases within the turrets overlooking the bay to catch sight of them. I smooth my hands down the dark blue chiffon that flows around me like midnight waves. My back is bare aside from the thin draping chains that connect the fabric. Two golden cuffs fashioned to look like two dragons flying toward the north star adorn my upper arms, and the dragon cuffs from Cayden hug my wrists. A sapphire on the bodice sits between my breasts, just above a small triangular cutout, and matches the circlet gifted to me on my wedding day that rests across my forehead.

Cayden steps up beside me, sliding his steel into its sheath strapped across his back, offering me his arm. He's also wearing the same crown he did at our wedding, however I can't blame him for not having the patience for finery beyond that in this heat. His wavy hair is untamed as a result of the wind, and he wears another black linen shirt with matching loose pants tucked into his boots, but I think he looks like a dangerous dream.

"King Cayden and Queen Elowen Veles of Vareveth!" Ophir announces as we stride down the gangplank and meet a steward at the base of the promenade leading to the castle.

"Welcome to Galakin, Your Majesties," the man says, wearing a red tunic embroidered with yellow and orange that complements his dark complexion and even darker hair. His eyes linger on Prince Zarius, but he thankfully doesn't say anything. We thought it best to introduce him to the royals ourselves before his identity is confirmed to their court. "I'm here to escort you to the royal family."

We begin our ascent of the hill lined with streams and flowers as the dragons fly overhead. My thighs burn by the time we make it to the top, and my eyes are spared from the blinding sun when we pass through a parted set of orange curtains that leads to a room open to the air on all sides and filled with regal furniture and palms.

We're led through curved halls decorated with painted tiles and across several bridges bordered by trees with butterflies and colorful birds flying around. The sun warms my shoulders when we step onto a patio with a long rectangular pool filled with lotus flowers and lily pads that stretches in front of a pavilion framed with House Ilaria banners. Servants back away from the royals when they note our presence, taking with them bowls of melon and trays of iced lemonade.

"May I present King Erix, Queen Cordelia, and Crown Prince Zale of House Ilaria," their squire declares from his place beside the steps leading to the platform.

Queen Cordelia rakes her brown eyes over us as she sips her drink. Her red gown covers the chaise she reclines on, and like all furniture within, it matches the House Ilaria colors. "I thank you for making such a journey to attend our ball." She rises from her perch and takes her husband's arm to descend the steps and kiss both my cheeks. My chest tightens, but I force myself not to stiffen.

"Thank you for inviting us, Your Majesty. I've always wanted to visit Galakin, though the tales I heard pale in comparison to its beauty."

Her hands remain on my shoulders as she faces Cayden, her smile straining as King Erix reaches out to shake his hand, and says, "I believe congratulations are in order, for freeing the dragons, acquiring your crown, and your new bride."

Cayden clasps Erix's hand, though he doesn't return the smile as Cordelia cuts in again, "Yes, my sister wrote to me about how beautiful the ceremony was. It was a shame we missed it."

"With war approaching we believed it best to solidify our union as quickly as possible."

"Of course," Cordelia responds, her auburn curls draping down her back like spilled wine as she turns to gesture her son forward. "We won't keep you long—I'm sure you want to get settled after such a long journey—but may I present the crown prince." A man who looks to be around my age leans down to kiss my hand, causing my discomfort to heighten.

"The conqueror king," Zale says, regarding Cayden. He is only a few inches taller than me, has the same eyes as his mother, and has curly hair like his father though it's brown instead of gray.

"Prince," Cayden responds. "There is also another in attendance." He gestures behind us, and our newfound friend steps forward. "Prince Zarius Liluria of Thirwen."

Erix lifts a brow and Cordelia's hand tightens on his arm.

"I thought Prince Zarius died with his mother," the king says.

Zarius gives a dry smile. "Sorry to disappoint."

Cordelia's eyes burn holes into Zarius, but she remains silent, her chest rising and falling unevenly. Erix nods slowly, regarding the prince like he doesn't know what to make of him. "You stand with your father's enemies willingly?"

"I owe my father nothing." Zarius juts his chin in my direction. "The enemy of my enemy is my friend."

"So it seems." Cordelia's lip curls before she masks her features. "We will discuss your presence in my kingdom later."

Calithea flies above us, screeching as she perches on one of the tallest domes, keeping her silver eyes locked on me.

"I've always wanted to see a dragon." Zale's tone is filled with awe as he gazes up at her.

"Her name is Calithea."

"Incredible." He smiles. "If you'd like to see more of the castle I can take you on a walk through the gardens before dinner."

We're here for an alliance, I remind myself. Cordelia loves her son, and I snubbed their informal marriage offer at the alliance ball. There's so much you can hide behind a smile, and I'm realizing that it might be my sharpest weapon when facing a court. Not every battle can be fought with a blade; some require weaving the correct words together to form a web to trap your prey. "That would be lovely."

Cordelia seems pleased as she gestures for a servant to lead us to our chambers. Every room and corridor of the castle is bathed in warm tones and regal touches, and I look down at the river running below the bridge that leads to our rooms as the servant unlocks the door. Similar to the rest of the structure, the windows don't have glass, and sheer orange curtains flutter in the breeze. The sitting area is circular, leading to a balcony overlooking the ocean, and our bedroom is behind gilded doors.

I spot Delmira swooping in the skies just in front of the balcony and I step through the opening to greet her. Seagulls squawk in the distance, and waves crash against the base of the tower.

"Hello, Delly." I lean forward, dropping my arms to the banister, and watch as she flips and turns for me. Her sky-blue wings should blend in with all the shades around us, but she stands out despite that. Cayden presses a hip into the railing and tucks his hands into his pockets. The dragons must sense him because in a blink four more are added to the show.

"You give them too many treats."

He shrugs. "I needed to get into their good graces somehow."

"No, you just love to spoil me and them by extension."

"I make no apologies."

"Mhmm." I straighten up to face him because he clearly has something to tell me.

"I don't like the way they look at you," he says, but he doesn't have to specify who.

"You don't like the way anyone looks at me. I think you'd be happy to consider it a criminal offense." He narrows his eyes but doesn't deny it. "I didn't like the way Cordelia looked at you either."

"Why?"

"She stared at you as if you didn't deserve to be here, to wear the crown, to stand beside me. You're more deserving than any of them. You won your crown; theirs were given to them. I—"

"El." He frames my face with his hands, running his thumbs over my cheekbones. "I'm a bastard—which I don't doubt they know—a criminal, and referred to as a demon. I'm not unused to people glaring at me or being unnerved by my presence. In fact, I prefer it because I don't have to pretend to care about who they are or what they're saying."

"I care," I whisper, clearing my throat. "I care about how they treat you."

He lifts my chin when I try to drop it, and my heart pounds so fiercely I'm sure he can feel it. I don't know why it makes me nervous to admit things like that. I told him I loved him and yet it feels like I'm ripping myself open all over again, no matter how simple the confession. Perhaps because my feelings have been weaponized against me throughout my life, I've never felt like they truly belong to me. "What you think of me is the only opinion I care about," he replies.

Be that as it may, I don't want people looking down on him just because of where he comes from. I lick my lips before pressing them to his quickly and step into his arms to watch my dragons. He stiffens at first, but then he relaxes and tightens his embrace. There's not a single place in the world that's ever felt more like home for me than his arms. I've been lost for so long, but when he looks at me, it's like I've finally been found.

CHAPTER
FIFTY-ONE

ELOWEN

"I MUST ADMIT, PART OF ME DIDN'T THINK THE DRAGONS were real," Zale says as I lean down to smell one of the flowers. They paint the earth in shades from the deepest pinks to the lightest yellows. The garden is thick and lush, no doubt from the amount of rain this kingdom gets. "I was there when the seer issued the prophecy and they hatched around your cradle, but I was too young to remember anything."

I straighten up to look at him. "Do you know the seer who issued it?"

"I do." He faintly smiles, and the wind billows through his light, elegant vest. His pants are made of the same mustard material, embroidered in a mixture of red and orange. "Mae is like a grandmother to me. She keeps to herself mostly, and there are some days when she's indisposed, but I can take you to see her if she's well enough for visitors."

"That would be wonderful." Maybe I can finally get some answers to the questions I've asked for years. "Thank you, Prince—"

"Just Zale," he cuts in.

"Zale," I finish. "You can call me Elowen. Do you know any of Mae's symptoms? I can try to help."

He sighs, tucking his hands into his pockets. "It's the visions. They deteriorated her mind over the years and sometimes she doesn't know what's real and what's in her head."

"I'm sorry." My lips turn down. There's nothing I can do for that. "That can't be easy to watch."

He offers me another small smile as we continue walking down a row of thick green palms. The banquet hall is just a few paces away and open on all sides now that the curtains are pulled back and secured with thick gold ropes. I feel Cordelia's eyes spearing me like a knife as I interact with her son. Zale's youngest siblings run through the grass while servants chase them to avoid them muddying their clothes, and the adolescents lounge under palm trees with paper fans. He has eight siblings in total, six sisters and two brothers. I can't imagine what it's like to be part of such a large family.

"I heard rumors you were able to wield dragonfire," Zale says, calling a small flame to him as we pass a torch. It flickers just an inch above his index finger, moving as he bounces it back and forth on his hand. "Care to demonstrate?"

I swallow the sense of failure clawing up my throat as Zale makes flame-wielding seem as easy as breathing. "Perhaps another time."

He regards me with suspicion, but doesn't voice whatever is in his head. I don't know if that's better or worse. "Shall we join the banquet?"

He offers me an arm, and I hesitate only a moment before taking it. I have a feeling offending Zale will put me on the worst side of Cordelia. It's bad enough I brought the son of her enemy here. Both of our arms are bare, and the feeling of someone's skin brushing against mine makes me want to run the other way until my chest stops tightening, but I keep the smile on my face as we step under the archway.

CAYDEN

I remove Elowen from the prince's arm the moment she's close enough to do so. It took every ounce of self-restraint in my meager reserves to not succumb to my possessiveness the moment Zale came to escort her. She releases a shaky breath only I'm able to hear, keeping that impenetrable smile on her face as she accepts a drink made of rum and pomegranates from a servant.

"Your wife is very lovely, king," Zale says to me. "Thank you for the walk, Elowen."

He turns on his heels and strides toward his mother, awaiting him under one of the many arches painted with small yellow suns. "Elowen? How informal."

"Don't start."

I snicker. "Did he do anything to bother you?"

"No, he was a perfect gentleman." She takes a sip of her drink before ducking close to my chest to hide her disgust. I take the glass from her and look around to make sure nobody is watching before dumping it into a potted palm tree. "I think that might kill it."

"Better it than you," I remark. "Why do you seem so on edge?"

"I just don't know why this family is so touchy."

I run my hand down her other arm. "Stick close to me. I'll ward them off." She must be desperate because she doesn't make any quip about being able to take care of herself, just nods. "And I'll get you a better drink."

"Zale said he'll take me to the seer who issued the prophecy when I was a baby," she says as I escort her to a table set before a larger one where the other members of our party along with the rest of the Ilaria family will eat. I don't believe in seers, but if conversing with the seer will calm something within her then so be it.

I wave off a servant who rushes forward to pull out Elowen's chair and claim my spot beside her at the head of the table with legs fashioned to look like sea serpents. Cordelia and Zale sit across from Elowen and Zarius, and Erix is across from me. Servants step forward again, placing small crystal bowls stacked with balls of honeydew and cantaloupe before us and filling the matching goblets with wine.

"Will none of the other kingdoms be joining us?" Elowen asks.

"Feynadra is due to arrive tomorrow," Cordelia says. "I believe it's best we speak business before my sister arrives. It's clear you came here with ulterior motives, considering a prince of *our* enemy kingdom sits at my table."

Zarius takes a long drink of wine, staring at Cordelia over the rim of his glass. "I believe I've been called prince more in the past twenty-four hours than I have since I was exiled. What an interesting turn of events."

Erix overlooks Zarius's tone and fixes his gaze on me. "I assume you're looking for our alliance? Use of our navy? Thirwen aligned with your wife's father, so you think we'll want a part in this war due to our longstanding animosity with them."

I'm thankful we're getting right to business. I'm not a courtier, and don't know how to make pleasant conversation for the sake of filling silence. I also don't possess the ability to pretend I'm interested in anything anyone is saying to me and am sure that's evident on my face. It's played in my favor in the past—I never wanted to converse with anyone and preferred being alone—but Elowen made me promise to attempt a cordial alliance before we resort to threatening them . . . something about how she never would've been given her dragon eggs were it not for the king and queen.

"I think you'll want a place in this war when we tell you what you'll get out of it," I respond. "Our goal is to restore Prince Zarius's claim to Thirwen and he has agreed to pull the navy back from your border and reopen trade with your kingdom. Trade with Imirath will also be an option, as my wife is the only living heir of Garrick Atarah."

Erix runs a hand over his lightly stubbled jaw, but Cordelia cuts in to address Elowen. "You knew what we wanted," she hisses. "You could've had your alliance through marriage. You're not a stupid woman, and I believe I made my intentions quite clear when I saw you last, but instead you not only insult my offer, you bring the spawn of my enemy to eat at my table."

"You are correct," Elowen evenly states. "I'm not a stupid woman, and Zarius is not his father just as I am not mine."

"And yet you chose a bastard over a prince!"

"I chose a king." Elowen's tone drops. "I chose a man."

It's unusual to watch someone else fight for me when I've spent most of my life waging my own battles.

"I would have been willing to overlook your indiscretions and would've turned a blind eye until an heir needed to be produced had you married my son."

"How generous of you."

My temper rises, thrashing against the cage I promised Elowen I'd lock it in, but Cordelia speaking to Elowen as if she had some claim over her fans the flames of rage within me. If Elowen hadn't agreed to be my queen, I would've slaughtered whoever I had to in order to keep her safe, even if she had been nothing more than my ally. "Call me a bastard all you want; I'm sure it frightens you to see just how high one can rise. But you will watch your tone when speaking to my wife." I lean forward and note the way the guards step closer to their rulers. "If you were so interested in Elowen then perhaps you should've mobilized your navy when she was locked in a dungeon after *your seer* relayed a prophecy to a tyrant."

"We couldn't have known what Garrick would do," Erix argues. "And we couldn't risk countless lives for one girl."

"Then you don't deserve her."

"And that bastard you insulted didn't risk countless lives, he risked his own," Elowen shoots out. "We have come for your alliance, but I warn you not to make an enemy of us. Most do not survive."

"You would threaten my parents in their own castle?" Zale incredulously asks, looking toward the guard behind Elowen. I draw my sword as he steps forward. To do what, I don't know, but his hand freezes on the hilt as I point the tip of mine beneath Zale's chin. Chairs scrape behind me and more steel is drawn.

"Elowen did not issue a threat; she made a statement, but I'm not as kind as her. If your guard takes another step toward my wife, your prince will bleed for it."

"To spill blood here would be an act of war," Erix declares. "Your army is across the sea."

"How insightful."

"You would never leave this banquet hall alive."

I leave my steel pointed at the prince's throat as I cut my eyes to Erix. "Neither would you or your precious prince."

An emerald-scaled body slams into the earth, visible through one of the archways. Sorin is her protector, as all the dragons are, but him most of all. Elowen once told me their imprisonment began the day Sorin bit off Garrick's pinkie finger after he raised his hand to her. Venatrix follows a second later, crushing the perfectly sculpted rows of flowers beneath her claws. The pair of them shove their heads through the two openings behind Elowen, roaring loud enough to wake a sleeping god. Several Galakin soldiers drop their weapons and mutter a prayer.

In the silence, Elowen speaks, "I suggest you all sheathe your steel. My dragons will not stand down until they know you mean me no harm, and though they listen to me, I do not control them. I ride them, but I don't stand in the way of their prey."

Erix's eyes flash to Elowen, who sips her wine, looking entirely re-laxed as she lounges in the chair. "Stand down," he orders, and the dragons cease growling as everyone stows their weapons and takes their seats again. The guards step back. The beasts remain in the gar-den, forever watchful of Elowen. She gives me a subtle nod, and I sheathe my sword before yanking her chair closer to mine and taking my place again.

To my surprise, it's Zarius who speaks first. "Galakin is a godly kingdom, same as Thirwen. King Cayden and Queen Elowen were declared a divine union when the God of Death, Water, and the Moon showed his favor on their wedding day by overtaking the sun. It is evidenced by their markings. This is the strongest sign we've received from the gods in centuries. I'm aware of the bad blood between our kingdoms, and how much has been spilled into the sea, but animosity must give way to peace if we want to move forward."

"Move forward?" Cordelia echoes incredulously. Erix places a hand on his wife's shoulder, but she shrugs it off. "My sister is lost to me forever. I cannot move forward when a piece of me lives within her corpse."

"Then avenge her," Elowen states. "Instead of blaming Prince Zarius for events that transpired before he was born, face your enemy on the battlefield with us and win."

Silence hangs heavy in the air and Elowen stands from the table. It's clear none of us can sit down for a meal after all that's occurred; the tension is too high. Our party follows suit, waiting for Elowen's command. "We can discuss your decision after you've had time to speak among yourselves, but I will not sit here and listen to you insult my king and marriage. Cayden has proven that the life of one bastard is worth a thousand kings, and he deserves respect. Most rulers wouldn't be on their thrones if they had to fight for them instead of being granted a crown at birth."

Elowen takes my arm, and I start to lead her out of the banquet hall, looking over my shoulder to regard the king and queen one final time. "We've come for your alliance but speak to my queen again in that manner and you won't have time to make peace with your gods."

The guards don't protest as we move through the castle and down the staggering hill leading to the docks. There's not a chance we're sleeping in the castle. Dark ships rock in the harbor all around ours as we step onto the deck and Elowen releases me to walk toward the bow. I pull my eyes away from her retreating form to face the prince of Thirwen.

"You stood by us."

"We're allies," he responds, his crimson eyes made brighter by the night. "I have something to gain from the success of this war, and I may not like Galakin, but their navy is necessary."

"You're much easier to deal with when you're sober," I remark before striding toward Elowen, who stares at the Galakin castle like she wants to burn it down.

"I need to ride," she says once I'm close enough, and I cut off a probably ill-timed innuendo when she sticks her hand out to me and

Basilius perches on a rock. He's so massive that he's taller than the masts of the ship.

I don't remember much of what occurred with Elowen between the ritual at Port Celestria and waking up at the inn, but as she releases me to climb up the dragon's lavender wing and settles herself on his back, excitement rises within me as she beckons me up. I'd never ask her to let me ride a dragon—she's had so little to keep to herself in life—but if she's willing to share then I won't deny myself.

She tucks her legs to one side, and the beast growls as I climb up behind her, wrapping my arms around her as she coos and strokes his scales. It doesn't take her long to calm him, and he kicks off the rock. His wings spread wide and he glides along the surface of the ocean, dipping his back claws into the breaking waves before tipping up and bringing us closer to the stars painting the sky. My heart pounds as if I'm charging into battle yet my mind quiets as he careens to the side, swooping through mossy cliffs speckled with tropical flowers.

Elowen's head falls back against my chest, and she lets out a long sigh, her lips curling up. It's as if being in the sky lifts the burdens from her shoulders, and I can understand why. Flying is a feeling I'd never be able to describe to anyone who hasn't experienced it. It's ... it's ... liberating. Elowen peeks an eye open, and the moment is only made sweeter by her laugh.

I grasp her chin, tilting it up and dropping my lips to hers. It's a slow kiss, and she deepens it, tangling her hand in my hair and sliding her tongue into my mouth. I move my hand, gliding my knuckles down her cheek and pulling her closer, breaking apart only to press my forehead into hers.

She smiles up at me with stars in her eyes and kisses me again.

CHAPTER
FIFTY-TWO

CAYDEN

DAWN GENTLY CARESSES THE CABIN AS I BLINK MY EYES open. Judging by the lack of thumping, hardly anyone aside from the guards stationed on deck are awake. I clear the roughness from my throat as Elowen drags the tip of her finger down my cheekbone. The last time she did this was when she got drunk after the alliance ball and I carried her to bed. I doubt she remembers any of it, but she traced my features with one hand and used her other to lace our fingers together. She even held my hand as she slept, and I spent the night sitting beside her bed to keep hold of her like I promised.

"How may I be of service, wife?"

"You can release me from your death grip so I can get the letter that slid under our door," she responds, and I tighten my arms for good measure, making her laugh before begrudgingly letting her go. I sit up, resting my back against the headboard as Elowen rejoins me and settles the sheet over her waist. "It has the Ilaria seal."

I grab my reading glasses off the nightstand and snatch it from her hands, breaking the wax serpent coiling around the sun to unfold the letter. How . . . interesting. Prince Zale requests our presence at a café in Zraka for breakfast without guards, stating that friends don't need soldiers between them. I knew we'd hear from the king and queen regarding our offer, but I didn't think Zale would ever speak to us again after I held my blade to his throat.

Pity.

I suppose I'll have to do something worse next time.

"Dear Cayden, go home, bastard, and leave your promiscuous wife behind so my son can make an honest woman of her. All my love, Cordelia. What a generous offer from such an intelligent woman."

Elowen rolls her eyes and steals it, her brows rising as she scans the words. "I didn't realize holding someone at swordpoint was a sign of budding friendship."

"You've drawn your knives on me multiple times and I'm your husband." I shrug. "It builds character."

"I also didn't expect him to apologize on behalf of his parents. He wouldn't risk putting this in writing if he didn't mean it."

"I'm interested to see what he'll say when he's not acting like a lap dog in front of his parents."

"Like the little ratty ones I've seen in court."

I chuckle, tucking an arm around her waist to pull her to my chest. "He requested Zarius's presence as well, so I think his offer is sincere."

She sighs, pushing away from me without relaxing, and rises from the bed. Much to my dismay, she dons the robe I tore off her last night. No matter how many times she lets me into her body, the need to touch her is never sated. This desperation lives within me like a growing flame and Elowen's presence is the oxygen that gives it life. Water sloshes in the porcelain bowl as she begins wetting her disheveled curls to begin her morning routine. "We should leave in an hour so we're not late. Can I trust you to let Zarius know?"

"Yes, love, I believe I'm capable of relaying a message." My feet press into the plush rug beneath our bed, and I pull a fresh pair of pants and a white linen shirt from my trunk, throwing both on before shutting it and lacing up my boots.

"I know you're capable of relaying a message, I just don't know how amicably."

"That depends on him." I kiss her cheek and dip out of the cabin, requesting a servant send coffee so she's not a monster by the time we make it to breakfast. Rhys and Zarius's room is in the same hall as ours and I pound on the door, heedless of the early hour. Rhys yanks it open, revealing the prince of Thirwen sprawled out on his small cot, snoring loudly with his mouth open.

"Well, I see why you're already awake."

Rhys gives a half smile, the first I've seen in his presence. "The prince is not a graceful sleeper. I assume you have a message for him since you're here so early?"

"Zarius needs to be awake and ready to leave in an hour. He's been summoned along with Elowen and me to meet Prince Zale in the city for breakfast."

"Not at the palace?"

I run my tongue along my teeth. "I doubt he wants his mother and father bearing witness to this meeting."

Rhys was there last night, seated at the long table with our soldiers and members of the water cult. Though even if he hadn't been, I have no doubt Zarius would have informed him of every detail once he made it back to the ship. The pair of them are often whispering to each other, and despite the rockiness between them when our paths first crossed, when sober the prince often seeks the knight's counsel and company.

"You need the support of Galakin if he's to ascend the Thirwen throne. His enemies won't be able to take on both of your kingdoms and those in Thirwen who support his claim."

"Speak plainly," I begin. "Do you honestly think many in Thirwen will support his claim?"

Rhys rolls his lips, looking down to hide the rare show of emotion, and clears his throat. When he meets my eyes again, the years he's spent on this earth seem heavier on him. "Many loved Ruella. They will support him because he's her son."

I quirk a brow at the informality with which he spoke of the late queen of Thirwen, but he doesn't balk. "So the rumors are true."

Rhys holds my stare, the lines around his mouth tightening as he looks over his shoulder to ensure the prince is still sleeping. "Not all of us have the power to overthrow a kingdom for the ones we love, demon. Sometimes we love them in secret, but even secrets have a way of never truly belonging to us." His eyes harden, and his fists clench. "The prince isn't my son if that's what you're insinuating, but that's never stopped me from viewing him as such. His claim is legitimate, as is he."

He's lying.

And that's why he stayed with him in exile. Not as a knight, but as a father protecting the one thing left in this world that connects him to his lover. I doubt Zarius knows; if he did he probably wouldn't be so eager to take the throne, especially considering King Fallon has other children.

"You don't have to reassure me of anything. The blood that runs through his veins is of no concern to me as long as it doesn't complicate my plans." I knew I'd never beat the game until I cheated all the players who stood against me. Zarius needs to figure out how to do that in Thirwen. There's nothing that threatens someone who inherited power more than someone who won it. "Ready the prince to leave."

I'm halfway down the hall when Rhys speaks again, "We both know what it is to suffer for wanting a woman who never should've been ours."

I look over my shoulder, waiting for the man to finish.

"Hold on to yours. From one bastard to another, I pray you never know the pain of fate when it comes to take what you've stolen."

CHAPTER
FIFTY-THREE

ELOWEN

THE CAFÉ ZALE INVITED US TO IS RIGHT ON THE WATER. A server leads us to a veranda overlooking the white sand and sea between pillars covered in orange and light pink blossoms. In the distance, a pod of dolphins flips through the crystalline waters, disappearing only when my dragons' shadows overtake them. It seems Zale was true to his word; no guards are either inside or on the road.

Zale stands beside a table with his hands clasped behind his back, his posture stiff though he tries to draw attention away from his nerves by smiling at us. He's in a similar outfit to last night, the red linen complementing his deep brown complexion and hair.

I take a seat across from the crown prince, and though the table is circular it's clear Zarius and Cayden deliberately sit closer to me. Zarius doesn't do so out of loyalty, and he has a hard time hiding his sneer when regarding Zale. A woman sets a pitcher of orange juice at the center of the table along with a coffee tray filled with sweeteners, milk, and a small bowl of chocolate.

Zale clears his throat, placing one of the chocolates in his cup and dousing it in coffee. He notes my intrigue, and says, "It's the preferred way of having coffee in Galakin since chocolate and coffee are the crops we take most pride in." He flips a cup up. "Try it."

I blankly stare at him, lifting a brow and waiting for him to speak. If he thinks I'll entertain him before acknowledging how he sat by while his mother practically called me a set of open legs and threw the word *bastard* around like a curse, then he's mistaken.

His throat bobs, and he looks down briefly before straightening his shoulders. "As I stated in my letter, I wished to apologize for how my mother and father conducted themselves last night. It was entirely inappropriate, and I'd never come between your marriage."

Oh, sweet gods.

I exchange a glance with Cayden, who makes no attempt to hide his thinning patience as he says, "Does the wind whistle through the empty space between your ears like an abandoned temple?" Zarius chokes on his orange juice, and I press my lips together to keep from laughing. "Tell us why you wanted to meet because I'm assuming it wasn't to inform us of how you take your coffee."

As a peace offering, I lean forward. The markings on my arms shimmer as I grab one of the chocolates. Steaming coffee melts it, and I stir with the small spoon looped through the handle to ensure no bits are left. The scent alone is enough to make my mouth water, and the taste is even better.

He seems pleased by my reaction and speaks with a newfound confidence. "I want to train you."

"Me?" I laugh again. "I didn't have tutors who used dulled swords, prince. I learned to fight to survive."

"In magic."

I set the cup back on the saucer and rest my folded hands on the table. "To wield fire?"

"I cannot wield dragonfire but teaching you how to wield earthly fire may help you hone your abilities. You wielded your fire in a moment riddled with emotion. You need to be able to call the fire to you as you sit here." He does exactly that, pulling the flame from somewhere in the restaurant. "You need to sense it even when you can't see it and let it become part of you."

"What do you get in return?" I ask, knowing everything comes at a price, but the offer is so tempting I'd be willing to pay just about anything. Fire floods my veins but has nowhere to go. It lives within me like an eternal flame, and I can either burn from the inside or conquer it.

He looks between all three of us as another server places a three-tiered tray of savory and sweet breakfast options on the table. "I'm going to convince my parents to join your war. It's not your fight alone." His gaze settles on Zarius who looks incredibly impassive, picking an invisible piece of lint off his shirt. "Our people fought before we were born and still hold on to their hatred, but it won't solve anything. All it will do is inspire that same malice in future generations, and countless lives will be lost because rulers could not find a way to lead their people into a better world."

"I'm not sure your parents will have such a progressive perspective on the events that began the war between our people," Zarius says. "Need I remind you that it was never proven my uncle stole your aunt away. She may have left of her own volition."

Zale sighs. "And we may never know that answer, but . . ."

"We cannot create a better future if we live in the past," I finish for him. "Leaders should aim to alleviate suffering, not perpetuate it."

"Yes." Zale nods. "Exactly that."

"This is all very heartwarming," Cayden flatly states, drumming his fingers on the table and draping his other arm over my chair. "But I want to know how many ships you can promise."

"Five hundred."

"Eight," Cayden replies.

"Six."

"Eight."

Zale sighs, sticking his hand out. "Eight hundred ships."

They shake on it. "You'll be informed of the battle plans once the treaty is signed and I see the ships with my own eyes."

"I have high expectations, having heard previous plans conjured by the demon of Ravaryn."

Cayden's face remains neutral, giving away nothing as to what's going on inside his mind. It's a tactic he uses to unnerve others, and it's certainly working on Zale as he clears his throat again and faces Zarius.

"Do you have any terms regarding our alliance?"

Zarius's lips are set into a firm line as he assesses the prince he must've been conditioned to hate since birth. "Pull your ships back in the Dolent when this is done. We sail to one war; I doubt either of us wishes to return to another if your promises of peace are to be believed."

Zale nods. "You do the same with your ships and we won't have an issue."

"How are you able to speak as if you're the king?" I ask, drawing his eyes back to me. "You cut deals with us in a café, not a castle. Do your parents—the owners of the navy you've promised us—know you're here?"

"My parents will see reason," he says, finishing off his coffee and standing from his seat. "Though you and I have more pressing matters to attend, queen."

I untie the straps of my sandals that travel up my calves as sand spills into the leather soles. Finnian trails his fingers over the bow slung over his shoulder as he studies the secluded beach for any sign of a trap, but only Zale stands a few paces above the wave marks on the shore as he lays out several dried logs.

Braxton insisted on accompanying us to this training lesson, but Zale didn't have any guards within the restaurant, and I'd rather keep the fragile peace. Zarius stayed behind to debrief with Ser Rhys, and Ryder wouldn't leave Saskia alone with him—despite there being several guards on board. I only hope the ship isn't burned to a crisp by the time we return, since Cayden isn't there to mediate. Once he knew Finnian would accompany me, he strode down the gangplank, claiming he had a quick errand to run. For Cayden, a quick errand can range from killing someone to picking flowers for me, but he was gone before I had the chance to question him.

I kneel across from Zale, my blue gown with a large diamond cutout on my stomach fanning around me. Finnian sits on a piece of driftwood a bit farther back, watching closely as Zale lights the logs between us with some flint. It starts out small but grows as Zale moves his hands around it.

"Fire needs oxygen to grow, but as a wielder, you breathe life into it instead," he says.

"When did you first know you were a wielder?"

He chuckles softly. "I accidentally lit a curtain on fire when I was a child. It was also a moment riddled with emotion, like your first experience. However, mine wasn't as complex as nearly losing someone I loved. My younger brother stole the stuffed monkey my grandmother made me, and that I kept under my pillow. He ran through the halls, showing all the other children my most prized possession and I was humiliated."

"Do you still have the monkey?"

"*That* is not the point of the lesson today," he answers, and I laugh when he doesn't deny it.

"What was its name?"

He gives me a flat look. "Pascal."

"Oh, that's precious," I coo, and he groans while pinching the bridge of his nose, gesturing to the fire again.

I reach forward, settling my hands on either side of the gathered logs and focus on the shape of it, the warmth, the scent of embers glowing at the base of the sandpit, but my body locks up when Zale wraps his fingers around my wrists, and Finnian rises to his feet.

"Release me," I quietly command before turning to Finnian. "I'm fine. You can refrain from sending us into another war."

He smirks while releasing his hold on the bow and taking a seat again. "Anything for you, Ellie."

I laugh softly and turn back to Zale who has his eyes fixated on Finnian. "Friend?"

"More like a brother." When people describe great loves, they often talk about romantic connections, but friendship can be just as epic. "If you could refrain from touching me throughout the lesson, it would be greatly appreciated."

He slants his dark brows, and nods as understanding washes over his features. "I apologize if I made you uncomfortable. It won't happen again."

I tilt my head, regarding the prince in a new light. "Thank you."

He nods and mimics my position, calling the fire toward him, cradling and curling it in his palms. "Focus on your breathing. Many think that fire is destruction but it's also life and balance. It has the power to heal. Without the sun we wouldn't be able to live, and without the stars we'd never find our way home."

He cups a small flame in his hands and deposits it in mine, but it's gone in a blink, leaving nothing but smoke wafting toward the sky.

I sigh, trying to quell the mounting frustration within me, but it's pointless. I reach my hands forward again, calling out to the flames and waiting for my power to awaken, but I feel nothing. I squeeze my eyes shut, forcing everything around me out of existence, and inhale the smoke through my nostrils. Within the darkness of my eyelids, I let a singular flame flicker until it widens and becomes a wildfire.

A dragon does not fear fire, nor will I. Flames are encased in their scales, just as they're embedded within my soul. The only way to defeat my enemies is not to let the doubt they instilled in my mind be stronger than my capabilities. They have tried to limit me, to stifle me, and I will burn them to the ground for it. My vengeance will be a realm of ash and blood.

I am the queen of flames, and fire answers to me.

"The only lesson we'll handle today is holding fire. You can't wield it if you can't hold it." I open my eyes as he cups the fire again. "Did you know you didn't become a ghost in Galakin as you did in Erebos? Here you became a legend. The lost dragon princess who would bring dragons back into our skies." He holds the flames above my cupped palms, and I breathe deeply, keeping my mind quiet and calling the flames that live within me to the surface. "The fire is who you are. Do not fear it."

He drops the flame into my hand, and I hold it.

CHAPTER
FIFTY-FOUR

CAYDEN

I F THERE'S ONE LESSON I'VE LEARNED, IT'S NEVER TO TRUST anything or anyone. A person can make empty promises sound as good as gold before you realize their pockets are as empty as their words. A prince isn't a king, and Zale can preach about the future he wants, but he's never had to fight to see his next day. He's hopeful because he's never had to face the cruelty of the world without a safety net.

I tug on my watch chain to check the time before replacing it in my hand with the grappling hook looped on to my belt. The curved metal wooshes through the air as I swing it in wide circles, keeping my eyes on the guards monitoring the ramparts above from the dense palms surrounding me.

I count the seconds down in my head before a rumble shakes the ground, and a shrill bell clangs through the air. "Fire! Bring water! Fire!"

The guards patrolling above rush around the tower to get a look at what's happening. Tragedy calls to humans like flies to honey. People love to watch the demise of others because for that brief moment, the universe's spiteful nature is reared at someone else. They can relax because they know for the duration that fate bites the jugular of an-other, its claws won't sink into them.

The grappling hook sails through the air before it latches on to the banister, the sound drowned out by the bells and flowing river that runs beneath the bridge. Yanking on it a few times before determining it'll hold, I press my boot along the castle wall, using the shade the bridge provides to my advantage, and pull myself up. Sweat beads on my forehead and slides down my spine, but I keep my pace quick. I'd rather not kill guards in a kingdom I'm trying to forge an alliance with, but if they cause a commotion, I'll find a way to shut their mouths and make them disappear. It's just another task that I don't need added to my list, and though I wear all black, blood is always a bitch to get out from under your nails.

I swing my leg over the side and crouch behind the ledge as I wind the rope and attach it to my belt again. If I walked up to the front gates, I'm sure I would've been let inside—I'm a visiting king, after all—but I'd probably have to wait for Cordelia to return from greeting the Feynadra ship that docked in the harbor. I can keep my temper in check when she insults me, but Elowen is a hard line that I don't let people cross.

I hustle across the stone bridge and through the parted curtains that lead to the royal wing. The castle guards aren't as vigilant as the royals believe them to be. I've been spying on their property since I left Elowen at the beach. I never made my presence known to avoid her inevitable questions and only followed her to ensure Zale hadn't planned an ambush. I didn't leave until I saw her hold a flame in her cupped hands. I knew she'd learn; she's already proven herself capable after wielding dragonfire, but I look forward to the day I'm able to watch her incinerate our enemies.

The curved tile-lined halls act as a sound tunnel for the crashing waves and gulls that fly above them. Nautical-themed paintings adorn the walls in elaborate gold frames, and hissing sea serpents line the halls like pillars. Two guards round the corner, and I dip into an alcove hewn into the wall between two serpents, containing only a tall potted palm. I call on the shadows dancing along the wall as the plant sways in the ocean breeze, but I feel nothing. There's no connection.

The guards pass and I pull out the sleeping powder Elowen and I used at Kallistar Prison, not giving the soldiers stationed in front of the king's study time to realize what's happening before I blow the dust into their faces. The magic seizes them immediately, and I step back as they fall haphazardly at my feet.

Without knocking, I shove the door open and stride into the study. The worth of an idea is determined only by the outcome, so time will tell if this was all for naught. Erix abruptly stands from behind his desk, and quickly overturns paper spread across the surface. It's set in front of a semicircle of arched windows with gently wafting gauzy red curtains, and the ceiling is a mosaic of a sunset. The study resembles the rest of the castle, accented with shades of their house colors—red, orange, and yellow—with regal and oceanic detailing expressed through the carved wood molding and fabrics in the sitting area.

"King Cayden," he says. "I wasn't aware we had a meeting."

"It wasn't scheduled," I respond, gesturing to the whiskey on a high rounded table, relieved to see the familiar amber alcohol in this rum-plagued kingdom. "But I believe we have much to discuss so I took it upon myself to find you."

"So in other words, you're not supposed to be here."

"I'm not supposed to be in a lot of places." I pour myself two fingers of whiskey. "And yet I find those are the most beneficial places to be." His eyes dart toward the closed door. "Call for your guards if you wish, but it'll take them awhile to respond." He moves to step around his desk, but I pin him with my gaze. "Sit down, Erix. If I wanted to kill you, I would've done so already."

"You are a horrible diplomat," he mutters, dropping into his seat again as I claim the one across from him. "And yet I find myself not entirely loathing you."

"Your kindness is enviable." I drop my elbow to the arm of the chair, the ice in my glass clinking as I swirl it slowly. "I assume you know your son hosted a meeting this morning?"

"Indeed." He mirrors my position, relaxing in his chair while placing a smoke between his lips and lighting it by summoning a flame from the lantern along the wall. "And I'm assuming you're here to solidify whatever my son promised you?"

"One thousand ships to me, trade between our kingdoms, and both he and Zarius agreed to pull their ships back from where they clash in the Dolent Sea."

The wood of Erix's chair strains under his grip before he slackens it. "Can you trust Prince Zarius? How am I supposed to know for sure that he'll pull his navy back from clashing with mine?"

"I don't trust Zarius, and neither should you." I take a sip of the whiskey. "But I know he wants to be king and that he'll do whatever he needs to get us on his side. As for a trade agreement, I'd sign one right now if you presented it to me."

Erix drums his fingers along the desk, letting his eyes drift to the sea that sprawls to the horizon. "And if I disagree?"

"Despite Cordelia's words at dinner, Elowen will always hold Galakin in a higher regard than other kingdoms because you presented her with her dragon eggs." I trail my tongue over my lips, taking time to mold my next statement. "However, your wife's hatred for bastards makes me believe you have a few hiding within the kingdom, and well . . . if a bastard with the blood of commoners can take the throne, imagine what a royal could do if given the right opportunity."

Erix's nostrils flare and his eyes narrow on me. "You have no idea what you're speaking of. I could have your tongue for that."

"You'd be dead before you rose from your chair." I take another sip, placing a boot over my knee as I lean back. "I don't care where your cock has been. The only reason I'm here is to ensure my wife has the highest chance of survival in the battles to come."

I can take on their armies, but it's Elowen who will face the navy while on dragonback. Galakin can aid her efforts in ways I can't while fighting on land. After almost losing her in the last battle, I need to take every precaution to ensure that never comes to pass.

"And do you intend to achieve that by threatening me?"

"I mean to achieve that by whatever means possible, and always remember that no threat of mine is empty when it comes to her," I state. "My loyalty is not to a crown or a kingdom; it will always be to my wife."

Erix takes a deep drag of his smoke, looking to the sea again as he blows it out. "Though I don't agree with your methods, I respect you as a man." I remain silent, not really caring about what he thinks of me. All I want are his ships. "Love has always had a way of bleeding duty dry. As king your duty is to your kingdom, even at the expense of those you love. The crown on your head must always come before the ring on your finger."

"You were born into a role I claimed with my sword, and considering you have bastards, I don't regard any of your advice on how to conduct myself as a husband highly."

His nostrils flare. "I never admitted to that. I love my wife."

"You didn't have to, and I don't care."

Erix knows he'd be a fool to make an enemy of me. With Elowen claiming the Imirath throne, our kingdom along with the southern isles will become the largest kingdom in Ravaryn. Not only that, but its queen is bonded to five dragons, and the flame-wielders of Galakin can't wield dragonfire if Elowen's revenge finds them next.

"A treaty must be drawn up," he says. "But I will aid your naval force *only* with the guarantee that trade will be established and Thirwen's ships will be pulled back from where they skirmish with mine."

I finish off the whiskey and place the empty crystal on the edge of his desk. "A pleasure doing business with you, Erix."

I yank open the doors to the study and step over the still-sleeping guards. They're in Erix's command so he can deal with them however he sees fit.

"Your Majesty!" someone calls out behind me, but I keep walking, eager to get out of this castle. "Your Majesty!"

I glance over my shoulder, and sure enough, a servant has her eyes on me. She pauses for a moment to catch her breath when she's close. "I only wanted to ask if you're lost. I know the towers can be confusing."

"I was just on my way out."

"But the queen has just arrived," she says.

"Queen Cordelia is busy with her sister, and I suggest keeping her occupied until I'm gone."

"No, sire. *Your* queen. Her majesty has arrived with Prince Zale and Commander Finnian."

CHAPTER
FIFTY-FIVE

ELOWEN

INCENSE BURNS MY NOSE, SO POTENT I CAN PRACTICALLY taste it. Mae's chamber is darker than most, but the woman is nowhere to be seen. Gold chimes hanging in the windows create a soothing melody . . . so I don't know why goosebumps dot my skin. It's the same feeling I got while crossing into Zraka. It feels like I'm forgetting something, like I'm meant to be somewhere else but can't remember where to go. Aside from the chimes, everything in the suite is red. It reminds me of Asena's robes, and I wonder if Mae has any ties to the fire cult.

I fist my skirts to keep from tripping over several floor pillows surrounding a low table and pause when Zale holds a hand up before disappearing onto the balcony.

"I think I'm going to sneeze if I stay in here a moment longer," Finnian whispers.

"I lived with you in your teenage years so this smells pleasant in comparison."

He glares at me while resting a finger beneath his nose. "Rude."

"Mae?" Zale calls out, and I peek through the gossamer curtains to watch him round a small lounge facing the ocean. The canopy overhead provides the elderly woman some reprieve from the sun, but I try not to gag when another wave of incense washes over me. Sticks of steaming wood rest in several golden bowls all around her. Her frail shoulders are wrapped in a shawl and rise when Zale steps into her vision. "I brought someone who wishes to speak with you."

"Elowen Veles and her brother have come to pay me a visit," she says in a wobbly voice as she reaches forward to cup his cheek. "Come here, girl. Let me see you after all these years."

I exchange a glance with Finnian, but Zale hardly seems unnerved as he gestures for us to come forward. I wipe my hands down my dress and straighten the straps on my shoulders as I do as she says. Deep lines are etched into her brown skin, and age spots dot her cheeks, but her eyes are warm and kind.

"Elowen Atarah. Elowen Veles." She says my name as if she's testing the weight of each syllable to determine which she prefers while resting her hands on my cheeks. "Elowen Veles. Prisoner, princess, dragon rider, queen."

"It's nice to meet you, Mae," I say as she releases my face but takes hold of my wrist to examine the lines of my palm. "I know we met before, but I was too young to remember it."

"But you remember your dragons. You can never forget your dragons."

"Yes, that's true. They're my earliest memory."

"The magic in your veins keeps you from forgetting," she mutters. "You can't forget any of it. Neither could he." I glance at Finnian again, but Mae pulls on my wrist as she shakes her head. "Bastard, criminal, commander, king."

My brows furrow. "What does Cayden remember?"

"He will know soon."

Zale claims the spot beside Mae and gently eases her hand away from my wrist. The woman seems to be calmed by his presence, a smile sliding onto her ruby-red lips. It's the only makeup she wears. "Mae, Elowen wanted to ask you some questions. Do you feel up to it?"

"Yes." She pats the other side of her, and I don't object. The cushion sinks beneath my weight, and Finnian moves to stand closer to me.

"It was said the gods came to you in a dream and told you to give me the dragon eggs. Do you remember any of it?"

Her brows crease, and she points toward the tea set in front of her. Zale leans forward to pour her a cup, and she sips it before speaking, hugging the porcelain as if she's freezing. "It was not the gods, it was one. The Goddess of Flames, Life, and Stars said it was time for dragons to reawaken. You were born to bring them into the world. You will keep them safe. The warrior with a fierce and gentle heart."

"But why not anyone else?" I ask.

"The fire in your soul," she insists. "What is meant for you will never miss you. It has a way of making you aware of its presence before you even know what it is." She taps her bony finger into my ribs, right where I felt the tug while sailing into Zraka. "A woman's intuition is rarely wrong. Trust in yourself to navigate your path. Only you can decide what is right, what breaks you, and what strengthens. To find the answers you seek, you must let go of doubt and embrace who you are."

My eyes flicker in the direction of where I felt the tug, and Mae nods. "Let the dragon rise from the ashes," she says. "A wrong was righted when they found and chose you. A thread torn in greed was mended with your birth."

The more she speaks, the more confused I become, but what I do know is that I want to investigate what lurks in Galakin, and why I'm so drawn to it. "What wrong?"

"The gods fought against one another, and it led to both their doom and the destruction of dragons. The skies are empty without dragons to claim them. A kingdom is nothing without a strong ruler on the throne."

Zale gently takes her hand, drawing her tender eyes to his. "But what was the thread torn by greed?"

She blinks at him, and it's clear she won't answer the question. I pinch my skirts between my thumb and index finger since it's less distracting than tugging at my necklace. I don't think it would be smart to push her—she seems so frail—so I bury my curiosity and ask a different question.

"Where did the dragon eggs come from?" She opens her mouth, but rears back as if someone slapped her. "Mae?"

She begins shaking her head, looking to the canopy blocking out the sky as she covers her ears. A noise coming from deep in her throat reminds me of a wounded animal, and Zale wraps his arm around her shoulders. I move off the couch and stand in front of Finnian, staying close just in case Zale needs assistance. I know she'd be no match against Finnian but protecting him will always be my first instinct.

"Mae!" Zale calls out when her eyes roll back in her head, and he gently pats her cheek. "She hasn't had a vision in years, I don't know what's happening."

"Do you want me to fetch a healer?" I ask.

"No, there's nothing anyone can do once a vision takes hold."

The curtains leading to her room part, and to my surprise, Cayden steps through. "I thought you had an *errand.*"

"I did," he answers as he cuts a path toward me. "I secured our alliance. I'll tell you the details later, but what the hell did you two do?"

"All I did was ask her some questions about the dragons and then this happened. We only just arrived."

"Loved by the gods. Hated by the gods. Loved by the gods. Hated by the gods," she chants under her breath. Cayden opens his mouth to say something but shoves me behind him when Mae springs forward and grabs on to his shirt. Pain twists her features, and I wish there were something I could do to help her. "The sun will be bathed in blood and the shadows will shroud the day. Ashes to be washed away by the waves. Old eyes watch and new eyes shut." Her voice comes out shockingly low, almost like it's not her relaying the message.

Zale pulls her away from Cayden when her irises reappear in the whites of her eyes. She collapses against him shaking and coughing as Zale wraps one of the many blankets around her. My heart pounds through my body so fiercely I can feel it in the tips of my toes and fingers. *Oh, gods.* I'm grateful the prophecy wasn't directly related to me as the one issued years ago was, but still, I could've lived happily never hearing another fall from anyone's lips.

I don't even know what this one means. The prophecy I received when I was a child was straightforward; there was nothing to decipher. I'm not sure if the state of her mind influences the clarity of her visions, but I don't know how the sun can be bathed in blood, or the probability of anything else she said.

"Y-you said we have an alliance?" Finnian asks, pulling his eyes away from the woman.

"I spoke to King Erix to ensure we got what we wanted."

"You *spoke* to my father?" Zale asks as the threads of his anger are sewn. "Or you threatened him?"

"Save your anger for the battlefield, Princey. You'll have the opportunity to bloody your sword in more than just practice rings if your mother has nursed you long enough."

Zale's face reddens and he stands from the couch, making sure Mae is propped up with enough pillows. "Did you threaten my father?"

"Perhaps you should ask him that question. I believe it's a matter of perspective."

"Perhaps I will," he shoots out.

"Enough," I cut in, stepping between them. "We all got what we wanted and I'm not going to babysit grown men while I have a war to fight. Either learn how to get along or keep your mouths shut."

Finnian steps around us to fix Mae's blanket, and Zale's stare tracks him. "Can I get you anything, my lady?"

Mae looks at him, her frail body still racked with shivers, and shakes her head. He nods, standing to his full height and rejoining our group as we walk closer to the railing. "Does anyone have any idea what the vision meant?"

"Mae often gets confused and lost in her head," Zale says. "I don't know if the vision was entirely accurate."

"She spoke clearly, even if the message wasn't," I respond, forcing my nerves down. The last time I received a prophecy, it led to me being chained up and ripped away from my dragons. "However, we have more pressing matters than visions from sleeping gods."

I try to put it out of mind, I really do.

But the shadow that's been following me like a dark cloud on the horizon for weeks grows darker, and I'm worried the rain will soon begin to fall.

CHAPTER
FIFTY-SIX

ELOWEN

I REST MY HANDS ON THE RAILING, STARING IN THE DIREC-
tion of where Mae told me to investigate. I can't see it from here,
but when I think of the dense forest at the base of the mountains,
I feel a tug on my ribs again. I'm supposed to be getting ready for the
ball, but every time I try to direct my steps below decks, something
brings me back here.

I hardly slept and spent the night lying on my side while staring out
the window in our cabin. Mae's voice echoed in my skull into the wee
hours of morning. We informed Saskia, Ryder, and Zarius of the
prophecy once we returned, but the only one who believes in prophecies is Zarius. He seemed unsettled, but had no theories as to what it
could mean.

A prophecy is what altered the course of my life. I was born to rule
Imirath and beaten before the throne. My blood has seeped into the
stones of the castle, and I live within its walls, its crevices, its very
foundation. My presence beats like an invisible heart buried so deep
the pulse drives my father mad, knowing one day I'll come to take
what's mine.

Some prophecies don't come to pass for years. Others are so vague
nobody knows if they truly did or are still awaiting fate to fulfill the
messages given to seers. The dragons fly in the direction I'm looking
but always alter their course to return to me, and I wonder if they

sense something as well. Something lingers out there, and it feels like I'm swimming in dark waters, unable to see into the inky depths monsters inhabit, waiting to drag me down.

"Lead the way, princess," Cayden says, striding up to me and leaning a hip into the railing.

"What?" I ask, clearing the fog surrounding my brain.

"It's clear you need to see whatever is out there, and you're not going without me." He points at the dragons. "I also can't climb onto one of them without dying so make your decision."

I bite my lip. "How long do we have before the ball?" The day was spent discussing possible battle plans with Zale and Zarius, and the sun is already setting.

He pulls out his pocket watch, quickly doing the math in his head. "If we're taking into account the several hours you'll need to get dressed, not enough."

I roll my eyes. "Deduct the several hours you'll spend practicing your glare in the mirror and we'll be grand."

He tucks it back into his pocket. "We have an hour."

I nod. "The dragons are uneasy so give me some time to calm Basilius before getting on."

Calithea may have carried him on her back while he was unconscious, but I don't think she'd accept him as willingly while conscious. The dragons can sense my emotions, and probably knew how desperate I was to get him out of there. All the dragons adore him, most likely because he arranges for their favorite meats to be brought to them and constantly sneaks them sweet treats, but I don't want to risk their wrath if he tried to ride them, even with me in the saddle. I begin humming the soothing tune that calms them when they awaken from nightmares and press my forehead into Basilius's as his claws sink into the harbor and he shrinks to my height.

All the dragons are large, but Basilius is massive.

Cayden watches as I continue humming and drag my fingers down his scales as I move along his body and climb into the saddle. He bristles beneath me, growling low in his throat when Cayden steps onto his wing, but I press my hand into his neck and continue the melody, gesturing Cayden forward with my other.

Once he's settled behind me with his arms wrapped around my torso, Basilius splashes through the low waves and kicks off the sand, flapping his lavender wings to carry us over the gate in the harbor and into the sky. The people of Galakin stop in the streets as the dragons fly above them, casting the shadows of their wings over their city. Some look at them in wonder and awe, while others run for shelter. To those who worship fire, the dragons must seem like gods.

The buildings give way to palm trees, and Basilius takes a right when I spot the river that separates Zario and Zraka. The banks are lined with sun-bleached rocks where bright-colored snakes sun themselves. I shudder. Snakes have always unnerved me. Sorin overtakes Basilius, followed by Venatrix and Delmira zipping past, but Calithea remains and nudges Basilius with her snout, making him hum happily.

The forest opens into a clearing and a crystal lake catches my eye, as do the ribbon fish swimming within, their long tails swishing behind them in colors of purple, pink, and yellow. They're beautiful but, like most brightly colored creatures, extremely venomous. Two stone buildings stand on either side of the lake and are connected by a wrought iron bridge that glitters in the sunlight. As we get closer, I realize they're temples. One has a crescent moon at the top and the other has a star.

It must be a worship site for the gods who blessed us.

The moon temple is on the left, hewn from stone so black it must be pure obsidian, and on the right is a white temple with blue veins running through it. *They remind me of our thrones,* I realize. Obsidian and moonstone. Basilius lands along the shore, and the fish dart into the depths. The forest is humid, and the air itself is sticky. I gather my curls in my grip as I slide off Basilius, fanning the back of my neck before letting them go.

"Let's check there first," I say, gesturing to the obsidian temple that Cayden hasn't removed his gaze from. Skulls are chiseled into the base of the pillars that line the entirety of it, and the phases of the moon are displayed above the entrance, reminding me of the tattoo he has on his ribs. I wouldn't consider it to be in ruins, but vines creep along the forgotten site, over fallen pillars and the chunks of the ceiling that have collapsed.

We climb up the steps that are as dark as a starless night, dodging the moss and weeds peeking through the cracks. It's completely bare inside aside from the altar made of the same black stone and a dried-up pool at the center. Cayden draws his sword, though it looks like no soul has been here in centuries, and spins in a slow circle as he nears the altar. He drags his hand over the slab, clearing the dust, dirt, and yellowed palm fronds. A faint pulse is absorbed by my sandals, and the hair on the back of my neck stands on end as Cayden reads the words etched into the altar.

"Nobody can escape the darkness, it awaits us all," he says. "I translated it from Ravarian so it may not be exact."

The temple groans as if coming alive from Cayden's voice, and he rushes toward me, pressing one hand into my back and keeping his blade extended in front of me. My chin jerks up at sudden movement, and water begins cascading from the tops of whatever pillars remain. Some arc over our heads and fall into the shallow pool that runs the length of the floor. Cayden lowers his weapon as a gust of wind slams through the open archways and dots our skin with droplets.

It's incredible.

He looks down at me as I lift my lavender skirt and step into the pool, finding my footing in the knee-deep water before releasing it. The slim golden chains hanging from the top of my two-piece shift against my stomach as I wade farther. Cayden's dark eyes track my movements, but he's unnervingly still as his pulse hammers in his neck. Power radiates off him as shadows stir like coiling snakes in the corners. The markings on my hands and arms pulse in time with my heartbeat when he steps into the pool and slowly walks toward me.

"I feel as if I've seen this in a dream," he says.

"I didn't think you dreamed." I circle one of the falls. "You're usually restless at night."

"Not often." His voice is gravelly and rough. "But whenever I do, you're always in them." The obsidian water ripples around us, but I can't tell if it's because of Cayden or the water that continues pouring. He may not think he has any magical abilities, but he believed in me when nobody did, not even myself, and this is me returning the favor. "I think I dreamed of you before we met. I never saw your face, but I knew it was you."

"How did you know?"

"The peace I felt." He catches me before I can dip behind another fall and presses me to his chest. His eyes are nearly black, and his skin is feverishly hot. I slide my hands along his shirt and hook my finger through the chain of his arrowhead necklace. "I've only ever experienced peace in your presence."

"Is peace what you're feeling right now?" I ask. He wraps a hand around the back of my neck, and my markings tingle as he brushes his lips over mine. "I know the magic within the temple is affecting you. I know you can feel it."

"I can assure you that the gods are the last thing on my mind right now, and what I'm feeling has nothing to do with them." I shake my head, but he uses his other hand to grab my chin and stops my movements. "Only you can bring me to my knees in worship, Elowen Veles."

I shiver, but it has nothing to do with another breeze sprinkling my skin with more droplets and all to do with the unyielding intensity Cayden possesses. The pull to him is so strong that it's nearly painful, but he doesn't release me from this immobilizing hold.

"To the next?" he asks, though the water hasn't stopped flowing.

"Only if you want to leave."

He steps back and threads our fingers together to help me out of the pool, but the distance between us doesn't lessen the lure to him. The drenched hem of my skirt sticks to my legs as we cross the arched bridge, and with each footfall amplifying the draw to the moonstone temple dedicated to the Goddess of Flames, Life, and Stars, my senses are pulled in two different directions.

"Do you think they formed an alliance because they share the night?" I ask.

"It seems possible."

"You've never read anything about the relationship between them?"

"No," he answers with a slight shake to his head, drawing my attention to the red scar on his cheek. "I don't think it was transcribed anywhere. Gods aren't allowed to fall in love with each other, so even if they did have a relationship, it would've been forbidden."

To live for eternity seems more like a punishment than a blessing if you must do it alone. I'd rather live a mortal life with a full heart than spend eons walking the earth, becoming numb to my surroundings and losing my humanity. The dragons screech as I press a sandal into the first step of the temple, and a chill snakes up my spine.

Similar to the temple dedicated to the God of Death, Water, and the Moon, the Goddess of Flames, Life, and Stars has an altar, but instead of a pool, it's an empty space. I release Cayden's hand, and blue veins dance throughout the floor as I walk toward the moonstone slab, bypassing a fallen pillar and brushing the palm fronds and dust from the surface. Sweat coats my hands and I read the words aloud.

"To endure fire is to walk within the flames and not fear burning," I translate the Ravarian aloud.

The temple rumbles, like a great crackling fire overtaking a forest as logs split into embers. Two rows of light blue flames shoot forward and curve around the perimeter of the temple as three within the center carve circles into the floor, creating the triple flame symbol associated with the goddess. *It's starfire.* Perhaps this is why I felt drawn here, to this element. I remember the man I bought the perfume from telling me starfire in its purest form doesn't exist in Ravaryn anymore, but it still does, and it was awakened by my presence. My dragons swarm above the ruins, shooting dragonfire into the center of their circle, cocooning me in flames as vibrant as their scales as I step around the altar, submerging myself in the sparkling flames streaked with silver.

It reaches for me but doesn't burn when it touches my skin and begins crawling up my arms. The starfire around me grows until the flames are as tall as the pillars and mingle with the dragons'.

I understand.

Fire can be chaos but can also be peace. Warmth is something all humans search for, but similar to love, too much of it can be deadly. There must always be balance in the elements, and balance in the way you regard them.

I sit at the center, watching the fire arch above my head and shoot around me like fireflies. The fire parts briefly to let Cayden enter, the only person who has never looked upon my power with fear. He strides through the flames to reach me, far more confident than anyone should be while walking through something that could kill them. He drops to his knees as the blue storm rages around us and cups my face, dragging his thumbs over my cheeks as his chest heaves.

"My love," he murmurs a second before pressing his lips to mine.

The kiss is feverish, dominating, and gentle all at once. The power I began feeling in the God of Death's temple amplifies, and I claw at Cayden's shoulders. I didn't know such a powerful love could be delicate until I met him. He lays me back on the cool stone floor amid the flames and pushes my skirt up my legs. If I thought his gaze was dark before, it's nothing compared to how he looks now. He yanks my hips off the ground and dips his head between my thighs. My lips part in a prayer as if the temple is dedicated to him.

Starfire shoots through my veins as he crests my pleasure, murmuring his devotion against my skin.

I wrap my legs around his waist once he sets me down, needing him closer. He pins my arms on either side of me, and the fire shifts to accommodate his grip. His hips grind into mine, and I moan into his mouth.

"You are more radiant than any goddess who has ever lived," he whispers against my neck, dragging his tongue across the swells of my breasts pushed together by my top. "I'm convinced there is no Goddess of Beauty because your existence would put her to shame."

I arch into him as he reaches down to untie his pants and rubs his cock against my wet center. The fire surging through me becomes stronger, hotter, more chaotic as he thrusts into me. I clamp one hand onto his shoulder and the other on the hilt of his sword still resting across his back as he takes me. Nothing has ever felt more perfect than being with him. The power thrumming inside my bones calls out to his as he looks into my eyes and presses our foreheads together. Cayden may not understand it, but I do. I see him. He covers my lips with his again and doesn't stop until the fire has burned out and the stars splatter the sky.

CHAPTER
FIFTY-SEVEN

ELOWEN

NOTHER SET OF GUESTS DESCENDS THE STEPS LEADING
to the patio made of red and white mosaic tile. Matching
lanterns are hung across the party, casting a warm glow over
everyone in attendance, glittering the dresses and crystal glasses filled
with wine and rum. Zarius looks just as bored as the rest of us, sitting
at the base of the tree I lean against while nursing his fourth serving
of rum. Saskia scrunches her nose in disgust.

"Should we dance?" Ryder asks.

"Thanks for the offer, but I'll pass," Cayden answers, earning a
laugh from Finnian.

Ryder glares at him. "I didn't mean with you."

Cayden takes another sip of rum. "However will I survive."

The rulers of Galakin should be joining us soon; they've been in
prayer for almost ten hours to honor each of the ten gods and the
winter solstice. Statues dedicated to each god are scattered through the
perfectly manicured garden. A faceless woman with a babe suckling at
her breast is dedicated to the Goddess of Marriage, Love, and Fertility. To her right is another faceless woman but on her knees with her
head bowed and covered in a veil: the Goddess of Grief and Sorrow.
To her left is a third woman with threads woven around her fingers:
the Goddess of Souls, Mercy, and Destiny.

"Walk with me?" I ask Cayden, who nods in response. The ball hasn't even started, and I already need a break from the amount of eyes that find me.

I fist my skirts and stride toward the torch-lined path to get a closer look at the artistry. Cayden silently follows at my side, his hand pressing into my back as he scans the thick greenery for any sign of a threat. Orange and red flowers wrap around the trunk of a large tree at the back of two statues that are clearly dedicated to the God of War and Strategy, given the drawn swords and helm obscuring his face, and the God of Illusion, the Mind, and Memory, which seems to shift colors depending on the lighting.

We step over a bridge that arches over a small river and leads to a semicircle-shaped patio with the remaining five gods, all still faceless. First is the Goddess of Air and Storms with her hands raised and lightning shooting from her palms, next is the God of Earth and Harvest with roots growing along his legs and arms, and after that is the God of the Sun and Light, with the most offerings at his feet. A golden crown rests upon his head and a flame burns in each hand, an homage to his ability to wield both earthly fire and sunfire.

"You're looking at the statue as if you wish to murder it," Cayden says, diverting my gaze to him. "I'd really rather not be jealous of a stone slab, sirantia."

I laugh softly and brush off his touch as we walk to the part of the alcove that has the clearest view of the sea. After Asena revealed that the God of the Sun tried to chain dragons as my father did, I'll always hate him, real or not. The wind carries the scent of night-blooming jasmine, irises, and starsnaps growing at the base of the two gods who presided over the night. The river snakes along the mossy ground and mingles beautifully with the music that continues to play.

I stride closer to the pair, feeling drawn to them knowing that they've supposedly blessed Cayden and me. The Goddess of Flames, Life, and Stars has three fires burning above her head, her hair spills to her mid-thighs, and in her palms sit two stars. Twin dragons curl around her arms and perch on her shoulders. Beside her is the God of Water, Death, and the Moon. The five phases of the moon are chiseled above his head and two skulls rest in his palms. I suppose this plot was chosen for him because of the proximity to both the river and ocean.

The markings on my arms shimmer as I crane my neck and reach forward to trace my fingers along the stone. It's smooth and cold despite the warmth of the kingdom. The holiday would've looked so different if we were back home. I've always associated it with ribbon-adorned trees, fresh baked goods washed down with hot cocoa, and sitting in front of the fire while watching snow fall, but it's too warm to even think about such things here. The people of Galakin can host their festivities from the beach if they wish.

Footsteps pound against the ground, and I reach for the dagger beneath my skirts as Cayden steps closer to me, his sword already unsheathed.

"Hold the charge." Saskia huffs when she struts over the bridge and sees our weapons. "I can't spend another minute with the others if neither of you are present. I have nobody to look at when they say something idiotic." I laugh while sliding my arm through hers and leading her back to the party. "Let's find something to eat before the royals arrive and politics must be dealt with."

My anxiety has nearly robbed me of my appetite, but I don't want her to venture off alone. We may be allying with Galakin, but we must remain vigilant. Our ensembles ripple in our wake as we rejoin the party and cut through the throngs of people. Saskia is clad in an elegant blue gown that cascades over one shoulder, and panels of sheer fabric dotted with diamonds flow behind her. I'm in a similar color, but my bodice and wrist cuffs are made entirely of pearls with thin strands that clasp around my neck and over my shoulders. Fabric drapes from my bodice to my wrists, flowing as effortlessly as my skirt, and matches my sapphire-and-moonstone dragon crown.

Finnian catches up to us, looping his arm through my free one and tagging along to the table filled with various vibrant fruits, flatbreads, and spreads. A servant piles a crystal dish high with an assortment of tropical delights, and I nearly groan while trying a strange-looking green one that I'm told is a kiwi.

"I might rethink the marriage offer from Cordelia if it means I can always have this fruit," I say after swallowing.

"Please don't say that any louder. I'd really rather not have to deal with fighting our way out of another coup," Saskia mutters, glancing in Cayden's direction to make sure he didn't hear.

"Calm down, Sas. A bit of violence keeps the evening interesting." I laugh when she groans.

"Who are we fighting?" Finnian asks as he rejoins us, shoving a mango slice into his mouth.

"Nobody at the moment but the night is still young," I respond, leading our way back to the group. "Lots of opportunities for one of us to piss someone off."

Lyres and string instruments alert guests to the impending arrival of the royal family, and the entirety of them flock to the base of the grand staircase in anticipation. We do the opposite, keeping away from the masses and rejoining our group. Cayden steals my grapes, and I glare up at him as he tosses them into his mouth, pulling me closer to kiss the side of my head.

"What did you get?" Zarius asks Saskia, smirking into his glass when she bristles.

"Nothing that would interest you, considering it doesn't come in liquid form and isn't served at a tavern."

"That's not true," he answers. "You can juice fruits."

She scoffs and moves to the opposite side of our gathering as I raise my brows. Cayden shakes his head. "Not our problem. Not our business."

"Saskia is my business," I say, biting another kiwi before Cayden decides he wants to steal that as well. "And it's so intriguing."

"Don't be so dramatic."

I narrow my eyes. "You think I'm dramatic?"

"Does the sun rise at dawn?"

A trumpet blares and I offer him my middle finger while turning away.

"House Ilaria would like to take this opportunity to thank you for joining the royal ball in celebration of the winter solstice," a squire announces before four more trumpets blare. "King Erix, Queen Cordelia, and Crown Prince Zale are accompanied by the entirety of their house and King Lycidas and Queen Nasha of Feynadra, our beloved queen's sister."

Erix, Cordelia, and Zale appear first, all in elaborate, jewel-encrusted finery reflecting the colors of a sunset. Sea serpents made of flames slither through the sky like shooting stars as they walk. The various princes and princesses follow, and then Nasha on the arm of her king. She catches my eye in the crowd and subtly dips her chin in acknowledgment.

Cayden places my dish on a low-hanging branch, and I take his arm so we can greet the royals together. Zale's smile widens when he spots us, but his gaze skims over our heads briefly. I turn to see what he's found and realize he's looking at an unknowing Finnian while he converses with Ryder. When I turn back to Zale, his gaze is elsewhere.

"King Cayden and Queen Elowen," Erix says as his people part and he steps closer to us. "I've drafted a treaty for you both to sign as well as a separate one for Prince Zarius. I will then publicly announce our allyship to those gathered to celebrate the longest night of the year."

"I believe it will please the gods," Cordelia says, her tone far more cordial than the last time we spoke. Her mouth is set into a firm line, but venom no longer laces her eyes. "I will never deny that I had hoped you would marry into my family, but the gods had a different plan for you. As you know, I have harbored guilt about what transpired in Imirath after my seer announced your prophecy, and helping you dethrone him is how I'd like to offer my apology, should you find our terms acceptable."

"The apology for my father's actions is not necessary," I reply.

She nods while waving a servant forward and presents us with two folded pieces of parchment. "You can take them inside if you'd prefer a quiet place to read."

"You'll have your answer shortly," Cayden responds before escorting me back to our group and dropping Zarius's treaty in his lap. "Are you sober enough to read that?"

"Oh, I'm grand," Zarius responds, ripping it open and stumbling to his feet so he's able to read it alongside Ser Rhys, who has remained silent throughout the gathering. I can't imagine how I'd feel if I were in his position and making peace with Imirath, so I'm not surprised he's turned to what I suppose is his favorite medication: rum. The two begin muttering quietly as I step into Cayden's arms, pressing my back to his chest so we're able to read the treaty together.

"It's a basic list of goods and a tentative schedule. Some of the tariffs are slightly higher than I'd like but considering we're getting one thousand ships I'd say it's fine," he surmises.

"One thousand?" I ask. "I thought Zale agreed to eight hundred."

"He did, but the king didn't know that," he responds. "Zarius, sign yours."

"I haven't finished reading it," Zarius tightly answers.

"I don't care. You're getting a throne through this, and pulling your ships away from the Galakin border strengthens their commitment to us."

Zarius opens his mouth to speak, but Saskia cuts him off. "You have nothing to offer us but your name, so sign it."

His slow blinks are clearly weighed down by too much alcohol, but he grits his teeth. "Let's get this over with."

He scribbles his name at the bottom and follows Cayden and me along the edge of the dancefloor where revelers dance to a melody created by sitars, tanpuras, and bansuris. The dancers clap their hands and clang the jewelry on their arms as they weave in between one another.

"ATTACK!" A palace messenger rushes to the top of the steps that the royals just descended, and the dancers awkwardly pause as the music cuts off. "Thirwen used magic to sneak past our wards and is attacking Zario!"

"Fuck," Zarius growls under his breath, scrubbing his hands over his face and slapping his hands into his cheeks.

"Stay in the castle, princeling," I command. "You're no use to us dead, and you can't fight a battle after you've drunk as much as you have."

"You'd be surprised how much I've survived while inebriated."

"I'm sure it's an invigorating tale you'll have to save for another day," Cayden says. "El is right."

The dragons roar overhead, sensing the enemy in the distance as my muscles tense, preparing for the battle miles away in a city we traipsed through mere days ago. It was so full of life and will now be plagued by death. Cayden catches Erix's eye through the crowd and holds up both signed treaties.

Erix raises his voice above the crowd. "The Dragon Kingdom fights with us! We take our enemy as one!" Cheers and calls for blood ring out, though I doubt many people here will be rushing to the battle. Everyone is nobility and will likely be sending soldiers to fight in their stead. "The gods have shone their favor on Vareveth, and they are on our side in this battle and those to come. For glory and Galakin!"

Cayden hands the treaties off to a servant and takes my hand, leading me back to the others so we can change out of our finery and don extra weapons. I grit my teeth, remembering how badly the last battle ended, and force myself to keep moving forward. If Nykeem is here, I'll flay his flesh from his bones, and no poison will stop me.

CHAPTER
FIFTY-EIGHT

CAYDEN

BLOOD SPLATTERS THE WHITE BUILDINGS AND DRIPS BE-
tween stones on the street. Smoke hangs heavy in the air, so
thick you can taste it in the back of your throat. I push onward,
keeping a firm hand on the reins of the borrowed horse from the royal
stables. I quickly unsheathe a knife from my thigh and throw it, watching as it pierces the back of a Thirwen soldier chasing down a man
carrying his child toward Zraka where they'll find refuge.

Corpses line the streets—men, women, and children—the closer
we get to the beach. Catapults fire flaming rocks into the city, crumbling the buildings and crushing those fleeing for their lives. Calithea
roars above us as she locks her claws with a wyvern, shoving it beneath
her while bathing it in silver flames. I've seen magic wielded and known
several legendary warriors, and yet I've never seen anything quite as
powerful as Elowen mounting a beast that would bring even the bravest person in existence to their knees.

"What's the plan?" Ryder asks as we make it to the top of the hill
that leads to the vast beach, and curses when he takes in the sight.
Ships as far as I can see, sand soaked with blood, and more Thirwen
soldiers spilling onto the beach as they climb out of rowboats.

"Kill as many as you can and try not to die."

The feral urge to kill and the instinct to survive flood through me,
sharpening my senses to every sword around me both bloodied and

sheathed. I lead the Vareveth charge down the dune, and steel sings through the air as I lock my blade with an approaching enemy, unsheathing another knife to slice his throat beneath his helmet. Blood shoots from the slit, spraying my face and dripping down my chin as I push forward.

The ocean splits in two as Calithea burns a line into the surface, swallowing up several rowboats as Elowen sits atop her. An explosion shakes the ground, and I throw my arm over my eyes to keep the sand out of my gaze before unsheathing a second sword. I swing them both, not looking as bodies hit the ground. Everywhere I turn, there's another enemy pressing forward, but they underestimate how much I enjoy this. I was born for battle and bloodshed. Gore coats my clothes and skin until I look like the monster this world made me into.

A volley of arrows takes out my horse, and I jump off his back before the beast crushes my leg, quickly getting to my feet while slamming my sword through someone's stomach. I shove them back with my boot to take on the next.

"The bastard king," he hisses through his blood-splattered teeth as our blades lock in front of my face. The tide laps against my boots as the waves crash against the sand. Messing with your opponent's mind is half the fun of battle, so I stick my tongue out, gliding it along my bloody lips instead of spitting the blood out.

I raise an unimpressed brow at *the irrelevant soldier.* So much blood has been spilled it bubbles on the surface of the tide and shore. He stumbles over a corpse floating face down when he takes a step back and unsheathes a second blade to match me, but it's shaky in his grip. My father once handed me a rock after I lost a fight and gave me the option to either break my right hand myself or let him do it. I smashed my own fingers that night until they were crooked and gnarled. He wanted me to be equally lethal with both, and it's clear this soldier didn't have my same training.

He lets out an unnecessary battle cry, and I knock the sword out of his weak hand, using the same blade to block his other while shoving mine through his mouth.

"In your next life, I hope you offer me more of a challenge." Blood gurgles up his throat as I yank my blade free, letting his body bleed out and sway in the small waves.

I squint into the sky, watching Calithea flip upside down and drag her claws down the belly of a wyvern. It doesn't kill it, but there are so many more than last time. I bite the inside of my cheek, unable to tear my eyes away. They're swarming her, and though the dragons are formidable, my heart nearly stops as I watch Elowen duck under a spiked tail with venomous points before she rears back and hacks it off with her sword.

The beast cries out, and it's only then that I notice it doesn't have a rider. None of them do. I tighten my hand on the hilt of my blade and scan my surroundings. For the mages to have the beasts in their thrall, they'd need to be close by, and I doubt they'd risk keeping them on the ships considering the graveyard of wood Elowen left behind in Port Celestria.

The wounded wyvern flies low, and despite its grave injuries, whoever is controlling it must be pushing the beast until its last breath. Its black eyes spot me on the beach where the red tide continues lapping against me. I chuckle under my breath as it begins flying straight at me. Blood continues pouring from its stomach as it coasts even with the surface and pulls its black gums back to expose rows of fangs.

I swing my blades and crouch into a defensive position.

It roars in answer and snaps its sharp teeth that crave my blood.

My blades are steady as is my pulse, monster against monster, an even match.

There's a flash of silver above and I risk glancing up, but Calithea darts away with an empty saddle. Elowen plummets through the air with her sword raised and mouth parted in a vicious battle cry. She slams the steel through the wyvern's skull while landing on its back, using the hilt to keep her steady as blood sprays from the wound, painting her beautiful face in crimson streaks. Sorin rushes to her, always the protector, and slams the wyvern from beneath her. Elowen jumps from it as Sorin shoots forward and catches her on his back.

The wyvern crashes into the surf as Elowen hooks herself onto Sorin, and the lifeless body drifts toward me. El looks over her shoulder and blows a kiss to me as I sheathe one of my blades to retrieve her sword from the wyvern's corpse. I catch the kiss after extracting the blade and press my hand to the steel, and I can't hear her laugh from here, but I can feel it.

That's my wife.

Forcing my mind back into battle, I notice a shadowed cove in the distance. A small sandbar covered in rocks juts into the surf, making it the only place to hide on the beach. I begin fighting my way toward it, submerging myself in a red haze. I make it to the bend, and wish I could wipe my eyes, but my hands are just as bloody as my face, and I don't want to risk releasing my weapons.

It's quieter over here. I'm able to make out the sounds of uneven breathing as I silently creep over the rocks. Two soldiers guard two mages kneeling in the water, and though their backs are facing me, I imagine their eyes are as white as Elowen's when she mindwalks. I climb down the cliff and dip my boots into the water without being noticed.

Their souls are mine to take. Their blood is mine to spill.

I move with the tide, using it to hide my footfalls as the sand sucks at my boots. It's too hot in this damn kingdom for armor, which makes it easier to move. Both soldiers' gazes are transfixed on the sky as they watch Elowen fend off the swarm. I jam my sword through the back of the one closest to me, the blow killing him instantly. I discard his body like a piece of driftwood and face the next.

The soldier shoots his blade forward, and I knock the pointed tip away from my torso. He's more skilled than the others I faced on the beach, removing a knife from his waist and slicing it through the air. He manages to skim my bicep, but it's not even deep enough to require stitches, and some sick part of me wishes it were, knowing Elowen would be the one to sew me up. It also tore the shirt she gifted me when she said I needed to incorporate more color into my wardrobe. It's dark blue, but it's the principle of it.

"You dumb cunt," I mutter.

He slams his blade into mine, but I keep hold and use my second to jam the pommel into his temple. He stumbles in the sand, and I shove him down, using my boot to keep him pinned beneath the surface and watch the life leak from his eyes as he thrashes. I jam one of my swords into the ocean and grab another knife from my thigh, throwing it at the mage farthest from me. It spears her right between her eyes, and she crashes into the graveyard of my own making, but not as gracefully as I hoped. Her shoulder slams into the remaining mage, and the blue returns to his eyes as the wyvern the other must've been controlling screeches.

I jam my remaining sword through the soldier's throat, forever pinning him beneath the surface, and launch myself at the mage as he reaches for the dagger at his waist. The salty sea sprays me as I tackle him, prying the knife from his bony fingers while wrapping my hand around his neck and yanking him up.

"Did you think I wouldn't find the people trying to kill my wife?" He spits water into my face, but I hardly register it through the firestorm raging within me. My sanity walks a fine line most days, but looking down at someone hurting Elowen, having them in my grasp, it renders my mercy nonexistent. "Where are your ships?"

"Fuck you."

I shove him beneath the water again, keeping him pinned there for several seconds before pulling him up again. He's sputtering and coughing, but I want some fucking answers. There may be a plethora of ships in the bay, but it's not enough to account for all the soldiers, and Thirwen wouldn't make the same mistake of sending an entire fleet to shore when they know Elowen is here. I dig the tip of his knife into his cheek. "You know who I am. I can make this very unpleasant, and I'll take my time doing it. Before you die, I'll make you forget what it's like to wish to survive. I'll make you crave death."

I shove him beneath the surface again before jerking him up. "Where are your ships?"

"Blockade." He coughs up a lungful of sea.

"Is Imirath with them?"

He gives me a delirious smile, confirming my suspicions. "You'll never make it back to Erebos. You may be blessed by a god, but you will die in this sea before you ever make it home."

I do not fear death, having learned how to die a long time ago. "Only one of our corpses will be left to feed the fishes."

I shove him below again as his eyes go white. A beast screeches in the distance, and sure enough, when I look over my shoulder a black-scaled body is coming right toward me. My vision goes red, and I grip the mage's neck, squeezing and squeezing until his veins are protruding from his forehead and his bones snap in my hand.

The beast continues flying at me despite the enchantment being severed upon the mage's death. I steal the bow off one of the fallen soldiers, nocking in two arrows and keeping my hands steady as I aim.

Hold it.

It screeches again. It's so close I can make out the shape of its individual scales and the blood coating them.

Hold.

I quiet my mind, fixing my eyes on the one place where I can hit it that'll make a difference. Its jaw unhinges wider, and when it's close enough for me to smell its rank breath, I release the arrows and dive to the side as it plummets forward. Its wounded cry pierces my ears, making them throb and ache, and I push myself up from the sand, taking hold of my two swords again as I face the wyvern. Blood gushes from the eye socket I managed to hit, and I duck as it swings its venom-tipped tail at my head.

I try to will the tide as Elowen has wielded flames, but it remains unresponsive. I grit my teeth, accepting that all I have is steel. It's all I've ever had. I've never needed the gods; I've never needed anything. I'm not blessed by death. I am death.

"Come on," I mutter as it snarls. "Come on!"

It snaps its head forward, and I spin out of the way, slicing one of my swords below its neck. It screams again, jerking its head away from me before I can cut its throat again, but I slice its wing, adding more blood to the already red ocean. It swings its tail again, and I sacrifice a blade to jam it through the armored flesh, pulling my hand down just before venom is injected into my wrist.

In one last effort, it snaps its head forward, skimming my shoulder with its canine as I shove my final blade through its second eye. I jam it to the hilt and keep pushing until I spear its brain. The final roar dies on its lips, and it crashes into the waves as I fall to my knees to catch my breath.

I don't often experience pity, but I do now while looking at the beast. I know what it's like to be caged, to be controlled, but I made it out.

I press a hand to its snout. There are no winners at the end of a battle, just haunted survivors. I caught Elowen crying on the ship after the first battle where she had to kill wyverns, and the memories have chased her from sleep on more than one night. She had to choose between the survival of her dragons and them, but the wyverns aren't acting of their own volition; they're being controlled.

"May your soul cross the river and find peace," I say while removing my blades. I move to stand beside the beast and dig my boots into the sand, pushing it farther into the tide to give it the only burial I'm able.

CHAPTER
FIFTY-NINE

CAYDEN

I WALK THROUGH PUDDLES OF BLOOD AS I STEP OVER DEAD bodies, listening to people call out for loved ones. The battle is over, and despite us being able to defend Galakin from invasion, the death toll on both sides is substantial, and that's not accounting for the citizens in the streets.

Where is my wife?

A knifelike sensation twists my gut as I look at the sky void of dragons. They often circle wherever Elowen is. My mind is my own worst enemy, conjuring images of her either dead or captured, and madness thrums within me. I've prepared for this war my entire life, and yet I know I'd give it all up for her. I'd find a way to live with hating myself if it meant she'd be safe.

I whip my head in all directions, my heart pounding so fiercely it nearly drowns out all the shouting. I don't catch a glimpse of her curls or colorful markings anywhere. It's always been easy for me to spot her. My gaze is often drawn to her in any room she enters and even seeks her out when she's not there. It doesn't matter how many people separate us. I was blessed with the ability to see only to catch sight of her; it's wasted on anything else.

Fucking hells.

I follow the curve of the beach, keeping my eyes sharp. Once, I found peace in violence and felt a sense of tranquility at the end of battle. My muscles would burn, and my body would be too tired to listen to my mind, but a storm rages within me that won't be quelled until I spot her.

My breath rushes from me all at once. "Elowen!"

She doesn't hear me, speaking heatedly with Finnian who rubs his hands down her arms before she kneels in the sand, flipping over another dark-haired soldier with shaky hands. Her shoulders slump after she takes in his features.

Oh, angel.

"El!" I call out again, louder this time. Finnian sees me first, and even from here I note the way the tension leaves his body. Ryder stands from where he was crouched looking through the bodies and presses a hand to his chest.

But it's Elowen I can't move my eyes from once she whips toward me. Her brows knot, and her face coats in an emotion I've never seen before. It's too powerful to be relief. Trembles rack her body as she rises to her feet and begins sprinting toward me.

My knees go weak under the weight of what it feels like to be loved by someone like her, and yet I remain standing. I step forward like I'm in a trance, only breaking free of it when I sweep her off her feet and crush her body to mine. Her heart beating against mine is the reassurance I need right now, and it still doesn't feel like it's enough.

She chokes on a sob as she buries her head in my neck.

"It's all right, angel. We're all right." I skim my hands over her body to make sure there aren't any wounds.

"I couldn't find you. Nobody knew where you were." She pulls back enough to look at me, and she frames my face with her hands as I set her on her feet and apply pressure to the back of her neck, massaging it slowly to ease her anxiety.

"I'll always find my way back to you. No matter where you are. Never doubt that," I say, pressing my blood-covered forehead to hers as the dragons circle the air around us. "I don't plan on dying in battle now that I have someone waiting for me when it's over."

I drag my thumb over her bottom lip once, twice, and then she smiles, and it feels like everything will be all right. She remains close to me as Ryder and Finnian reach us, pressing her back to my chest to face them.

"There is talk that the king of Galakin joined the battle and that he's wounded," Ryder says. "He was going to accompany us to Imirath but now it'll probably be Prince Zale leading the force."

"Zale will be easier to deal with," I respond.

Ryder nods. "I want to get back to the castle to check on Sas."

"She's in the stronghold and has Ser Rhys to protect her," Elowen says. "She'll be more worried about you."

Ryder shakes his head. "I don't trust him or the prince."

"I don't think any of us ever will." I thread my fingers through Elowen's and begin guiding her up the beach. "But he knows it would be a death sentence if Saskia died while left in his protection, and if any harm comes to her, Zarius won't get his throne. He'll get a pyre."

Finnian dips his hands into the ocean to wash off the blood before following us. "Were any Imirath soldiers here? I only recognized Thirwen, but there was no sign of Nykeem."

"I didn't spot any Imirath ships as I flew, and nobody bore my father's sigil."

"It was all Thirwen, but Imirath is with them." I fill them in on what I found out about the blockade as we look for horses to ride back to the castle. With Galakin's aid, and the advantage of surprise, I'll come up with a plan to get us through. Imirath will be focused on protecting their southern tip, so the full force of their navy won't be present, but Thirwen's numbers will be vast. We grab the reins of three riderless horses on the beach and mount the blood-covered saddles. I keep Elowen in front of me, not wanting to release her just yet. Sorrow and relief surround us as we ride, wading through the ever-confusing aftermath of war as some reunite with loved ones and others lose everything. Elowen wipes a tear off her cheek as a man hoists a little girl covered in ash out of the rubble, holding her to his chest as he blinks back tears and she wraps her small arms around his neck. I wonder if

Elowen is thinking of her father, or maybe Ailliard, two men who let selfishness and fear get in the way of loving her.

We follow the procession of soldiers riding back to Zraka, keeping quiet out of respect for the fallen. We could've boarded a ship at one of the various docks, but the wounded need to sail more than we do. Ryder is practically vibrating with anxiety when we make it to the long stone bridge shaped like a sea serpent that connects the castle to Zraka. We're forced to slow our pace to avoid trampling some wounded being escorted across, as well as citizens seeking refuge. Healers hustle throughout the courtyard, their magic shining like golden orbs in the night.

I help Elowen dismount and guide her toward the front entrance. Ryder runs ahead of us, hardly dodging those in his path, but Finnian sticks beside us. Elowen threads her arm through his and leans her head on his shoulder, and though she doesn't see it, he stares down at her adoringly.

"Sas!" Ryder calls out, his voice echoing throughout the vast entryway lined with floor-to-ceiling gaps to provide a view of the ocean. Saskia jerks her head up from where she kneels on the floor to hand out cups of water. The ladle tumbles from her grip as she jumps to her feet to wrap her arms around Ryder. Ser Rhys and Zarius lean against a pillar a few paces away, the latter pulling his now sober eyes away from the back of Saskia's head to look in my direction before facing the sea.

Saskia throws her arms around Elowen next, not caring about sullying her gown as she presses Elowen's dark blue and black leathers against her. The sheer cape that stops at the top of her thighs must've been torn during the battle.

Finnian stays beside her as I stride toward the white-haired prince. "There will be wounded soldiers from your kingdom being brought to the dungeons for questioning if they're of high enough rank."

His red eyes flash to mine. "I will not kill them if you—"

"Give them the option of taking a blood oath," I cut him off. Killing them would only turn Thirwen against him. "When you face your father on the battlefield, don't do so with only my soldiers surrounding you, do it with your own."

"My father will most likely be cowering in the castle," he says. "He has a penchant for killing those who are unarmed, not soldiers."

"Even more of a reason to differentiate yourself from him. Don't tell your people to follow you, show them why they should."

He glances around the room. "Will Thirwen soldiers already be in the dungeons?"

"Yes. We rode back, but they would've put the prisoners on ships to avoid them escaping."

"And you know where the dungeons are?"

I jut my chin toward the hall, and both he and Rhys follow. I know just about as much of the castle layout as a servant after spying on Erix. We need to act quickly, before Galakin orders their execution or they die in the interrogation process. The air is humid, making the dried blood on my skin itch as we stride toward the eastern tower. Like every other tower, it's built of white stone and topped with an orange dome, only there are no open windows, just small slits covered in bars. The guards let me pass, and the putrid scent of human waste makes me long for the smoke and gore of battle the moment we cross the dark threshold.

"I'll have to kill them if they oppose me," Zarius says, his voice echoing throughout the musty hall.

"You'll also have to kill Thirwen soldiers on the battlefield if they raise a sword against you. Get used to it."

"I'll grant them the mercy of a quick death. I won't leave them to rot in a cell."

"The only ruler wearing a bloodless crown is a corpse," I respond, as I spot our intended target in the distance. I jerk my chin, signaling him to step forward and order the guards aside.

To his credit, he doesn't balk or shy away as one might if they were taking on a role unknown to them.

"Step aside," he commands, but the Galakin guards don't move. The Thirwen soldiers do their best to catch a glimpse between the bars of who's speaking but can't quite make it out yet. "I am Prince Zarius Liluria of Thirwen, firstborn son of King Fallon and rightful heir to the throne. I signed a treaty with your king and unless you'd like for that agreement to be dissolved due to your insolence, step away from my soldiers and leave us be. I will be the judge of their fate."

The guards eye each other warily, and I rest my hand on the hilt of my blade for good measure, sending the pair of them scampering off with their tails between their legs.

"Are you sure the King of Galakin will approve this?"

"Ask for forgiveness, never permission," Elowen says, stepping from the shadows and startling Zarius and Rhys.

"Gods, where did you come from?" Zarius asks, placing a hand over his chest.

"A loveless marriage." She gestures for Zarius to step toward the door, and whispers to me as he complies, "Did I scare you?"

I don't want to crush her hope, but I knew she was there the whole time. "Mhmm."

Her triumphant grin has me shaking my head as I follow her into the cell filled with eight prisoners. Only a small barred window provides fresh air in the overly crowded cell with wounded men and women pressing their backs into the walls.

"So it's true," the woman closest to us says. "The prince lives, as does Ser Rhys."

"Why did you come here?" Zarius asks. "What was the purpose of the invasion?"

"Officially, to seek revenge upon the dragon queen for burning our fleet." She licks her pale lips. "However, there were rumors you were alive. Your father sent us to kill you." I rest a hand on my sword in tandem with Rhys, and Elowen takes a step closer to Zarius, who holds up a hand to ward off our protection as she addresses Rhys. "We thought you died in the battle."

"It was fabricated by King Fallon when I was away from Prince Zarius. His intention was to kill us both, along with"—he clears his throat—"Queen Ruella. We escaped. She was not so lucky."

"Queen Ruella died of fever," a man in the corner states.

"Then why wasn't she given a pyre as all monarchs of Thirwen are?" Rhys's voice becomes rough, rigid. "If he wanted to properly mourn his wife, he would not have buried her in the crypts and married another woman in a fortnight."

"Queen Ruella," the soldiers surrounding the cell mutter, placing their fingers to their lips before pressing it to their hearts. Zarius and Rhys follow suit.

Zarius continues after a pregnant pause, "The dragon queen was doing her duty and is an ally to the crown prince of Thirwen." None of them challenge his claim, which is a good sign. "You have the opportunity to join me by swearing a blood oath, or you will face the sword."

A soldier in the corner speaks first. "If I am to swear to you, I'll have to fight against my kin." He lifts his head, blood spilling from a gash in his forehead. "I cannot spill their blood."

His shackles rattle as he stands and kneels before Zarius with his head bowed. Rhys steps forward to take the burden off his shoulders, but a subtle shake of Zarius's head stills him, earning a bit of respect from me. A second soldier moves to kneel beside the other, but the remaining six offer up their palms to him, prepared to take the blood oath.

"King Fallon committed treason in killing our queen," the woman who first spoke says. "We will avenge the good queen by placing her son on the throne."

Zarius moves to each soldier, slicing their palms open as they let their blood soak into the stones below and give their oath to protect, serve, and never betray him on pain of death. Zarius turns his sword on the kneeling soldiers, placing his blade at the neck of the first and saying the words I spoke to Elowen weeks ago, and to the wyvern tonight: "May your soul cross the river and find peace."

CHAPTER
SIXTY

ELOWEN

THE BELLS OF THE CASTLE TOWERS RING OUT TO WISH their prince farewell, and a sea that was riddled with blood yesterday is now filled with flowers. The people of Galakin stand along cliffs, shores, and boats to cheer as our ship cuts through the floating garden with more petals raining down. I have no doubt Zale is on the main deck, giving his best smile and waving at the people he'll one day rule. I needed silence, craved it, after being surrounded by the screams of battle and the wounded in the aftermath. I healed as Nyrinn taught me, not yet trusting my magical abilities enough to attempt tending to wounds with anything other than remedies known to me.

Saskia stands beside me on the small, private deck located at the stern of the ship, a frown turning her lips down. "I don't understand why people cheer for war. They throw flowers as if in celebration when many will die."

I drum my fingers along the railing, dragging my gaze over the Galakin fleet following us. Their orange sails billow in the breeze, enlarging the red sea serpent coiling around the yellow sun. The king and queen also gifted Zarius five ships to transport Thirwen survivors who bent the knee to him and took a blood oath. Zarius kept his family's sigil, but inverted the colors, making it a red kraken wrapping its tentacles around a matching ship on a black sail. "I think life becomes a series of trying to make the unbearable moments bearable, and most often that comes in the form of hope, even if it's a lie. They may throw flowers in what looks like celebration, but flowers are also placed on graves or threaded through a corpse's hands before their pyre is lit. It's a goodbye, even if they don't want to speak it plainly."

Her eyes rest heavily on my profile, and though she doesn't reach out to touch me, she takes a step closer as the red-tinged and scorched coastline of Zario fades away and we begin the journey back to Erebos. Not home. Vareveth soldiers will meet us in Port Celestria to push forward into Imirath.

The door creaks open behind us, and we both turn toward the sudden breach of peace. Zarius freezes in the doorway as his gaze settles on us. "My apologies, I thought the space was vacant."

He moves to turn away, but I stop him. "You don't have to run, Zarius. We're locked on this boat for a week, we're bound to cross paths."

One of his hands tightens on the wood when his crimson eyes settle on Saskia briefly, but he releases it, and strides toward us, taking the vacant spot on my other side. He doesn't say anything, opting to stand in silence as he watches the small waves created by the vessel. I hate thinking about what could be lurking within the shadowy depths. I've seen my fair share of monsters on land. I'd hate to find out what swims where no person has ventured.

"Why is the kraken on Thirwen's sigil?" I ask, wanting to say anything to break the now uncomfortable quiet.

Zarius's eyes move to the dragons flying just behind the ship where I can keep sight of them all. "Several centuries ago, it was said the first queen of my house was bonded to the kraken. It was her familiar."

Saskia narrows her eyes. "I heard that was a children's tale."

Zarius doesn't look at her when he speaks. "There's often truth in tales, even those meant for children."

She scoffs. "I prefer factual texts, not fairy tales."

"How dull your library must be, my lady."

Saskia looks to the sky in what seems to be a plea for mercy before addressing me. "I'll be on the upper deck."

She breezes through the door, her black gown trailing behind her, leaving Zarius and me in silence again. If he's bothered by her swift dismissal, he doesn't show it, but the silence between us is still irksome.

I lick my lips. "Do you have a familiar?"

He flinches, though it's barely noticeable. "I had a familiar. Many years ago."

I glance at him from the corner of my eye again before mirroring his position, facing forward to watch the dragons cut through the sherbert-colored clouds. The only comfort I was able to find in exile was knowing the dragons were alive. I forced myself to survive because I knew they needed me. His loss is one I can empathize with, and I pity him in this moment. "I'm sorry, Zarius."

I can't imagine my bond being severed. The hollowness I'd be forced to live with . . . I don't even know if I'd be able to survive it. It would be like walking through life with five permanent knives in my chest, always bleeding, never healing.

"Thank you," he says, sounding sincere before clearing his throat. "She's still with me. Those that are bonded to us never truly leave us."

"Will you ever be able to form an attachment to a different animal?"

"No, and I wouldn't want to," he adamantly states.

"I understand." I swallow thickly. "When I was separated from my dragons, I never spoke of them because it was too painful. I know we aren't exactly friends, but if you want to talk about her with someone who understands animal bonds, you can talk to me."

To be misunderstood is an awfully lonely feeling. You can say exactly what's in your head but feel as if you're talking to a brick wall when saying it to the wrong person. Zarius has no ties to home aside from Ser Rhys, and I can empathize with that as well, not having anyone in Imirath.

He turns away from my dragons, and though his face doesn't change from impassive I note the respect trickling into his eyes as he dips his head. "Have you thought about what you'll say when you see your father again?"

I grit my teeth while contemplating the uncomfortable question. After all these years, I'm putting an end to the war he started between us. "They don't deserve words when all they have given us is blood. Let your vengeance and sword speak for you. It's the only language they know, so don't ponder what you'll say, ponder what you'll do when the time comes to take the crown he ripped from your grasp."

His white waves brush across his face as he regards me but doesn't move to tuck them away. "So you are as bloodthirsty as they say."

"I'm a woman. My taste for blood stems from the need to replenish what was drained from my body when men decided I was not a person, I was property." I tilt my chin up, taking a step closer to the prince. "The only way to survive this world is by becoming more powerful than those who stand against you. Indecisiveness is the death of success. All it takes is one moment of hesitancy for failure to find you. Use this journey to make your peace with what you must do, and how your life will change, and see it done."

I turn toward the door, leaving Zarius to contemplate my words, but the boards creak beneath my feet when he calls out my name, halting my movements. "Thank you."

I look over my shoulder, raising my brows. "For encouraging you to kill your father? That was entirely selfish. I don't want to be the only ruler Ravaryn curses as a kinslayer when we ascend our thrones."

"For your candor. Flowery language seems to be the default when speaking of difficult topics."

"Ah, well if it's honesty you value then I vow to put you in your place whenever needed, princeling."

He grants me a half smile—the first he's given me since we met. "Noted, dragon queen."

CHAPTER
SIXTY-ONE

ELOWEN

THE SUN SETS ON OUR THIRD DAY ON BOARD, MARKING IT almost halfway through the journey. Finnian snores on my shoulder as we soak in the dwindling warmth through our thick sweaters. My neck aches from sitting straight-backed against the wall for so long, but I feel bad moving when he's so peaceful.

Ryder strides toward us, Cayden and Saskia not too far away. He taps Finnian's cheek, and a snore catches in his throat as he slowly blinks his eyes open to glare at Ryder.

"I was sleeping," he grumbles.

"Yes, I believe we all heard you," Ryder replies before addressing us all. "We need to begin discussing how we're going to get through the Thirwen and Imirath blockade. Ophir was able to wield the tides to get a sense of their coordinates and we're due to hit them in the early hours of morning."

Zale joins our group as well, and Finnian subtly hides himself behind my hair to wipe his face.

"You didn't drool," I whisper.

"I don't trust you anymore after you didn't wipe my face when the vextree poisoned me."

"I have boundaries in this friendship."

"Since when?" he hisses.

"I don't actually know."

He tugs one of my curls, and I bat his hand away as we turn back to the others.

Zale could've sailed with any vessel within his fleet, but he opted to travel with us, as did Zarius. It makes it easier to plan for battles as a unit, but Zale and I have also been meditating every morning at sunrise to help me locate the well of power within me.

"What if Elowen just did her thing and flew ahead and burned all the ships?" Ryder asks.

"She can't fly into battle entirely by herself when we don't know their numbers," Finnian shoots out.

"The soldiers who swore allegiance to Zarius informed us that their boats are charmed against earthly fire, and dragonfire is unpredictable. It burns hotter and takes longer to dissipate. Even with the help of the water mages to increase our speed, it'll add days onto our journey if we alter our course and we can't risk sailing the fleet through a firestorm," I say.

"It will be a battle of blades, not dragons," Cayden adds. As much as I love flying, I've missed fighting on the ground . . . well, if you can consider a ship to be ground.

"You may not be able to use the dragons, but I believe I have a way to aid our efforts," Zarius says, clasping his hands behind his back.

"Do you even know how to wield a sword?" Ryder asks, his tone dripping in condescension, but to his credit, Zarius doesn't rise to the jab.

"Quite well," he answers evenly. "However, I'm not speaking of blades. I'm speaking of magic." My brows furrow and I cross my arms. I wasn't aware he possessed any magic.

But my curiosity gives way to shock . . . because Zarius *disappears.*

There's nothing but an empty space where he was standing.

"All hells," Saskia mutters before abruptly screaming when Zarius reappears several paces from where he stood, holding a sword to Ryder's neck.

"As I said, I'm very proficient," he says while sheathing his blade, earning a murderous glare from both Saskia and Ryder, but I'm intrigued.

"You're an illusionist," Cayden says.

Zarius nods. "I'm able to manipulate the perception of those around me."

"Then why didn't you do that the night we met?" Saskia demands.

"He did," Cayden cuts in. "When I first saw him, his hair was blond, but it changed soon after he left the gambling den."

"I was piss drunk," Zarius flatly states while looking at Saskia. "I need to fully concentrate for the illusion to be believable. One wrong detail and everything could fail. It's extremely taxing, and I won't be able to wield a blade as I work."

"So that's how you stayed hidden in Galakin." I drum my fingers against the barrel. "You'd alter your features so nobody would know who to look for, even if they had an idea of where you were."

Zarius nods. "I chose Galakin because it would be the hardest kingdom for my father to send assassins to, but I was still an enemy prince no matter my standing with my father."

"Were you born with that ability?" I ask.

"It developed over time," he answers. "My people worship the God of Illusion, the Mind, and Memory. It's believed that my ancestors on my mother's side were gifted a drop of his blood, giving us our red eyes and, occasionally, magical abilities."

"Are you sure you'll be able to mask the entirety of the fleet?"

"If given the proper space to prepare, yes."

"Worst-case scenario, you fail and we die." Cayden shrugs, leaning back between my thighs. "It'll spare you from living with the shame unless your father ordered you to be captured alive."

"What a lovely vote of confidence, Cayden. I'm so glad you joined this conversation."

"Anytime, my love." He pats my leg.

"You'll still need to be prepared to fight once the illusion is unmasked. If we're to put you on the throne, then prove you'll survive the battle," Ryder says, bringing the conversation back to where we started. "You didn't fight when we first captured you."

"As I stated, I was piss drunk," Zarius reiterates. "And who's to say you're the best soldier I'll face?"

I laugh and follow it up with a cough in an attempt to cover it up.

Ryder tugs his shirt over his head and throws it to the side. "I'm not a soldier. I'm a general."

Zarius says something under his breath that I'm not able to hear as he mirrors Ryder's actions, removing his shirt to expose panes of lean muscle and a tattoo of a roaring snow leopard that takes up the entirety of his back. The tail coils around his waist, and its front claws are raised as it stands on its legs. This must've been his familiar. It's a memorial of what he lost forever inked on his skin.

Rhys steps forward as Zarius grabs a practice sword, as do the six guards who swore to Zarius in the prison. They were of higher rank and are now his king's guard, which is why they're sailing with us. They've had to take up bunks below decks where the crew rotates sleeping, but they're making it work. So long as nobody knocks on my door and asks to sleep in my cabin, I don't care how they sleep.

I glance between Rhys and Zarius, the older knight staring at the prince with unabashed pride. It's the look I've seen countless fathers give their children. Sometimes it's easy to identify an emotion when you've never known it. It stands out more, perplexes you. There's a nagging sensation to identify what it is so you can decipher why you've never experienced it or if you ever will.

Zarius's hair is white, wavy, and cropped beneath his chin, though he always pulls the top half back and leaves two pieces to frame his crimson eyes. Rhys's hair is shorn close to his scalp, but from the black undertone to his gray wisps, it's obvious he once had a full head of dark hair. I suppose their eye shape is similar, both deep set and angular, but not identical.

I just can't shake the way Rhys not only looks at Zarius but treats him.

I wrap my arms around Cayden's shoulders and press my chest to his back to lean close to his ear. "Rhys and Zarius . . . do you think . . ."

He crosses his arms over his chest. "I knew you'd realize it."

"Cayden Veles, did you know a secret and not tell me?"

He smiles over his shoulder. "I was waiting for you to figure it out."

I glare at him. "I'm going to light the lavender lingerie you wanted me to wear on fire."

His eyes narrow. "I'll put it on a shelf you can't reach."

We face forward again as steel collides, and the two men begin circling each other. Ryder's sword shoots forward, but Zarius blocks it. Ryder has more power behind his swings, but the prince is swift. It's clear Rhys trained him and catered to his strengths. If Ryder could go for the kill, Zarius would've been dead already. He has the battle experience that Zarius lacks, but sparring is much more drawn out.

"I was waiting for this to happen," Zale mutters, cocking a hip on Finnian's barrel.

"I think we all were." Finnian answers with a chuckle. "They've been at each other's throats since they met."

"Why?"

"He drunkenly complimented Saskia."

"I have sisters." Zale cringes. "I can't blame Ryder."

"I got over it." Finnian pats Cayden's shoulder and is quickly swatted away.

"All of my compliments to Elowen were made while sober," Cayden states.

"You drink whiskey like it's water," Finnian answers.

"I wish you would. Maybe you'd pass out and stop talking."

I roll my eyes. "You all make me look forward to battle just to get a break from this incessant bickering."

Zarius locks his blade with Ryder and darts his eyes to Saskia. A rare smirk forms on his lips as he says something that makes Ryder growl and shove him back. A sword drops to the deck, and Ryder's fist slams into Zarius's mouth.

Zarius wipes the blood from his lips. "For such a dignified general, I didn't think you'd resort to such a juvenile response."

"Fuck you," Ryder grits out.

"There's that sparkling eloquence."

Finnian sighs, shoving himself off the barrel to step between the two. "That's enough. Go take a walk."

The pair of them continue glaring at each other as they stalk off toward opposite ends of the ship. Saskia sighs while shaking her head, muttering about stupid men. I can't say I disagree. This vessel feels a whole lot smaller than when we first set sail.

"Both of you walk overboard to spare me a headache," Cayden calls out.

CHAPTER
SIXTY-TWO

ELOWEN

Z ARIUS STANDS AT THE BOW OF THE SHIP, HIS FINGERTIPS twitching as he stares out at the black horizon. I slide more knives through my waist belt, watching as fog begins to creep along the surface of the sea. The entirety of the fleet silently douses all lanterns as he works, not wanting Thirwen or Imirath to spot us on the horizon.

Sweat soaks Zarius's shirt as he works, making the snow leopard tattoo visible through the fabric as the mist thickens. It clings to the air around us and reminds me of the mist that once surrounded Aestilian, but I'm able to see through this. It must have something to do with Zarius's magic. It would be useless if we couldn't see the enemy, rendering us just as blind as them. I command the dragons to remain quiet and camouflage their scales as Zarius instructed earlier.

One by one, a blanket settles over a thousand ships, swallowing us whole. Thirwen and Imirath will see a storm approaching, but they won't know it is blood and fire that will rain down upon them. The dragons fly just above the masts of the first five ships, Venatrix remaining over ours, as the torches of the blockade flicker in the distance. I dust my fingers over my knives again as the silhouettes of the anchored ships appear.

Cayden nods to Ophir standing beside the railing, who responds by cracking his knuckles and clasping his hands together before shooting them out on either side. The ship sways beneath our feet as Ophir manipulates the tide to sail our ships through the rows in the enemy's blockade. On board the deck, steel slowly begins unsheathing the deeper we get into the guarded territory. Soldiers relax on the decks we float past, drinking and joking as the fog swarms them, entirely unaware of our presence. We're surrounded by purple and red sails on all sides, and I don't risk making a single sound.

Zarius's hands shake as he tries to hold the spell, but it can't last forever.

"They wanted war, give them hell," Cayden whispers before kissing the top of my head and stepping forward as Zarius falters under the weight of his fading spell. "Fire all cannons!" The illusion fades in a blink as blasts vibrate the deck beneath my boots. "Keep her steady, Ophir."

Bells clamor as the two ships on either side of us begin taking on water rapidly, their decks sinking into the abyss as my dragons descend, ripping into several ships with their claws and pushing them beneath the surface.

I pull two knives from my sheaths, kissing the blades in a silent goodbye as Finnian threads an arrow through his bow. "Shoot straight."

"Throw true," he responds with a smirk.

I whirl my blades upon the enemy, spearing two soldiers rushing to man their cannons, and throw two more at a pair swinging onto our deck with the ropes attached to their ships. They lose their grip and tumble into the dark waters below, taking my blades to their graves. Finnian picks off several more, and I grab my crossbow from where it rests at my feet to fire beside him.

Saskia rushes to an unmanned canon on our deck, crouching behind it to aim after the man beside her loads it. The bang booms like thunder as an iron ball shoots out and splinters the wood right where a ship meets the water. The pair of them quickly repeat their movements and send water gushing into the vessel.

"Sas!" I shout in warning, but I have no arrows left. I toss my crossbow aside and unsheathe another knife, aiming it at the soldier rushing at her back from where he landed on our deck. I cock my arm back, but an arrow pierces his neck before I have the chance to throw. She shrieks as blood splatters her cheeks and looks over her shoulder to the upper deck, and though nobody is facing us with a bow drawn in the air, one rests by Zarius's feet as he drags a blade from its sheath.

Zale steals my attention as he runs to the railing and swings his arms in a wide arc, sending a long blade made of flames shooting forward, and though the ships don't catch fire due to the enchantments, it severs fifteen soldiers in half.

"You had me holding fire when you could've taught me that?" I call out after disarming an enemy and slicing them down the middle.

"All in good time," Zale answers.

The next two ships we cross anticipated us while we fended off the previous, and soldiers swing onto our deck on both sides. Cayden and Ryder are there in an instant, leading a combination of Thirwen, Galakin, and Vareveth soldiers into battle. Blood coats the boards as steel clangs through the air. I throw myself into the chaos, becoming one with my blade as I've done since I had my first kill.

A female soldier sprints toward me, and I dodge the knife she throws at my face, ramming my blade into her stomach when she's close enough. Gritting my teeth, I push her toward the railing and kick her over the side. Ships sink all around us from the efforts of our soldiers and my dragons shredding them with their talons. Their snouts are covered in blood from ripping people apart, sometimes swallowing them whole.

A symphony of war is brought to life through the screams of those burning, bleeding, or thrashing in the water as sharks and monsters drag them under.

"Princess," an Imirath soldier croons as he steps into my path along with another mirroring his large stature.

"Prick." I unsheathe a knife and drop to my knees, spinning before the one who spoke realizes what's happening, and jam it through his thigh. One of the most valuable lessons Ailliard taught me was that it doesn't matter the size of a person, even a small serpent can take down a mountain of a man if they strike fast and hard. My lethality comes from striking quick and accurately. I don't need long to take down an enemy, just a blade.

He cries out and fists my hair to the point of pain as a knife cuts right for my neck. I wrap my free hand around his wrist while kicking my leg out to fend off his partner. I toss my sword high, flipping it through the air to grip the hilt and jam it behind me. Blood spills down my shoulders and back and I let his body hit the floor as I tug my blade free.

My head snaps to the side, but I manage to stand my ground as my cheek throbs. Blood trickles down my face, and I lick it away from my lips. "Now is that the proper way to treat your princess?"

"The ruination of Imirath is not my princess," he spits, crouching into an offensive position while slamming his sword forward.

I tsk, smirking at him between our locked weapons. "Someone should've taught you manners."

I knee him in the stomach and follow it up with a kick to his jaw. I manage to slice him in the stomach as he recovers, but it's not deep enough to kill him.

"Blood for blood," I say with a smile. "It's only fair."

He charges at me and steel clangs as he forces my back against the wide mast at the center of the ship. Splinters dig into my arms as I fend off his hold, and his sword shimmers as he rears it back and aims for my face. I free myself enough to duck, and a dull thwack vibrates my back as he embeds his weapon into the wood. Taking advantage of his poor swordsmanship, I shoot up and shove my blade through his chest, yanking it free and fisting his hair to bend him over in his final moments.

"It's proper protocol to bow to your princess."

I pat the Atarah sigil burned into the leather on his upper arm before letting him collapse on the deck.

A cannonball rips into our deck, and I drop to my stomach beside the corpse as wood rains down upon me. Blood soaks through my clothes, and I can't wait for all this to be over so I can bathe.

"You all right, love?" Cayden calls out, and though I don't spot him in the chaos, I'm not surprised he has one eye on me.

"Never better." I grimace while peeling a clump of hair off my sticky arm and shoving to my feet, taking hold of my weapons again.

In their desperation, a mixture of Imirath and Thirwen soldiers throw torches at our ship, knowing they're going to die and wanting to take us down with them. Zale orders the fire-wielders under his command, and they send the earthly fire back at our enemy. Their ships don't catch fire, but their sails do, which sends hot embers and sheets of billowing fabric onto those on the decks. I feel my power surge within me as I watch their movements, imagining it like the tide pushing and pulling as I let the magic flow through me.

The hair on the back of my neck rises, and I let my instincts guide me until my gaze catches on light blue flames flecked with silver billowing on a torch in our path. We're almost through the blockade, and though we've lost some ships, the element of surprise aided us in an invaluable way. The battle is nearly over, but I need to ensure we're not lost to it in the final moments.

Fucking gods.

Zale can't wield starfire—I don't even know how they got it—and it's just as unpredictable as dragonfire. I'm not willing to run the risk of failing, and rush to the edge of the ship as Zale and Finnian call out my name, but I ignore them, creating some semblance of a most likely horrible plan as I stab and dodge.

Honestly the best plans are born from absurdity and are only considered good if they work out.

"I need you to aim at that ship exactly like you have been," I shout above the battle while wrapping a rope around my fist and stepping onto the railing.

"Elowen." Saskia speaks my name as if she's trying to coax a feral animal not to bite. "What the hells are you doing?"

"Possibly creating a diversion, possibly dying, we'll see."

"Elowen!" she screams, trying to catch my ankles, but I leap forward with my sword drawn. Arrows fly all around but don't manage to hit me as I vault over the gap between ships. My boot slams into a woman's face, and the starfire torch falls from her grip as she collapses on the deck with my feet on either side of her. I jam the heel of my boot into her temple to knock her out, muttering a curse as another soldier recovers the torch before it hits their deck.

I'm swarmed in an instant, swinging my blade without looking just to keep enemies away from me. Someone else sails over the railing, barreling into the three soldiers on my left as arrows are fired from behind.

"Always surprising me, angel." Cayden offers his back to me so we're able to battle together.

"It keeps our marriage interesting." I stab someone through the throat and flick a bloody curl out of my face. "No thanks necessary for my service and devotion."

Corpses pile up around us as we fight dirty, watching from the corner of my eye as our ship sails safely past and Finnian's arrows no longer reach me. My limbs burn nearly as much as my lungs, and an axe flies above my head, splitting a charging soldier's face in half.

"I had him!" I shout.

"No thanks necessary," Cayden replies.

The blazing starfire captures my attention again as the soldier now holding the torch rushes toward the railing. We're too far to pry it from their grip and douse it. I call to the flames, beckoning them toward me as the man carries them farther away.

You are mine.

You belong to me.

You answer to me.

The flames flicker, slowly inching toward me, but the connection is severed when Cayden's arm wraps around my waist and he throws a knife through the person's neck. Starfire swallows the ship in an instant and singes the back of my arm as Cayden vaults us over the side, sending us crashing into the shark-infested waters.

The cold swallows me whole, and my ears ring at the sudden silence. He keeps us beneath the surface, the corpses and sunken ships illuminated by the firing cannons and blazing starfire. Even beneath the waves, I can feel the heat. The salt burns my eyes, but I don't risk closing them. Sharks swarm beneath my ankles and I force myself to slowly blow out the final breath I took, needing to savor the oxygen.

I cling to Cayden and force the scream that bubbles up my throat to stay locked behind my lips when a tentacle shoots up and wraps around a dead body, and then two more, dragging them down where I can no longer see. Two eyes that look like rubies blink open and stare at us. One eye alone is as tall as Cayden, and it's so dark that I can't see the full size of the monster's body. Though maybe that's a blessing considering at least fifty tentacles fan out around its rounded head. Cayden shoves me behind him, keeping a hand pressed to my back, rendering me immobile as the ancient creature gets closer. My lungs beg for air, but the fire is still too thick, and I don't think it's smart to offer whatever monster this is our backs.

Black spots dance in my vision and a soundless scream flies from my lips when another tentacle shoots forward, wrapping around Cayden's boot, but he doesn't stab it with the sword still in his hand. I tug at his shirt to free myself from his hold so I can stab it. I'm not proud enough to believe I can best a sea monster in its domain, but I'm not going to watch it drag Cayden down without a fight. His thumb rubs against my back, but he doesn't let me move away.

The monster clacks its razor-sharp teeth, the eerie sound vibrating and echoing throughout the space and sending the sharks darting away. It retracts its slimy tentacle while creeping up farther from the shadows and Cayden pulls me to the surface in time to see it wrap its tentacles around a handful of Thirwen and Imirath's ships. It drags some beneath the sea but swallows others whole, feasting on whatever soldiers swim to the surface.

"All hells," I say in a daze. "What did you do?"

He shakes his head, still keeping an arm around me as we swim through the burning wood and bodies. "I didn't speak to it or command it as you do your dragons."

"You did something," I sputter. "You never told me you speak fish."

He stops his paddling to glare at me. "Don't start."

"I've already begun and will not cease."

His sigh echoes against the water as he begins swimming again. "All it did was look at me."

"Maybe it thought you were pretty." He groans in response like he's debating leaving me behind to fend for myself in the sea, but he tightens his hold, smiling in spite of himself. "Do you know what monster that is?"

His eyes ping to Thirwen's sails, many of them burning in the aftermath of Zale's efforts. "I think . . . it's the kraken."

"I'm never swimming in the gods-forsaken ocean ever again."

Cayden manages to get us back to our ship and shoves me onto the ladder. The dragons sink their claws into the ships of the final line, sinking them as we enter open ocean again. I pull myself up and tumble onto the deck in a heap, and Cayden isn't too far behind. I'm too exhausted to even care that the wood is covered in blood, or that it vibrates as people surround us. I crack my eyes open, and Saskia, Finnian, Ryder, Zale, and Zarius are all staring down at us.

"This is my own personal hell," Cayden states as he sits up to avoid their gazes, but I remain reclined.

Zale shakes his head and is the first to break the silence. "You crazy bitch."

I'd be offended if his words weren't drenched in a mixture of astonishment and respect, and instead, I laugh.

CHAPTER
SIXTY-THREE

ELOWEN

M Y COAT FANS OUT ON THE UPPER DECK AS I LIE ON my back and stare up at the stars. They're so bright tonight that my dragons' scales glisten as they fly. I couldn't sleep which isn't unusual, but it's our final night on board. Aside from the battle, it feels as if we've escaped into our own world when we're on the ocean. I'd like to see more of Ravaryn when the war is over, and though the challenges will always come, I look forward to the day when I can wake up and enjoy my life.

I've never fought for glory or to be known as one of the greatest warriors in the history of Ravaryn when scholars simplify my life into a few paragraphs. I fight because I was hurt, as were the people and creatures I love, but I long for the day when I won't have to worry about whether they'll make it to the next. I want mornings in my garden, afternoons beside the lake, and evenings by the fire. I want to read all the books I consistently save for another day and try the recipes I've written on parchment.

I want to live, not just survive. If war was preferred, we wouldn't crave peace in the midst of it.

I pull the fur-lined fabric tighter around me when a breeze blows off the sea, and I'm thankful I remembered gloves before leaving the cabin. Cayden had to run a plan by Zarius, and I know I could've gone with him, but I wasn't in the mood to speak. Sometimes I crave silence like air. But aside from that, hearing Cayden's battle plans reminds me of what we'll face when we dock and it's like an invisible hand wraps around my neck. My breathing always picks up, as does my pulse, and the walls feel like they're closing in on me.

I couldn't lie in bed, in what was suffocating silence, and needed to find a quietness that calmed me. Cayden can fill me in on his plans when we dock, but I just want one more night of pretending we live the kind of life where I don't have to fear him dying from a blade. In another life, I'd really like to be ordinary with him.

The door below me squeaks on the hinges, and I know it's Cayden when his scent floats up to me.

"Wife," he says by way of greeting, claiming the spot beside me and placing a wrapped box between us. He rests an arm over his bent knee and places his other hand by my head. "Before you say that I buy you too much, I don't care, and this is your winter solstice present. So just open it."

"You have such a sweet way with words," I say while sitting up. "Your present is wrapped and under the bed."

"Is it lingerie?" he asks.

"Why? Do you want to wear something pretty for me?" He tugs on one of my curls, and I smack his hand away. He laughs, and I don't know why I'm taken aback by the sound. Maybe because it's so rare to see a smile on his face . . . but to see one so entirely unburdened is even more so. I hoard them like little treasures in my mind, keeping a portrait gallery of all the moments I pray I'll never forget. "Behave and I'll give you what you want. *After* I give you your actual present."

I had Blade forge a sword from an obsidian steel found in the caves deep in the southern Seren Mountains. The pommel has an oval sapphire framed by two dragon wings. He scratches the back of his neck, and his smile becomes tighter. Maybe one day it'll be easier for him to receive gifts, but I doubt it'll be anytime soon.

He avidly watches my fingers untie the lavender bow and unfold the matching fabric keeping whatever is inside hidden from me. He swallows and runs a hand through his hair again, plucking a knife from his thigh to twirl it between his fingers.

Gods, what's in here?

I lift the lid, revealing a thick leather-bound book with five dragons burned into the center and vines along the edges. My curiosity mounts as I hoist the heavy gift from the box and trace the divots. I flip the cover open, revealing a single word written in delicate script: *Hatchlings.*

I look at him, but he averts his eyes to the knife as he clenches his jaw.

When I flip the page, my breath is ripped from me as if I've been punched in the stomach. I trail my shaking finger over the small dragons staring back at me. They're so tiny they could fit in the palm of my hand if they hatched today rather than when I was an infant. I turn another page, and a detailed description of Sorin follows: his breed, his size, how his egg was incubated, his strengths, weaknesses, and personality traits. They're all details I've shared with Cayden in passing, thinking nothing of it as I rambled about my memories or things I learned.

Several drawings of Sorin in various positions and from different angles fill the parchment, followed by more pages dedicated to the other four. Judging from both the weight and size of the book, I think all twenty-four years have been illustrated, and I wouldn't be surprised if the twenty-fifth year is there as well considering our birthday is only a few weeks away. I'm a year older, which is so strange to think considering I view them as oversized babies.

I keep flipping as my heart fills to the brim and overflows, hugging the book to my chest after looking at an aged seven Venatrix so my tears don't bleed through the page. Cayden reaches forward to wipe them from my cheeks, looking as if I've stabbed him.

"I didn't mean to upset you," he murmurs. "If you hate it, you can toss it into the sea, and we never have to speak of it again."

I shake my head. "H-how?"

He licks his lips. "It was nothing, don't worry about it."

"This isn't *nothing*," I adamantly state. "This must've cost a fortune."

"You mentioned how much it hurt you to not know what they looked like as they grew up." He shrugs. "I just wanted to try to give you back a piece of what Garrick stole. I know it's not the same as—"

I shut him up with a kiss, climbing between his legs with the book still pressed firmly to my chest. His pulse thunders through him, and he threads his hands through my hair. I pour all the worries and anxieties that drove me up here into him, letting his love burn them away. I want to be here with him, not lost in my head or worrying about a future that hasn't come to pass. But even the sweetest fruits ripen and rot; nothing lasts forever, but clinging to him makes me feel like I can alter that inevitable path.

"You don't hate it?" he asks, pulling away.

"I love it." I blink away the remainder of my tears. "You have no idea how much this means to me."

"Fuck," he breathes, the tension fully melting from his broad shoulders as he tightens his arms around me and pulls me into his chest. "Thank the gods. For a second I debated jumping over the railing with the book."

I scrunch my nose. "I think I'll keep you around for a bit, Veles."

"Mmmm," he mumbles. "How generous."

He kisses me again, threading his fingers through my hair and holding me against him while I flip through the book. There are times when it gets to be too much, where the pain is overwhelming and I have to set it aside, but he continues holding me as dawn breaks over the horizon and I've read through it all.

CHAPTER
SIXTY-FOUR

ELOWEN

ALL TOO SOON, THE GRAVEYARD OF SHIPS I LEFT BEHIND in Port Celestria juts from the ocean and I send the dragons forward. Their flames burn what remains, and we hoist anchor to sail through the ash, getting as close to the shore as possible before filing into rowboats. Vareveth soldiers fill the beach and begin cheering as they spot their king and queen coming to shore with an armada at our backs. I'm buried in my dark blue-and-black leathers and furs with my sapphire and moonstone crown resting over my forehead. The cold feels even stronger after spending all that time in the Galakin sun.

"How are you holding up, princey?" Finnian asks Zale.

"I'll let you know if my balls freeze off," he mutters through a shuddering breath.

"I eagerly await the update."

Zale snickers in response as our boat wedges itself in the wet sand, and I step out onto my land, onto my home. I kneel and coat my palm in the coarse sand, rubbing it through my fingers. I will have the life I want after I spill the blood of those who try to take it from me.

"The wards are gone," I say. "As is their army."

"Garrick and Fallon must've ordered the army to retreat to Zinambra. They'll have a better chance at facing our army as one considering we have our full force," Cayden answers.

"So it all comes down to one battle."

One battle to determine the fate of thousands.

The fate of the Imirath throne.

The fate of everyone I love.

Finnian steps up beside me. "They'll cower behind their walls as they send their soldiers to do their bidding."

"Nobody will be left to guard their walls once the battle is over," Cayden says.

"And I'll smoke them out like the rodents they are if they try to hide," I add.

"Fallon is mine," Zarius states while climbing out of his rowboat, Ser Rhys and his king's guard following. He didn't touch a drop of alcohol on the journey home and trained on deck daily. He may not be the most skilled warrior, but he can hold his own. The illusion he created spared us substantial casualties and damage to the fleet, so anyone who denies his strength or request would be a fool.

"He's yours to do with as you wish."

He nods, but his shoulders don't loosen.

"We should advance," Ryder says. "I'm sure spies are in the woods, and we shouldn't risk an ambush. It'll take us at least two days to reach Zinambra if we stick to main roads and ride hard. The soldiers can rest when we reach the outskirts of the city."

Cayden nods, gesturing General Autumn forward.

She bows. "My king."

"Make sure the army is ready to march within the hour. We ride to battle."

"I'll see it done." She slams her fist into her chest twice as she turns away from us to begin her task. Zale squints into the darkness of the town consisting of small stone cottages along winding roads. It reminds me of Avaloria, the coastal town in Vareveth we flew to after the battle was over. They're not so different, and it's the people who inhabit towns like this who are crushed under the weight of their rulers' hubris and hatred. Candlelight flickers in the windows, adding a sense of life to the ghostly village. Snow floats down from the sky and coats roofs and overturned boats as smoke rises from chimneys.

"Do you see that?" Zale asks.

"See what?"

He juts his chin forward, walking with me until sand gives way to stone, and we begin hiking up a steep hill. Cayden, Ryder, Finnian, Saskia, and Zarius follow, not that I'd expect them to stay back. Not only are we in dangerous territory, but they're all unbearably nosy.

"The Atarah colors are purple and gold, yes?" Zale asks.

"Yes," I answer. "A purple banner with a golden trident spearing a crown."

My breath puffs in front of my lips when I slow my steps and take in the sights around me. Strips of dark blue fabric are tied around doorknobs, and bed sheets stitched with the Veles sigil hang along laundry lines draping over the streets, billowing in the wintery breeze. One by one, curtains are drawn back, and several sets of eyes land on me standing in their street. I can feel their fear through the glass, and perhaps they're wondering if we're here to harm them. I'm sure my father has spread tales of my ruthless nature, forging me into a monster that would harm the innocent through his ire.

I stride toward the door closest to me, unwrapping the blue fabric from the knob and using my teeth to tie it around my palm. I press my hand over my heart before lifting in the air, wanting to show them that they're safe from me, my dragons, and my army. A window creaks open, and a handful of ribbons in various shades of blue twirl through the air as they land beneath my boots.

"It's Princess Elowen," a little girl whispers.

I swallow the lump in my throat. I never thought I'd be welcomed in the land that was meant to be my home, but whoever sits on the throne doesn't define what that kingdom is. The people and the culture are what breathes life into land.

I smile warmly at the young girl in the window and wave to her. More windows begin sliding open, and more ribbons and fabric scraps join the others on the road. *Princess Elowen* is whispered until it becomes a cheer, a welcoming, and a reckoning all in one.

They grow bolder, coming out of their homes in long cloaks and boots once they see I'm not a threat. My group follows me on the road as I walk forward and freely through a kingdom that I was once a prisoner of. I thought I'd be received with hostility if I ever returned, but I'm received with warmth. I wonder what Garrick told them about me, if he said I'd burn their homes and slaughter their children. I'm aware I've done questionable things, but only what is necessary to survive in a world that has done everything in its power to remove me from it. I don't remember the names and faces of all those who have tried to kill me, but here I stand, in Imirath.

In the kingdom I never thought I'd step foot in again, let alone rule.

The people do not call out for my father, they call out for me. The lost princess who has returned to take what is hers.

CHAPTER
SIXTY-FIVE

CAYDEN

WE SLOW THE HORSES AFTER RIDING THROUGH THE night and the entirety of the following day with only small breaks during the journey. The closer we get to the castle, the fewer citizens populate the towns. They must've fled to the mountains to seek shelter from the battle. The roads are covered in muddy boot and hoof prints from the soldiers and their horses that pulled back from the border. It serves as an omen: one army flees and another approaches.

I kneel down to grip a soaked, bloodstained blue curtain with our sigil stitched upon it. Elowen strides beside me, the ribbons from her homecoming still laced through her thick braid, and a frown pulls at her lips as she regards what I'm holding.

"I won't be my father," she whispers. "I won't leave this world worse than how I found it."

She says the words like a reminder, like she fears seeing her father's traits in herself when she takes his throne. "You already have made it better." Elowen is ruthless, but the difference is that she is so out of survival, Garrick is so out of his hunger for power. If two thieves commit the same crime, their morality can often be found in their motives. I let the curtain slip from my grip, glancing toward the clearing up ahead where the army will camp. "Hope is like a drug. Once you experience it, you'll search for it in everything and crave it in your most vulnerable moments. You give these people hope. It's why they fled. They know a better world is coming and want to live to see the day it dawns."

"I didn't think you believed in things like hope."

"I don't." I grab Koa's reins and walk beside Elowen, leading him beyond the town. General Gryffin transported him from the castle stables so I can ride him into battle. "But I've always believed in you."

The dragons screech, drawing her attention to the sky as I tie Koa off on a post where I'll pitch our tent. "We should make a fire. Finnian asked me to go on a walk earlier, so we'll gather some wood."

"I'll get Ryder and Saskia," I answer, watching as she shakes out her hands and walks across the row to Finnian's tent, threading her arm through his as she erases the anxiety from her features. She's putting on a brave face for his sake. I catch Braxton's eye and jut my chin in their direction. He nods and trails them from a safe distance. The pair of them may be warriors, but we're too deep into enemy territory for me to take any chances.

Crackling flames fill the silence as the five of us gather a few leagues from the merriment of camp, sitting on downed trees as the last rays of the day are snuffed out. We all know what's to come, and it makes our group more somber. We walked this path to free the dragons, knowing it would lead us back here, but I don't think any of us anticipated how quickly we would return.

I've never had anything to lose, and now it feels like I have everything to lose. I tip my tankard against my lips, twirling one of Elowen's curls around my finger as she rests between my legs. She moves every few minutes to stir the stew in the pot resting in the embers. I'd offer to take over, but I know completing tasks eases her nerves.

"You're all acting like we lost the battle before it's even begun," she sighs, pouring some food into a dish for Finnian and handing it off to him.

Ryder spoons some into his mouth. "My apologies if the eve of battle is a dull affair, sunshine."

"Apology accepted." I don't know how she manages it, but Ryder's face cracks into a grin. "There is nothing tragic in this moment, so don't borrow tomorrow's pain for today's peace. If my world is to end tomorrow, there isn't anyone else I'd rather spend my last night with." Sorin and Calithea land in the woods behind us, huffing. "And you too, sweetlings."

The emerald and silver dragons curl themselves around our small gathering as the other three circle in the air above us. Elowen smiles, broad and beautifully, and it steals my breath before I drop my gaze. The woman with the biggest heart I've ever known will be the biggest target on the field. She's been a target all her life and gods, I know she can handle herself, but I never knew it would be this hard to watch her fulfill the deal we struck. Part of me wishes we had failed and lived in exile together as outlaws.

But she'd never be happy.

She'd never be whole without her dragons.

She loves those beasts more than most mothers love their children.

Finnian looks around at all of us. "This isn't my worst day, nor is it any of yours, so let's not sit around with sour moods and regret it in the morning."

"When I was locked in the dungeon," Elowen begins, and all of us pause. It feels like the world stops. She never speaks of her time in Imirath. "After the particularly bad beatings, I'd whisper, *Just one more day.* All I had to do was survive just one more day, and maybe the next I'd see my dragons, I'd find a way to break free. I wouldn't have the life I do if I gave up while fighting for it."

I bite my tongue and curl my nails into my palms to keep from charging the Imirath castle this very moment. She deserves so much more from this wretched world, and once the war is won, she'll have it.

"No matter what happens"—Ryder shakes his head—"I wouldn't give up this time with you all for the world."

Finnian raises his tankard. "To the families we choose."

"And to one more day with them," I finish.

I bury my unease and kiss her cheek when she takes her place between my legs again. Then someone lurking beyond the dragons speaks. "Do you have room for one more?"

Elowen's eyes glow gold and Sorin lifts his tail to let Zale into our small circle. "Always, princey."

Saskia's brows rise. "I thought you'd be spending the night with your soldiers."

"They regard me as a prince, and I care little for formality on to-night of all nights."

"So you enjoy it when you're not on the brink of battle?" Finnian asks.

Zale shrugs, taking some stew from the pot and nodding his thanks to Elowen. "I don't despise it. Would you if you were a prince?"

Finnian purses his lips. "Can't say I've thought much about it, since I'm an orphan-turned-commander."

"I never thought I'd relate to you on anything," I mutter.

"Isn't it amazing?"

"Try annoying." Elowen pinches me in the thigh with her surpris-ingly sharp nails. "Gods," I mutter, snatching her hand. "Yes, Finnian, I'm immensely glad we are both warmongering orphans. Happy now?"

"Immensely," she responds, mocking my voice and sending a wave of laughter washing over everyone in the group.

I bend down to tap my finger on her lips, lowering my voice so only she's able to hear. "Keep running that mouth, love. You're making me think of all the ways I'd love to shut you up."

"I'm counting on it." Her eyes spark with a challenge, and she bites the tip of my finger before turning back to the group and snuggling into my chest.

Sorin growls when a twig snaps. "Fucking hells," another familiar voice bites out, and Elowen calls the dragon off.

"Hello, Zarius," she says.

"I'm only here because I want to make sure you're not plotting without me, not because I wish to spend time with any of you," he says, claiming an empty spot at the base of a tree. "I didn't expect to nearly be burned alive."

Elowen rolls her eyes. "Sorin didn't even lift his head."

"They can still breathe fire while lying down."

"If it offers you any consolation, he already had his fill of goats so he probably wouldn't have eaten you."

Zarius's gaze cuts to the green beast staring back at him as he drawls, "Yes, that's quite comforting."

"We're not plotting without you," Saskia states. "Friends have dinner on occasion, though I doubt you'd have experienced that given your repellent personality."

"If *you* found a way to accomplish this feat, I'm sure I'll catch on."

Elowen hides her face in my chest to laugh, but Finnian sees her and it sets him off, followed by Ryder, because Finnian snorts like a damn pig. I wrap my arm around Elowen's shoulders to hide my face in her hair, but Saskia still sees.

"I hate all of you," she grumbles.

Her anger melts over the course of the night, and she laughs along with the rest of us at various jokes at one another's expense and stories we trade. But the pile of logs disappears, and then the second, and the third. When the camp has gone quiet, the gravity of the moment weighs heavily on us all.

The flames die out, leaving only glowing embers, and the cold creeps in. A sliver of the moon hangs high in the sky, and all of us know it's time to get some rest, but none of us moves—not Finnian, leaning against a tree; or Ryder, with an arm tucked under his head as he stares at the stars; Zale, as he finishes off his ale; Saskia, swaddled in a blanket beside me; Zarius, prodding the embers with a twig; or Elowen, with her head resting on my thigh.

"No goodbyes," Ryder says, getting to his feet and brushing off his pants. "I'll see all of you in the morning." He offers a hand to Saskia as Sorin and Calithea take to the skies again, nodding to us before he escorts his sister to her tent.

"I'll walk back with you two," Zale says to Finnian and Zarius. "It'll save me from the married couple."

Finnian snorts, kissing Elowen's forehead as he disappears into the darkness with the princes. I thread my fingers through Elowen's to tug her to her feet and drape my arm around her shoulders, tucking her against my body. Soldiers cease sharpening weapons and conversing with each other to dip their heads in our direction as we stride through rows of tents to get back to ours. I part the heavy fabric for her and let it fall behind me after ducking inside. There's nothing in here aside from a pallet of furs and a low-burning lantern, but that's really all we need for one night.

Elowen unclasps the buckle on her coat with shaky fingers, letting the fur-lined mass of dark blue fabric slide to the floor followed by her leathers and tunic. I mirror her actions, as she slips under the furs without a stitch of clothing. I'd probably be panting like a dog if I weren't so worried about her.

"El."

"Hmm?" she hums, staring blankly at the canvas wall.

"Angel." I sit beside her, gathering her in my arms, and tap the side of her head. "Don't leave me stranded while you're braving the storm alone."

She sighs, tracing the markings down my neck and over my shoulder. "You'll get tired of my ramblings one day."

"You could read off dry political texts for hours and I'll still be interested because I'd be watching you and listening to your voice."

She smiles, but it's weighed down by too many emotions. "I'm going to war against my father because of what he did to me and my dragons when I was a child, but I can't stop thinking about the soldiers who will never go home and the grief their loved ones will suffer all because I couldn't move on like Ailliard expected me to do."

I quell my rage at the mention of that sick bastard and focus on her. What she needs is not a rant about how much I hated the man. "Imirath has pushed against Vareveth since before we were even born, and before I became commander, they used to regularly raid Ladislava. Many of the soldiers fighting with us now have lost immensely at the hands of Imirath."

She nods and sucks in a deep breath. Thank the gods I'm getting better at using my words. "Maybe in another life we won't have to fight wars. Maybe we'll be happy and unburdened and simple."

"I don't want a different life with you." I press my lips to hers. "I want this one, and after tomorrow we will be happy and unburdened and simple. I swear it. I'll give you whatever you want."

"What do *you* want?" she asks, still tracing my markings. "What do you think of when you picture the future?"

I lick my lips, tucking a hand behind my head. "I told you that I've never let myself think all that much about it. I never really thought I'd have one."

"Think," she insists. "I know that's a hard concept for you to grasp but I trust your capability."

I lightly yank one of her curls. I always thought I'd die young, like I was living on borrowed time, so I never bothered thinking of a future beyond getting revenge. "All I see is you happy at home surrounded by books, pastries, and dragons, while wearing little to no clothing, but I'm open to negotiating how covered you are." She tilts her head, looking at me like she wants me to say more. I run my tongue over my teeth and loose a sigh. "Why don't you tell me these grand plans that you have, to give me some inspiration."

She bites her lip again. "We never talked about"—she swallows—"children. Everyone keeps throwing the term *heir* at us, but we've never spoken of it."

My gaze darts away from her, and I clear my throat. "You want them?"

"I don't know," she answers quietly. "When the dragons were taken away from me . . . their screams . . . I can still hear them, and they sounded so much like children. I can't go through that again."

"I don't think I'd be a good father, but I'd never let that happen," I say, a wave of protectiveness flaring up within me. There are some people in this world who would make it a better place by not procreating, and I truly believe I'm one of them, but what I do know is that I'd *never* let harm come to my children. "I won't be him."

"Him?" Her gaze softens. "Your father."

I fixate my eyes on the canopy above me. The walls in my first apartment were paper thin and I heard the screams of women as they gave birth, heard the sobs of their husbands when they bled out on the bed. Thinking of Elowen in that position . . . I can't.

She presses her lips to my heart. "You'll never be anything like your father." The urge to refute her statement rises in my throat. I look just like him. I'm wretched and selfish like him. I'm incapable of loving nearly anything in this world aside from the woman in my arms. "You stood beside me when it would've been easier for you to hand me over to my captors. You fought for me, and since we met not a day has gone by when I didn't know I was safe with you."

"I love the very bones of you." I force my eyes back to hers, a desperation clawing at my chest. "You know that, right?"

"I do."

"The world could be caving in right now, and I'd still stay right here with you, Elowen Veles." I press my lips to hers again, sitting up to switch our positions. "If this is my last night in this world, I need you to know that meeting you has been the most wonderful part of my life."

A tear leaks from her eye, but I place my lips to hers before she has the chance to respond. I need to feel her. I need to take care of her. I wrap my arm around her waist, pushing her chest into mine as she arches off the furs. I want to keep her like a secret, hidden from the world and all to myself. Gliding my knuckles up her cheek and sliding my fingers through her curls like we have all the time in the world instead of being on the brink of battle.

With one arm, she tightens her grip around my shoulders and trails her other hand down my chest to grip my length. Her hand languidly slides up and down, sending blood rushing to my cock. I dip my fingers inside of her as she strokes me, pumping and curling them as her moans press against my mouth.

"Please," she pants. "I need you."

"I know, love."

I line myself up with her entrance, slowly pushing inside. Normally I'd spend more time teasing her, but I need her, too, like I've never needed anything, never allowed myself to. It's terrifying, but I wouldn't give her up for anything. All my life I warded myself against vulnera-bility, but I'd strip off every piece of armor and hand her a blade.

Her legs tighten around me as I thrust into her, taking her in long, unhurried strokes. Making love not only to her body, but to her soul. I press my signet ring to her clit, and she whimpers against my lips as her thighs begin to shake. Circling it, I increase my pace, parting our faces just enough to watch her eyes roll back in her head as she calls out my name.

I wrap my hand around her jaw, forcing her gaze back to mine and fuck her through her peaks of pleasure, not letting myself finish just yet. I want her limp by the time we're done.

I turn her on her side and lay behind her, hooking one of her thighs over my arm and sliding back into her. She arches her back, and I fist her curls to bring her lips back to mine as I snap my hips forward. I force anything beyond this woman out of my mind, losing myself in her. She wraps her arm around my neck to keep us close and bites her lip. Her eyes are heavy with desire as she shoves her hips back into mine.

Maybe the people were right. Perhaps she is an enchantress. I taste divinity when our lips meet and between her thighs, and with every moan and hitch of breath I fall more into her thrall. When her skin is pressed against mine and she lets me into her body, I feel like a born-again believer performing a sacred ritual to a goddess.

I release her curls and slide my arm beneath her, needing to run my hands along her body. "You make me mindless for you," I say like an accusation, and roll her peaked nipple between my fingers. "Do you know how hard it is to be surrounded by people, knowing what it feels like to have you wrapped around me, and have to pretend like I don't want to pin you down and do exactly this?"

"Would you?" she gasps.

"Needy girl, you'd like that." I smile against her lips. "I'd never let anyone who's seen you naked leave with air in their lungs, but what a beautiful sight to keep with them in the underworld. But yes, Elowen"—I thrust hard—"if you let me, I'll come up behind you and slide my cock into you. In the garden, the library, the kitchen ... all hells, I'd stop a meeting just to sit you on my desk and spread your thighs."

My hand seeks her clit once more, crooking my fingers upward to crest her pleasure. She pants and squirms in my hold, burying her head in the crook of my neck. But I force her out and glide my tongue from her shoulder and up her throat, biting down on the spot that she loves just below her ear. She arches against me again as I suck, wanting to mark her. "Give me another, beautiful. You're almost there."

She comes undone, calling out my name and pulling me over the edge with her. Fucking gods, *this woman.* I'm ruined, have been since the day I met her, and I am irrevocably damned with every breath I take. She doesn't even have to be in my presence because she's in my mind, enchanting me like a temptress, and when I think of the legends of sailors who threw themselves to the tides when they heard a siren's song, I understand why. I'd follow Elowen anywhere, even to death.

I ease myself out of her and pull her onto my chest, running my hands through her messy curls. "Sleep, mia sirantia. I'll be here when you wake up."

"I love you," she murmurs, passing her thumb over her wedding ring and draping her leg over mine. Her blinks grow heavier, and I dust my fingers over every inch of her.

"I love you more than you'll ever know," I whisper after she falls asleep.

I'm wide awake, and I don't plan on sleeping a wink, not wanting to miss a second of savoring the feeling of Elowen's heart pulsing against mine.

Tomorrow I'll become the worst version of myself to fight for our future.

But tonight, all I am is hers.

CHAPTER
SIXTY-SIX

ELOWEN

I TIE MY BRAID OFF, FLICKING IT OVER MY SHOULDER AND letting it fall down my back. A golden House Veles sigil rests at the center of my forehead along a simple band. The same knives I've strapped to my legs every day rest against me, and I don black armored accents over my blue tunic for extra protection—a steel chest plate; shoulder, arm, and thigh guards all designed with draconic elements. They're thinner than a foot soldier's armor in favor of mobility while I ride, but still strong.

I've fought for my crown, bled for my kingdoms past, present, and future, and I will have my vengeance. I think of the dungeon, can smell the coppery blood pooling on the floor, hear chains rattling and the taunts of my father's guards, and feel a cane slapping into my flesh. I force myself to conjure the image of my dragons being dragged away from me, to feel the burning of my throat as I screamed.

I will not cease until the city flows with red rivers of my making. The princess of destruction can rise from the ashes as the queen of salvation.

The tent flaps part, and Finnian dips inside. He's wearing a full suit of armor with his bow strapped across his chest and a sword at his waist. "Scouts have reported the enemy has mobilized. Cayden sent a summons for all rulers to attend one final council meeting before the battle commences."

I nod, checking on my crossbows to ensure they're loaded properly, and swing a quiver of arrows over my shoulder. He holds the tent open for me and I hand my weapons off to a waiting soldier. "Attach these to Venatrix's saddle. I've already handled all the others." I let her see my eyes glow gold for good measure as I issue the command through the bond. "I've commanded her to let you approach, so you have nothing to fear, but don't linger."

"Yes, my queen." The woman bows, her black-and-blue armor glinting in the sun as she follows my orders.

The camp is a series of tents in the house colors of our allied forces: blue, red, and orange. Finnian leads me to the largest structure, with three peaks at the top, and though my leathers are lined with fur, the fire blazing within is welcomed. Cayden's helm rests on the table, as does the sword I gifted him for the winter solstice, and his obsidian armor easily makes him the largest man here.

Our generals bow their heads as I pass them, taking my place beside Cayden at the center of the long slab of wood covered in a map of Zinambra. The silver armor and red capes worn by Zarius and his generals are a stark contrast to Galakin's gold.

"You won't be with the fleet?" I ask Zale, taking note of his heavy plate. Naval soldiers favor leathers, considering they'll sink like a rock if they fall overboard.

"I'll be leading a battalion into battle. I want Thirwen and Imirath to see that their enemies are united against them on all fronts," he responds. "However, my fleet is mobilized." He points to the southern tip of Imirath. "There are no sightings of ships from the southern isles and our goal is to surround the fleet. If they flee to shore—"

"I'll burn them alive. They'll be like sitting ducks on the beach," I state before turning to Cayden. "I can command two dragons to remain with the army."

"No, you need to utilize their full force to monitor as much ground as possible. We cannot risk Garrick or Fallon escaping on a boat and raising supporters elsewhere. This war ends today."

"We should march soon," Ryder states. "It won't be long before they reach us, and they'll have an advantage if we don't get to the top of the hill."

"We will march soon, but we'll be marching to the base of the hill we stand upon," Cayden answers, and the tension grows within the silent tent as seasoned soldiers glance at one another.

"The base of the hill?" Ser Rhys asks. "I beg your pardon, Your Highness, but——"

"Mind your tongue and there will be no reason to beg," Cayden cuts him off.

Rhys bristles. "I'm aware you have experience, but standing at the base of a hill is suicidal."

"We will see Cayden's plan through," Zarius cuts in, and I manage to keep the surprise off my face. "He is the most notorious swordsman and would not have become the demon of Ravaryn through faulty plans."

Cayden dips his chin, and Zarius does the same. Something unknown to me is communicated through their eyes. Though it seems it's unknown to all of us. If I didn't trust Cayden to lead the ground forces, I'd pull him aside and demand to know what he's thinking, but even before I knew Cayden, I knew of him. His mind is as lethal as his sword.

"We would be fools to believe Imirath and Thirwen don't have as many scouts monitoring our camp as we have theirs, and not every plan can be spoken aloud," I say. "Cayden will not begin this battle at a disadvantage. If you can trust in anything, you can trust in his reputation."

Ser Rhys bows but doesn't say anything as battle horns blare in the distance, accompanied by the sound of thousands of boots and hooves slamming into the earth.

"Garrick and Fallon were not sighted with their armies, and I imagine their queens are with them," Cayden says to me. "Do what you must to force them out. I'll command a battalion to search the field for Nykeem and eliminate him. I'll be ready for the rulers when they flee the castle upon your assault."

I nod before glancing to Zarius. "As I said, the fates of the rulers of Thirwen will be up to you."

"Nobody marches before my command," Cayden states. "Any who disobeys will be shot down on my order. Ensure your soldiers are aware of this and begin preparations."

Everyone slowly filters away from the table to take to their individual tasks, and the dragons screech overhead. Their sharp eyes must be able to see the enemy already. I turn to Finnian first, now that only five of us remain. His throat bobs as he looks down at me and reaches forward to wrap me in his arms. He presses one hand to the back of my head and the other around my waist, hunching over a bit to accommodate our height difference as I stand on the tips of my boots.

"We survive together," he says. "Today is no different."

I hug him tighter. "Against the world, Finny. You and me."

He presses his forehead to mine, squeezing my hands as he blinks his teary eyes. "No other words. No goodbyes."

I press my palm to his cheek, letting the love in my eyes speak the words neither of us can manage to get out. I don't think there's a proper way to thank someone for loving you when you felt unlovable, becoming your family when you had no one, and morphing into a home when you didn't know what to look for in one.

"I promise to let you drag me to every tavern in sight when the battle is over."

His brows knot as he laughs, and we leave it at that. I won't be able to mount a dragon if I even contemplate a world without Finnian. We exist through what and who we love; it fills the cracks hatred chisels within us and gives us a reason to trudge through our worst moments. Even when you can't find the strength to live for yourself, you can for someone else.

Ryder and Cayden are the least emotional, and perhaps it's because they fight beside each other every battle, or maybe it's due to their experience. But Saskia has had to say goodbye to them an equal amount, and it's clear she's having a hard time reining in her feelings.

"I'm with you," Ryder says.

"I'll be on your left," Cayden responds, reaching forward so he and Ryder can clasp each other's forearms. "To battle, brother."

Ryder turns to Finnian, offering him the same goodbye gesture he gave to Cayden. "You'll be manning the archers atop this cliff?"

"Until the lines get too mixed, then I'll join the battle."

"Good. You've got the best aim out of anyone so at least I have a slightly lower chance of being hit with a rogue arrow." He sighs, stopping in front of me while pointing skyward. "You give those bastards hell and keep a wyvern from mangling my pretty face."

"You have my word you'll be just as pretty when the battle is over."

"Something to live for." His smile widens, but twitches when he turns to face Saskia, staring up at him with misty eyes. "None of that."

She blinks faster, her dark lashes glistening with the tears she's desperately trying to suppress as she flings her arms around his neck. Ryder tightens his hold around her waist, kissing the top of her head before he lets go. I throw my arms around Saskia next, breathing in her jasmine scent before taking one last look at a group of people who have come to mean more to me than I ever imagined.

"I'll see you soon," I say as Cayden threads his fingers through mine and leads me from the tent. Soldiers have already begun forming their ranks, and a mixture of House Veles, House Ilaria, and inverted House Liluria banners flap in the wind. They patiently wait for their leaders to escort them to the battlefield, prepared to fight, prepared to die.

I'm not one for speeches, but I release Cayden's hand and step forward knowing this will be my final chance to address the army before I take to the skies.

"Soldiers of Vareveth," I begin, raising my voice enough to ensure they can all hear me. "You are of the dragon kingdom, and you must fight as if the very fire that resides within the winged beasts lives with you. A dragon does not cower in the presence of steel, and nor shall you." They slam their swords into their shields twice. "I was born to House Atarah, one of the oldest ruling houses of Ravaryn, but at the end of this battle it will be House Veles banners adorning this city. It will be ours!" The soldiers slam their steel together again, raising their voices in a cheer as I persist. "To our allies who have come here to join our fight, the loyalty of a dragon is not a fickle thing. You stand with us today, and we will not forget your bravery. In being here, you help free the people of Imirath—my people by blood—from the grip of the tyrant Garrick Atarah. When the sun sets on this day, you will stand as the victors of a new world anointed in his blood!"

The cheers are deafening as I look back at Cayden, and he takes hold of my hand again to escort me through the lines. Soldiers look to us with respect and adoration. My heart pounds in time with the war drums vibrating the earth as the battalions call out for vengeance, for retribution, for the death of their enemies.

I hope my father can hear them from where he cowers in his castle.

I hope he's looking to the skies with fear, waiting for me to descend.

I have come for my throne, and I will not cease until the Imirath crown is ripped away from him.

We step through the tree line, and anxiety tightens my throat. I can put on a brave face for the soldiers but not for Cayden. He's going to be down there on the field leading the charge, and our enemies will be pointing their blades at him. I know he's strong. I know he's survived countless battles. But all it takes is one second for your life to change and tragedy to strike.

"Please don't," I whisper in a thick voice, looking down at his boots when we stop beside Venatrix. "We said everything we needed to last night." I don't care that he doesn't know what our future looks like because I want to live it. I won't let Garrick take away someone else I love. *I can't.*

"I'll only say this once." He frames my face with his hands to keep my gaze locked on his. "None of this is worth it if you don't walk off that field. I have no intention of dying, but I need you to know that if I meet my end today, no grave will ever claim me and my soul will never find rest until it's with yours again. I will always find a way to get back to you, even in death."

I don't know who moves first, but in the next second my arms are around his neck and his are around my waist, and our lips collide. He kisses me like he'll never see me again, like he wants to pour every ounce of his love and protection inside of me to keep me safe.

I'm breathless when he pulls back, and he leans in to give me another quick kiss as if he can't help himself. "If you don't get on her in the next thirty seconds, I don't trust myself not to tie you to a tree again."

A half smile weighed down by far too many emotions stretches across my lips, and letting him go is one of the hardest things I've ever had to do. It feels like something is severed between us when I break the contact, pulling away from him sooner than I'm ready.

"Show them why you've been named the demon of Ravaryn," I say, looking over my shoulder with one boot on Venatrix's wing. "Be every bit as bloodthirsty as the whispers claim you to be; do whatever you must to survive and come home to me."

"I will," he answers as I settle myself in Venatrix's saddle, and watches as I hook the straps to my harness. "And you must show them who you are, El. They were fools to make an enemy of you. Now slaughter them for it. You are the dragon queen; you are everything your father feared you'd become. Force him to watch as you burn his reign to the ground."

CHAPTER
SIXTY-SEVEN

CAYDEN

*T*HUMP.
> *Thump.*
> *Thump.*

Thump.

The sun illuminates the pebbles and dirt raining down from the peak of the sloped terrain. Our horses stomp in place; most of them are battle-seasoned and know we're at a disadvantage. Horns blare, closer now, signaling the cavalry to prepare to charge. Banners displaying both the House Atarah and House Liluria banners crest the top of the hill, and a long row of soldiers follows.

A horn blares again, and they stop at once. The line stretches back as far as I can see. I nudge my horse in the side, signaling Koa to step a few paces in front of my army. The soldiers grow antsy around me, and I can't blame them—they don't know what's happening. Zarius has made sure of that.

"Hold your ground!" I command. I couldn't risk revealing the plan to anyone aside from the water and fire cults who helped it come to pass. Their blood oaths forbid them from betraying Elowen and me. If Ryder or I had worked on it, we would have been noticeably absent, but Zarius was able to shroud the surroundings while the cults worked.

"Archers!" I shout, giving Finnian the command.

"Nock!" Finnian orders as the charge begins. "Loose!"

A volley of arrows flies overhead, spearing through several horses and enemy soldiers. I watch as some are trampled beneath their on-coming army, their bodies swallowed up in seconds. I unsheathe the blade strapped across my back, but keep it lowered at my side as thousands of battle cries fill the air. Another wave follows upon Finnian's command, taking out several more as the enemy aims their spears, coming at us with the promise of death on the ends of their pointed tips.

"Steady!" I call out. My soldiers can't move yet. Even one mistake can ruin the plan.

I take a moment to glare up at the obsidian spires of Imirath's castle cutting through the clouds. I began this fight for my mother and for myself, avenging two deaths that took place that day despite only one soul crossing into the underworld. Becoming the worst version of myself was necessary for survival, to get myself to this moment, when a boy born with nothing to his name can challenge a king.

"Do not fight for me—fight for yourselves, fight for your families, and fight for whoever you left behind who will suffer if you fall today! Don't fight for glory—fight because each enemy you kill is another threat eliminated. I do not fight with you as only a king; I fight with you as a man avenging his wife, and a son avenging his mother. Fight with the outrage of those who were trampled under the weight of this war and the corruption of Garrick Atarah." I shout above the symphony of war as the enemy continues to near. "Ride with your swords drawn and bestow death upon those who challenge you! You show no mercy, you give no grace, and you kill every last bastard who stands between your queen and her rightful throne!"

Hundreds of branches snap, exposing the trap as a mixture of Imirath and Thirwen soldiers fall into a cavern hidden by various things from the terrain: twigs, snow, rocks, moss, and leaves. They're unable to slow their horses given the speed they gained from charging down the hill. Their eyes widen with fear as they jerk on the reins, but it's in vain. Bodies upon bodies pile on top of one another, helpless and immobile, stacking up like bricks.

Ophir and Asena commanded their cults to dig as deep as they could, both using their element-wielding to their advantage. Water mages pulled on the water within the damp earth to create the curved trench, and the hill at our back prohibits the army from surrounding us, even if they could manage to jump the gap. Fire mages melted through boulders and defrosted the earth under their fingertips the farther they dug. Zarius utilized his illusion magic to mask the entire plot, and didn't have to use it to shroud the trench.

The mages blended it perfectly with the earth around it.

I raise my sword high into the air when the trench is stuffed to the brim. Hundreds of dead on their side, and not a single casualty on ours yet. "CHARGE!"

CHAPTER
SIXTY-EIGHT

ELOWEN

"Zayèra!"

Venatrix's red flames cut a line down the beach, engulfing the enemy soldiers climbing out of rowboats and trying to run toward the battle. Our allied forces advance on the tide, firing cannons to push Imirath and Thirwen back as they fight for position. Smoke rises where I patrol the beach and castle in the clouds, and though we've put a significant dent in their navy, the remaining ships are still numerous and filled with skilled sailors. I unhook the crossbow from where it's strapped on Venatrix's saddle and command her to descend.

The wind screams in my ears, nearly drowning out the warning made by a soldier on deck. "Dragon! Dragon approaching!"

I tighten my hand on the saddle horn, aim at a woman manning the cannon pointed at the peak of Galakin's fleet, and pull the trigger as Venatrix rips into the deck with her claws, gouging deep enough to send water spilling into the vessel as she pushes it down into the sea.

Her tail drags through the ocean as she uses it to steer herself through the slim gaps between ships. My saddle straps strain when she flips upside down, letting another volley of arrows deflect off her armored scales before righting our position again.

I look over my shoulder to ensure we're far enough from our fleet to give the command. "Zayèra."

Her flames spill from between her lips and engulf seven ships and whoever was stationed on them. The dragonfire doesn't simply burn the soldiers, it melts the flesh from their bones and then blackens them. When dragons fly to war, they become the gods of it. Mortals and steel are mockeries of their might.

Bells ring out from behind, and I look to the Vareveth fleet. They have the advantageous position; they shouldn't be calling for aid. I order Venatrix to fly above the masts to grant me a better perspective and I blink slowly while staring out at the horizon filled with purple sails . . . but it's not Atarah sigils stitched upon them . . . it's the crescent moon of House Vellgrave, the deceased house of the southern isles before they were conquered.

My hands tighten on the saddle horns.

It's considered treason to fly the sigil. If they were loyal to Garrick, they'd be sailing under Atarah banners, but I can't ignore the possibility of a trap. We haven't heard anything of the southern isles aside from the initial rebellion, and the territory is claimed by Garrick. I look to the Vareveth fleet again, and unease prickles my palms. Our navy will be pressed between Imirath and the southern isles fleet if they haven't come to fight for us.

"Solka." I command Venatrix to fly out to them and summon Sorin and Delmira to follow. We soar over our navy and quickly gain on the approaching fleet. Venatrix roars at the head of the pyramid, but I force her not to burn them yet, and our bond strains. She rebels against the command; mercy is not in her nature. "Lotas, Venatrix."

She obeys the command when said in Ravarian. It carries more weight in their minds.

Bile rises in my throat when I look closer and realize the bowsprits of each ship are not adorned by carvings . . . but bodies. Blood soaks through Imirath soldiers' armor and drips down the bow of each approaching vessel. I descend, needing a closer look before deciding whether I think they're truly here to fight with us.

Venatrix's claws sink into the deck of the ship leading the fleet and it nearly capsizes under her weight. She lets out an ear-piercing roar, sending everyone on board to their knees. "One wrong move and I'll burn you alive."

"We've come to fight for the demon king and dragon queen," someone cries out in desperation, and I take a moment to look them over. All on board are in bloodstained ordinary clothes, looking more like fishermen than a naval force, but it's their builds that make it known they're fighters—their scars as well.

"And if anyone tells a lie, I'll feed them to my dragon," I state. "Venatrix is a bloodfury—she craves it—and even your entire crew won't fulfill her appetite."

Wood creaks as a man rises from where he knelt, and I pull my crossbow free and aim it at the upper deck. He pauses and holds his hands up while awkwardly crouching. "What my soldier says is true, Your Highness. We have come to aid your efforts against Garrick Atarah."

"I take it you're the captain?"

"Yes, my queen."

I aim the loaded bolt at his heart. "Why should I trust you? I don't want to burn you, captain, but I can't let you near my fleet if I perceive a threat."

"Your king is a southerner."

"Half," I correct. "We got word of your rebellion, but Cayden's name was not stated when you called for your rightful king. He has no relation to House Vellgrave."

"House Vellgrave is gone, but King Cayden Veles is the only ruler I will bend my knee to. He has the blood of the southern isles in his veins. Noble, commoner, it matters little to us. Long have we suffered under the reign of your father. He pulled the soldiers who patrolled our land to Zinambra in preparation for the battle, and we rebelled, knowing you and King Cayden were coming."

It sounds too good to be true, but not only would I be a fool to execute them, I'd also be no better than the man they're desperate to be free from. The man I'm desperate to be free from. I look around the ships that sailed from their isles and not a single weapon is drawn against me, not a single arrow pointed at my throat.

They sailed here for freedom, and for Cayden. I wish he could witness the people from his father's land choosing him in a way his own father never did. I think he can learn to love the southern isles, to honor their culture as Garrick never did.

"If you are with us, then split your ships and help us surround the peninsula. Garrick and Fallon cannot escape." I don't have the time to stay here and speak. Calithea and Basilius continue monitoring the beach and burning whenever necessary, but I need to get back to watching the castle. "If you turn your cannons on my fleet, you will not live long enough to see the end of this battle."

The man presses a fist over his heart before placing both hands on the helm. "To the king!"

"To the king!" the crew echoes, and Venatrix flaps her wings to rise off their deck. I fly above them, watching as their ships slice through the surface. My breath rushes out of me as their fleet splits in two and they follow my command. The southern isles truly rebelled, and they did so to bend the knee to Cayden. It's now four kingdoms against two in the water, even if our Thirwen numbers are extremely low. Immense pride swells within me. Oh gods, I can't wait to tell Cayden, but I need to focus on getting through the battle first. There hasn't been any sign of my father or King Fallon.

I unhook myself from Venatrix and jump onto Sorin's back. Venatrix is out for blood, so remaining on the beach will fulfill her craving, but I need to be on my fastest dragon in case I spot Garrick. We leave the sand behind and cross into the city. Citizens of Zinambra run along the canals and narrow streets, screaming under the shadows of my dragon's wings. They duck behind barrels and flee into shops and homes . . . as if mere stone and wood could protect them if I decided to burn the city. But I will not sit upon a throne surrounded by ashes of the innocent. I want only one corpse at my feet today. Sorin lands on a tall building, his talons wrapping around the edge as he roars at the castle.

Everything looks so similar to the way it did when we were here last. Dragon sconces still line the roads and curved stone bridges that stretch over the canals. Islands within the bays still house estates, restaurants, and extravagant shops. The dark stone houses are just as lovely as they always were, but there's one thing marring the otherwise beautiful city: *the castle.* My heart pounds in my chest as I look at it, and Sorin cries out again, sensing my growing unease as the memories flood me. My lip curls while looking at the dragon statues still bordering the entrance. I thought Garrick would've removed them after hearing of my and Cayden's sigil, but perhaps that's why he didn't. He didn't want to seem like he was scared.

Yet he cowers behind the same walls he locked me in, clinging to his throne like a lifeline while his soldiers fall on the field. I was born here, bled here, fled here, but I won't be able to rule here until Garrick dies. I'm no longer a ghost, or the princess in chains. I am Elowen Veles, the dragon queen, and my father can scatter stone dragons throughout his kingdom in hope of projecting their might upon his reign, but he will never ride a dragon. He will never be one with the beasts that are fire made flesh.

I want him to face me.

I want him to see the monster he created.

I want him to fear me as I once feared him.

Sorin leaps from the roof, spreading his wings wide and carrying us closer to the structure that was once nicknamed the impenetrable castle. He should've known that one day his monster would return to break her cage. Fleeing wasn't enough; it will never be enough. For as long as I live, I will think of this place and never see its beauty. All I see is death, and I want everyone to see it as I do.

Sorin glides toward the entrance, tipping his wings up to fly to the top of a towering obsidian spire. We rise above the castle, and Sorin fully extends his wings while screaming, screaming, and screaming again. The agony laced through the sound pulls at my heart and twists it. I tighten my grip on the saddle horns as he sharply dives and spits green flames down the spire, twirling around it. It crumbles and crashes into the earth as he continues his destructive pursuit. Calithea joins him, raking her claws down the front of the castle and roaring through the gaps she cleaves. Venatrix and Delmira remain at the beach, but Basilius's humongous lavender body descends upon the bridge leading to the main entrance, ripping it with his claws as he melts the dragon statues by the entrance that were almost as tall as him.

I keep the bond open, letting their anger and pain flood through me as they burn and decimate our prison. Garrick tried to take everything from me, from us, but I sank my claws into fate and ripped it to shreds. My anger has simmered for years and boils from me now, scalding all in my path.

"Face me, father!" I shout. "I traveled all this way; will you not say hello to your daughter?"

After all the spires have fallen, Sorin bathes the roof in a blaze so hot I feel it pulsing against my cheeks. Smoke stings my eyes, and dust floats into the air as, stone by stone, half the roof collapses in on itself. Sorin latches his claws on to the crumbling ledge, throwing his head back and roaring.

"FUCKING FACE ME!" I stand on Sorin's back, but all that does is give me a fresh perspective through the green, silver, and lavender flames. With the state of the castle, my father will be forced to flee. Towers tumble into the canal at the base of it, blazing ramparts fall haphazardly, and what's left of the structure wobbles and sways as the assault continues. I project Garrick's face into my mind and keep the bond open in my chest as I take my seat again. Even if he escapes my sight, he will never escape the dragons.

Sorin's head cuts to the left and the ledge collapses in his wake as he shoots us toward the ground on the eastern side of the castle. Mad laughter bubbles up my throat when I realize why he acted so abruptly.

Garrick Atarah is finally outside his precious castle walls.

Calithea bursts through a crumbling tower, roaring as she joins us, and I command Basilius to attack the wyverns now flying toward us. Wyverns are naturally smaller than dragons, but compared to Basilius, they look like hatchlings. Perhaps my father thought he could escape into the Seren Mountains as Cayden and I once did, but the senses of a dragon are too sharp to be evaded by men.

Wards in the shape of a small dome glow at the center of the small royal party, leaving eight guards from Thirwen and Imirath to fend for themselves. They're not the ones I came to kill, but perhaps there's some truth in being in the wrong place at the wrong time. They chose their fate when they followed my father and the rulers of Thirwen out of the castle. To their credit, they don't flee, but their drawn swords are pathetic as Sorin descends upon them and scorches their flesh and the earth beneath them in green flames.

When they clear, nothing but charred bones surround the wards that are still intact. I command Sorin to land in front of them, and Calithea takes the rear. The pair of them slam their tails on either side, locking the rulers and mage within a circle of green and silver scales. They're shouting at the distressed mage within, and I smile while meeting my father's dark, fear-filled eyes.

"Zayèra."

CHAPTER
SIXTY-NINE
ELOWEN

GREEN AND SILVER FLAMES SLAM TOGETHER AND STRETCH high above the trees, pushing against each other, mingling and melding, as black-and-white sparks rain down. Within the fire, I listen to the mage scream under the weight of my dragons' power as she desperately tries to remain strong. Sorin and Calithea continue blowing, but instead of remaining on Sorin, I slide down his wing.

This is our fight, together.

My power pulses under my skin and I close my eyes, picturing a building wave, letting it start out as nothing more than a crest along the surface and watching it become a tidal wave strong enough to swallow a mountain.

I am made of fire, and I do not fear it; I become it.

I open my eyes again, calling Sorin's and Calithea's flames to me as I stand evenly between them. Silver flames coil around my left arm and green around my right, and pool in my hands. I meet my father's gaze though the dragonfire as the tidal wave crashes on the shore, shattering the earth beneath its might. My hands shoot out on either side of me before I slam them together as Zale did back on the ship, and a blade of green-and-silver flames forms between my palms.

It flies forward, and the wards shatter into what looks like a thousand glass shards. My dragons jut their wings out to protect me, the membranous tissue illuminated by the blast, and don't move from their position until they're sure I won't get burned. I step forward as they slowly slide their wings back, keeping them close to me as Sorin snarls low in his throat. My eyes glow gold as I stare down at the group of five sprawled out in the snow. Calithea bites the head off the mage while Sorin swallows her body. Asena told me not every mage has the ability to portal, and I doubt she did or she likely would've done so while surrounded by fire, but I can't risk Garrick being whisked away.

Queen Aveline of Thirwen clings to King Fallon where they've collapsed, and a woman shrieks and sobs while grasping at Garrick's cloak. *Ah, his new wife.* She doesn't show signs of pregnancy, but that doesn't mean she isn't.

"Don't fret, lady," I say. "I didn't plan on calling you mother. I had one of those already and well . . . let's just say the name is a bit of a curse coming from my lips."

"Don't speak of your mother," Garrick states, the first words he's said to me since I fled Imirath over a decade ago. His voice raises the hairs on the back of my neck, makes bile churn in my stomach, but I show no outward sign of being bothered. Never again will I let him think he has any power over me.

"Or what?" Though I'm looking at my father, it's through the eyes of an orphan. I never watched his dark hair begin to gray. I never noticed when the lines in his face became etched over time. He may have sired me, but he's no father of mine. He stands to his full height, which isn't that impressive, and doesn't bother offering his wife a hand up. "I see you're just as charming as you were when I left." I chuckle. "I thought you'd be taller."

The other rulers manage to clumsily get to their feet. Fallon keeps a protective arm around his wife. His long blond hair clings to his face, wet from the snow, and her dark hair does the same.

"What will you do to my children?" Queen Aveline asks, her blue eyes blown wide as she glances between the dragons.

"Their fate is not mine to decide. That duty is allotted to your son." I look to Fallon. "Prince Zarius. Heir to the Thirwen throne."

Fallon's lips part in a snarl, but before he has the chance to spit vitriol, Calithea shrieks to drown out his voice. "Have some manners, Fallon. Threaten or insult me, and my dragons will be quick to end you."

"And you won't?" my father's wife asks, the tremble in her voice evident.

"I prefer to toy with my prey."

Stones from the castle continue falling all around us as I look at my father again. It seems fitting that both he and his precious castle will share the same fate on the same day. It's said that captains go down with their ships, and my father will forever haunt the decimated and broken halls of this place.

I order Calithea through the bond, and everyone takes a step back when my eyes glow gold again. She resists, not wanting to leave me while in the presence of the enemy, but I hold firm in my command. She nuzzles her snout into my side, and I caress her scales without taking my eyes off Garrick.

Calithea closes one claw around Fallon and Aveline, and another around my father's wife, giving me one last look before taking to the skies to carry them back to our camp. They scream and beg for mercy they won't find from me. I need Thirwen's soldiers to see their king and queen have been captured, and for Imirath to see my father's wife. It'll get into their minds and fester, and no matter the state of the battle, they'll have nothing to fight for because they'll know they've lost. Swords will grow heavier, swings less precise, and eventually their blades will slip from their fingers as they begin the journey to the underworld.

Garrick lifts a brow, the first change in his stoney expression since I've seen him. "You sent a dragon away."

I unsheathe the blade at my waist. "I've never needed flames to kill you." He remains still and stone-faced, not moving to grasp the blade strapped across his back. His pristine armor makes me laugh. "That's a lovely costume but I think you're a bit old to be playing knight. Draw your sword."

His nostrils flare, but he obeys. The hilt of the golden blade is encrusted with purple amethysts, and I wonder if he's ever used it. "What I did, I did for the good of Imirath."

"And how's that decision working out for you?"

"The prophecy has come to pass," he hisses. "You have destroyed the seat of our house and sullied yourself with a bastard."

"Your house," I amend while twirling my blade. "My name is Elowen Veles, and I'd rather be the queen of a bastard than daughter to a king who couldn't hold a throne that was handed to him. Even now Cayden is on the battlefield while you try to scurry away like vermin."

"But you *will always* be my daughter." I grit my teeth. "You will always be an Atarah, no matter your name. Your heirs will be Atarahs. You will never escape the blood that runs through your veins."

"Perhaps not." I tighten my grip on the hilt. "But you shouldn't be so concerned with my blood when yours will soon coat my blade."

I don't wait for him to advance and swing my sword. He juts his forward and the steel vibrates, sending small shockwaves up my arms. I'd love to draw out his death, make it last for days, keep him in a cell and make him beg, but his death will end the war. He's not worth losing sleep or peace for. He's just a pathetic little man with poor footwork. It's clear he's never truly faced a skilled swordsman. He moves as if fending off an instructor, not fighting for survival.

Sorin growls as we circle each other, no doubt hating having Garrick this close to me. Sorin has always had a protective streak woven into his soul, even before he bit off Garrick's pinkie; it would show whenever my father was nearby. As a hatchling, he would perch on my shoulder and scream his head off whenever Garrick was present. I still have the scars on my shoulders from his tiny talons sinking into my flesh without him realizing.

I move again before Garrick can react, utilizing the full capacity of my skills and cutting him across the thigh. He cries out through clenched teeth but manages to stay upright as he juts his sword at me.

I spin away with ease and click my tongue while slicing just above his chest plate.

"If you're going to be a warmongering cunt, at least have the decency to practice your swordsmanship."

He swipes for me again, summoning some force within him, but he's still no match for me. "You hate me so much, and yet we are so similar."

I raise my brows. "I'm much prettier."

"I heard you killed Ailliard," he pants. "I would've done the same thing. If someone tried to take my crown from me, I would've brought war to them."

"And yet only one of us knows how to win a war." I shove him back with our locked blades, and swing again, severing his bone. His four-fingered hand thumps on the ground as his screams thunder throughout the forest, mingling with my laughter spilling through clenched teeth. *This* is the man who chained me. *This* is the man who ordered my torture. "Where's your boldness? Does it disappear when I'm out of shackles? There is no one for you to cower behind, Garrick. There is no one to save you from me."

I slice his other hand clean off and jam the hilt of my blade between his shoulders, sending him tumbling into the snow. "You're pathetic."

I command Sorin to wrap his claw around Garrick and hoist him into the air, squeezing and squeezing until he's choking and sputtering, begging for release. Drool dribbles down his chin as his eyes bulge out of his head. Sorin releases him a fraction, just enough for him to find reprieve, and tightens his claw again.

As he's extended in the air, I slice through his boots, adding his feet to the appendages littering the ground. "Just in case you had hope of escaping."

Sorin lowers Garrick so he's at eye level with me. "Throw him down."

Garrick's arm snaps from the force of the impact, made worse by landing on what might've belonged to a wall of the castle. He screams, and I watch as tears run down his cheeks. Just as I did with Robick, I commit this image to my memory. This is the man who should have loved me, and instead spent years of my life torturing and hunting me. He sent men into my cell to break me and only stepped in when they wished to rape me because he wanted to sell me off to the highest bidder on the marriage market.

"I want you to know something before you die," I say. Sorin's head stretches above mine as he spreads his wings on either side of me. "If you had been different, I never would've fought against my kingdom, but the prophecy was true." His eyes find mine, gaze flickering between me and my dragon, flooded with fear. "I am the ruination of the old Imirath, your Imirath, the Atarah's Imirath, and I will bring its salvation through my reign. I would have lived in peace, but you started a war between us, and now it's time to end it."

"Elowen—"

"Do not speak my name."

He gurgles on his blood, but it's not enough. I need to hurt him more.

I drop my blade and call upon the fire that lives within Sorin, summoning it through his scales. A web of green flames stretches between us and weaves around my fingers. I press the fingers of my free hand into the hollows of Garrick's cheeks and force his mouth open as he sobs, keeping the green flames burning in my other hand well within his sight.

"I hope making an enemy of me was worth it, father." I tighten my grip when he squirms. "You've lost. Imirath is mine, and it belongs to House Veles. I'm loath to teach you an invaluable lesson mere moments before you die, but if you're going to order an execution, be the one to swing the sword. If not, you risk failure, and nothing festers hatred quite like time."

"The prophecy—"

"Do you know what happens to a rat when it's burned, father?" I chuckle, cutting him off. "The same as it does to everything else."

I slam my hand over his mouth, commanding the fire to grow through him like vines. He jerks and screams as I force the fire to continue burning him alive. It floods his veins and boils his blood. The skin of his face reddens and splits, veins burst and blister as I continue shoving my power into him until he's unrecognizable.

His final whimper presses against my palm, and with his eyes on mine, Garrick Atarah dies within the remains of his castle.

I let his lifeless body fall to the ground as I stand over him.

It's over, I tell myself. *He's dead.*

It's so strange looking down at him now. When I was a child, I used to think he was the largest man in the world, an unshakable force, but I beat him. I survived him. I thought I'd feel relief, but I don't. I think it'll take me some time before I can accept Garrick is no longer alive. I spent so much of my life protecting myself from him that I don't know what it is to live without armor.

Sorin attempts to curl his talons over my shoulder, but they're as tall as me now. My dragons are safe. A small smile curls my lips, and I reach up to stroke the scales of his wrist. "You're far too big for that now, my sweetling."

Flames continue billowing along what remains of the castle, and the ground rumbles as more stones fall. Cayden once promised me that he'd help me rip it apart brick by brick, but dragonfire devoured everything Garrick loved. I hope his last sight of this world haunts his soul in the underworld, for it was a scene conjured from his nightmares. A queen returning to reclaim her throne with a dragon at her back and others in the sky.

CHAPTER
SEVENTY

ELOWEN

I TURN AWAY FROM GARRICK AND PRESS MY FOREHEAD INTO
Sorin's when he drops his head. The scent of charred flesh stings
my nose and eyes, but I focus on Sorin's presence as the walls that
once caged us crumble and the man who ordered it all lies broken at
our feet.

"We should get back to the battle to finish this once and for all," I
say, and Sorin presses his head harder against mine before I kiss his
snout and climb up his wing. He takes to the skies after I strap myself
into the saddle, rising above the buildings along the canals with Garrick's body in his back claw. Venatrix and Delmira continue burning
the beach, and I fly over the ships to ensure they know that their king
has fallen.

Basilius and Calithea fight against wyverns over the battlefield in
the distance, ripping them to shreds and discarding the leathery bodies over enemy lines. Sorin cries out, jerking back but not quick enough
as a wyvern springs up from the roof just under him and latches its
jaws around his neck. Fear floods through me in an instant.

"Sorin!" I unhook my harness and unsheathe a knife before jolting
forward. The beast jerks, and I wrap one arm around Sorin's neck to
stop myself from falling while raising my other hand to plunge the
knife into the wyvern's eye. Blood bubbles up and coats my skin as I
repeat the action until the creature is in too much pain to hold on.

It shrieks as it unlatches itself, and though blood coats its fangs, the wounds aren't deep enough to kill Sorin.

I remain perched on Sorin as he lunges forward and sinks his fangs into the wyvern's neck, just as it bit him. He shakes his head, decapitating the creature as its bones snap under Sorin's strength, and its body crashes into the canal far below.

I scan my surroundings for other threats, but my pulse doesn't calm down. The sky around us may be empty but Sorin's scales are cold, and growing more so by the second.

Something is wrong.

Dragon scales are never cold; being close to them is like sitting in front of a roaring hearth.

"You're all right, my love." I run my hands down his neck as I drop back to the saddle. "You're okay."

He screeches and thrashes his head side to side like he's trying to shake something off, but nothing is here. I scream his name as we lose altitude, and my stomach flies into my throat before he recovers. My heart pumps so fiercely that I can feel it in my fingertips. We're still in enemy territory, and we're flying too low. Sorin cuts to the left at the last possible second to avoid crashing into a building and keeps shaking his head as he takes us higher again.

Something is very, *very* wrong.

I cry out in time with Sorin and grab my chest. It feels like someone is trying to hack our bond in two. It's pulled on, knotted, and yanked, but whoever is doing this amplifies their magic, and the pain morphs into thousands of knives stabbing at the unbreakable force. I gasp for air as Sorin falters again, too lost in my pain to be frightened. I haven't felt this kind of sensation since my father hired a mage to try to break the bond between me and my dragons—the day my mother died after the spell rebounded. Ailliard freed me from the dungeons after that. I can't imagine how much worse the torture would've become after the queen was killed.

I don't remember my mother before my imprisonment. The only detail I can recall of her was that she stared at the wall and sat silently by my father while I was tortured in front of the throne. She never came to my cell in the middle of the night to sneak me some scraps of food when the king was asleep. She didn't even try to run when the dragons began blowing flames. Sometimes I think she wanted to die.

The bond twists again and Sorin cries out. I rub at my chest to try to ease the piercing pain, but even breathing too deeply hurts. I force myself to fall forward, but I move too late. An arrow that I was too distracted to spot manages to skim my ear, but the droplets dribbling onto my shoulder aren't what worry me, it's the fact that Sorin didn't see it at all. He would never let anything hurt me, ever since I was a child.

The mage that my father hired to break the bond was from Thirwen. I don't remember his face, but I do remember that.

Oh gods.

What if it was the mage who nearly killed Cayden? I glance down at my arms despite them being covered, but the markings that swirl around my arms are proof of what I did in the wake of Nykeem's bomb.

You will be cheating death, and there is always a price to pay, Sage's voice enters my mind as Sorin cries out again.

No.

No.

Oh, gods, but it makes sense. Cayden is the most protective man, and Sorin is the most protective dragon. Sage spoke of balance. I saved one protector only to lose another.

Not Sorin.

Sorin cannot be my price.

I will not let anyone take Sorin from me.

"I'm with you, sweetling, just hold on," I manage to say through the pain and focus all my power on the bond, trying to pull it away from whoever is toying with it. A wyvern with the first rider I've seen in this battle aims straight for us. "Zayèra!"

Dragonfire spills from Sorin, but the force is blocked by the same kind of wards that protected Garrick as he ran from the castle. I reach for my crossbow and fire it, but the shield shoots up again. I don't want to risk summoning dragonfire myself right now knowing that Sorin needs me to grasp the bond, and I can't do both. My hand tightens on the saddle horn as we gain speed, and once we're close enough, my suspicions are confirmed.

Atop the wyvern sits Nykeem. I remember seeing his face through the wards, and the horror that coated his features as I melted them. Each time I've fought a wyvern and their mount, the rider had white eyes like I do when I slip into my dragons' minds, but Nykeem is fully conscious.

Flames won't work here. Sorin needs to attack. I command him to discard Garrick's body, and the king of the conquered kingdom crashes into a watery, unmarked grave. My crossbow will be of little use, so I attach it to the saddle and tighten the strap around my waist. "Vetàs."

Sorin's front claws shoot forward, tearing through the shield as he blows more dragonfire. His bottom talons lock with the wyvern's, rendering it immobile given that it has only two legs. It bites Sorin, utilizing its only defense left, but Sorin rakes his other talons down its chest and belly as we tumble to the ground. Neither the mage nor I can reach for our weapons as they plummet.

The pain in my chest lessens, and Sorin's scales begin to warm in Nykeem's distracted state. I shove his hold out of us. Sorin unlatches his claws from the wyvern's and throws it to the ground before taking to the skies again, but Nykeem isn't with the corpse of the creature when I look down. My head throbs painfully in the aftermath of the manipulation and I summon Calithea as another wyvern rides for us without a mount. Something is still wrong with Sorin, and I don't see Nykeem anywhere. I need to get Sorin on the ground and behind our lines. The battle isn't far, but it's impossible for me to spot anyone I love from this altitude.

Pain shoots through my chest again, and I look down to ensure I haven't been wounded. Nothing is there. It's burning hot, like someone is pressing a brand fresh off the fire into my ribs. Sorin screams along with me, his flight faltering, and my stomach rises as he sharply dips. He thrashes his head again, crying out like he's in more pain than me, and his scales are *freezing*.

Calithea is too far away for me to wait. I know I've been caught in a trap, but I can't lose Sorin. If I slip into his mind, I won't be able to defend myself, but I know that's the only way I can help him fight off this assault. Thirwen's magic is rooted in mind control and manipulation, and they often slip into the minds of their familiars. My dragon will not pay the price for saving Cayden—I will, no matter the cost.

I look to my wedding ring and drag my thumb over the stone before pressing it to my lips. Sorin cries out again, and I can't take it anymore. Sorin would never abandon me, and I won't abandon him. If he plummets to his death, then he'll be taking me with him.

"I've got you, sweetling," I say soothingly and Sorin *whimpers*. "I'm right here."

I take one last glance at the battle still several yards away and let the world fade around me. I follow the bridge between our minds, which looks like a forest made entirely of emerald-green wisps. Where Basilius's mind was tranquil, Sorin's is chaotic, made even more so by the unwanted presence spreading like decay. It withers the vibrant green as Nykeem tries to take hold of Sorin's mind by smothering his soul.

I send out a wave of power and light to fight off the darkness trying to swallow him. Nykeem is no match for our bond now that I've fully immersed myself and can throw him out. The colors of my markings fill the space—silver, gold, lavender, and blue—and shield the green wisps that curl around me. Sorin's always protected me fiercely, and I will not leave him to fend for himself. I slice through the black webs, forcing the mage back in this battle that nobody else can see.

Something pulls at me and tries to force me out, but it's not Nykeem. It's something beyond Sorin's mind. I don't know what it is. I don't even care. I stay until no trace of an intruder remains and fortify it with a shield of my own to prohibit anyone else from entering again. I'll have to do it with the other dragons once the battle is over—and after I kill this fucking mage.

I uncurl myself from Sorin as I retreat into my own mind, but the world rushes around me when I regain my sight. Wind whips through my hair as Sorin flies *at* me. The severed straps of my saddle flap around my waist. The ground quickly rises up to meet me as I plummet toward the battlefield. Blood rushes from Sorin's neck from the previous puncture wounds and arrows jut out of his wings. He's the fastest dragon, and if he can't catch me, none of them will. He screeches, pained and panicked as I spread my arms out on either side of me and keep my eyes locked on his.

It's okay, I say down the bond. *I love you. No matter what happens.*

He screeches again as his claw wraps around me, and I cry out. My chest and side throb painfully as he hugs me to his body, and we fall from the sky together.

CHAPTER
SEVENTY-ONE

CAYDEN

N°.

No.

Elowen has never fallen, but she is now. She tumbles through the air with her hand outstretched to Sorin who flies faster than I've ever seen him as arrows protrude from his wings. The other dragons flock to her, but they're too far away to catch her before she hits the ground. Her torn saddle straps hang around her waist in scraps. I don't know what happened. One moment she was flying back on Sorin, and the next she was falling.

Darkness rumbles beneath my skin as I watch the woman I love fall to her death. I need to reach her. I need to help her. Sorin extends his claw and manages to wrap his talons around her, but they're too close to the ground. He curls his body around Elowen and levels out his wings, but all it does is slow them slightly before they crash through the treetops of the forest beside the battlefield.

A battle cry climbs up my throat and a red haze coats my vision. I swing my blades, fighting without precision or mercy, and leave a massacre in my wake. I barrel through the lines, fighting my way to the trees in a violent frenzy. I'll take on the whole fucking army with my bare hands. I'll rip them apart limb from limb and leave them clawing their way through the mud.

Desperation lights the fire within me and rage like no other breathes life into it. I'll cleave this world in two before I let anyone take her from me.

I break through and my blood-covered chest heaves as I sheathe one of the blades on my back, keeping the other in my hand as I run into the woods. I ordered General Gryffin to mount Koa when he was wounded, and I'm wholeheartedly regretting that decision now.

"Elowen!" I shout. "ELOWEN!"

Sorin hums, and I follow the sound, sprinting over rocks and vaulting over fallen trees. Steam rises from the pools of Sorin's blood along the forest floor, melting the snow. Elowen lays beside him, stroking a shaking hand down his scales.

"My baby," she murmurs. "You're okay, my baby."

Sorin's not mortally wounded, though arrows pierce his wings and wounds puncture his neck . . . but Elowen.

"HEALER!" I shout over my shoulder, ripping off my helmet and gauntlets.

"Cayden," Elowen rasps, blood trickling from the corner of her lips as she turns to face me.

My heart sinks further. She's pale. She's so fucking pale and her hands are covered in her own blood. "Hello, my love."

I drop to my knees beside her, my stomach rolling while taking in the three arrows made of glowing green metal piercing her ribs. Pulling them out could injure her further, but that poison . . . *oh gods.*

"Garrick is dead, but I don't think I killed Nykeem." She cringes in pain. "His eyes weren't white when I saw him, so I think another mage controlled his wyvern."

I don't care. I don't fucking care about anything. "I'm so proud of you," I gently state, taking her into my arms. She groans weakly and settles her head in the crook of my arm. "I'm going to get you help. You just have to hang on until I get us back to camp, all right? You're okay."

"Cayden," she says my name again, blinking through the mist coating her eyes. "I'm a healer. I know when a wound can't be mended, even if they weren't made with this poison."

I try to lift her, but she cries out, and I sink to my knees again. "I'm sorry, sweetheart. I don't want to hurt you." I turn over my shoulder again. "I WILL KILL EVERY LAST HEALER IF SOMEONE DOESN'T STEP FORWARD!"

"Cayden—"

"You're fine," I rush out. "You're going to be fine. Stop talking to me like you're going to die."

I can't fathom a world without her when she is my world. Her heartbeats are the only thing keeping it turning. I tighten my hands on her, watching her pulse and kissing her forehead as a healer makes it to the forest and kneels on Elowen's other side.

"I had to save Sorin," she whispers. "I couldn't let him die. I couldn't leave him. I'm"—she inhales sharply—"so sorry."

I shake my head, speaking through my tight throat. "You have nothing to apologize for."

I'm being as gentle with her as I possibly can, but my emotions rage within me. I feel helpless, watching a mage from the fire cult press her glowing hands into Elowen, but they fade and flicker without removing the arrows.

Please don't take her, I pray. *Please don't take her away from me. I know she's too good for this world but let her stay in it.*

"Why isn't your magic working?" I growl.

"Nykeem made the arrows, and I can't heal a poison I can't identify," the woman whimpers with teary eyes on Elowen. "And I can't remove the arrows without killing her."

"Then find someone who fucking can!"

She looks at me then, her eyes filled with so much dread that I already know what's coming before she says it. "Nobody can."

"Portal the mage who healed me. I'll do the same ritual."

"Go," Elowen whispers, tilting her head to face the mage as the other four dragons surround us, calling out to their rider.

"Don't take a fucking step away. Heal my wife." I press her closer to me without moving the arrows. "DO SOMETHING! Please, I'll give anything, I will be in your debt eternally, just fix her."

"I wish I could." Tears stream down her face as she clasps Elowen's shoulder. "I'm so sorry."

"She can't do anything." Elowen chokes, and the mage runs away when I face Elowen again, pushing her hair behind her ear. "And the soul bond can be used only once."

"Send Nyrinn and Zale," I shout after the mage's retreating form. My frustration breaks through my tone. "Why would you waste it on me?"

She gives me a half smile, more blood trailing down the corner of her lip. *No. No. Fuck.* It needs to stop. "Saving you could never be a waste."

"You didn't save me. If you die it will all have been a waste. I won't stay in this world without you."

"Zale can't heal the poison," she whispers. "He can only heal what he can identify."

I yell through clenched teeth like a wounded animal, setting her down gently to unsheathe a knife from my thigh. Though I hate hurting her, I slice open her palms and do the same to mine, not even feeling the bite of steel. I clasp our hands together as she did before performing the ritual, but nothing happens. There's no force locking our flesh together.

"It's not going to work," she says softly.

"El, my love." Tears begin sliding down my cheeks. I didn't even think I was capable of crying anymore. "Please don't leave me."

"You remember what I said at our wedding? I will wait for you in every lifetime, Cayden Veles. I'll see you again, and I'll love you again."

"No, you won't." My tears worsen, dotting her cheeks with rivers of sorrow as I cradle her in my arms again. "I won't get this lucky again, so you have to stay here with me." She laughs, but it's weak, and strained, and all wrong. "We're going to have our future together just like we talked about last night. I'm going to smother you with gowns and pastries and books, and we're going to have boring days together."

She nods, the corners of her lips rising as her brows knot. "Keep talking."

"We can have a cottage in the mountains and the sea just for us. I know how overwhelmed you get when surrounded by people, so we can go there to escape court. We'll be happy, just the two of us, and if you decide you want to have children, I'll pull myself together to be good to them and do right by you, but I need at least a decade with you before anyone else joins the picture. I'll give you anything you want, angel, you just have to stay with me. I don't care what my life looks like as long as you're in it. That's all I need."

Life leaks out of the woman who has always been so full of it as she stares up at me with stars in her eyes. "I know you think yourself unworthy of me, but I need you to know that I could never love anyone the way I love you." Nyrinn runs through the trees with Braxton and another soldier at her side, the general falling to his knees when he sees the wounded queen in my arms, removing his helmet to press it against his chest.

The other soldier mirrors his actions, but it's different for Braxton. He was the first soldier to step forward and swear himself to Elowen after she was attacked in Ladislava. He was the only soldier who stepped forward to address the way Ailliard treated her. Braxton never had children, and though Elowen is a grown woman, I think guarding her fulfilled some part of him.

Elowen continues even after Nyrinn kneels beside her, keeping her eyes on mine. "Never doubt that I wanted everything with you. I'd have spent my life proving you're worthy in all the ways you think you're not."

I cradle her face, kissing her forehead again. "Shh, love. Save your breaths."

We'll have it all.

We'll have everything.

Nyrinn does her best to keep the emotion off her face, but her shaking hands give away everything.

"What have you gotten yourself into this time, my girl?" she asks, gently.

"At least I'm far away from your pretty floors."

Nyrinn offers a strained smile, wrapping her hands around the first arrow, and looking at me with a tortured expression. "We have to try."

I bite my tongue, knowing this will be excruciating for Elowen, but I can't let her die. I don't know where Zale is, I don't even know if he's alive. Nyrinn pulls a heap of fabric from her pack, and I lean Elowen against Sorin's cheek. Elowen looks around to all her dragons, her eyes glowing gold as her lips quiver and she sucks in a shuddering breath.

"Stop saying goodbye," I command.

"I have to."

I take the fabric from Nyrinn, balling it up tightly and pressing my arm across Elowen's chest to keep her from thrashing. "I have to make this as quick and clean as possible," Nyrinn says. "Cayden will press the fabric to try to stop the bleeding, but we need to get these arrows out of you."

"Mhmm," Elowen mumbles, her blinks growing slower as does her pulse.

Nyrinn sucks in a sharp breath, wrapping both hands around one of the arrows. I press my lips to the side of Elowen's head, murmuring against it, "I've got you, angel. It's my turn to heal you and you'll be back to tormenting me in no time."

"Tell Finnian I love him," she says.

Nyrinn rips the arrow free, and Elowen screams through the blood gurgling up her throat, spilling down her chin. I press the wad of fabric against the open wound but there's so much blood. Too much blood.

It coats my hands until I can't see my skin.

The dragons cry out, their screams mingling with her agony.

"I'm so sorry, my love. Just hold on for me a bit longer."

"ELOWEN!" Finnian bellows, running through the tree line. He throws his helmet to the side, his bow too, nearly falling over himself as he rushes to get closer to his best friend. He collapses beside Nyrinn, tears running through the blood on his cheeks. "What happened? Why isn't anyone using magic to heal her? ZALE!" he shouts desperately. "ZALE!"

"Fi"—she chokes—"nny."

"I'm here, darling." He looks to Nyrinn, who prepares to pull out the second arrow. "What the fuck are you doing?"

"We can't leave them inside her!"

"There's too much blood!"

Elowen's head lolls on Sorin's scales, and I pull it up, locking my gaze on her glazed irises. "I"—she chokes on more blood—"l-love . . ."

Her words drop, and her eyes cloud over. She's not looking at me anymore. No. *No.* "Elowen." I slap my hand against her cheek. "ELOWEN!"

Tears continue spilling from my eyes, but I don't move to wipe them as I take her in my arms again. Elowen hates when I let her go during the night, even if it's just for a few moments. She told me it's the only time she feels safe enough to rest.

"Come back," I beg, my voice hoarse from screaming.

Finnian screams and punches the ground, cursing every god who took Elowen from this world. The dragons wail so sharply, tearing apart the forest and bathing it in flames as they take to the skies to circle their rider. The woman whose soul called to them and brought them into this world. It's like they're screaming in hopes that Elowen will find them again to remedy their pain as she always did. Sorin nudges her leg, pleading for her to wake up, and moves on to her hand, trying to place it on his snout, but it falls away.

"Come on, El." I rock her body back and forth. "Show me those pretty eyes, angel. Please. Don't leave me."

She doesn't move, her empty eyes staring at the skies she once flew in. "Breathe, my love, please breathe." I pat her cheek more and jostle her in my arms. "ELOWEN!"

She can't be gone.

This isn't real.

I press my head to her blood-covered chest, but there's no heartbeat.

Claws rake through my heart and lungs. I can't fucking breathe. Everything hurts. I thought I knew what it was to be angry before, but it's nothing compared to this. I've never known pain until this moment. I cannot endure whatever this feeling is. I will not survive it, and what would even be the point?

We were so close to the life we wanted. She was so close to getting the life she deserved . . . and she's just gone, and everything good within me has been taken with her.

I rear my head back and scream. The ground rumbles beneath me as icy rage continues to pound through me. It's not hot, as one would think, it's cold like death. My agony awakens something in me, awakens something in the world surrounding me, and every shadow in the forest moves to cling to me. They wrap around my arms like snakes and hold Elowen's body to mine, like the darkness of the world clings to the light as it leaves.

My power is spawned from suffering and forged in rage. Elowen was right, and she's not even here to see it. In the back of my mind, I can hear her triumphant laughter, but it's so far away. I lost everything, and now I want to take everything. I have nothing left, not a shred of humanity or happiness, and the darkness fills the empty shell of my living corpse.

Nykeem did this.

He took her from me, and not a single shield will save him from my wrath.

There is not a corner of this world he can cower in because I will lurk in every shadow, ready to strike.

Elowen doesn't need me to hold her right now; she needs me to avenge her.

I kiss Elowen's forehead one more time, whispering my vow against her skin. "For you, my love, I will break the world."

CHAPTER
SEVENTY-TWO

CAYDEN

I DRAW MY BLADES AGAIN AS THE SHADOWS CREATE A WALL AT my back and circle the steel, stepping through the tree line as a shell of the man who entered it. I died with my wife, and all that's left is the need for vengeance. As it did on our wedding, the moon overtakes the sun and plunges the world into darkness. Maybe even the sky mourns Elowen, knowing she will never mount her dragons and fly through it again. Her laughter will never caress the moon. Her smile will never be lit by the stars.

Elowen took everything that made me human when her soul left her body, creating a void for power to fill. I sense everything, the water in the earth and in the bodies of the soldiers around me. I see the darkness within them, and I want to kill them all.

I don't simply crave death.

I've become it.

I swipe my sword through the air, sending out a blade of shadows that severs a battalion in half. My boots sink into bloody entrails as I continue advancing. Someone calls out my name, but it's not mine anymore. Nothing is aside from this power. I raise my hands, summoning the water within the layers of the earth and sharpening it into points. I listen to the terrified screams of those on the wrong side of the war, and I let the shards hang in the air for several prolonged seconds, relishing the sound before slamming my hands forward.

Ice shards spear their throats, eyes, legs, and armor. Death hangs heavy in the air, such a fulfilling smell.

I watch the world crumble through the holes of my helmet. The female dragons fly to the castle again, but the males most likely remain to guard Elowen. Even in death, they will never leave her. They burn and rip apart what remains of the stone until not even the outline of the structure remains.

Elowen's revenge is carried out by those who will not let her die in vain.

Screams rise like the tide and wash over me like a wave. The opposing army tries to run from me, and I utilize the shadows to drag some back. The darkness wraps around their necks like ropes. I let the others run for a bit, give them a shred of hope, before I manipulate the water that courses through their bodies to boil them alive.

No soldier who has picked up a sword against us today will be spared. They will suffer for what has been done. I don't care if they weren't directly responsible. I want them all to die. Each death makes me crave more, and I gorge myself on their agony, knowing it will never compare to mine.

"Bring me Nykeem!" I roar, my voice not sounding like my own. It's so dark that it sounds demonic, and with the horns on my helmet, perhaps I've entered my true form. I was not made for happiness. I was made for war.

I send out another wave of shadows, killing countless soldiers in the span of a second.

They return to me, swirling around my arms and gathering around my hands as I continue trudging through the massacre of my own making. The field is entirely red, and bodies upon bodies are piled everywhere. Within my mind, I imagine the shadows as an army, an endless battalion of darkness, and will them to take on human forms. My power obeys, and their essence molds into soldiers with blades of ice, marching behind me as I begin slicing my way through my enemy and sending the shadows to do my bidding.

"BRING HIM TO ME OR I WILL PEEL YOUR FLESH FROM YOUR BONES!"

The lines in front of me part, making way for Nykeem to step forward. A fresh wave of anger rushes through me, consumes me, and eats away at my morality that was already meager to begin with.

I'm nothing without Elowen, not even a man, and I want to reduce this mage to *nothing*.

I remove my helmet and toss it aside as the shadows shield me from a volley of arrows. I don't want to miss a moment of this, and I want Nykeem to see my face as he dies. Nobody can save him, and if they try, I'll cut them down.

I jam my bloody swords into the mud and leave them behind. I don't want to bleed him dry; I want to drain the life out of him, rip it from him, and feast upon his screams.

I look down at Elowen's name inked upon my finger and swipe away the mud and blood marring my skin. It creates a sticky rim around my wedding band, but I've never felt right taking it off. A shadow curls around it, like it longs to find any part of her and keep it close.

"For Elowen," I say, charging forward.

Talons made of wispy darkness form at the tips of my fingers, and I claw my way through his magically made shield. Pulling it apart like wet clay, as Elowen once did. I never cease my movements as the mage tries to re-form it to keep himself safe from me.

I don't need to get through it to kill him, but once it's shredded to ribbons, I step forward and drag him up by his neck. He gasps and sputters, and I cock my fist back before slamming it into his face, adding fresh blood to Elowen's name like an offering. This is all I can give her. I didn't save her. I promised to protect her, and I failed. She died in my arms, bleeding out and in blinding pain, choking on her death while she tried to tell me she loved me.

If I had never found her, she'd still be alive.

I did this.

I roar, losing myself in violence, in the pain flooding through me sharper than any wound I've ever received or inflicted. He drops to the ground when his face is unrecognizable, his nose crushed and his teeth littered around us. My army of shadows still slays the enemies remaining, and the dragons return to the battle to fight alongside them, blowing dragonfire and scorching flesh and earth.

I kick him in his throat, and watch him grip it, sucking in breath like a wounded animal on his hands and knees. It's not enough. It will never be enough. I pull upon my newfound powers, seeking the water within him, and shove it into his lungs, drop by drop. He cries out, clawing at his chest, lying on his back as he gasps for air. I swipe my hand, ordering the water to retreat to grant him the illusion of survival before doing it all over again. Water pours from his mouth, and I order it to retreat again.

"Please," he begs, sobbing and crawling toward my boots. "All I did was serve my king."

"And all I'm doing is avenging my wife." I jerk my leg back and kick him in the face. "You took her from me." I step on his throat, slowly crushing his windpipe. "There is nothing human left within me, and the monster that resides in my flesh relishes in your agony."

He claws at the leather covering my ankle, and I begin flooding his lungs again, keeping the pattern going as the sky turns red upon his death and the war is over.

Not won.

I lost everything.

CHAPTER

SEVENTY-THREE

CAYDEN

EVERY PATH I'VE WALKED HAS ALWAYS LED TO ELOWEN, and as I push myself up from my knees with the hilt of a sword I pry from the fingers of a corpse, I turn in the direction of her again. The decimated army is all around me, and yet I feel nothing but grief. Devastation.

My chest physically hurts despite my only wound being a slice on my bicep. I don't recall someone cutting me. I barely even notice it now. Blood leaks from the gash and down my arm, and I hope whatever parts of me soak into the earth find Elowen and keep us together where life has torn us apart. Flowers will grow from her spilled blood whereas mine will leave behind a barren land to starve anyone who hopes to find any shred of mercy. She is blessed by life, and though I'm the one with air in my lungs, each breath I take brings me closer to death and I'm thankful for it.

I trudge through the bodies and forest, needing to be with her again.

Elowen's curls spill over Finnian's lap, and Ryder does his best to console a screaming Saskia, but he's in no state to offer strength. They look at me when I emerge, I see it in the corner of my eye, but all I care about is my dead wife.

My wife.

The woman I vowed to protect. The woman who was my only happiness in this world.

Twigs snap as Ryder and Saskia approach.

"Don't touch me." The words are raw, hollow. Clawing their way up my throat that feels like sandpaper. The last person I held was Elowen, when she screamed in my arms. I grit my teeth, dragging my hands through my hair and pulling at the roots, welcoming the pain.

"I'm so sorry," Ryder whispers.

I shake my head, unable to hear any of this. I can't speak of her as if she's dead when her love lives within me like a flame.

Saskia tries to open her mouth to say something, but a whimper cuts her off.

I step around them, returning to Elowen's side. Nyrinn must have removed the final arrows after I left. Finnian's vacant eyes stare forward, entirely drained of hope. Venatrix lands behind her and roars. What was once mighty is now broken, and I understand the beast more than I ever have.

Finnian doesn't move as I lift her, cradling her in my arms and walking back to camp. One by one, as if setting loose a wave of devotion and devastation, soldiers drop to their knees at the sight of their lost queen. The sky opens, weeping for her, and Sorin *screams*. I wonder how much he understands about what's happening, if he knows Elowen sacrificed herself so that he would live.

"We can take her, Your Majesty," a woman steps forward. "We can clean her."

"Nobody touches a hair on her fucking head," I darkly state. "And whoever follows me will be slain on sight."

I walk through the camp, not stopping until I make it to an abandoned cottage along the road. It's quaint, smelling of cinnamon and firewood, and I duck under a low-hanging beam to a room in the back. I kiss her forehead while placing her on the bed and begin drawing a bath in the en suite tub.

"I know you hate the feeling of blood on your skin after it dries," I say, moving to the small armoire in the corner. Whoever lived here must've left in a hurry—everything seems untouched. My heavy hand tugs a simple lavender gown off the hanger with bell sleeves lined in white fur. The same kind Elowen always wears. "I don't think I ever told you that lavender is my favorite color. It has been since the moment I saw you in the gown you wore to your first dinner in Vareveth. Ever since then, I think of you whenever I see it."

I keep my back to her, and for a moment I pretend that her big brown eyes are fixed on me, hanging on to every syllable and waiting for more. "I didn't know how to speak my feelings aloud, but I'd hear music when I looked at you. I have sheets upon sheets of melodies I'd conjure from the simplest moments we spent together."

I squeeze my eyes closed, resting my forehead on the wood after I slam the door shut. She's not here. She's not fucking here. She was supposed to survive and run to me like she did after the battle in Galakin. I can still picture her in the upcoming summer, making bouquets with the flowers she grows and sprawling out on the grass with her dragons.

I remove my armor until all I'm left in is a black shirt and pants, and gently strip her leathers and armor off. Pain shoots through me at the sight of her blood-covered torso. Black markings from the poison stretch across her chest but have begun to fade now that it's done its job, I suppose. I press my lips together, hoisting her in my arms again and testing the water before placing her inside.

I run soap through her hair, detangling the curls matted from the wind and blood. *So much blood.* "I'll take care of you. Don't you worry about a thing."

The words taste like acid, and I turn away from her to retch into a bucket. The bile burns my throat, and I wipe my mouth and rinse it before finishing what I started. The first thing she does after every fight and battle is strip out of her leathers and bathe. I dry her body and place her back on the bed to dress her wounds with a roll of gauze. My hands shake as I wrap her. I don't know how to not take care of her. I don't know how to let her go. I don't know how to accept that she's not just sleeping.

I drop to my knees after sliding the gown up her body and settling it on her shoulders.

"Always so beautiful." I run my knuckles down her cheek. "Elowen, love, I won't survive this."

I take her cold hand in mine and bow my head to rest it against her stomach, my tears soaking the fabric. I thought I had nothing once, but I would take the days of endless fighting and starvation over this without a second thought. I feel as if I'm a rotting corpse with a heartbeat, like fate has bestowed upon me the one enemy I can't draw my sword against.

I look out the window, to where the sun paints the sky red as the darkness of the eclipse and shadows remains. There must be something I can do to help her, to bring her back. I force my mind to conjure everything I read on necromancy when I was younger. In most cases, mortals bargained with the Goddess of Souls, Mercy, and Destiny to save a loved one from death.

A red sky.

Where have I heard that before?

In Galakin.

Mae's prophecy.

The sun will be bathed in blood and the shadows will shroud the day.

Something sparks within me. What else did she say . . . I force myself to think beyond Elowen, sending my mind back to Galakin. I didn't seek Elowen out all those months ago because of the prophecy that she would be the ruination or salvation of Imirath. I believed in facts, one of them being that the woman bonded to five dragons hated the same man as me, but I'll take anything right now. Even if it makes me a superstitious fool.

Ashes to be washed away by the waves.

Could that be the rain over the battle? The ramparts of the castle? My hands washing the gore from Elowen? Does it even matter?

Old eyes watch and new eyes shut.

New eyes . . . Elowen. Pain lances through me again. "Old eyes," I mutter, dragging my hand through Elowen's hair. The oldest eyes of Ravaryn would be the gods.

Have my powers awoken something? Someone? Desperation will make a person believe in anything, I suppose.

The earth rumbled as I screamed, and the gods feast upon the sorrows of mortals.

I'm moving before I even know what I'm doing, but I must do *something*.

I lift Elowen in my arms again, carrying her out of the house, and follow the sounds of wailing dragons. A hand clasps my shoulder, and I balance Elowen in one arm to draw my sword, pointing it at the neck of whoever approached. Feeling more animalistic than human.

"It's me." Ryder holds his hands up in surrender, more tears falling from his eyes as he takes in the state of me, the state of Elowen. I must look as deranged as I feel. "Where are you going?"

"I'm getting her back."

A helpless sound crawls up his throat. "She's gone, brother. I'll build her pyre with you."

"She will not burn!" I roar, tightening my hold on my sword despite it being at my side as Finnian and Saskia rush forward. I lock eyes with her best friend, maybe the only person who will understand my anguish. "She wanted me to tell you that she loved you." Tears glimmer in his eyes and he chokes on a sob and drops his gaze from Elowen. "I'm getting her back."

Saskia steps forward, and I clutch Elowen tighter, my protective instincts flaring up, intertwining with possession. Saskia's eyes latch on to mine, and she holds up a single purple flower in silent permission. I breathe slowly, nodding only once, and she steps forward to tuck it behind her ear and kiss her forehead.

"I will miss you every day that I live," she whispers.

"I'm getting her back." I need to believe that this will work. I need to try. If I lose hope now then I'll take her back to Vareveth and dig our grave behind our house, not a pyre. I'll keep my eyes on hers as I pierce my heart and curl my body around hers. One day, when some-one finds us when we're nothing but bones, they won't know where I start and she ends. Too intertwined to ever be separated. Decay and time will attack our mortal flesh, but our souls will reside somewhere sorrow can't find us, and I'll keep her there, loving her until the very essence of what breathes life into our bodies is snuffed out.

"Please," Ryder says. "Don't force us to live with the loss of both of you."

"I'm already dead."

I stride past, ignoring him as he calls out my name, only turning around when the sound of struggling replaces his pleas. Finnian shoves him back, not allowing him to follow us, and Saskia drops to the grass to bury her head in her hands. A flash of silver rushes forward, and Zarius drops to his knees beside her.

"Don't look," he says, forcing her to turn around.

"Cayden!" Ryder calls out from where Finnian pins him against the earth. "CAYDEN!"

I feel nothing.

Not a shred of regret or remorse.

And I turn away.

The dragons must sense where Elowen is because they land in a circle around me, snarling and snapping their teeth. Maybe I should be afraid, but I'm not. It would be a mercy to be relieved from the torment within.

"Help me," I whisper. "Please help me."

I know they can't understand me—the only person they can under-stand is Elowen—but she swore they could sense emotions and per-haps my devotion to her. I've ridden Basilius before, but to my surprise, it's not he who lowers his head, but Venatrix. The fiercest of them all. The red queen.

I climb up her wing and settle us in the saddle, keeping Elowen's body cradled against mine as I grip the saddle horns.

"The Etril Forest," I say as she takes to the skies. How she knows where I need to go is a mystery that I don't have the energy to think about. She flaps harder, flying us over the scorched and bloodied earth, leveling out as we make it to the beginning of the forest behind the castle that Elowen and I ran through. When she first summoned Sorin and I swore I was looking at a goddess. Snow swirls around the peaks of the Seren Mountains that sharply cut through the clouds.

"I should've grabbed you a cloak," I mutter, pulling her into my body to try to keep her warm, covering her hands with mine and breathing onto them now that Venatrix is level. "I can feel you pulling me to you, beckoning me, and I'm going to find you, angel. I promise."

Venatrix calls out to the others, dipping low to land on the forest floor at the base of the temple ruins. The sky is just as bloodred as it was over the battlefield, and shadows still cling to me. I don't know what's happening, and I don't have even an iota of curiosity.

I think about the last smile she gave me.

I think about the kiss before the battle.

I think about every fucking regret, and I form them into blades in my mind, sheathing them at my side, and carry her into the temple.

Wind whips through the broken pillars, scattering the bits of white rock that must've chipped off of them when they cracked. Some still stand, but others stretch into the forest. They might have been reclaimed by greenery at one time, but now are smothered in winter. I force myself to set Elowen down, her dark curls splaying through the unmarred snowfall like a sleeping angel.

I will see her again.

I unsheathe a knife as I walk toward the altar, slicing my palm open and letting my blood dribble down. "I, Cayden Veles, King of Vareveth, summon the Goddess of Souls, Mercy, and Destiny to strike a bargain."

CHAPTER
SEVENTY-FOUR

CAYDEN

WHEN I LOOK AROUND THE RUINS, I NOTICE SWIRLING marks along the walls and floor taking on a silvery glow. The wind stops howling, and the world goes quiet aside from the growling dragons perched upon the crumbling structure. I walk back to Elowen, taking a protective stance in front of her body and sheathing the knife in favor of a sword.

The dragons take to the skies as the stones rumble beneath us. The fallen white pillars rise from the ground, as does the collapsed ceiling, as if pulled by some invisible force. Eerie, chilling laughter floats through the newly formed structure as if it had never been in ruins. The dragons perch around the perimeter, still able to see through the tall archways.

Cayden Veles, the voice goads. *What has your anger done this time?*

Silver wisps sparkle through the air until they band together, forming a portal that resembles a whirlpool of liquid metal. A woman steps through, clad in a draping dress made of fabric that matches the conjured portal. Her red lips mirror the blood I spilled to bring her here. Pale hair is pulled away from her face and her skin is even paler; it's like she wishes to blend into everything around us.

"You summoned me, king," she says, stepping around the altar to look around her temple as if she's seeing it for the first time.

"You are the Goddess of Souls?" I ask, still not willing to believe the gods are real despite the display of power.

Her pale blue eyes glow silver as she settles her gaze on me. "And you are a man reeking of desperation. My favorite kind of mortal to make deals with."

"Bring my wife back," I demand. "If you truly are a goddess then I'm the man who woke you, and you are in my debt. If you require further payment, take my life in her place."

She tilts her sharp chin to the ground, clicking her tongue. "And you would force her to live with that? Don't you think she has hurt enough?" Her icy eyes return and drift to Elowen. "Such a pretty soul, so bright, and yet so broken."

"Her soul is mine," I state in a low tone, summoning the shadows from the depth of my pain and curling them around my arms, letting them snake across the floor and coil in the corners like vipers ready to strike.

She laughs in a girlish way, light and aloof. I always thought the gods would be more threatening and formidable, but the Goddess of Souls looks like an ordinary woman aside from the silver eyes. "I can taste your suffering. There are those who still slumber who will wish to inspire your agony."

I clench my jaw. "If you don't bring her back, I will reduce this world to nothing. I will kill every last bit of life and take away everything that makes you a goddess. You will be as powerless as I am at this moment. I will rip away everything you hold close and force you to watch it die. You will rule over a wasteland because I'll be here with my sword and shadows, ready to wage a final war on the gods."

She tilts her head, intrigued rather than perturbed. "Do you truly think you could win?"

"It's not about winning." A cruel sort of smile lifts my lips. "It's about creating the most suffering before death claims me."

She purses her lips. "I cannot take your soul because you have a destiny to fulfill."

I dryly chuckle. "If you refuse to strike a bargain that ends with Elowen's soul being returned to her body, you will have made an enemy today and believe me when I say I am the last person you want working against you. You won't have to worry about destinies because I will rip this fucking world to shreds. The gods may be back, but they will not go to sleep next time; they will die at my hands."

"As I said, not *all* the gods have returned." She smartly takes a step back as my shadows slither closer to her. She waves her fingers through the air, and something pulls in my chest. "How far are you willing to go for her?"

"Farther than you can fathom."

"Fine," she says. "I want you to kill someone for me, and once that's done, I require your services to find some lost objects."

"Give me a name."

She laughs again. "Cayden Veles."

Easy. "How will I know you'll return her soul to her body, and how will I fulfill your quest?"

"So devoted to her," she mutters. "As it always has been."

"What do you mean by that?"

She smiles in response, filled with sharp teeth and a suspicious glint in her eyes. "You will find her yourself," she says, ignoring my previous question. "If you can. I cannot interfere, and your success is entirely up to you. The underworld is *vast.* If you fail, you'll be forced to wander the underworld for eternity in constant search of your lost love. You will never be reunited with her, you will never rest, you will always hunger and thirst in a way that can never be quenched, no matter how much you try."

I searched the world for this woman since I was a boy. I won't fail. I conquered a kingdom to have her, and I'll conquer death as well. I'll make hell my kingdom and crown her as my queen in this world, the next, and all to come.

"What object do you want me to find?"

"All in good time, my friend," she giddily states. "Before you do this, know that a soul can't die. You can be wounded in your pursuit and feel as if you're on the brink of death, but it will never be granted. Nothing suffers more than a soul. When the body is wounded, it can be bandaged, but when a soul is wounded, it rips you apart from the inside."

Nothing can compare to what I feel right now. At least when I'm in hell, I'll be in the same realm as her. I'll have something to fight toward. I'd rather crawl through hell to be with her than fly through life.

"I accept your bargain," I say.

"Lovely." She snaps her fingers, and a silver band forms around my wrist as a black cloak settles over my shoulders. "There are ten layers to the underworld. That band will grant you access to each as you pass through."

"It will get me to her, but will she be able to leave if she doesn't have one?"

"First you must worry about finding her. I will offer you no information or aid beyond the band."

I grit my teeth and turn away from the goddess to return to Elowen's side. I slide her rings off her fingers and loop them onto the chain of her moonstone necklace before fastening it to my belt. I settle her in my arms again as I did moments before she died, with her head balanced in the crook of my elbow. "What will happen to her body? I will not have atrocities committed against her if I'm not here to stand guard."

"We struck a deal," the goddess says. "Your bodies will remain under my protection. No harm will come to either of your mortal remains, but if you come back, well . . . I believe you'll find yourselves changed." Her eyes show a hint of sadness when she glances at Elowen. "For what it's worth, I do not relish the prospect of your failure."

I ignore her, focusing my attention on Elowen, cupping her face in my hand and unsheathing one of her dragon daggers I sheathed on my thigh. "In every lifetime, Elowen Veles, and in every world."

I wrap her hand around the hilt, covering it with mine and pointing it right over my heart as I scan her face again, committing it to memory, not knowing when my eyes will be blessed with the sight of her again.

"I once promised you that I would defy death itself to keep you with me, and I will claw my way through it to get you back."

I press my lips to hers and stab myself through the chest.

CHAPTER
SEVENTY-FIVE
CAYDEN

I STARE INTO THE STAGGERING OBSIDIAN ARCHWAY, SWIRLING with mist, and unsheathe the sword at my back, taking my first step into the freezing pits of the underworld.

In the distance, there's the smallest orb of light, but it's gone so quickly I'm not sure if I hallucinated it.

I'll see you soon, my angel.

A monster growls within the darkness, and my lips part in a snarl of my own as I raise my sword against the domain of death.

ACKNOWLEDGMENTS

THIS BOOK TRULY WAS MY MOUNT EVEREST. *Wrath of the Dragons* has been with me through some of the hardest moments of my life. Writing has always been a crutch that I used to get through the hard times, but there were days when I felt so empty that I didn't know if I'd ever be able to write again. However, I found my way back, and I poured my soul into this book once I found my rhythm again. Love is such a strong element to this story because I believe that during this period I learned the true meaning of it. It's what got me through my darkest moments and filled my cup when it was empty. It's sprinkled into our everyday lives: baking with my mom, walking with my dad, catching up with my brother, having dinner with my fiancé, and getting coffee with friends. You don't need to have a good day to find something good within it, and you should never take a single moment for granted with someone, no matter how small it is.

There are many people that I want to thank so here we go:

To my fiancé Tanner, my mom and dad, and my brother Andrew: I'm grouping all of you together for this one because I truly could not wish for a more supportive foundation to stand upon. I'm so grateful for all of you. No matter what has happened, we've always made the best of it, and we've always had each other. Thank you for supporting me and lifting me up in all your own ways. I don't know who I would be without your love, and I'm so thankful I'll never have to know. Each of you add so much happiness to my life and make me look forward to every day.

To my critique partner, Imani Erriu: Imani, thank god you slid into my DMs to tell me that my dog is cute because I don't know where I'd be without you. You have been instrumental in this journey, and I'm so grateful we're walking it together. Watching your success has been so wonderful, and I know the best is yet to come. Thank you for coming into my life when I didn't know what I was missing.

To my editor, Shauna Summers: thank you so much not only for your guidance and advice but for never failing to tell me how much you loved this story. I'm so thankful to have an editor who not only believes in my book but in me and my career as well. You are always so amazing to work with.

To my agent, Jessica Watterson: first I want to thank you for every "lol" and "hot" that you commented while reading *Wrath of the Dragons*. It was like getting a glimpse into a reader's annotations, and I loved it so much. You have been so supportive throughout my indie-to-trad journey and are always in my corner cheering me on, and I'm so thankful for you.

To Nicole Platania: I should be typing this while making avocado toast since it's our daily ritual. Watching your success has also been so amazing, and I can't wait to see all you accomplish in your career. Thank you for being one of the first people to read *Wrath of the Dragons* and scream about it with me when I needed it most.

To Ashley Cotto: my assistant, makeup artist, soul sister, manager— and the list really goes on and on. Thank you for always being there for me since we were fourteen. I'm so proud of you for chasing your dreams, and I'll always be your loudest cheerleader. I can't wait to see you again so I can hug you since we haven't been apart for this long since we met.

To Andrès Aguirre Jurado: the man who designed the stunning map at the beginning of the book and the House Veles sigil within the interior. Bless the Instagram algorithm for leading me to your page.

You are such an amazing and talented artist and add so much life to the story with your visuals.

To Lucy Walls: the extremely talented artist who drew the wedding scene of Elowen, Cayden, and the five dragons that you see on the endpaper. Lucy, I cannot thank you enough for capturing all the little details within the scene and bringing it to life. You were so amazing to work with! Thank you so so so much for such a stunning piece, your kindness, and your dedication.

To Brianna Kusilek, Taylor Noel, Megan Whalen, Mae Martinez, and Emily Siegmund: my amazing team at Delacorte Press! Thank you all so much for all the work you do, I truly appreciate it so much.

To Hozier: I wouldn't have gotten through writing this book without your music. Thank you, king. <3

Lastly, I want to thank all the designers and editors who have worked on this book, and every reader who picks it up. I promise I'll be working on the next book day and night after leaving you on that cliffhanger, ha ha. Oopsies. Sorry not sorry, xoxo.

All my love,

Olivia Rose Darling

ABOUT THE AUTHOR

OLIVIA ROSE DARLING is the *USA Today* bestselling author of *Fear the Flames*. Darling developed a passion for writing from a very young age, always scribbling poems onto napkins and short stories into her school notebooks. She graduated from Pace University and attained a degree in English with a concentration in creative writing. She's always on the hunt for a new fantasy world to escape into, a large mug of tea, and time with her loved ones.

oliviarosedarling.com

@itslivdarling

ABOUT THE TYPE

This book was set in Centaur, a typeface designed by the American typographer Bruce Rogers in 1929. Rogers adapted Centaur from a fifteenth-century type of Nicholas Jenson (c. 1420–80) and modified it in 1948 for a cutting by the Monotype Corporation.